"This is never going to work," Steve said, as he sat in the cockpit of the Fury.

"Better hope it works," Tyler said.

The space fighter plane lurched to the side and nearly tumbled off its landing gear.

"I hereby rechristen this flying ship 'The Tub,'" Tyler said.

"What we have here is a system that's not designed to work," Steve said. "It's sometimes possible, in an emergency, for two pilots, who are both experienced and who have worked together well, to both control a bird. This is completely different. This is impossible!"

"We have to make it possible," Tyler said.

Steve started to reply, then looked up as one of the ground controllers started waving.

"I've got an incoming call," Tyler said. "Since I told my plant to restrict..."

"Same here," Steve said. "General?"

A Horvath ship has just cleared the gate, the CJCS said.

"Oh...crap," Tyler said. "They just fired."

"What?" Steve said, closing his eyes.

The view Tyler was accessing was from the VLA which had devoted a portion of its system to observing the solar system's latest visitor. As they watched, the Horvath cruiser started dumping small objects into space. Objects which quickly accelerated and disappeared.

"That's a planetary bombardment," Tyler said, softly.

Get off the ground, the CJCS said. *Now!*

"Yes, sir," Steve said. "Goodbye."

"We still need to load rounds," Tyler said, sending an order to start loading.

The rounds had been kept nearby just in case of a worst case scenario. Worst case seemed to have hit.

BAEN BOOKS by JOHN RINGO

LEGACY OF THE ALDENATA: *A Hymn Before Battle* • *Gust Front* • *When the Devil Dances* • *Hell's Faire* • *The Hero* (with Michael Z. Williamson) • *Cally's War* (with Julie Cochrane) • *Watch on the Rhine* (with Tom Kratman) • *Yellow Eyes* (with Tom Kratman) • *The Tuloriad* with Tom Kratman • *Sister Time* (with Julie Cochrane) • *Honor of the Clan* (with Julie Cochrane) • *Eye of the Storm*

MONSTER HUNTER MEMOIRS (with Larry Correia): *Monster Hunter Memoirs: Grunge* • *Monster Hunter Memoirs: Sinners* • *Monster Hunter Memoirs: Saints*

BLACK TIDE RISING: *Under a Graveyard Sky* • *To Sail a Darkling Sea* • *Islands of Rage and Hope* • *Strands of Sorrow* • *Black Tide Rising* (with Gary Poole)

TROY RISING: *Live Free or Die* • *Citadel* • *The Hot Gate*

COUNCIL WARS: *There Will Be Dragons* • *Emerald Sea* • *Against the Tide* • *East of the Sun, West of the Moon*

PALADIN OF SHADOWS: *Ghost* • *Kildar* • *Choosers of the Slain* • *Unto the Breach* • *A Deeper Blue* • *Tiger by the Tail* (with Ryan Sear)

MORE SERIES by JOHN RINGO

SPECIAL CIRCUMSTANCES
INTO THE LOOKING GLASS
EMPIRE OF MAN
PALADIN OF SHADOWS

To purchase these and all Baen Book titles in e-book format, please go to www.baen.com.

LIVE FREE OR DIE

JOHN RINGO

BAEN

LIVE FREE OR DIE

This is a work of fiction. All the characters and events portrayed in this book are fictional, and any resemblance to real people or incidents is purely coincidental.

Copyright © 2010 by John Ringo

All rights reserved, including the right to reproduce this book or portions thereof in any form.

A Baen Book

Baen Publishing Enterprises
P.O. Box 1403
Riverdale, NY 10471
www.baen.com

ISBN: 978-1-4391-3397-2

Cover art by Kurt Miller

First paperback printing, November 2010
Sixth paperback printing, July 2018

Library of Congress Control Number: 2009039759

Distributed by Simon & Schuster
1230 Avenue of the Americas
New York, NY 10020

Pages by Joy Freeman (www.pagesbyjoy.com)
Printed in the United States of America

For Aunt Joan
May you find a cozy spot by the fire
where the door never closes, the owner
runs credit, the taps never run dry
and the piano is always playing.

As always
For Captain Tamara Long, USAF
Born: 12 May 1979
Died: 23 March 2003, Afghanistan
You fly with the angels now.

ACKNOWLEDGEMENTS

The first acknowledgement is that this book is a total rip-off.

For many years I have been a fan of webcomics. Previous readers who have googled Bun-bun know of my affection for Sluggy Freelance.

Now go look up Schlock Mercenary: www.schlock mercenary.com. Go ahead. I'll wait.

For a looong time. Because Schlock has been peacefully (not) trundling along under the pen of one Howard Tayler, bon vivant and man about Salt Lake City, since June of 2000. And unlike some webcomics (and some authors who shall remain nameless), Howard has been able to stay on focus and deliver consistently amazing stories. Every. Single. Day. People talk about my output but I really don't have a clue how he does it. It's like voodoo. Sickness? Injury? Nothing has stopped Howard and I hope nothing does for a longer time. May he be given the gift of eternal life.

But while I like Schlock and Tagon's Toughs, what really intrigued me as a writer was the first contact period which is only lightly touched upon. What *would* happen if an alien race suddenly trundled a gate to other worlds into our solar system? And Howard wasn't perfectly clear what happened in the immediate aftermath. Instant "one-world"ness is, in my opinion, unlikely.

The next thing I love about Schlock: Back in the day in SF, people were willing to think *grand*. Since we've had problems with getting off this mud ball, writers seem to think that we have to think small. Howard (and I) disagree. Space is mind-bogglingly huge and vast and neat and scary and neat and huge. The main character in this book is a person who, possibly because of his stature, thinks "Cheops was insufficiently ambitious." This is a book about *grand* vision. The hell with microsats. Give me vast fleets of roaring spaceships! Give me the vision to terraform worlds! Give me battles that make a human feel their tiny little cosmic insignificance and characters that shrug it off and go "Yeah, but we *created* these engines of war so who is *really* larger?"

And if I can't get that in near-earth, near-term SF from anybody else, well, damnit, I'll just have to write it myself!

The last thing that I love about Schlock is that Howard isn't afraid to dive right into the science part of science fiction and dig hard. So you can expect a certain amount of science in this here science fiction. Get over it.

This is not a book for people who love the "other." There are no "original" concepts of how otherworldly aliens would be. One of the nice things about Schlock is that aliens are just people. Not particularly good or bad, not particularly great or menial, not particularly otherworldly. Just people. As are Howard's humans.

They haven't changed themselves into something unrecognizable. They're just people doing their jobs. (In the case of Tagon's Toughs, killing beings and breaking things for as much money as they can squeeze.) And in this book and the others that I hope follow, that's what you're going to get. People being people and aliens being not so much different.

Is this the prequel of Schlock? That's up to Howard. With his permission, I'm sort of playing about in his universe. And loving every minute of it.

The second acknowledgement, very much as great as the first, is to the people who helped me with this novel. I believe, firmly, that if you're going to write science fiction, you should get your science right. Don't get me *started* on people who *think* they can write SF and don't know basic chemistry, physics or astronomy. (M. Night Shyamalan comes to mind.) Alas, even my own knowledge of all three is limited. I am not, as Robert Heinlein was, an engineer. Nor an astrophysicist like David Brin.

Thus when I get big, crazy space ideas, I need help. Lots of help. In the Vorpal Blade books, that is ably supplied by Dr. Travis Taylor, Ph.D. Alas, Doc has a very busy day job currently and his own projects. In this case, I had to refer to others for assistance.

The most notable of the many people who gave input on this novel are assuredly Bullet Gibson and his lovely wife Belinda. Between the two of them they took a very rough manuscript and, without any support but thanks, fixed not only the many problems of mass, volume and velocity but my (numerous) grammatical errors.

Any mistakes remain mine. But you should have *seen* what they had to *work* with!

Enough. Let the insanity begin.

FOREWORD BY HOWARD TAYLER

If you ask any two witnesses exactly how events unfolded at the scene of the crime, you are going to get two different stories. The less contact the witnesses have with each other prior to your questioning, the further divergent the stories get. Hair colors, car colors, even skin colors and names may change between their accounts.

The longer you wait to question these two following the event, the more their testimonies will begin to sound like tales spun around different characters in different universes.

In the Schlockiverse it has been a thousand years since the Gatekeepers barged in on Humanity and installed a new front door for Sol System. My own memory of that event is pretty fuzzy. Who am I to say that John doesn't have it right? And if he got some of the hair colors, skin colors, or names (or species) mixed up, well...I'm pretty sure the tale is true in spirit.

It is often said that Truth is stranger than Fiction. This is not an aphorism. It is a formula. If this book isn't the truth about how we go about carving the phrase "Humans ~~were~~ ARE here" on the great edifices of Galactic Society, it's because Truth read John's Fiction and said "Okay, I'll have to do better."

THE MAPLE SYRUP WAR

PROLOGUE

It is said that in science the greatest changes come about when some researcher says "Hmmm. That's odd." The same can be said for relationships: "That's not my shade of lipstick..."—warfare: "That's an odd dust cloud..." Etc.

But in this case, the subject is science. And relationships. And warfare.

And things that are just ginormously huge and hard to grasp because space is like that.

* * *

"Hmmm . . . That's odd."

"What?"

Chris Greenstein, in spite of his name, was a gangling, good-looking blond guy who most people mistook for a very pale surfer-dude. He'd found that he was great with the ladies right up until he opened his mouth. So his public persona was of tall, blond and dumb. As in mute. He had a master's in aeronautical engineering and a Ph.D. in astrophysics. The first might have gotten him a really good paying job if he could just manage to get through corporate interviews without putting his

3

foot in his mouth. The second generally boiled down to academia or "Do you want fries with that?" He had the same problem with academia he had with corporations.

Chris was the Third Shift Data Center Manager for Skywatch. Skywatch was an underfunded and overlooked collection of geeks, nerds and astronomy Ph.D.s who couldn't otherwise find a job who dedicated themselves to the very important and very poorly understood job of searching the sky for stuff that could kill the world. The most dangerous were comets which, despite having the essential consistency of a slushee, moved very fast and were generally very big. And when a slushee that's the size of Manhattan Island hits a planet going faster than anything mankind could create, it doesn't just go bang. It turns into a fireball that is only different from a nuclear weapon in that it doesn't release radiation. What it does release is plasma, huge piles of flying burning rock and hot gases. Over a continent. Then the world, or the biosphere at least, more or less gets the big blue screen of death, hits reset and starts all over again with some crocodiles and one or two burrowing animals.

One comet killed the dinosaurs. Most of the guys at Skywatch made not much more than minimum wage. It gives one pause.

The way that Skywatch looked for "stuff" was anything that was quick, cheap and easy. They had databases of all the really enormous amounts of stuff, comets, asteroids, bits, pieces, minor moons, rocks and just general debris, that filled the system. They would occasionally get a contact from someone who thought that they'd found the next apocalypse. Locate, identify, headed for Earth? yes/no? New? yes/no? Most of it was automatic. Most of it was done by other people: essentially anyone with a telescope, from a backyard enthusiast to the team that ran the Hubble was part of Skywatch. But thirty-five guys (including the two women) were paid (not much more than minimum wage) to sort and filter and essentially be the child of Omelas.

Chris was a nail biter. Most people who worked for Skywatch for any period of time developed some particular tic. They knew the odds of the "Big One" happening in their lifetime were *way* less than winning the lottery fifteen times in a row. Even a "Little Bang" was unlikely to occur anywhere that it mattered. A carbonaceous asteroid with a twenty-five megaton airburst yield like Tunguska was unlikely to occur over anything important. The world is seven-tenths ocean and even the land bits are surprisingly empty.

But living day in and day out with the certainty that the fate of the world is in your hands slowly wears. Most people stayed in the core of Skywatch for fewer than five years if for no other reason than the pay. Chris had started as a filter technician ("Yes, that's an asteroid. It's already categorized. Thank you...") six years ago. He was way past his sell-by date and the blond had started going gray.

"It's a streak. But it's a really odd streak. The algorithm is saying it's a flaw."

The way that asteroids and comets are detected has to do with the way that stars are viewed. The more starlight that is collected the stronger the picture. In the old days this was done by having a photographic plate hooked up to a telescope that slowly tracked across the night sky picking up the tiny scatter of photons from the distant star. Computers only changed that in that they could resolve the image more precisely, fold, spindle and mutilate, and a CCD chip was used instead of a plate.

When you're tracking on a star, if something moves across your view it creates a streak. Asteroids and comets are closer than stars and if they are moving across your angle of view they create such a streak. If they're moving towards you it creates a small streak, across the view a large one. The angle of the Sun is important. So is the size of the object. Etc.

Serious researchers didn't have time for streaks. But any streak could be important so they sent them to Skywatch where servers crunched the data on the streak and finally came up with whether it was an already identified streak, a new streak, a new streak that was "bad," etc. In this case the servers were saying it was "odd."

"Define odd," Chris said, bringing up the data. Skywatch researchers rarely looked at images. What he saw was a mass of numbers that to the uninformed would look something like a really huge mass of indecipherable numbers. For Chris it instantly created a picture of the object in question. And the numbers were *very* odd. "Nevermind. Albedo of point seven three? Perfect circle? Diameter of ten point one-four-eight kilometers? Ring shaped? Velocity of...? That's not a flaw, it's a practical joke. Who'd it come from?"

"Max Planck. It's from Calar Alto. That's the problem. Germans..."

Calar Alto was a complex of several massive telescopes located in Andalusia in southern Spain and was a joint project of the Spanish and German governments. The German portion was the Max Planck Institute for Astronomy and despite its location, Max Planck did most of the work at Calar Alto.

"Famously don't have a sense of humor," Chris said. He looked at the angle and trajectory again and shrugged. The bad part of working for Skywatch was worrying about "The Big One." The good part was that nothing was ever an immediate emergency. Anything spotted was probably going to take a long time to get to Earth. "Mark and categorize. It's not on a track for Earth. Angle's off, velocity is all wrong. Ask Calar to do another shot when they've got a free cycle. And we'd better keep an eye on it because with that velocity it's going to shoot through the entire system in a couple of years and if it hits anything it's going to be *really* cool."

"You know what it looks like?"

"Yeah. A halo. Maybe it's the Covenant."

Chris picked up his phone groggily and checked the number.

"Hello?"

"Chris? Sorry to wake you. It's Jon. Could you come in a little early today? We've got a manager's meeting."

"What's up?" Chris asked, sitting up and rubbing his eyes. Jon Marin was the Director of Skywatch. He knew his managers didn't get paid enough to be woken up in the middle of their equivalent night.

"It's Halo. There's been an . . . anomaly. We'll talk about it when you get in. We've got a video conference with Calar at four. Please try to be there."

"Yes, sir," Chris said. He looked at the time and sighed. Might as well get up, day was shot to hell anyway.

"Good afternoon, Dr. Heinsch . . ."

Jon Marin, in spite of his name, looked and sounded like the epitome of a New York Jewish boy. Which was what he was. His first Ph.D. was from NYU, followed by MIT and Stanford. His brother was a top-flight attorney in New York who pulled down a phone number every year. And his mother never let him forget it. He kept trying to point out he was a doctor, to no avail.

"Dr. Marin, Dr. Eisenbart, Dr. Fickle, Dr. Greenstein . . ."

"Doctor." "Doctor." "Doctor." "Doctor."

"As first discoverers we have named the object the Gudram Ring. This will, of course, have to be confirmed. But there is an anomaly we are having a hard time sorting out. We had a cycle that was doing a point to that portion of the sky but when we attempted to find the ring, it appeared to have disappeared."

"Disappeared?" Chris said. "How does something ten kilometers across disappear?"

"We wondered the same thing," Dr. Heinsch replied soberly. "I was able to get authorization to do a sweep for it. It took three full sweeps."

"Your sweeps cost about . . . ?" Dr. Marin said.

"A million Euros for each. But something that was once there and now is not? We considered the outlay appropriate. And we were right. We finally found it. Here is the new data."

The astronomers leaned forward and regarded the information for a moment.

"It slowed down," Chris said after a moment. He finally found a finger that wasn't chewed to the quick and started nibbling. "Was there . . . It didn't have anything to cause a gravitational anomaly. It's coming in from out of the plane of the ecliptic."

Most of the "stuff" in the inner Solar System lay along a vaguely flat plane called the "plane of ecliptic." Earth, Mars, the asteroid belt, were all formed when the Sun was a flattened disc. The outer layers cooled and congealed into planets and then life formed and here we are. We are all star stuff.

If the ring had been coming in along the plane it might have passed a moon or planet and had a change in velocity, what was referred to as a "delta-V." But there weren't any planets "up" in the Solar System and it was inside the Oort Cloud.

"Correct," Dr. Heinsch said as if to a particularly bright child. From the point of view of "real" scientists, those who can, do, those who can't, teach, and those who can't do or teach, work for Skywatch.

"Is this data confirmed?" Dr. Marin asked very cautiously. Skywatch generally only made the news when they screamed "The sky is falling!" Since every time they'd screamed that, it hadn't, they'd gotten very cautious. And this wasn't the sky falling. This was...

"Absolutely," Dr. Heinsch said. "However, we have sent it to you in raw form. We have also contacted the Russian, Japanese and Italian Institutes."

"Yes," Dr. Marin said, nodding. "I think we need to stay very cautious about this until we have a confirm all around..."

"It's a *space*craft!" Chris blurted.

"We need to be very *cautious*," Dr. Marin said, turning to glare at Chris.

"But it's *decelerating!*" Chris said, waving at the screen. "At the current rate of delta it's going to come to rest somewhere near *Earth*!"

"It appears to be headed for the Earth/Sol L2

Lagrange point," Dr. Heinsch said, nodding. "What it does then, of course, is the question."

"We need *definite* confirmations on this before we take *any* action," Dr. Marin said.

"I'm sure we will have those quite quickly. I would request that you contact Palomar for their take. Good day, Doctors."

Planning for shots by the big telescopes of Earth's major countries is blocked out months and even years in advance. They also cost a lot of money.

As the terminator circled about the globe that night, all such scheduling was put on indefinite hold and dozens of telescopes pointed to a very small patch of the sky.

There was, of course, a huge outcry amongst "real" researchers who had grants to study oxygen production of Mira Variables that, naturally, were more important than anything else that could possibly be happening especially with those bunglers at Skywa—A WHAT?

And then the press found out.

"The Gudram Ring has settled into a stationary position in the Sun-Earth L2 Lagrange point," Dr. Heinsch rumbled, looking at his notes. "The position it has taken is not entirely stable but it seems to have some form of stabilization system. Since it was able to maintain delta-V such as to decelerate into the system, that ability is self-evident. However, the L2 point creates a stable point of gravitational interaction which is why so many space telescopes are placed there. Power output for stabilization is, therefore, reduced. As of now, we have no idea as to its method or purpose. Questions?"

"What is it for?" the first reporter asked.

"And I repeat, we have no idea as to its method, we don't know how it works, or its purpose, we don't know why it is here. At this moment, it is as enigmatic as the monolith from *2001*..."

"Office of the President. If you would like to leave a message for the President of the United States, press one. For the Vice President, press two. For the First Lady, press three..."

The phone bank for the general contact number for the White House was not in the White House. It was in a featureless office building in Reston, Virginia. There a group of seventy receptionists, mostly women, received calls from the general public directed at the President.

In the early days of telephone, all calls were listened to, notes taken and daily they would be collated and tracked. This took a lot of people looking over the notes and figuring out what they meant. But there were general tenors. Do a three-part scale. "I love the President so much I want his sperm." "The President's an idiot." "The President is going to die at four PM on Friday." So then there were standard forms. Then computers came along. And Caller ID and voice recognition and automatic voice synthesis and phone trees and...

What the seventy people did was mostly let the computers handle it.

But if you worked the phone tree hard enough, you could get a real human being.

"Office of the President."

"This is not a prank call," a robotic voice said. "This system cannot normally block Caller ID. Please look at your Caller ID."

The receptionist looked at the readout and frowned. The Caller ID readout was a random string of numbers.

"The penalty for hacking the White House is—"

"Please contact your intelligence agencies and confirm that this call is coming from a satellite and has no ground-based transmission. We are the Grtul, the People of the Ring. We come in peace. In five days, on your Thursday, at 12 PM Greenwich Mean Time, we will call your President through a more secure means. This should give him time to clear his schedule. This will be a conference call with several of your major leaders, all of whom have been contacted or will be contacted. Please ensure your President is informed of this call. Thank you. Good-bye."

"So...do we know *which* secure line they're calling?" the President asked.

The Secure Room in the White House was, like most of the rooms in the White House, small. And compared to some secure rooms, not particularly secure. It had been repeatedly upgraded, but when you started off with a concrete basement in a limestone building built in the 1800s there was only so much you could do. The Joint Chiefs much preferred the Tank in the Pentagon.

"We're ready no matter where it comes in, Mr. President," the chief of staff said. The room was more or less at capacity since nobody knew the agenda for the meeting. State, Defense, the Joint

Chiefs, NSA, DNI, himself, even Treasury and Commerce had horned in. About the only member of the "core" cabinet not present was Interior. Surprising even himself, the Director of NASA *had* managed to get a seat.

"Nobody talks but me," the President said just as the phone rang. He took a deep breath and pressed the button for the speaker phone. "President of the United States."

"Waiting... Waiting... Present are the presidents of the United States and Russia, prime ministers of Britain, France, Germany, Japan, China, India, Brazil. Each have staff present. We will not be responding to questions. We are the Grtul. We come in peace. The ring in your sky is a gate to other worlds. We produce these rings and move them into star systems. Use of the ring requires payment. The payment schedule will be sent to you. There is to be no use of hostile energy systems within three hundred thousand kilometers of the ring which are capable of damaging the ring. Anyone who pays may use the ring.

"In seven days we will make a general broadcast to the people of your planet on the subject of the ring. This will give you sufficient time to make your own statements and prevent panic.

"You have a distributed information system. We will establish a document on the information system which will give the full rules, schedules and regulations of the ring. We will include a list of answers to questions. In the last ninety million years we have been asked most conceivable questions. We will now answer the three most common questions asked and then we will terminate this call.

"By 'anyone can use the ring' do we mean that another species can use it to enter your system? Yes. Does that mean that hostile or friendly forces can use it? Yes. Are you allowed to block the ring? No. Goodbye."

"Hell," the President said as the phone went dead. "Those *were* my top questions. NASA? Input?"

"There is a real philosophical question whether there *can* be hostile species at the level to be able to use interstellar travel," the director said. "The energies involved mean that survival as a species if you are innately hostile becomes difficult. If you can create a spacecraft that can go three hundred thousand miles in any reasonable time frame, you can more or less destroy a world. The biosphere at least. Over time, hostile species will tend to wipe themselves out."

"That's a great philosophical point," the Chairman of the Joint Chiefs said. "But the fact that the Grtul mention hostile species and not fighting near the ring probably means you're more or less dead wrong. Pun intended. And according to my people, *we* can't even *get* to this thing."

"Oh, we can get there," the director said. "We're working on a proposal for a manned spacecraft capable of the journey."

"Time and budget?" the President asked, wincing.

"About five years and . . . well, the budget is still being worked on."

"Under or over a trillion?" the national security advisor asked.

"Oh, under. Probably."

Two Years After First Contact

(NASA has completed preliminary studies to the studies necessary to begin preliminary design phase of the bid phase on a potential ship to reach, but not enter, the Gudram Ring. Cost: $976 million dollars.)

The prime minister of Britain picked up his phone without looking. It was the ringtone of his secretary.

"Yes, Janice?"

"Actually, my name is Andrilae Rirgo of the Glatun. I am the captain of an exploratory vessel which has just exited your Grtul Ring. We come in peace and are interested in trade."

The prime minister looked at the handset then at the phone, which was registering a random string of numbers from the Caller ID. Just as he was getting over the shock the door opened and his secretary started waving her arms frantically. He was able to read her lips well enough to get the words "Gate emergence." The rather graphic hand motions, not to mention his current conversation, helped. He nodded at her and went back to his conversation.

"Well, uh, Mr. . . . Rirgo did you say? Welcome to Earth."

"So we really don't have anything they want?" the President said.

"No, sir," the commerce secretary said. "The computer chips they're offering are centuries more advanced than anything we produce. Enormous storage and something close to infinite parallel processing. They also integrate with terrestrial systems seamlessly. Somehow. The IT experts are scratching their head as to how. But why they can just take over our systems is now pretty obvious. The chips are more like viruses than computers. But what they mainly want is precious metals. Specifically the platinum group which are pretty rare. Also gold."

"Do we mine those?" the President asked.

"We do in small quantities," Interior said. "More in Canada. Most are extracted from nickel and copper mining. Most of the world's deposits are in South Africa or Russia."

"Damnit."

Three Years After First Contact

"This had better be important," the President said as he entered the Situation Room. The Secret Service had practically yanked him out of a meeting with the Saudi ambassador.

"We've had a gate emergence," the Chairman of the Joint Chiefs said over the video link.

"We've had those every few months for the last year," the President pointed out. "Mostly what I suppose could be tramp freighters, no offense to our Glatun friends intended."

It had quickly become apparent that even tramp freighter captains could access any electronic transmission. This had less to do with the super advanced chips they traded for enormous amounts of heavy metals or anything else that seemed of some worth than their software systems and implant technology. Efforts to duplicate their information technology had so far been unsuccessful and most experts put humans as at least five hundred years behind current Glatun technology.

"Not Glatun. The ship looks like a warship and isn't responding to our standard hails."

"Is it... big?" the President asked. He'd been elected on the basis of his domestic programs and wasn't quite up to speed on international affairs much less interstellar.

"It really doesn't matter how big it is, Mr. President," the admiral in command of Space Command responded. "We still don't get the engineering of the Glatun reactionless drive or their power systems. So we're grounded. If it's a warship it's going to be able to hold the orbitals. And who holds the orbitals, holds the world."

"Oh."

"All stocks of precious metals," the secretary of state said. "Private, corporate and governmental. We can keep enough stock of gold to keep the IT industry running but that's it. We pointed out that it would make us more efficient at extraction and they accepted the argument, but palladium, which turns out is important for hard drives, has to be turned over. That's for all the world's governments. Or our cities get what Mexico City, Shanghai and Cairo got. Pony up and the Horvath won't nuke the rest of the world."

"Technically they weren't nukes," SpaceCom pointed out. "They were kinetic energy weapons. Practical effect is similar but no fallout, thank God."

"Why those three?" the President asked. "Did they say?"

"No, sir," SpaceCom said. "But if you've ever seen a night shot of the world, it's pretty obvious. They picked the three that are most noticeable. Since we're in a shield room I'll point out that that was a pretty poor choice on their part. I don't think they'd developed full intel on the planet. Doesn't really matter but it's a potential chink in their armor. They're not gods."

"True," the JCS said. "But we also can't fight them. Recommendation of the JCS is that we pay the tribute and try to get the Glatun to intervene. We just *can't* fight them."

"So are we going to have them landing here?" the President asked. "If so there's going to be a major security situation."

"So far we haven't even seen the Horvath," the secretary of state said. "All discussion has been electronic or with their robots. As to where they are landing..." She nodded at the secretaries of commerce and interior.

"We and Canada will ship our small amount of production to South Africa, which will handle the transfer," Commerce said. "There will only be landings in South Africa and Russia. And only to pick up refined metals. They appear to want to keep the world running so that we can fill their holds. Not that we can; the whole world's production amounts to a few dozen tons a year."

SpaceCom looked a bit irritated for a moment, possibly because his aide had touched him on the arm, then grunted.

"What I don't get is why they're getting them on the planet," SpaceCom said. "According to my experts, most of this stuff is to be found in asteroids. We've got a ton of asteroids just cluttering up the damned system. Most of what we mine is from asteroids that have crashed into the Earth. Why not just mine the asteroid belt?"

"Possibly because then slaves don't do it for them,"

the President said dryly.

"It's a matter of what your world calls realpolitik," the Glatun representative said politely. The Glatun was a bit over a meter-and-a-half-tall biped with blue skin, red eyes, a vaguely piglike head and snout and a mane of white fur running down his back. He was dressed in an informal tunic for the discussion which was, in diplospeak, "non-binding and informal." Which was where all the really serious binding resolutions were always hammered out.

"We have called for the Horvath to remove themselves from your world's orbitals and they have chosen to ignore our requests. Since Earth is, to them, a very good conquest, relatively rich in heavy metals compared to Horvath, they won't leave absent either armed confrontation or, possibly, a trade embargo. Since Earth has, essentially, little or no value to the Glatun Federation, we have a sufficiency of strategic metals, and there are negative aspects to both choices on our part, we must unfortunately state that we remain neutral in this dispute."

"We have . . . an extensive asteroid belt," the under-secretary of state for interstellar affairs said, throwing in her only bone. "We believe it to be rich in the platinum group."

"For which you should be grateful," the Glatun replied. "Most inhabited systems are mined out. However, our laws, and long experience, prevent us from mining your asteroid belt as long as there is not a centralized, or at least effectively sovereign, system government. The Horvath meet the definition, not the United States of America. Certainly not the

UN. The Horvath have, also, offered the asteroid belt. Be equally grateful that we declined that offer. There are enormous problems with asteroid mining. It requires quite large lasers and fabbers and is fuel and energy intensive. To make it worthwhile for a Glatun corporation to invest in this system would require long-term leases. In the current security and political situation the Glatun Federation would not permit such legally binding contracts."

"We're on our own." The USSIA finally said, becoming decidedly informal. "We have sixteen million dead, three major cities in ashes and you're *neutral*?"

"Since we are speaking frankly..." the Glatun said. "The decision of our policy makers is that Earth is simply sufficiently unknown and unnoticeable to take the chance of losing credibility in a minor dispute. The reality is that the Horvath, who are not much more advanced than Earth, would probably leave if so much as a single Glatun destroyer entered the system and ordered them to do so. However, if they didn't and shots were fired, much less loss of Glatun life, there would be questions asked in Parliament, AI queries, and of course the press would simply go wild. It is easier and safer to do nothing. Absent Earth becoming more of a hot topic in the Glatun Federation or becoming in some way strategically important, yes, you are on your own."

ONE

Tyler dropped his chainsaw and pulled out his cell phone. He'd barely felt the vibration and it was impossible to hear over the saw. He looked at the Caller ID and tried not to curse. Three missed calls from the same ... Arrgh!

"Tyler Vernon."

"Tyler, it's Mrs. Cranshaw. How are you today?"

"Just fine, ma'am," Tyler said, squeezing his eyes shut and waiting for it. She always started nice. "And you?"

"Fine, just fine," Mrs. Cranshaw said. "Fine weather we're having. Getting cold. The frost should bring out the leaves a treat."

"Yes, ma'am," Tyler replied. *Here it comes.*

"Speaking of it getting cold, I think I asked you to bring by some firewood."

"Yes, ma'am. And I said I'd get it over there on Friday."

"Well, it's gone Wednesday. Are you going to *be* here on Friday?"

"When I say I'm going to be there, I'll be there, ma'am."

"Well, I asked for it last week. Seems you could have got it here before Friday. You're not doing much else."

Just working at the market, part-time, working in the bookstore, part-time, working at the mill, part-time, cutting wood, splitting wood, by hand, and answering your damned phone calls every damned day. Oh, and the rare consulting gig. But other than that I've got all the time in the world! I suppose I could point out that I could have delivered it Sunday night at 10 PM but she'd go and tell all her friends I'd been snippy with her and half my clientele would dry up rather than go up against her vicious tongue.

"Gotta work at the market this evening, ma'am," Tyler said politely. "Couldn't get it by until late. Tomorrow I'm going to be working at the bookstore all day and then in the market that evening. I'll be there at one Friday if the job I've got to do at the mill don't take too long. No later than four."

"You'd better be here by one," Mrs. Cranshaw said. "I don't want to be without wood this weekend."

"Yes, ma'am," Tyler said.

"You be with the Lord, Tyler Vernon," Mrs. Cranshaw said and hung up.

Tyler closed the phone and swung it back and forth in his fist, wanting to crush it and the whole damned world that seemed to be determined to do nothing but ruin the life of one Tyler Vernon.

Tyler Alexander Vernon was five foot two, one hundred and thirty-five pounds and long over the problem of having three first names. He'd been born and raised in Mississippi, graduated from LSU with a master's in computer science and, after applying five times at NASA, ended up working for an internet backbone center in Atlanta. That had led to various positions in the IT field and a pretty steady corporate advance culminating in a senior manager position at AT&T in Boston. Then came the real breakout: *TradeHard*.

He'd had it made in the shade. He and his wife, okay, had some issues. But even if money couldn't solve everything, it could solve a lot. He'd never thought that his webcomic was going to be anything other than something to fill the time and maybe make its nut. How was *he* to know it would take off like a Delta rocket? The awards, the adulation. He'd really not cared that much about the money. He really hadn't. It was more about making a change in people's lives. But as it turned out...

No, that was unfair. Petra hadn't cared about the money. She cared about the lifestyle the money brought in. She'd hitched her wagon to a rising star at AT&T back before he'd been doing much more than scribbling. Dug in there though the tough years, reveled in the good. Tyler hadn't really wanted the cabin in New Hampshire but he was glad they'd bought it. And paid it off as the money got better and better and...

A science fiction based webcomic about a free-trader ship. One of the few that had gotten national syndication. A small TV show. A movie deal in the works.

And the gate opened. And science fiction, as an industry, died.

Well, there was always IT. Five years was a lifetime in IT. Catching up was possible but hard. He'd been *making* it.

And the Horvath came. And the inevitable depression that followed the orbital bombing of three major cities. Not to mention the stripping the world of all its heavy metals.

And like one of those rocks tumbling towards the planet below, his life had gone into freefall. The fiery reentry culminating in the plasma explosion of the divorce.

And now he lived in a cabin in the woods and saw his kids when he had any time between working five jobs.

He put his phone away, picked up the saw, yanked it into life and applied it to the oak he was chunking. Hard.

"Tyler, Chuck needs you to work on Saturday."

Steve Moorman was the night manager of Mac's Market in Franconia. Tall, stooped and prematurely balding, his life ambition seemed to be to retire as the night manager of the Mac's Market in Franconia. Tyler considered him lacking in ambition. But despite his current downcycle, Tyler considered most people to be lacking in ambition.

Since it was Chuck that needed help, that meant day-shift and there was an "issue." He had a gig at a con in Reading on Saturday. The greater SF market may have suffered the fate of the dodo but fandom just would not let go. There was even some anime still going.

He did some quick calculations.

He wasn't getting paid for the gig; the only reason he was invited as the Artist Guest of Honor was that he was somewhat famous, local and cheap. But he still could move some merc in the dealer's room and people still bought his sketches of Gomez, Frank and Forella. The market was a little saturated but he'd still make more sitting on his butt in the dealer's room than working it off in the store. And Saturday sucked. The ski-birds from Boston and NYC would be flooding in and asking "Why don't you have arugula? Where's the couscous?"

The flip side being that if he said no, not only would one of the other stockers get asked the next time some extra time came up, but Steve, the passive-aggressive asshole, would probably start cutting back on his hours.

Short-term money or long-term money? More like medium-term because he was *not* going to retire as the night manager of Mac's Market.

Somehow the con co-chair had gotten a Glatun to attend. That decided it. The chance to talk to a real-live alien wasn't one to pass up.

"Steve, I'm really sorry but I'm already scheduled for something on Saturday," Tyler replied, diplomatically. "I'd love to work but I've got a gig in Boston."

"Uh, huh," Steve said, slowly. "Isn't that one of those . . . convention things?"

"Yes," Tyler said, just as slowly. "It's one of those convention things. I can work the evening shift—"

"No, that would be too much juggling in the schedule," Steve said, puffing out his cheeks. "I'll just ask Marsha."

"Sorry about that," Tyler said. "Anything else?"

"There's a spill in produce," Steve said. "Help Tom clean the oranges."

"Right away."

Tyler took the two crisp twenties from Mrs. Cranshaw and nodded.

"Thank you," he said politely.

"Forty dollars seems an awful lot of money for a cord of wood," Mrs. Cranshaw said. "Not like I don't already own plenty."

Owner of five maple sugar distilleries and over four thousand acres of maple forest and white pine, one of Mrs. Cranshaw's noted peculiarities was that she was so tight with money she made the buffalo squeal.

"Going rate, ma'am," Tyler said. He'd wondered when he started delivering wood to her why he'd been chosen rather than one of the local lumberjacks. You know, people who *worked* for the old witch.

The answer being, nobody else would put up with her.

"Forty dollars is just robbery for firewood," Mrs. Cranshaw said. "When I was a girl, Cokes were a nickel. A nickel, I tell you!"

"Yes, ma'am," Tyler said. If you tried to stop her she got mean. Best to just ride it out.

"And the winters is getting worse. It's these damned aliens."

At best the orbital bombardment of Shanghai, Cairo and Mexico City had dropped global temperatures by .0001% according to Glatun-backed studies. It took a lot more than a few megatons of rock and, okay, some really major secondary fires, to disturb Earth's climate.

"Yes, ma'am."

"I'm thinking about selling this place," she said. "My old bones can't take these winters."

She'd apparently been saying that since before her fourth husband died. They'd all been wealthy, they'd all left her all their fortune and they'd all died of natural causes. Anyone who suggested anything different had better move out of the county. Besides, after husband three there'd been a pretty thorough investigation and the final result was "dead of stress."

"Yes, ma'am."

"Everything seems to go up but maple sugar land," she said angrily. "Wood isn't bringing what it used to, not at all. Nor maple sugar. Damn aliens. Hate those damned aliens."

"Yes, ma'am," Tyler said. He bit his tongue to keep from adding: *And so do the Chinese, Egyptians and Mexicans.*

"They're listening to everything we say," she said, looking at the sky nervously. "They're up there right now, listening to us."

While the Horvath information systems did seem to be able to track just about any conversation made around an electronic device, Tyler rather doubted that they were personally listening in on this one. He had a moment's empathetic thought for any Horvath who was and quashed it rather automatically.

"Yes, ma'am."

"Well," she said, relenting a bit. "You did stack it neat. I like a good neat stack of wood."

With most people when you delivered a cord it was "Here you go" and get it off the pickup as fast as possible. All done, that'll be forty bucks.

Not with Mrs. Cranshaw. That firewood had better be stacked in a neat and tidy cord on her back porch. Which took about five times as long as just dumping it in the yard.

Speaking of time.

"Ma'am, I'd love to stay and chat. But I've got an event in Boston where I'm the speaker and I need to be going."

"Speaker?" she asked, incredulously. "About what?"

"The webcomic I used to do," Tyler said evenly.

"Oh, yes," Mrs. Cranshaw said, with the most perfect note of neutrality that descended past condescension and straight to contempt. "You used to do that comic thing."

"Yes, I used to do that comic thing," Tyler said. "And now I'm going to go talk to people about doing comic things."

"Used to run in the paper," Mrs. Cranshaw said. "Never did get what was so funny about it. And I didn't like all them alien names. Couldn't figure them out."

"Yes, ma'am," Tyler said.

"Well, if you've got a commitment you best be to it," Mrs. Cranshaw said. "Can't hardly figure out what you're going to talk on seeing as there's real aliens now. But you do go on and talk about comic things."

"Yes, ma'am," Tyler said. "See you in a couple of months, then?"

"Sorry I'm late, Mr. Du Vall," Tyler said, shaking the con-chair's hand. "Got hung up doing some server work."

"Not a problem," the convention co-chairman said. James Du Vall was 5'11", AmerAsian and shaped something like a large bear. He had black hair, a white and black beard, and it was patterned in a very familiar way. Tyler had never met him but could just about guess his nickname . . . "Call me Panda. Everybody does. You're just in time for opening ceremonies, which was your first panel."

Tyler had gotten a peek into the ballroom as he was walking in and shook his head.

"I thought you said this was a small con. There must be a thousand people in the ballroom."

"I'd say they're all here to see you," Panda said with a shrug. "Truth is they're mostly here to see—"

"A real-live Glatun," Tyler finished, gesturing with his chin at the alien standing in a corner and watching the "pros" straggling into the small, walled-off area. "I won't ask how you got him to attend."

"Simple," Panda said, smiling thinly. "I paid him. More than I'm going to get out of the con but that wasn't the point. Science fiction isn't dead, it's just become reality. And fandom is still where people who want to work for the future gather. I could go on but we've got to get going."

"Lead on," Tyler said.

Panda headed up the steps to the stage and the other "Special Guests" sort of straggled after him.

There was the usual series of tables flanking a podium and the usual milling as people tried to figure out where to sit. And Tyler had his usual flash of annoyance at it. *They're chairs. You sit in 'em. Sit. Heel.*

Since the Glatun looked particularly puzzled, he caught its eye and waved to a chair, pulling it out. Fortunately Glatun and human design were similar enough a human chair worked just fine. The Glatun sat down and Tyler snagged the chair next to it by right of conquest. Worked for the Horvath.

"Ladies and Gentlemen and honored extraterrestrials..." Panda said to some cheers at the last part. "Welcome to MiraCon..."

"You are Tyler Vernon," the Glatun whispered as Panda started into what sounded like it was going to be a very *long* speech.

Tyler noted that the voice, which was fairly human normal, was coming from a small pod on a collar and the Glatun had not, in fact, opened his mouth. He'd heard that they mostly communicated through their implants but it was still a bit of shock.

"Yes, I am," Tyler whispered back.

"I am Fallalor Wathaet, captain of the *Spinward Crossing*. A pleasure to meet you. You used to write *TradeHard*, did you not?"

"Yes," Tyler said, shocked again. "How did you...? *Why* do you know that?"

"The security situation on Terra for traders is good," Wathaet said. "But if I was going to be dealing with people, I wished to know who I might be near."

"We are, after all, potentially dangerous locals with bizarre and disgusting customs," Tyler said.

"'Who will do anything to screw us out of our credits. Our job is to be better screws.'"

"You *read* the comic?" Tyler was still recovering from the earlier shocks. This was water on a duck.

"It is one of the few times when I have understood human humor," the Glatun said. "Perhaps in part because it struck so close to home and was so true. Although banks do not routinely send mercenaries to collect your ship. There are people in our government who do that quite well, thank you."

"It was a rare situation," Tyler pointed out. "But... thanks for the compliment."

"I almost stopped reading in the first few panels," Wathaet said, "because I did not understand the cultural conditions of stealing the infant's candy. When I was able to grasp it fully, though, I very nearly had an accident. Rule Nine: If the other guy doesn't feel screwed we're not doing our jobs. I printed that out and put it up in the mess. We all got it. But I personally feel it's more of a guideline."

"Same here," Tyler said. "If I'd really been a back-stabber I would have been a VP."

"Why did you stop writing?" Wathaet asked. "I was only able to find the comic on an archive server and there were no notices to explain your cessation."

"Whew..." Tyler said. "Big answer. Basically, it was an economic decision. As soon as the gate opened, everyone in the industry quickly saw that anything SF was falling off. So I got dropped like a hot potato in most of my markets. The website traffic and merch fell off sharply as well. Then with our Horvath protectors requiring a very high payment for protection, server space started getting expensive. Eventually it simply wasn't economical."

"You have very few new drawings on your personal system," Wathaet said. "Sorry about looking. But your information systems are so primitive that it's a bit like trying not to look through a plate glass window. Once I'd scanned all your available archives on other systems, I set my system to find more and only realized I was in your personal system when I saw many of them were partials. But I think you haven't had much time. Your personal and business finances are terribly screwed up. My apologies. Again, it's rather hard *not* to look."

"No problem," Tyler said, gritting his teeth. "On another subject, was trading good?"

"No," the Glatun admitted. "With the Horvath control of your heavy metals, which were paltry anyway, your world has virtually nothing to trade. Despite that, every time one of our ships comes here we have to first meet with members of your senior governments who ask if there's anything we, the traders mind you, can do about the Horvath. No, there's not. Then we meet with senior corporate representatives who have gathered such things as we might be interested in and we trade. The pattern is always the same. And, really, what am I going to get for folk art?"

"The Venus de Milo is hardly folk art!" Tyler said. He'd seen the news. "Not to mention the paintings." He paused and sighed. "Sorry. I really do understand the situation. Probably better in some ways than those 'senior representatives.'"

"Hmmm. From your comic I would say that is the case, but how exactly?"

"Look up Polynesian contact with the West," Tyler said. "I assume that is..."

"Yes, the similarities are there. We do not carry diseases but..."

"You're trading iron nails for pearls," Tyler said. "Well, you were. Now our Horvath benefactors receive the pearls as an honorarium for their defense of our system. And we only have coconut husks and carvings to sell."

"Do you really think the Horvath are your benefactors?" Wathaet asked.

"Of course I do," Tyler said, smiling. "Our Horvath benefactors who find our systems as porous as you do and are listening to this conversation on my cell phone are our *friends!*"

"Ah," the Glatun said, making a noise something like a sneeze. "Don't worry. The Horvath are most certainly not listening to any conversation *I* am involved in."

"Really?" Tyler asked.

"Really. Horvath systems are better than *yours*. But the information systems on what they call a battle cruiser, which is not much bigger than a Glatun admiral's landing barge, are no match for even *my* ship. And I'll admit I don't have galaxy class systems. The Horvath are most certainly not listening."

"In that case," Tyler said, smiling again. "Of course we're poor. They're stealing all our metals. What I don't get is why the Glatun don't throw them out so Glatun traders get the metals."

"Other than assuring the safety of trade, our military tries very hard to avoid nonstrategic entanglements," Wathaet said. "That has not always been the case and we've had times in our history of military adventurism and colonialism. But we've given that up mostly."

"I can understand that, too," Tyler said, nodding. "I know this is a shot in the dark, but have people sort of shown you, well, *everything* we have to trade?"

"What do you mean?" the Glatun said, then held up a hand. "Your turn to talk."

"Damn," Tyler said, getting up and trying to remember what he was going to say.

He managed to stumble through some remarks then sat back down quickly.

"You said something about everything you have to trade," Wathaet said. "Your produced items are rather crude and expensive for you to produce compared to fabbers. Not economical for us. There's not much mark-up in the market for things that are simply made by hand. A fabber can produce variation easily. We produce what you consider precious gems practically as industrial waste..."

"Got all that," Tyler said. "I mean, you *read* the comic. Covered that."

"True. And Forella really screwed those natives."

"Well, they deserved it. What about commodity materials?" Tyler asked.

"You mean foodstuffs?" Wathaet said. "I did read the comic. You know as well as I that your foodstuffs are chemically incompatible. We may have some similarity in appearance to terrestrial organisms but our chemistry is radically different. You covered that as well."

"Which is all very good theory but it hasn't been *tested*," Tyler said.

"Yes, it has," Wathaet said. "By the first contact ship. We're incompatible."

"Did they test *everything*?" Tyler said. "If not—"

"My turn to talk," Wathaet said, getting up. "Where is that...Ah. There's the speech..."

Tyler sort of tuned out his speech and thought.

"What are you doing before you leave?" Tyler asked as Wathaet sat back down.

"We leave on Wednesday," Wathaet said. "That's when we're picking up our last few trades. Not much on Monday. Why?"

"Let's check," Tyler said. "I'll load up my pickup with just...stuff. You've got something that can tell if it's poisonous, I'm sure."

"Yes," Wathaet said.

"I'll bring a bunch of...stuff," Tyler said. "It'll take a bit for you to check it but there might be something that you can find that's worth trading. If so, you make a profit and I've got the lock on a major extraterrestrial market. Unlikely, but why think small?"

"Intriguing," Wathaet said. "I'll do it. On one condition."

"Which is?" Tyler asked, warily.

"Can you...do a sketch?"

"Mr. Vernon?"

Tyler looked up from the sketch he was doing and smiled.

"Hey, how you doing?"

"Great," the man said, smiling. Six foot, short red hair, really Irish complexion, green eyes. Miskatonic U T-shirt and jeans. "My name's Dan Poore. I'm a really big fan."

"Glad to hear that," Tyler said, handing the previous customer his sketch.

"Thanks, Mr. Tyler," the kid said, forking over ten bucks. "This is great!"

"And thank you," Tyler said, ignoring the mistake in his name. "Would you like a sketch...uh..."

"Dan," the redhead said. "Uh...sure." He dug in his pocket and came up with two fives. "Could you do one of the Glatun?"

"Wathaet? Sure," Tyler said. Might as well get some practice.

"You guys were sure talking up a storm on the stage," Dan said.

"Turns out he did some research on the people he might be meeting and took to *TradeHard*," Tyler said, starting to sketch rapidly.

"I guess...a story about a group of space free traders would make sense to an alien free trader," Dan said. "Were you just talking about the comic?"

"That and why I stopped doing it," Tyler said. "And

he wants me to come over to the ship and do a sketch of him and the crew and the ship *TradeHard* style."

"Getting paid in atacirc?" Dan asked curiously.

"I wish," Tyler said, handing over the sketch. "Thanks for your continued support. Are you part of TradeCrew?"

"Uh, no," Dan said. "But I'd like to get a 'What's Your Score?' T-Shirt."

"Twenty-five bucks," Tyler said, handing over a large. "And thank you again."

"Must be a bit of a come-down doing small cons," Dan said, forking over the money. "I hope I didn't..."

"Just love the people," Tyler said neutrally. "Anything else?"

"No," Dan said. "Thanks."

Special Agent Daniel Nolan Poore got in the van and was swept head to foot before he opened his mouth.

"He's meeting with the Glatun. Didn't get into when. Says he's just doing a sketch of the crew and the captain."

"Why do they want a sketch?" the senior special agent asked.

"Said that Wathaet's a fan," Dan said, shrugging. "Makes sense."

"Write it up," the SSA said. "Longhand. I want somebody with a camera, and I shouldn't have to point this out, but a *chemical* camera, getting shots. I don't want the Horvath or the Glatun to realize they're under surveillance."

TWO

As he drove back to Boston on Monday, Tyler had to admit that he'd much rather work for Chuck on day shift. When he'd gone to the general manager and asked if he could scrounge through the rejects that were being returned, Chuck had just waved. Among other things, Chuck was a fan and while that didn't get Tyler many points, it allowed them to communicate better.

People generally didn't buy something in grocery stores that was dinged, scratched or otherwise marred. They'd eat stuff that had so little nutrition that they might as well eat the box but woe-betide if the box was crushed. So anything that wasn't visually perfect got sent back to the vendors and either got credited or sold through outlets. There were rules against giving it to most food banks for that matter. Most of it was just thrown away.

Most of the damage occurred over the weekend so Tyler had had plenty of stuff to pick through and he'd gotten just about one of everything. The likelihood of any of it being compatible with the Glatun, much less valuable, was small. But long shots occasionally hit and it was this or cut trees.

Tyler really wanted to wangle a ride on the ship. There was no way that was going to fly but it was a childhood dream.

He hadn't just come up with *TradeHard* on the spur of the moment, he'd wanted to *be* Wathaet from the time he was a kid. His grandfather was in his sixties before they ever met but he remembered the old man's stories like they were yesterday. Granda had been a crewman, eventually rising to captain, on tramp steamers that plied the South Seas trade back when they were still converting from sail to steam. His stories of trading for copra, fights with gangs in pre-Communist Shanghai and, as they both got older, beautiful island maidens, were some of the highlights of Tyler's childhood. That and books, mostly SF books once he found them. Combine Norton and Heinlein and Poul Anderson with Granda and you got *TradeHard*, what Tyler *really* wanted to do when he grew up.

He'd considered going into the merchant marine rather than college but it simply wasn't the same as when Granda was a crewman. American crewmen, especially, ran under so many rules, unions and regulations that it wasn't much different from being part of any other corporation. The soul was gone from it.

Space, though, had to be different. There was just too much variety available. Sure, there were problems. But they'd be bigger... grander.

"So for two fifteen-minute speeches you managed to make our gate fees," Drath said sourly. The ship's purser blew out a line of spittle and recovered it. "And that only by smuggling out that guy's stash of gold coins. How the hell did he hang onto those, by the way?"

"Look up 'survivalist,'" Wathaet said. "It's a really bizarre religion these people have."

"Unless we can find a rich buyer with a queer jones for alien folk art we're not going to make fuel! And that doesn't count the damned mortgage. We are so screwed."

"I know," Wathaet said, lifting his mane in a shrug. "I'm meeting that guy who used to do the *TradeHard* comic. He's bringing some stuff for me to look at. Not much chance any of it will be worth anything but at this point..."

"It's about all we can hope," Drath said. "Well, I hear Norada Lines is hiring. Back to being a cargo handler."

"Yeah, good for you," Wathaet said. "I'm not qualified on anything bigger than a class IV. I'm going to be doing the Tranat run for the rest of my life. I *hate* Tranat station! It's a damned *gas* mine! There aren't even any good bars!"

"Hi," Tyler said to the armed guard at the gate. The *Spinward Crossing*, which was smaller than he'd realized, was tucked into a warehouse in a half-finished industrial park near Reading. Why they'd picked the Boston area was anyone's guess. Most of the ships that had landed in the U.S. had landed near Washington or L.A. "Vernon Tyler. I'm supposed to meet with Captain Wathaet."

"Yes, sir," the security guard said, consulting a list. "Could I see some ID?"

"Why are there guards on the ship?" Tyler asked.

"Believe it or not, some people can't sort out the difference between Glatun and our Horvath benefactors," the guard said, handing back his ID. "So far we haven't had any protestors but there have been . . . incidents in other countries."

"Ah," Tyler said. "I'm not going to cause an incident."

"No, sir," the guard said, opening the gate. "Have a nice day."

"Captain Wathaet," Tyler said as he parked the pickup. He'd been directed to bring it actually *into* the warehouse so he was able to park it right by the ship. That was after another security check, which had searched the back and underside of the pickup, presumably for bombs.

"Mr. Vernon," Wathaet said, stepping down from the cargo ramp. "A pleasure to see you again. What have you brought?"

"Rare and costly viands from the four corners of the Earth," Tyler said cheerfully. "You'll understand if I don't get into exactly *what* rare and costly viands."

"Of course," Wathaet said as Tyler started unloading. "Bring them up in the ship. I've set up a table and some chairs. It occurred to me after we made this agreement that I was placing myself in trade against the writer of *TradeHard*. I'm not sure that's a good idea."

"Those who can, do, those who can't, write," Tyler said, pulling out a set of trays with Dixie cups on them. The Dixie cups had been the most expensive part. "I've really got no experience of this sort of thing. Even if we find something I'm pretty sure I'm going to get screwed. I have prepared two hundred and twenty-three different possible trade items for your examination. Each of them is of the highest possible quality and chosen from some of the rarest and most sought-after substances on Earth."

"You're behind on your cell phone bill and your ex is still looking at the e-mail she hasn't sent about being behind on your child support payment," Wathaet said, taking out a small hand scanner and starting to scan the cups. "I'm pretty sure that these are from the tossed out trash in the stockroom of your store. But it's not under surveillance or in inventory so I'm not positive."

"Bastard," Tyler muttered, setting the cups down on the table. It looked to be some sort of polymer and was sort of scratched and worn. For that matter the small...hold, he supposed, was beat to hell. "I hate it when people know more about my life than I do."

"Like I said," Wathaet said, "it's like trying not to look through an open window. Nothing, nothing, poisonous as hell which is interesting..."

"What's that?" Tyler asked.

"Thirty-seven."

"Wow. If we ever do get into regular trade with your people, don't ever *ever* accept a Coke."

"Thought that was what it was," Wathaet said. "We'd been warned. And our implants can process it. Would only make us mildly ill. This one is interesting. Not for us. It's compatible with Rangora systems. Not sure what it would taste like to them."

As he was scanning, he was picking up and sniffing anything that wasn't registering as toxic. He paused with one and set down his scanner. His snout practically turned inside out as he gave a long sniff. The mane that ran down his back stood up like a startled cat.

"This smells..." Wathaet said, carefully dipping a finger into the yellow-gold syrup. He took a small taste and rolled it around in his mouth. "This is..."

Suddenly he drove his snout into the cup and began licking frantically.

"You okay?" Tyler asked worriedly.

"Yeah," Wathaet said. His tone wasn't muffled because he wasn't actually opening his mouth. But it should have been because his snout, which was just a bit too wide, had ripped open the Dixie cup and was covered in a golden-tarry substance. A long, purple tongue emerged and began licking the substance off. "What *is* this stuff?"

On the long shot, which seemed to be playing out, that something would be compatible and interesting to the Glatun, Tyler had put the various foodstuffs into the cups and marked then with numbers. That way only he knew what they were. The "156" was barely visible since it had been ripped.

"Huh," Tyler said, consulting a handwritten list. "Dragon's Tears. *Figured* it would be that."

"What is Dr....Wha-buh...Wheeeeeeeeeeet." The Glatun shook his head and opened his mouth. "*Gar-glaaafawwowluple?*"

"What is Dragon's Tears?" the collar transmitter asked.

"Did you just *speak* Glatun?" Tyler asked.

"More or less," Wathaet said, shaking his head. "I couldn't handle my plants for a second. That stuff has a *kick*! I think we might be onto a winner here. What is Dragon's Tears? It's not anywhere on your information systems."

"Tears of a Dragon," Tyler said. "Nearly impossible

to get, very rare and almost secret. You have to make a dragon laugh and cry to get them. First you have to tell a dragon ten jokes it's never heard before. If you tell it one joke it's heard you have to start over again. And you'd better tell them fast and well or it will eat you. If you make it through that, then you have to tell it ten sad stories that make it cry. When it starts to cry you dash forward and catch the tears."

"You are such a liar," Wathaet said. "First of all, dragons are a legend like the trakal of my people. Second, if something was that rare and costly you couldn't afford it. Third, all my instruments say that this came from a plant."

"True, but it's going to make great marketing," Tyler said.

"You got any more?" Wathaet said, contemplating the empty cup with slumped shoulders. "Seriously, this is *really* good. Who knew?"

"I've got some more," Tyler said. No cameras that could see in the truck bed. "But, seriously, I do need some trade for it. I'll get some more out of the back of the truck and we'll trade."

When Tyler got back there wasn't one Glatun but three clustered around the table. He'd brought a squeeze bottle and some Dixie Cups.

"Why don't we try mixing it with a little water?" Tyler said. "I don't have enough to fill these cups. I'm thinking... hundred weight of atacirc per weight of tears."

"You've got to be joking!" one of the Glatun snapped. They pretty much looked alike but this one had a longer snout than Wathaet and darker blue skin.

"Hey, Tyler," Wathaet said, the collar transmitter faithfully replicating his slur. "Meet Drath. He's the purser. Han'les all the...cargo an' stuff. An' Fabet's a eng...enga..."

"Ship's engineer," Fabet said, leaning forward. "So what is this stuff?"

"Dragon's Tears," Tyler said, squirting a generous measure into a cup and handing it to the purser. If he was reading things right the purser was going to be the guy he needed as hammered as possible for the negotiations. "Very rare and precious."

"Not worth a hundred weight of circuitry," Drath said, taking a sniff. It was the same reaction as before. Light sniff, heavy sniff, nose dive. "Whoooooooo!"

"Guys," Tyler said, filling cups. "This stuff really *is* expensive. Slow down!"

"Here," Wathaet said, reaching into a pocket. "You guys like this crap. It's trash but is better than your trash." He rolled a handful of atacirc onto the table and waved. "Keep it. Go' anymore?"

Tyler carefully scooped up the fortune in circuitry and poured some more "Dragon's Tears" in the captain's cup.

"Goorbol computers on this planet," Fabet slurred. He'd had about three ounces total. "Total trash. Go' tha' stuff for scrap! Is scrap! Hah! Is, like, hundred years old! Hah! Is good stuff, this."

"Shhhh..." Drath whispered, waving a hand around. "Shhh...Humans can' know that! Think i's...kala stones or something." He appeared to sneeze several times.

"So...Drath," Tyler said neutrally. "This appears to have some trade value. It is, as I said, a very rare and costly viand on this planet. I think a hundred weight to one is perfectly reasonable."

"Me too!" the engineer said. "Stuff will sell for bazillion credits on Glalkod station!"

"Shhhh!" Drath said. "Shhhhh! Well, Mr. Vernon," he continued, straightening his harness, "this does seem to have some merit as you shay. But not gr... great and atacirc is, also, very rare and costly..."

"Your engineer just said you bought it for scrap," Tyler said.

"*Scrap!* And we're gonna get *rich*!"

"He exaggerates. I think that a rate of fifty weight of this... Dragon's Tears to one weight of molycirc would be more in order..."

"So... two weight of atomic level circuitry to one weight of Dragon's Tears," Tyler said. "We have a deal?"

"I dunno," Fabet said. "You got any more?"

"I think that is a fair trade," Drath said, slowly and distinctly. His head twitched several times rapidly.

"How do your people finalize such things under your laws, and are they considered binding?" Tyler asked.

"Tha's a little complicated..." Wathaet said.

"Binding contract shall be established by verbal confirmation of all parties in the presence of a Federally authorized contracting hypernode system," Drath quoted clearly. "All trade ships as well as banks and public places of consumption are required by law to have such locked systems present for the closure of contracts and such contracts are considered both proprietary and binding reference Federal Code One-One-Four-Seven-Nine-Eight-Three-L-Q-Five. Something like that."

"So, you guys agree verbally and you're bound?" Tyler asked.

"Try to get a judge out here," Fabet said. "Or, and this is an important point, a commercial authorities seizure party."

"Shhhh..." Drath said. "Are you in agreement or not?"

"I dunno," Tyler said woefully. "I'm feeling like you guys are going to screw me somehow. You've got the ship and all."

"We're not going to screw you, man," Wathaet said, waving a cup. "We're buddies."

"Okay," Tyler said mournfully. "I'm practically giving this stuff away but if that's as much as you'll go... I agree to two weights of atacirc for one weight of the substance designated Product One-Five-Six, nickname Dragon's Tears."

"Hah!" Drath crowed. "You're bound now, baby!"

"Agreed!" Wathaet said. "Feeling screwed?"

"Very," Tyler said, his shoulders slumping.

"You should," Drath said, taking a sip of the now watered down Dragon's Tears. "We're going to get rich with this stuff. How much can you get?"

"It *is* actually fairly rare," Tyler said. "And the real problem is the Horvath."

"They're not going to interfere with our trade," Wathaet said. "They know better than to mess with a Glatun ship."

"No, they won't," Tyler said. "But I can't get my hands on a full cargo of this right away. And if they find out what you're trading, they'll come and take it. If they can, because it's a lot harder to obtain than mining for stuff. War. Destruction. No Dragon's Tears."

"Point," Wathaet said, his crest fluttering. "So we smuggle it out."

"Good thing you're dealing with *us*, then," Fabet said.

"Look, it was only *once*, okay?" Drath said. "People act like I made a career out of it!"

"The Horvath own our communications," Tyler said. "And even if you can hack them . . . They're going to be paying attention to anyone who meets with you guys."

"Point," Wathaet said. "But *we* can disappear easily enough."

"You can?" Tyler said.

"To them, yeah," Drath said. "There's an open field which doesn't have much observation near your home. Meet us there . . . When can you get more of this?"

"Tell you what," Tyler said, thinking rapidly. "I'll bring as much Dragon's Tears as I can fit in the back of my truck. I can trade this atacirc for . . . I should be able to afford that much. The stuff really *is* expensive. You guys fill the back with atacirc and we're golden. You sure you can spoof the Horvath?"

"Yeah," Wathaet said, more clearly. "Even if they're paying attention to you, they won't see you leave your house. We'll try to make sure they don't know what you're picking up."

"And you'll forgive me if I point out I'm going to try to keep *you* from finding out," Tyler said. "I can probably get it by Tuesday night."

"Tuesday night at nine PM," Drath said. "It's called Homer's Farm. But there's no farm there."

"Long story," Tyler said. "Okay, I'll be there. Two weights to one. I'm being screwed."

"Great," Fabet said. "You're gonna bring more, right?"

⁂ ⁂ ⁂

As Tyler drove out of the industrial park he carefully pulled his cell phone out and set it on the dash where it could easily pick up his voice.

"Well, *that* was a bust! What the hell am I going to do for money *now*? Those stupid aliens! Damn Glatun! Laughing at me! Like they really liked the sketch. Bastards. What am I going to do now? Maybe Jeff Morris over at AT&T has got some consulting work? Since I'm in Boston, might as well check."

He felt like an idiot. But if he was going to get his hands on a truckload of Product 156 by tomorrow night he'd better hurry.

He kept a glare on his face as he fought his way through Boston traffic and tried very hard not to break out in gales of hysterical laughter.

"Hey, Tyler. Long time."

Tyler and Jeff Morris weren't exactly friends, they just knew each other. Both had started off in the industry about the same time. They'd worked together a couple of times in different companies. Sometimes they were competitors. A couple of times *while* working for the same company. IT was like that.

Right now, though, Jeff Morris wasn't looking exactly pleased to see his old acquaintance. Jeff had managed to not only survive when so many had fallen, he'd finally worked his way into an office, which in IT generally meant he could make hiring decisions. And he probably had every guy he'd ever sort of talked to at COMDEX begging for a slot. Any slot.

"Hey, Jeff. You mentioned that you had a project called Babylon you were working on and I might be interested," Tyler said, sitting down an picking up a yellow pad. He'd looked for cameras on the way in and the only one was on the monitor and it was pointed at Jeff.

"Babylon?" Jeff said, puzzled.

"Yeah," Tyler said, not looking up. "Had to do with a lass." He held up the pad which said in great big letters: SECURE ROOM! NOW!!!!

"Babylon!" Jeff said, slapping his forehead. "Sorry, we'd changed the project name. It's..." He paused and looked around for inspiration. "SeeFid! It's called SeeFid now. But it's really secure. We'd probably better talk in a shield room."

"SeeFid?" Tyler said as soon as he was sure the room was secure.

"C++ for Idiots," Jeff said. "It was a book on the wall. And you've got a lot of nerve making fun of that. A Lass Babylon? Jesus Christ. How did you even know I'd read that book?"

"Saw it on a shelf one time at a party at your house," Tyler said. "Only thing even close to SF so it caught my eye. How's Mel?"

"Pregnant again," Jeff said. "Nice to see you and all, as I said, but why is my department being charged a thousand dollars an hour to use the shield room?"

"This," Tyler said, pulling his hand out of his pocket and rolling the handful of atacirc out on the table. "I need a million dollars. Quickly. And I need a hundred grand of that in cash."

"Is this from the *Spinward Crossing*?" Jeff asked, picking up one of the chips gingerly.

"Where else?"

"You found something they want to trade," Jeff said. "It's not worth a mil. A lot, yeah, not a mil. Among other things, about one in ten of the stuff the *Spinward Crossing* has been selling doesn't work. And I can't authorize that sort of money."

"I'm going to have more. Quite a bit. I need AT&T to get some people in here to buy it from multiple companies. I'll cut AT&T in on one percent of whatever I make for being the house. And, obviously, we need to keep this quiet. Nothing electronic."

"Agreed," Jeff said. "But as I said, I can't authorize any of that."

"I know that, Jeff," Tyler said, sitting down. "Which means you need to shag your ass to the thirty-fifth floor."

"I also can't simply walk in on Weasley Rayl," Jeff said nervously.

"You can if you're holding a million dollars in atacirc in your hand," Tyler said. "Weasel won't mind. Really. Especially since this deal ends on Wednesday."

"Call him Weasel to his face and it won't matter how much atacirc you're holding," Jeff said, sighing. "Okay, okay. I'll need to take..."

"Take as many as you'd like," Tyler said, waving expansively.

"Mr. Rayl is in a meeting," the executive secretary said sternly.

"And if I'm wrong he'll fire me," Jeff said, breezing past her.

"I said stop!"

Jeff opened the door to the President of Northeastern Operations' offices and strode across the carpet to his desk. Mr. Rayl was, in fact, reading the *Wall Street Journal*. He looked up as the door opened, tilted his head to the side and set the paper down.

"This is either important or you've just pretty much killed your career," Rayl said mildly.

Jeff walked up to the desk and held his finger to his lips. Then he held out his hands, cupped, so the executive could see the atacirc for just a moment.

"It's about the SeeFid project, sir," Jeff said. "The one we used to call Babylon. Tyler Vernon used to work with me over at Verizon and I thought he might have some ideas. As it turns out, he does."

"It's okay, Bernice," Rayl said, waving at his secretary. "This really is an emergency. I'll be in...?"

"Shield Room Five."

"Mr. Tyler," Weasley Rayl said heartily as soon as the door was closed. "Pleasure to see you in the building again!"

"Pleasure to see you too, Mr. Weasley," Tyler said as Jeff winced.

"It's...Damnit. It's Tyler *Vernon*, isn't it? Sorry."

"We've both got the same problem with our names, sir," Tyler said, smiling. "No offense intended."

"None taken," Rayl said. "What have you got?"

"I have to meet tomorrow night, clandestinely, with the Glatun," Tyler said, sitting down. "I need to pick up a pickup's load of a certain product. Less than a pickup's load, actually. They will trade me a full pickup of atacirc."

"Christ," Jeff said. "Six *petabytes* of variable use memory, infinite parallel processor and the size of a match head. You could buy...Name a third world country. Name a *country*. I don't think anyone's seen a *case* of it in one place."

"More than that," Tyler said. "As you said, nobody

has seen a case in one place. You can replace a server farm with one chip. The value I saw someone calculate in *Wired* on a standard dry bushel of it is a hundred *billion* dollars. Which *nobody* can afford. A pickup load is going to distort that price. I still need a million dollars, at least a hundred grand in cash. That's for those. AT&T gets some serious players that can pay for the rest. I'll take a check. We'll negotiate for it here. AT&T gets one percent as the house. And I need to do this quick because time's awasting. Among other things, I'll need to get the money from a bank and they close soon."

"Banks stay open to surprising hours when the right people call," Rayl said. "It's not worth a mil. Among other things..."

"Some of it's bad," Tyler said. "I also got the information that it's their scrap and about a hundred years old."

"More or less what we thought," Rayl said, narrowing his eyes. "But that sounds like you got more information out of the Glatun than most governments."

"They are, surprisingly, fans of my series," Tyler said, shrugging. "I just remembered I owe them a sketch. That's beside the point. One mil."

"Two hundred grand," Rayl said. "The hundred in cash is no problem. I'll call JP."

"Not going to just give this away," Tyler said. "Nine hundred and that's flat. Novell is just down the road. And I know people there, too."

"Two fifty and I'll make sure you can breeze in and out of the bank. And twenty percent on the trades. Wednesday morning work?"

"Wednesday morning works, but if you think I'm giving you twenty percent, you've been drinking. Two percent, eight seventy-five."

"Eighteen and three."

"I'll tell you truth. I'm not going lower than nine and I'm not going higher than four. Take it or leave it."

"I'll leave it. But I'll get closer. Twelve percent and five hundred grand. Seriously, that's a good deal."

"Totally sucks. Five and eight hundred."

Rayl considered his opponent and shrugged.

"I'd be doing a disservice to the shareholders if I went lower than ten percent as house, there's going to be costs involved, and eight hundred is highway robbery. Six hundred."

"Seven fifty."

"Seven."

"Done. I'll geek to ten."

"Then we have a deal," Rayl said, standing up. "I'll need to go get the check cut personally. Eight AM Wednesday morning?"

"Can you get the right people here by then?" Tyler asked. "We're talking cases of atacirc. And it has to be all sub rosa."

"We've gotten used to working around the Horvath," Rayl said with a sigh. "They, fortunately, either don't pay as much attention as people think or can't count. We've simply *had* to sneak materials through the system beyond what they allow. We are, in other words, used to this sort of thing. I can get the right people here. *With* their checkbooks. Speaking of which, stay here. I'll go get the check."

Tyler tried not to bounce as he walked to his truck. He still had a lot of stuff to get done and if the Horvath were watching it still could get very sticky.

"Mr. Vernon! This is a surprise!"

"Uh, yeah," Tyler said, trying to remember the red-headed guy's name. No chance. "Good to, uh, see you again, uh..."

"Dan," the man said, holding out his hand as if to shake. In it was a badge. "Hey, could we talk?"

"Sure... Dan..." Tyler said, trying not to curse. "I'm sort of busy at the moment. E-mail me?"

"My van is right over here," Dan said, putting his hand on Tyler's arm. "Come on. Won't take a second."

Tyler, feeling both pissed and a tad nervous, got in the black-tinted van. It had been rigged as something of a mobile command post but what was interesting was that there were no electronics. There were some cameras that looked as if they were fifteen years old but super advanced at the time. *Chemical* photography cameras. And lots of paper.

"Mr. Vernon," a man in a suit said. Fifties and a bit chubby with an incongruous goatee. "My name is Senior Special Agent Aaron Spuler. Welcome to the command post of Project 4038."

"Which is spying on Tyler Vernon?" Tyler asked. "There are laws, you know."

"Which is spying on aliens who can... what was the phrase? Go through our most advanced firewalls so easily it's like 'looking through an open window,'" Spuler said. "And anyone who has interaction with them. Because every interaction with ETs is a potential national security problem as long as that God damned Horvath ship is in the sky."

"Which is pretty indiscreet of you to say," Tyler said.

"Give us some credit, please," Agent Poore said. "This is a shield car and we made sure you were not carrying your cell."

✳   ✳   ✳

"Maple syrup?" Spuler asked, incredulously. "They're addicted to maple *syrup*?"

"Shhhh!" Tyler said. "Christ, now everybody's going to know!"

"Our job is *gathering* information, Mr. Vernon," SSA Spuler said. "Not giving it out. And don't worry about congressional investigations or something. *Nobody* wants to know we exist."

"Their chemistry is incompatible with ours," Agent Poore said. "How can they metabolize it?"

"No clue," Tyler said. "But they reacted like it was booze or something."

"We saw the reaction," Spuler said, waving at the cameras. "But the problem is the Horvath."

"The Glatun apparently have as much control over Horvath information systems as Horvath have over ours," Tyler said. "Or so they say. We're going to meet tomorrow night. I need to go get some money and then, somehow, get my hands on a truck-load of maple syrup without the Horvath finding out. They'll come to me and give me cover for the transfer. Frankly, it feels a bit like a drug deal."

"Your truck?" Spuler asked.

"Yes."

"That should escape their notice as long as they are not actively watching you," Spuler said. "More would be harder. The flip side is that if this is popular among the Glatun, it could give us some leverage."

"I've thought about that," Tyler said, holding up a hand to forestall a reply. "Let me just be clear about something. I'm not going to play puppet to the government. By the same token, yes, I care about that damned Horvath ship and this country and the world and humanity. And I will do my level best to figure out a way to get it out of our sky. But right now, I need to go get some money and find six fifty-five gallon drums of maple syrup. In about thirty hours."

"We're not going to get involved in a purely commercial enterprise," Spuler said. "But this isn't, on one level. If you need our help, we'll be around."

"Thanks," Tyler said. "Can I get out, now?"

"Feel free," Spuler said, waving at the door. "Just... try not to get the world destroyed, okay?"

"Doing my best," Tyler said, yanking open the door.

When he got to his truck, Tyler picked up his cell phone and brought up his contacts.

"Hey, Petra," Tyler said, trying not to sigh.

"Tyler," Petra said. It was that tone. That "I'm unsatisfied with the situation but I'm not going to bring it up" tone.

"Sorry I've been behind in my payments. I'm going to slide some money over this week."

"Thank you," Petra said civilly.

"I'm doing some projects with AT&T, so the money should be better," Tyler said. "So... hopefully no more money issues."

"That would be nice. It's hard enough to make it on the settlement as it is. The girls are right here..."

Tyler thought about his kids every day. What he had *not* thought about, until that moment, was what that meant in terms of his current doings. It took him less than a second, a very brief pause, to make the hardest decision of his life.

He hadn't talked to his kids in two weeks. And he realized he might not be talking to them for months.

But when you sail in harm's way, you don't take hostages.

He squelched the screaming inside.

"Don't really have the time," he said airily. "Got to go. Bye."

Petra Vernon closed her cell phone and looked at it with a puzzled expression. She and Tyler might have had their differences and schedules might have prevented him seeing the girls much, but he *always* wanted to talk to them.

They'd been married for ten years and even over the phone she could read him like a book. Something was going on and it was very odd. And if he didn't want to talk to the girls there was a reason.

She made a face and put the phone in her pocket. She'd find out what was going on when it started to smell.

"Hey, Mr. Haselbauer!" Tyler yelled, waving at the tractor.

Jason Haselbauer was one of the old farmers in the district. A lot of people had moved in from outside the area of late. Most of those were Vermonters and people from the People's Republic of Massachusetts looking for somewhere cheaper to live. And immediately wanting to change things so they were as screwed up as Vermont and Massachusetts.

The Haselbauers, though, were descended from Hessians who'd decided they'd rather farm alongside the Scots and English of the White Mountains than fight them.

"Mr. Vernon," the farmer said in a slow New England drawl. "Pleasure to see you. Fine weather we're having."

"Great," Tyler said. "Leaves are coming out a treat."

"Be a good winter for the sap," Haselbauer said, climbing off the tractor. "Good leaves means good sap. And how are you doing?"

"Well, sir, well," Tyler said. For all he dressed like a homeless guy, Haselbauer probably owned more land than Mrs. Cranshaw. And, notably, a maple syrup distillery. And about as renowned for keeping his own counsel as Mrs. Cranshaw was for being a revolting bitch. He was also, Tyler recalled as he craned his head up and up and then up *again*, the single most *massive* guy Tyler had ever met. He looked more like a mountain than a human being. "I have a rather unusual request. Are you carrying a cell phone?"

"Don't hold with them," Mr. Haselbauer said. "If someone wants me they can call me at home. An if I don't answer they can come to find me if it's that important."

"Yes, sir," Tyler said. He'd heard that about Haselbauer as well. "Just rather not have anyone listening in on our conversation. Some people can listen to them even if they're turned off."

"Ayup," Haselbauer said, narrowing his eyes and adjusting his ballcap. "What have you gotten yourself into, young man?"

"Simple trade, sir, simple trade," Tyler said. "The thing is, I need to buy some barrels of maple syrup. But I need it to look as if I'm *not* buying them. I don't need anyone knowing my business."

"That's an odd request, young man," Mr. Haselbauer said, tilting his head to the side.

"Well, sir," Tyler said, shrugging. "It's got a bit to do with the Revenuers."

"Ah!" Haselbauer said, his face going hard. "*Them*, You need not say more. When do you need it?"

"I'd like to do it like this..."

"There's a spaceship landing in Homer's Field," Tyler whispered to himself in wonder as the stars were occluded.

The sky was clear and bright with a thin crescent moon. What the locals still called a smuggler's moon. New Hampshire had, back in the day, been a major supplier of corn whiskey to the lowland folks. Back when people considered a tax of fifteen percent on their hard work of running a still to be a slap in the face. There was more than one meaning to the state's motto.

A shiner's moon was gibbous, half full, to full. That was when you could see well enough by night to get the still running and the mules with corn up to the hollers. Up in the hollows of the hills the smell of the distilling was caught and held, keeping the Revenue Agents from finding you. Making shine.

To bring it down to the city folk with their silver you needed good dark to sneak past those Revenuers. A smuggler's moon.

"Do you have the stuff?" Wathaet whispered as he stepped off the cargo ramp.

"Six barrels of first quality Dragon's Tears," Tyler whispered back. There was no point to whispering, nobody was moving this time of night and Homer's field was back off the road. But the whole thing did have the feel of a drug deal. That was fine by Tyler. Granda had had a few stories about slipping past Revenuers here and there. Family tradition was being upheld.

"Awesome!" Fabet said, dragging something that looked like a cross between a broom and a forklift.

Tyler opened up the back of the truck and started to roll one of the barrels off onto the ground.

"Got it," Fabet said, sliding the device into place. He carried the six-hundred-pound barrel away through the air.

"Anti-grav," Tyler said with a sigh. "I want."

"Might be able to do something about that if this stuff takes off," Wathaet said. "By the way, when my head finally cleared I felt screwed."

"Come on," Tyler protested. "You're trading trash for something you're going to make a fortune on. And on that subject, we need to talk."

"What?" Wathaet asked. "You want my firstborn?"

"No," Tyler said. "I want your corporations."

"You want me to give this up?" Wathaet said. "No *way*!"

"Come back in about thirty of our days," Tyler said. "I'll have two of our heavy trucks loaded with Dragon's Tears. That's about enough to fill your cargo hold. But between now and then you need to contact your corporations. I'm going to get as much of a control on this market as I can. I am, hereby, willing to contract that the ship *Spinward Crossing*, crew thereof, will get five percent of any trade in Dragon's Tears in which I engage with other parties. If *they* will, upon determining that there is an economic worth to Dragon's

Tears, engage with major Glatun corporate partners for further trade. Bottom line, you get five percent of all the Dragon's Tears I trade for the rest of your life. Well, split however you split stuff. If I'm trading with multiple corporations I can get more than *you're* going to get me. Right?"

"Trade for *what*?" Wathaet said, thoughtfully. "I mean, you guys are trading for atacirc. Wow, I get five percent of all the atacirc you guys buy? No way!"

"Think I'm just going to trade for atacirc?" Tyler said. "I'm not sure how to do it, but I'm going to trade for whatever you guys use as currency, and not cheap, and then *buy* atacirc. New stuff that's not *crap*!"

"You guys don't have a hypernode point on the whole damned planet," Wathaet said.

"Then the first thing I'll trade for is a hypernode link!" Tyler said. "Wathaet, we've got a Horvath ship sitting on our *necks*. We need your big guys to sit up and take notice. That's not going to happen, sorry, because a small-time free trader got lucky. It will if *they're* making the profits. Think about it. Especially since sooner or later the Horvath will find out about this. And then they'll cut us *both* out. In my case, probably cut up. They'll take the m . . . Dragon's Tears, trade it to your big corporations and *you'll* be back to trading with primitive planets for coconut shells and 'folk art.'"

"All transferred," Fabet said. "Hey, can I . . ."

"No!" Wathaet said. "That last point has merit, I'll admit. I'll think about it."

"Oh, one more thing," Tyler said, going to his front seat and pulling out a jug. "Look, I know we're not contracted on this, but . . . That primitive folk art? Could I, uh, buy it back from you?"

"Hell, yeah," Wathaet said, hefting the jug. "For this? Sure. I don't get the night painting, anyway."

"The painter was kind of cracked," Tyler said. "It's the night sky the way he saw it."

Tyler started at the tap on his window and sat up, rolling down the window.

"Were you here all night?" Jeff asked, looking around the secure garage.

"I had Ireland's worth of atacirc in the back," Tyler said, wiping his eyes and yawning. "What was I going to do, sit at *home* with a shotgun on my lap?" He set the shotgun on the floor.

"Not to mention what you had up front," Jeff said, his eyes wide. "Is that...?"

"Yeah," Tyler said, getting out. "And two Goyas, a Matisse and some Italian guy from the Renaissance. I couldn't fit the Venus. Wathaet said he'd store it for me off-planet. I'd appreciate it if AT&T would do me the same service *on* planet. Lord knows I'm not going to keep them in my house. Maybe 'Starry Starry Night.' It'd look great in the kitchen."

"Well, come on up to the conference room," Jeff said. "We'll get some coffee in you."

"A donut would be nice."

"Gentlemen, welcome," Rayl said, nodding at the executives gathered in the shield room. "Sorry for the crowding but I think this is the appropriate venue. By arrangement with Mr. Tyler Vernon we have a rather large quantity of atacirc available. AT&T will be taking a ten percent cut on all trades. We will be bidding by lot which will be, pardon, a case by case basis."

"How many?" an Asian asked.

"Twenty-six cases," Tyler said. "All the *Spinward Crossing* could fit in my pickup. It was up to the roof. They're hauling them up here at the moment. There was a problem of spoofing the internal cameras so the Horvath wouldn't notice."

"Twenty-six!" the man had a British accent. "Bloody hell! I don't suppose you'd like to tell us what you're trading?"

"I'll let the term 'proprietary' hang in the air," Tyler said, sipping his coffee.

"The atacirc we are getting is, of course, not consistent," Rayl said. "As soon as it is delivered you will be given an opportunity to examine each case and decide what it is worth and then we'll get the bidding started."

"I think they went a little crazy off that one case nobody could find any faults in," Tyler said, riffling through the checks. They were the big kind so people could fit all the zeroes.

"Feeling a bit stunned?" Rayl asked in a contented tone. He was going to come out of this smelling like a rare hybrid rose. He'd just made a fair bit of AT&T's profits for the quarter in one day's work.

"It's not every day that a guy becomes an instant billionaire," Tyler said. "Multi . . . multibillionaire. In fact, I don't think anyone has ever become a multibillionaire in a day."

"So what are you going to do with it?" Jeff asked. "And is anyone else really in the mood for a drink?"

"Champagne would be about right," Weasley said. "Tyler's buying."

"I am in a mood for a drink," Tyler said. "But first I need to see a lawyer. Besides the tax implications, which are going to be large, I've got some stuff to buy. I'll need to take a rain check."

THREE

"Fabet!" Wathaet commed as they cleared the gate. "Fabet! Is he in the Dragon's Tears again?"

"Don't think so," Drast replied. "I locked it up."

"Did you get the jug?"

"Yes."

"Oh, hell," Wathaet said as a customs cutter approached.

"Ship *Spinward Crossing*. Heave to and prepare to be boarded."

"We're getting hit by the nosies," Wathaet commed. "Just stay cool, man."

"It's all good," Drath replied. "There's no special import duty on this stuff."

"There will be if they see Fabet."

"You seem to be in compliance with all applicable regulations," the customs bot said dubiously. "You are, however, officially notified of note of seizure by the Onderil Banking Corporation for nonpayment of mortgage on the *Spinward Crossing*. And you owe back payment for parking orbit charges of four hundred and eighty-four credits on Glalkod Station."

"I don't have that on me," Wathaet said. "I've got two and a half pounds of gold..."

"Checking. That is acceptable to prevent immediate lock-down. Full payment is required before leaving parking orbit. Your ship is... required to go to holding area Z-A-Four pending further determination."

"I have thirty days to challenge the seizure order," Wathaet said. He knew that one like the back of his hand.

"Correct. Your ship cannot be seized for thirty days. However, it will be held in orbit until full payment is made of back charges on mortgage including any appropriate penalties and unpaid parking including levied fines."

"Fine, fine," Wathaet said. "But I've got thirty days, right?"

"That is correct," the robot said, spitting out some forms and handing them over. "You are free to move to... holding area Z-A-Four. Have a nice day."

Wathaet didn't even want to open up his hypernode link. He knew what it was going to look like. But he had to call a cab to get to the station since they wouldn't even let them *dock*!

"Captain Wathaet, this is Agent Girinthir representing the Onderil Banking Corporation..."

As soon as his hypernode link was open *everybody* he owed money to knew it and their bots went to work.

"I've got to make trade before you can get paid," Wathaet commed back. "As soon as I can move my cargo you'll get paid. I confirm that I have been contacted. Any contact in less than one week's time will be defined as harassment."

"Very well, Captain Wathaet," Agent Girinthir replied. "I see that you have officially accepted note of seizure. Your ship will not be . . ."

"Got it," Wathaet commed. "We're done. Goodbye. Damnit."

That was a lot of bots.

"Captain Wathaet, this is the Lrdrgl Company. You are three months behind on your . . ."

"Damn!" Wathaet said, closing the call. "Vauroror Taxi . . ."

"Captain Wathaet, this is the . . ."

"DAMN!"

Fortunately, the taxi-bot was programmed to take metals in trade. That was one of the reasons he used Vauroror. They took any form of exchange and no questions asked.

On the other hand, he couldn't take the tubeway. He'd checked, and all his bank accounts, even the ones he thought nobody knew about, were levied and emptied. Any money going in those was down a black hole never to return. So anything that required a hyperpay was out.

That meant walking. Fortunately they didn't charge for air for five days or the security bots would see if he could breathe vacuum.

It took him about thirty minutes to reach Kolu's. When the door dilated he took a deep whiff. What a fine perfume. And all the usual suspects were lined up at the bar.

"Wathaet!" they chorused. "Where's my money!" "You owe me a round, you welshing bastard!" "That corbot you sold me was defective!"

"Glad to see you guys, as well!" Wathaet said. "Be with you in a minute!"

"You have a hell of a lot of nerve showing your face in here!" Kolu bellowed from behind the bar. "Where's my fifty credits?!"

"I have something better," Wathaet said cheerfully.

"This had *better* be good," Kolu said suspiciously. "Let's just say that the Gordont fire gems didn't exactly take off. Especially since they all *went out* the day after you shipped out!"

"This is good," Wathaet said, sitting down and setting a bulb on the bar. "Put some in some water. Just a bit. I *should* let you try it straight."

"Be a fine day when something can get *me* drunk," Kolu said, pouring a bit of the syrup into a cup and sniffing.

"What *is* this stuff?" he commed a moment later. He couldn't talk because his snout was stuck in the cup.

"Dragon's Tears," Wathaet said. "It's a rare and precious viand from a previously undiscovered planet."

"Like you'd take the chance on going through an unchecked gate," Kolu said, shaking his head. "Damn, it's got a *kick*, don't it?"

He pulled out a bunch of shot glasses, put a drop of syrup in the bottom of each, then filled them with water.

"Here," Kolu said, sliding the shots down the bar. "Try this stuff and see what you think."

"What is it?" Ingr asked suspiciously.

"Dragon's Tears," Wathaet said. "Try it. It'll put hair on your back. Sorry, Gurcaur."

"Screw you, Wathaet," the mangy Glatun said, taking a sip. "Holy Hell!" he added, dropping the shot. "Another, if you please, bartender. That is *fine* stuff."

"Money on the bar," Kolu said. "Five credits a shot."

"Five credits?" Ingr said. "You haven't even bought it from Wathaet. Hey, Wathaet. You owe me, like, fifteen credits. Seventeen with interest."

"Give Ingr four for free, please, my host. And we need to talk trade."

"Shmirg," Kolu said to the Rangora. "You've got the bar. Set 'em up. Drop of this...Dragon's Tears in each shot."

"Got it," the saurian said. "Don't know what you guys are getting so excited about. Try some sulfur petals!"

"I am *not* paying seven hundred credits for a barrel of this stuff," Kolu said. "No way, no how."

Everyone knew that Kolu owned about a hundred businesses on the station and the planet below. But he ran them all out of the dodgy little room behind the bar. And if he slept anywhere else nobody had found out about it. It was rumored that he had a pile of osmium under his bunk big enough to drive a battle cruiser.

"Hey, you saw how they took it," Wathaet said, topping up his glass.

"And I'm not going to get so hammered I say yes. Four hundred credits for the barrel."

"Isn't going to happen. I need a hell of a lot more than that to get my ship out of hock. Look, I'll give you this. Six hundred. Give me half now. I need to go get the barrel and I need enough money to get it from the ship to here. You can have the jug I brought for free. You're going to make more than six hundred off that jug alone. I'll give you one barrel at six hundred. And when I get more I'll keep selling you that stuff at six hundred. You know it's going to catch on. I'm going to sell the rest of it at bid. But for you, my old friend, I'll lock in the price."

"Five hundred. I think I've got that much in the drawer."

"Done. But I need it on a cash chip."

"You're asking a lot . . . What?" he asked as Shmirg stuck his head through the door. The room was soundproofed. It was now apparent there was a lot of shouting in the bar.

"You either need to get out here or call in Tugornc," the Rangora said. "I can't keep up."

"What do you mean you can't keep up?" Kolu asked. "It's just Ingr, Gurcaur, Hathan, Fandent and Bob. How much can they be drinking?"

"It *was* just Ingr, Gurcaur, Hathan, Fandent and Bob," Shmirg said. "But Ingr commed Mongogw and Hathan called his pair-brood and Fandent called his ship and . . . I need some *help* out here!"

"So that's five hundred, half now, half when I deliver and both on a chip?" Wathaet asked.

"I'll go get the chip."

"Holy hell," Wathaet said as the tractor-bot stopped. There was a line outside of Kulo's. Shmirg was now working the door, the saurian towering over the horde of Glatun.

"Go on through, dude," Shmirg said as Wathaet pulled the grav bar off the tractor. "Watch yourself. The party is in full swing."

"WATHAET!" about half the bar chorused as he pulled the barrel through the door. It was packed from side to side and most of them were hitting shots as fast as Tugornc could pass them out. There were two more Rangora Wathaet didn't recognize circulating with shots. Kolu liked Rangora because they didn't drink anything he stocked, and most species didn't give them crap no matter how drunk or stoned they were. The problem being when Rangora showed up for work *already* hammered. Then it was just call for security bots and clean up the damage.

"Get that stuff in the back room, fast," Kolu commed. "We're nearly out, and when we run out I'm afraid there's going to be a riot!"

"What kind of connection is this?" Kulo asked as Wathaet rotated the barrel up into a holder.

"It's called a screw," Wathaet said. "Primitive planet. Figure it out. I've got three more containers of Dragon's Tears. I'm going to head over to Thmmo and Uatha's. If they haven't heard about this, they will soon. But I'm not selling it for five hundred credits, that's for sure."

"Oh, hell," Wathaet said as he stepped through the air lock. Fabet was passed out in the passageway. "Drast?"

"Wazzip?" the purser commed.

"Where the hell are you?"

"Sec...Bzzzpt...*unable to process transmission.*"

"Secure room," Wathaet muttered.

He went down the passage and was unsurprised to see the door wide open. The purser was lying on the ground in a puddle of syrup. Fortunately, he'd gotten the cock closed at some point. As Wathaet walked in the room the purser rolled over on his side and started licking the deck.

"Oh, get up," Wathaet said, pulling him to his feet. "I need you to... Take a shower for one thing. *Curgo*. That's probably a couple of thousand credits of syrup you guys just drank! And spilled! And it's coming out of your share!"

"Bzzzpt?"

"Never mind."

He got the purser and the engineer into their bunks, rekeyed the door to his own codes and got down to work. He'd dropped off bulbs of Dragon's Tears at four more places. And he had enough money to placate most of his minor creditors. Not pay them off. Just placate them. The major ones were all on hold.

He'd taken one barrel to Kulo's. Drast and Fabet had broken into the one he'd been using for samples. But they couldn't really drink all that much of the stuff. More had probably spilled on the deck. So call it two-thirds left.

Four and two-thirds barrels. He dropped that for bid onto the hypernet to see what happened.

"This is a rather unusual request, Mr. Tyler."

Robert Lyle was a senior associate with Bertram, Bertram, Hudson and Slavens, a Boston law firm that had fought its first tort case in British court. He wasn't quite sure about his newest client, but when the CEO of Verizon calls and suggests that you arrange a meeting it was considered wise to do so. The conditions and subject, however, were bothersome.

"While we do sometimes have clients who might

have accidentally bent one of the numerous laws and regulations of the United States or international courts, we prefer..."

"I'm not trying to break or bend the law," Tyler said. "And I'm not sure I'm talking to the right person if you can't even get my name straight. Tyler *Vernon*. All I want you to do is arrange some perfectly legal purchases. I simply don't want those purchases to be reported as associated with me until they have all or mostly been completed. And they need to be distributed so as not to be obvious."

"This is quite a bit of land, Mr. Vernon, pardon me," Lyle said. "And a large number of operating businesses. And you simply wish that...the owners be unaware?"

"I need for *everyone* to be unaware," Tyler said. "*Totally* confidential. I'm talking to you. You don't even tell *your* people who is doing the buying. We'll figure out some way to slush the money quietly. It'll probably have to be through shell companies. As long as it is eventually reported to the IRS it's no problem, right?"

"Bit more than the IRS for *this* level of transaction," Lyle said. "And we're talking about a good *bit* of money."

"Yeah," Tyler said. "Money's not an issue. And your firm can't make the purchases directly. I chose you because you work some very big deals and you can probably cloak the purchases. Three or four other firms, brokers, etc. All behind proprietary layers."

"If the government isn't the issue..." Lyle said, looking puzzled. "Why are you cloaking these purchases?"

"Oh, the problem's the Horvath," Tyler said. "It's

the *Horvath* we need to not associate these purchases with me. At least for a while. As long as possible."

"Now you are getting completely out of my field," Lyle said. "Anything involving the Horvath has national, *international*, security issues."

"The government is generally aware of what I'm doing," Tyler said. "And not against it to the point that they can find a policy with both hands. All I'm doing is engaging in honest trade. Now are you going to take the job or not? Obviously the commissions are going to be..."

"Quite remunerative, yes," Lyle mused. "I'm sure we can manage this. As long as we are not in jeopardy of violating bar regulations. But I have to ask: Why do you want to own...how did you put it? 'Every single square inch of land that can produce maple trees?'"

"*Sugar* maple," Tyler said with a smile. "That is, as they say, proprietary. And there are some qualifiers on it. Anything that is currently on the market, buy first. Then concentrate on things which have been traded in the last ten or fifteen years and corporate holdings. Get as many of the new crew out of the area as possible. At that point, the price is probably going to be running up pretty solid and we'll be hitting diminishing returns, so the old families might start to sell. But try to keep other corporate entities out of the area.

"Most important of all, I want you to buy one *particular* piece of property for the absolute best price you can get it. Which means it should be one of the first properties bought. Put the best person you can find on it. Research the target. Find vulnerabilities. Blackmail. Anything. Absolutely screw her."

"Her?"

"Yes," Tyler said. "I especially want *her* land. Make sure you get it for a price that she'll go for but still feels vaguely screwed. She'll find out *how* screwed later. I'm not normally the sort of person to screw widows out of money but there are widows and widows. The name is Mrs. Angelina Cranshaw."

"We're rich!"

"We never have to work again!"

"If I can keep you guys from drinking it all," Wathaet said sourly. "And we've got to do one more run to Earth. *Then* we'll be rich."

Dragon's Tears was good. There was no question of that. But mostly it was new and different. Despite trading with hundreds of different species and despite Glatun corporate departments and AIs that constantly strove to find "the hot new thing," something truly new and different was rare.

Six thousand credits a gallon, though, was just *stupid*. And it wasn't even going to make it past Glalkod.

"Think of it this way," Wathaet said. "We can't even afford to get drunk on it. And we're sitting on enough portable cash that every crook in Glalkod station has got to be trying to think of a way to break into our hold."

"Egh," Fabet said. "When do we make the transfers?" No one bar on Glalkod station had been able to buy their full cargo.

"Tomorrow," Wathaet said then shuddered. "Security bots on the way."

"*Spinward Crossing, this is Athelkau. The value of your cargo has passed nonsecure storage threshhold. To prevent misadventure in the system you are being moved to secure docking bay One-One-Six-Dash-Alpha. Your cargo of Dragon's Tears will be moved to high security storage pending transfer to purchasing parties. A charge of one hundred and ninety-six credits will be added to your transfer fees. System overrides in five, four, three...*" And the ship started moving out of its current parking orbit.

Athelkau, the AI for Glalkod station, handled, well, everything. Parking, maneuvering, most transfers and commercial transaction assurance, air and water recycling and, notably, security. Athelkau saw all. You did not argue with Athelkau when it decided something needed to be done.

"We're surrounded," Fabet squeaked.

"Just stay cool," Wathaet said. "We haven't done anything wrong."

"*This* time!" Drast pointed out. "And if the nosies get involved they're bound to find *something*."

"Then let's not give them a reason to get any more involved than necessary," Wathaet said. "Athelkau, roger that override. Thanks. We were just discussing the security problem."

"*My job is to stay one step ahead of problems,*" Athelkau replied.

Wathaet got the tickle for a priority hypernet call and sighed.

"As my bots should have pointed out," he commed, "all bids on Dragon's Tears are closed..."

"Captain Wathaet, this is Niazgol Gorku. I wonder if we could get together for a chat."

"What?" Fabet asked as Wathaet's hair stood on end.

"Uh, Trader Gorku. It's, uh, a pleasure to com with you. Uh... I... yes... I..."

"Your ship is being moved to a security area at the moment. Why don't we have dinner on my yacht. I am, conveniently, parked right next to you. Isn't that a surprise? We'll be ... neighbors."

No surprise at all. Gorku was certainly the richest person in the Glalkod system and consistently rated in the top five in the Federation. That he could get Athelkau to park the *Spinward Crossing* next to him was no surprise. That was how the system worked.

The Glatun government was an enlightened plutodemocracy. There were various levels and branches of elected government that set general policy. Most of it was then administered by artificial intelligences like Althelkau. There were, of course, hosts of bureaucrats but most of them carried out tasks set by the AIs.

But it was recognized when the basic documents were being developed that "them that have, gets." So part of the assumption was that people who were more economically advanced would do two things: wield more power and work to consolidate such power.

The first was, in general, not a bad thing. Persons who have been raised to wield power are generally good at it. And the smart rich tend to train their children to be smart about being rich, getting more rich and generally tending the Federation as a garden.

But not always and not always for the general betterment of the Federation. So there were various processes in the basic set-up that allowed for change, such as the election of officials that, at the end of the day, could override the wishes of the functional oligarchy of wealthy elites if enough nonelite Glatun felt it necessary. And the AIs were, specifically, programmed to create niches and openings that "have-nots" could exploit if they were smart and ruthless enough. Thus they could be haves, some of the elites would slowly fall out of elite status, and there was turnover.

However, if someone was an elite, and Gorku was certainly one such, "suggesting" to the AI that the *Spinward Crossing* would best be parked next to one's yacht was no big deal. The surprise was that Gorku would take any direct interest at all.

"Yes, sir," Wathaet said, aloud. "I'd be glad to have dinner with you. What time?"

"Twenty-three forty work for you?"

"Twenty-three forty it is, sir," Wathaet said, pulling at his trans-collar nervously.

"It's a deal," Gorku commed, cutting the call.

"Your hair still isn't going down," Fabet said.

"What's up?" Drast commed.

"I have to meet with...Niazgol Gorku," Wathaet said.

"Oh," Drast commed. "You poor doomed bastard. We are so screwed."

"Are you enjoying the ndolul, Captain?"

Gorku was a short-nosed Glod like Wathaet. Wathaet wasn't prejudiced by any stretch of the imagination but about the only snotty stuck-up long-nosed Koorko he got along with was Drast, so it was somewhat comforting.

The two very large waiters were less so. They looked as if they were suckled on asteroids.

"Great," Wathaet said, taking another small bite. "Truly wonderful."

"Well, when one is rich one can afford good chefs," Gorku said. "And proper ingredients. The blag has to be very fresh. I had a ship bring it in just this morning. The reason for the query is that you don't seem to be enjoying it. Haven't eaten much. I assure you I do not regularly descend to cannibalism and both the servers are quite gentle for Rangora."

"No problem at all, sir," Wathaet said, trying to take a larger bite. No chance. All four stomachs were rejecting input.

"I am, of course, interested in the Dragon's Tears," Gorku said, taking a sip of same. "Lovely stuff. I assume you bought it on Earth."

"Yes, sir," Wathaet said, summoning just enough courage to defend never having to summon courage again. "And the Terran we bought it from has a binding contract with us!"

"Five percent of all Dragon's Tears subsequently sold by him to any Glatun or Glatun corporation," Gorku said. "Would you like to hear the seven ways that I came up with to get around such a contract? That was before my AIs became involved."

"No, sir," Wathaet said, his shoulders slumping.

"Dear, dear Captain Wathaet," Gorku said, bobbing his head. "I am not trying to steal your discovery. The same, however, cannot be said of my competitors. I am, rather, interested in Terra. Of course, I am interested in many things, you understand. But Terra is one of those. It has such potential and, of course, is quite close to Glalkod. Now that there is, in fact, something of worth to trade the potentialities increase. I simply wish to ensure that my companies are part of that potential. You understand?"

Most *of that potential*, Wathaet thought to himself.

"Yes, sir."

"What are your near-term arrangements?" Gorku asked. "In regards to further shipments of Dragon's Tears. Not what you plan on doing tomorrow with your money. I was a spaceman myself once."

"I'm to meet with my contact on Earth at a remote location on two-thirty-eight at ten-forty," Wathaet said, trying not to sigh. "He's to have most of a hold's worth of Dragon's Tears."

"Do you know how much of his world's supply that represents?" Gorku said. "We have identified it as a plant product, probably a sap. A sap of what is the great question. There are over nine dozen saps that are used for foods or industrial products on the planet."

"I do not, sir," Wathaet said. "I will say that he asked me to involve people...such as you in trade, sir. He wants our 'big boys,' as he said, involved so they might get the government to intervene with the Horvath."

"Over Dragon's Tears as a product, unlikely," Gorku said musingly. "But he's apparently fairly smart. More likely if corporations are involved than, pardon, a small free trader. Although you will get wealthy quickly, you don't have the established contacts, the methods... Hmmm." Gorku wrinkled his snout in thought.

"If he's that smart, he's also not going to want to trade with a single corporation," the financier said. "And he'll want more than trash atacirc."

"I think he wants to trade for credits and buy atacirc here on Glalkod," Wathaet said.

"Not impossible to arrange," Gorku said. "If we have regular trade with Earth, going around the Horvath of course, then establishing a commercial hypernode is a necessity. Very well. Meet with your...contact.

Make him aware that you have contacted corporations. When you return we will have arrangements completed to establish regular trade. And as contracted, you get five percent."

"Thank you, sir," Wathaet said.

"Less fees, of course," Gorku said with another wrinkle of his nose. "And the government will quickly designate it as a luxury good, which means higher taxes. But I think we will all make more than a bit of profit and that is to the good, is it not?"

FOUR

"Mr. Vernon," Mr. Haselbauer said, folding himself into the seat across from Tyler.

"Mr. Haselbauer," Tyler said, trying not to seem nervous.

"Weather's coming on fine, don't you think?" the farmer said as the waitress scurried up. "Adele, I could do with a cup of your fine coffee if you please. And just a touch of maple syrup."

"It's getting hard to find, Mr. Haselbauer," the waitress said, dimpling. "But I got some in the back just for you."

"The weather is indeed coming on fine," Tyler said, scratching his head at the notes on the pad.

One of the things he liked about Anna's was that there weren't any cameras in the restaurant. So the Horvath, even if they'd noticed changes in one Tyler Vernon, couldn't look over his shoulder at the notes he was making.

The problem was, trucks were tracked. Just about every tractor trailer in the U.S. had a tracker on it. And while the Horvath might not notice two trucks going to an open field in the middle of the night, *might* didn't really cut it. He somehow had to get two trucks loaded, quietly, discreetly, then to the pick-up point without any possibility of the Horvath noticing.

Then there was the product. He'd found it surprisingly hard to find two tractor trailer loads of *barrels* of maple syrup. Much of the production was small farms and distilleries. The few large distilleries sent most of their product out to distributors who then held it, in individual sized packages, and doled it out through the year. That Mr. Haselbauer had had six barrels was luck as much as anything.

It was driving him nuts.

"Strange doings in the area, though," Mr. Haselbauer said as Adele brought him his coffee. "Lots of land trading hands, especially given that things are a bit hard off at the moment. Didn't think that fine old lady Mrs. Cranshaw would ever sell her land. And she didn't get near much for it, neither."

Tyler tried not to chuckle. Turned out that most forensic departments, even going quite a few decades back, tended to store "questionable" samples from remains. And it was amazing what modern forensic systems could tease out of samples from the fifties. *Natural causes, my butt.*

"And you aren't working near as much as you used to just a bit agone," Mr. Haselbauer said.

"I've found some additional sources of income, Mr. Haselbauer," Tyler said.

"Found a few in my time as well, young man," Mr. Haselbauer said. "Known a few friends as did as well. Some of them thought they could just stop workin', found such good additional sources as they say. Thing about Revenuers, they look for such things.

Know a few friends didn't think on that. Don't get to talk much and I do sore miss the company. But Concord's a long drive."

Tyler looked up into blue eyes as innocent as a child.

"There are Revenuers and Revenuers, Mr. Haselbauer," Tyler said cautiously. "Some as have people running about the hills looking for additional sources of income. Some as think they can look for them from above. Waaay above."

"*Them* Revenuers?" Haselbauer said, tilting back his John Deere cap.

"Could be, Mr. Haselbauer," Tyler said, shrugging. "Because we are friends and have been for some time, I shall give you my own piece of advice if you will take it from a young man such as me. There may come some men from the city asking you what you would take for your maple trees and distillery."

"Have been," Haselbauer said.

"Don't. Sell. And tell such as you may find appropriate the same, Mr. Haselbauer. I'd have all such as you holding maple come spring. You will not *believe* what maple is about to be worth. Of course, this may involve some problems from . . . Revenuers."

"Them as you mentioned?" Haselbauer said.

"Them as I mentioned, Mr. Haselbauer," Tyler replied. "May be some great trouble from them."

"They don't take part," the farmer said musingly. "They'll be wanting *all*."

"Touch hard, that," Tyler said. "Touch hard getting all if the *right* people are holding."

"Hard in two ways, young man," the old man said. "Very hard."

"Yes, sir," Tyler said. "Very hard. Hard as granite.

This may seem a touch uppity, Mr. Haselbauer, coming from a newcomer such as I. But have you read your license plate lately?"

"Hmmm..." Haselbauer said. "This might be the most interesting winter since '56."

"Fifty-six?" Tyler said.

"Didn't make the history books," Haselbauer said, smiling in fond remembrance. "But there's some places up to the hollers do you dig down a bit you might find whole cars. Still occupied. Don't care for Revenuers not a bit. Shall be making some calls."

"*Discreet* calls," Tyler said desperately.

"Young man," Haselbauer said. "You are quite a smart young feller and for being a damned Rebel born you are a decent young man. Hard worker for a Reb. But when it comes to dealing with Revenuers you *shall* accept that I am neither stupid nor senile."

"Yes, Mr. Haselbauer. I apologize." Tyler paused and thought for a moment, then sighed. The old man was about to grab his cojones and squeeze, he just knew it. But experience was where you found it. "About them Revenuers, Mr. Haselbauer..."

"Wathaet," Tyler said as the captain came down the cargo ramp. At least he was pretty sure it was Wathaet. He was dressed differently and his Mohawk-like hair was cut differently.

"My good friend Tyler," Wathaet said, waving. "I hope that these friends of yours are very closed mouthed. We have the Horvath thinking we're still in Boston at the moment, but they are listening."

"Don't talk much," Mr. Haselbauer said, coming up out of the darkness.

"Captain Wathaet," Tyler said. "This is Mr. Haselbauer. Few of his friends are driving the trucks. We need to get started unloading."

"Fabet! Grab the lift," Wathaet said, stepping off the pad then looking up at Haselbauer. "You're nearly the size of a *Rangora*."

"Bigger," Mr. Haselbauer said. Fabet squeaked from the darkness, then Tom Haselbauer, who was simply a younger version of his grandfather, came by dragging the grav lift loaded with three pallets of maple syrup.

"He couldn't hardly pull it," Tom said. "Where you want it? And how do you get this thing to lift higher?"

"Is all well?" Wathaet asked nervously.

"Very well," Tyler said. "Mr. Haselbauer has me feeling very screwed but other than that, it's great."

"Twenty percent is cheap," Mr. Haselbauer said. "I should have charged you more."

"Did you talk to your big boys?" Tyler asked.

"I didn't have to ask," Wathaet said. "I was more or less told they were taking over. But we get our cut. They want to meet."

"I guess that same warehouse you were at in Boston would do," Tyler said. "We'll make all this stuff official then."

"What about the Horvath?" Wathaet asked.

"When the corporate reps arrive I'll explain why trying to steal this from us will work...poorly if at all," Tyler said.

"Don't give naught to Revenuers can I avoid it," Mr. Haselbauer said. "So they got cannon and machine guns and, I guess, rocks from up there? Don't give naught. Don't care for them a bit. And they'll be hard done getting this...Dragon's Tears, is it?"

"I've managed to get pretty close to a monopoly on all held stocks," Tyler said. "That's what I'll be trading for. There's about as much as can fill four ships your size. There won't be *any* more until next spring. So the Horvath won't have anything to take. And taking it will be...hard, even then. Getting it is hard and the people that collect it...don't respond well to threats. That's what I'll tell your corporate people. What they then do about that is up to them. But if the Horvath think we're just going to cough it up...They're wrong."

"They'll bomb your cities if you don't," Wathaet pointed out.

"Don't care for cities, neither," Mr. Haselbauer said. "Where do you think Revenuers come from?"

"We are encountering some resistance to sale of lands, Mr. Vernon," Lyle said. He still had a very satisfied look. The charges for arranging the transactions had been...astronomical.

"Good," Tyler said. "Then stop the purchases. I think we went in fast enough that most of the land and distilleries didn't get run up in cost that much. And anyone who is holding out for what we've been offering, it's because they like what they're doing. I'd like you to arrange a discreet surveillance of Mrs. Cranshaw, by the way. When she realizes what happened to her I'm going to have one very nasty and devious old lady with, apparently, access to exotic poisons, after my butt."

"Yes, sir," Lyle said, making a note.

"If worse comes to worst we can slide the information your consultants found to an ME and let things take their course," Tyler said. "So what percentage of the total crop do I have?"

"About sixty percent of land currently in maple sugar production," Lyle said. "In addition there is land currently in white pine and other timber farms which comprises an additional twenty percent of the total land area where sugar maple is harvestable. This comprises... well, a goodly bit of Maine, Vermont, Massachusetts, New Hampshire and the rural areas of Ontario. It is, I checked, the largest land purchase in recent history. I am still, obviously, curious as to your obsession with maple sugar. Not to mention where the money came from. Frankly, it's too much to be absolutely illegal, and given the companies who wrote the checks..."

"I think all will be clear soon," Tyler said. He'd blown through pretty much all of the money from the deal with Wathaet but he now had a *shipload* of atacirc. Well, eighty percent of a shipload, damnit. "But that's about right. I don't want to own *all* the maple sugar in the world. Monopolies just don't work well. But if things become... difficult and people want to sell because of the difficulties, be ready to start buying again. Now, to the next step. No, I've got a better way to do that..."

Tyler stopped on the sidewalk outside the attorney's office and extended one arm up and the other down. The one extended up he circled about his head while pointing to the ground with the other.

"Come on, figure it out," he said, looking around.

Before long a man in a slightly ill-fitting suit got out of a late-model sedan and walked over.

"Looking for us?" the man asked.

"Took you long enough," Tyler said. "In a few days, exactly when isn't quite clear, some Glatun will be visiting. They'll be planning on occupying the same warehouse in Reading as the *Spinward Crossing*. I'd appreciate you guys setting up a secure room somewhere nearby. Then we can finally get to *real* negotiations."

"And the Horvath?" the man asked.

"These guys the Horvath are *definitely* not going to want to touch," Tyler said. "Except for the initial exploratory ship, everyone we've been dealing with is bottom rung. Even their governmental people. These guys aren't going to be Donald Trump but they report to corporations and they're here for our maple syrup. All large stocks of which I've managed to lock up. They'll then have all winter to figure out if they want to confront the Horvath over maple syrup. Because, believe you me, the people that collect the stuff are not *about* to let the Horvath take more than a tithe of it."

"And if they nuke Boston and Washington?" the agent asked sarcastically.

"I'll do my best to avoid that," Tyler said.

"How?"

"I'm from the South. We have our little ways."

"What about Atlanta?"

"Okay. So sometimes they don't work."

"Gate emergence."

"What do we have now?" The colonel on duty leaned over and contemplated the screen.

"Looks to be one large ship," the sergeant said.

"Tentative ID is a freighter. No visible weapons. Four more ships, small freighters maybe? Not a class we've seen."

"Those are the visitors we were told to expect," the colonel said. "I hope."

"Sir?" the tech said. "What visitors?"

"Close held."

"Gentlebeings," Tyler said, breezing into the conference room. "I hope you have been well treated. We don't have much in the way of Glatun food products but there's Dragon's Tears."

"Thank you," one of the Glatun said. "We have managed to refrain."

"Oh, dear," Tyler said, waving to the people with him. "Gentle Glatun, Robert Lyle, my attorney of fact for this negotiation, Ms. Cody Castilla with our Treasury Department and Mr. Jason Haselbauer, who is representing a significant fraction of the remaining holdings of Dragon's Tears which I have not managed to procure. And you are?"

"Karorird Ongl, Onderil Banking."

"Canarorird Hetuncha, Gorku Corp."

"Lathmal Indendu, Hurin Corporation."

"Rolaut Orth, Limaror Corporation."

"We need name tags or something. First as to Dragon's Tears. The material is in fact maple sugar syrup. Please feel free to access relevant information on our network."

"Geographically and seasonally highly limited," Hetuncha said. "Excellent."

"Yes," Tyler said. "Because limited means valuable."

"And as of this morning, local time," the Hurin

Corporation representative said, "sixty percent of the operating distilleries and about thirty percent of the available growing land just transferred to the LFD Corporation, Tyler Vernon, Chairman of the Board. Masterful stroke, Mr. Vernon. I see that Mr. Haselbauer, yes, represents many if not all of the independents."

"And you and the independents represented by Mr. Haselbauer hold *all* of the stored stocks," the Limaror Corporation representative said sourly.

"For which we will be negotiating today," Tyler said. "Mr. Haselbauer and Mr. Lyle will be handling those negotiations. Ms. Castilla, who is an expert in banking, will be working on setting up appropriate banking systems, secure from the Horvath, so that we can engage in regular trade. But first a word about maple sugar..."

"Mostly collected by small farmers," Hetuncha said. The Gorku rep wrinkled his nose. "Geographically scattered, hard to gather. And it *has* to be gathered during a very limited period of time. Even if the weather cooperates, any resistance to gathering means a severely reduced crop."

"Which can be good and can be bad," Tyler said. "Less means higher price in general. But if it's simply *unavailable*, one can see the market dying. New product and all. You'll want to maintain your source of supply. I direct your attention to the initials of my corporation, gentlebeings."

"Various meanings," the Onderil rep said. "But in context, our AI says it refers to your tribal motto."

"Closer than you realize," Tyler said. "With everyone who was in it purely for money, or because they thought the Berkshires are pretty, out of the game the Horvath will find it rather *hard* to take. Even the Canadians that gather it are pretty stubborn folk."

"Aren't taking mine, that's for sure and certain," Mr. Haselbauer said. "Burn the trees first. And maple's practically religion to my family."

"I suggest you have your AIs study local tribal reactions to force," Tyler said. "And their relationship with the rest of the world. Especially, as they would put it, 'city folk.' Because what you are buying is *all* the maple syrup that's going to be available until next spring. You have a few months to process the cultural implications. Negotiation will be for Glatun credits, gentlemen, not atacirc. After that, we can trade with regular traders for atacirc and so on and so forth. And, of course, the usual taxes go to the..."

"Revenuers," Mr. Haselbauer said disgustedly.

"The problem is, we really don't know if we're getting a significant amount of credit for this or not." Cody Castilla was in her fifties and severe. Severe face, severe clothes and severe body language. "Their economy is still opaque to us. Our analysts are still trying to process the economic implication of most manufacturing being robotic."

"Not entirely," Tyler said. "Economics comes down to food in the end. What one standard meal costs is another way to say it. I asked Wathaet, innocently, if I visited his station and if I could eat Glatun food, which I can't, how much a cheap meal would cost. He said an ormo, whatever that is, was about a quarter credit. He also told me that his full cargo load of trash atacirc was around a hundred and twenty credits.

And, forgetting the earlier question, made like that was a huge amount of money."

"We're up to fifty credits a *gallon*," Lyle said. "We can buy five shiploads of atacirc for a gallon?"

"We got screwed by them boys," Mr. Haselbauer said.

"Which is why I insisted on more than one corporation being represented," Tyler said. "Dollars are not going to translate to credits but *work* will. How much will it cost to send some of our grad students to Glatun to learn their technologies? How much will it cost to get Glatun to come here to teach? How much will it cost for us to get starter plants and fabbers to make more? We should be able to buy more advanced technologies with this. Not much, but it's a start."

"We need to be able to buy advanced weapons, sorry as I am to say that," Ms. Castilla said. "So we can get the Horvath out of our sky."

"A Revenuer wanting to defend the country?" Mr. Haselbauer said, grinning. "Will wonders never cease?"

"Listen, you . . ."

"Enough," Tyler said. "We don't need tribal differences right now. We can't buy enough weapons, even with the full load, to matter. Probably. It's possible they have weapons we can set up there that mean no Horvath can survive getting through the gate. But I doubt it. For right now, we need to be important to the Glatun powers-that-be so that they will *bring* weapons. And Glatun that know how to use them. Which is why we're going to geek to fifty credits a gallon. Because they're going to make a very nice profit and they will *like* us. We've pushed the negotiations far enough that they won't take us as pushovers. Hopefully they'll be smart enough to see what we're doing. But if I'm getting their society, there is one more thing we need and I can*not* think of a way to get that!"

"What?" Castilla asked.

"You don't want to know."

"Mr. Vernon," the Gorku representative said. "It is a pleasure to meet you."

"And you, Mr. . . ." Tyler said, grimacing. "Sorry, terrible with names."

"Hetuncha," the Glatun said. "It is easier if one has implants. You really don't have to *remember* as you think of it."

"Nice ability," Tyler said. "How much does that cost, exactly?"

"Depends on the implants," Hetuncha said with a slight sneeze. "A basic implant set-up, were there any designed for humans, would be about fifty credits. Full standard civilian, with all the trimmings, as you would put it, runs about four hundred depending on your accessories. Can run more but such people are considered . . . strange."

"And an AI?" Tyler asked.

"AIs are somewhat limited," Hetuncha said. "Only a few thousand are produced a year and they have strict limitations on action. A very basic AI is several thousand credits and in your current unfortunate security situation the Glatun government would never permit an AI to reside in the system. There is one on the freighter which accompanied us, a Gorku freighter, I might add."

"Ah," Tyler said. "And a super-cannon to shoot the Horvath out of the sky?"

"There are ground-based defense systems, of course,"

Hetuncha said. "But they are of limited use due to orbital mechanics. Point-defense only. You wrote *TradeHard*. You know that."

"Just hoping," Tyler said.

"We also have laws against trade in weapons in most cases," Hetuncha said, working his snout.

"Heh," Tyler said. "See how long that lasts when White and Green mountain folk start having off-planet credit to burn. Like they won't find some free trader to supply ray guns? There are things, however, that I'd like to buy that I doubt would bother your government. Nothing weaponlike at all. But I'm not sure if it's off-the-shelf or something that needs to be customized. Also, I am in the near future going to be interested in doing some movement of . . . stuff to orbit. Again, nothing weaponlike in nature."

"What, exactly, do you need?" Hetuncha asked.

"A device that can attach to a satellite that will give a very low delta-V but can maintain a charge or power system for a very long time. Basically, something that can move a satellite around the system but it doesn't have to be fast. Slow, cheap and durable is the key. Also, obviously, with a long-range transmitter."

"I should, as you say, screw you," Hetuncha said. "But you're talking about a standard satpak. They're half a credit. That's if you're buying more than a thousand at a time. And don't try to negotiate, they are very fixed cost. They weigh about a half a pound and have a duration of seventy-three years. We have very good capacitor technology. But even if you put a lot of them together you can't get out of your gravity well."

"Not interested in that," Tyler said. "Lifting out of the grav well? By one of your ships?"

"Depends on when a ship is here," Hetuncha said. "And how big your satellite is, and mass. If the ship can just kick it out the door on the way to the gate? Five credits is standard up to three tons and the size of one of your cars. If they have space available. A few thousand of them and the ship isn't doing anything else and the same. There's a fuel cost to getting out of the gravity well, but if they're going that way anyway the extra mass isn't that much of an issue. The ship we brought has shuttles to pick up cargo. Normally there would be shuttles on the world but we, unfortunately, had to bring our own. Do you have satellites to boost now? I don't see you anywhere as involved in the satellite business."

"Not yet," Tyler said. "I'm thinking long term. *Very* long term. I need a thousand satpaks the next time a ship comes through. That's a registered contract."

"Well, you certainly have the credit."

"Last question," Tyler said.

"At this point I ought to be charging you," Hetuncha replied, sneezing.

"Feel free," Tyler said. "Because the answer is going to be long. And time is money."

"What's the question?" Hetuncha asked curiously.

"Tell me everything you can about the Horvath," Tyler said. "Carnivore, omnivore or herbivore? Reproductive methods? Culture. Monolithic or tribal. How long have they been in contact? What was their tech level before contact? United before contact? Everything..."

"That's two hundred and fifty-six thousand gallons off-planet," Lyle said smugly. "Which translates to twelve point eight *million* credits."

"Given the exchange rate as posted to their hypernet, that translates as the planetary economy of Earth," Castilla said, shaking her head.

"Because all we have is maple syrup," Tyler said distantly. "Mr. Haselbauer, I've sent a quiet message through the hypernet to Wathaet that maple sugar independent distributors now have Glatun credit to burn."

"Why thank you, Mr. Vernon," Mr. Haselbauer said.

"Also that some might want to buy atacirc for resale but that you have other interests," Tyler said. "I need to go. I have some people down south to see."

"Going back to your rebel roots?" Mr. Haselbauer asked.

"MIT for design," Tyler said. "*Huntsville* for production."

"In a remarkable development, Glatun traders are now swarming to Earth in search of . . . *maple syrup*? The tasty treat that kiddies love on pancakes seems to be *ambrosia* to our closest extraterrestrial trading partner, and the price of maple syrup has gone, well, *sky* high! This is Courtney Courtney with Headline News . . ."

FIVE

"You want *how many* mirrors?"

AMTAC was a small company in Huntsville that had managed to survive in a nearly extinguished market. Space mirrors had been well on their way to being a big business before the Horvath arrived. Mirrors were used for a variety of applications from directed-energy-weapon research to astronomy. Get a bunch of mirrors together that were well spread out, and you could get one heck of a space shot. The replacement envisioned for the Hubble was based on distributed mirror technology.

However, the Horvath habit of from time to time potting a satellite just for kicks had practically killed the entire space industry. And space mirrors had been the first to go.

James Raskob, President, CEO and Chief Engineer of AMTAC had managed to keep the company together, with a lot of layoffs, admittedly, despite the bad times. They also made ground-based mirrors and as the only remaining supplier of space designs they could pretty much set their rates. When they got any business. But this was a little kooky.

"I'd like to get up to production of one ten-meter mirror per day," Tyler said. "After we're up to one a day we'll have to start working on better mirrors. These don't need to be great. Just be able to reflect sunlight pretty well. And I'd prefer cheap since we're going to be making a lot."

"Define 'pretty well,'" Raskob said, wincing. "I mean, what sort of coefficient of thermal expansion? Albedo constant? Pretty well is a pretty loose—"

"I just need some pretty good mirrors," Tyler said, shrugging. "Right now I just need stuff that will reflect sunlight. Glass, nickel, whatever."

"Tracking systems? Maneuver? Boost requirements? How high a thrust during boost?"

"I think the Glatun are about our same grav," Tyler said. "They're supplying the tracking and maneuver systems and boost. Oh, and I'm going to need a ground station. You know any people in the ground system business? And you're probably going to need to build up some inventory, hire some people. I'll front you a loan or buy into the business. We're going to be making a lot of mirrors."

"Look," Raskob said, shaking his head. "I appreciate that and everything. But what do you want the mirrors *for*?"

Tyler wriggled uncomfortably, then shrugged.

"I want to melt asteroids."

"Ah . . ." Raskob said, sitting back and steepling his fingers. "Now you're making sense. You have the Glatun willing to boost for you?"

"You know the whole maple syrup thing?" Tyler said. "Well, I'm the maple syrup king. Yeah. I can get them to boost for me. And I'm buying standard satellite packs off of them. I'm also getting a supposedly user-friendly control package. Basic idea is boost a bunch of mirrors, focus them on an asteroid, melt it and pull off the metals."

"Which will belong to our Horvath benefactors," Raskob pointed out.

"Which I might just sell, in space, to the Glatun," Tyler replied. "Let the Horvath take it up with *them*."

"You are playing a dangerous game, friend," Raskob said.

"Well aware of it," Tyler said. "But it's the only game in town. Now, can you make the mirrors?"

"Easily," Raskob said. "But not the main array mirrors. You're right, those are anything cheap, light and shiny. You're going to have to have collectors, though. Those are going to be tougher.

"I'll subcontract for the main array mirrors and make the collectors here. We can easily do one of the main array mirrors a day. CTE isn't really a big thing since they're just moving light around. Collectors, one a month to start. And then bump up the production as I can get qualified workers and more equipment."

"Are we going to need really huge ones?" Tyler asked.

"No," Raskob said. "Just more collectors. You don't even have to have collectors all in one spot. And eventually, collectors that can collect from collectors. Two hundred main array mirror outputs pointing at one collector is about the limit of what one will be able to handle with standard materials. And you're eventually going to want collectors that can handle the power of thousands. Cryogenic beryllium's the thing for that. Problem is keeping it cryogenic in space. Which asteroids are you thinking of mining?"

"I was thinking the ones that are inward towards the Sun from Earth," Tyler said.

"Atens?" Raskob said, shrugging. "That works. They don't stay in there, you know. Very eccentric orbits."

"Main array down towards Venus orbit?" Tyler asked. "That way it's collecting more sunlight—"

"Without getting into the super-hot regimes," Raskob said. "Sure, that would work. I'd suggest up out of the plane of the ecliptic to keep it out of the way."

"Point," Tyler said. "I've got a thousand satpaks coming in a month. I'm not sure when I'll have ships to carry it up but there are more free traders coming these days. They're always willing to pick up a few extra credits. I can probably get a whole ship since all the maple syrup is gone."

"In a month I can have ten mirrors at least," Raskob said. "Primary array, that is. Maybe one collector. And, yes, I know people who do ground control. If they've got systems to support it," he added glumly. "Everybody's IT stuff is breaking down."

"I'm getting at least one hypernode connector as well," Tyler said. "And, ahem, I'm the world's primary supplier of atacirc. I assume they can integrate atacirc into their systems?"

"Oh, yeah. This is gonna be fun! As long as our Horvath benefactors don't get snarky."

"Well, that's always the problem," Tyler said.

"Admiral, thank you for taking my call," Gorku said. "Since I was ordered to do so I really didn't have a choice," Admiral Orth Glatuli said. The commander of the Glalkod defense zone did not seem especially pleased to be taking a personal call from one of the system's wealthiest individuals.

"Now, Admiral, I truly would not be bothering you if I didn't feel it was important to the Federation. I know how busy you are."

"I will take that under advisement," the admiral said. "What is the substance of the call?"

"I would like you to reevaluate the question of the Terran system," Gorku said.

"I continue to contend that maple syrup, popular as it is among my sailors, is not a reason to go to war with the Horvath. And war is certainly not a reason for you to make another megacred."

"Agreed," Gorku said. "But I would suggest strongly that you engage Ldria in a serious analysis of the humans in terms of not just immediate but long-term consequences to the Glatun Federation. Ldria is, after all, the only class five AI in the system."

AIs were broken down into classes, I through V, depending on the multiplicity and complexity of tasks they could perform. Large freighters, cruisers and passenger liners might host a class I AI. This went up in scale to class IV which were the highest, legally, permitted to corporations and those used by fleets. Class V were relegated only to military and governmental entities.

There were rumors that certain corporations had defied the ban and created their own class V and even class VI AIs. The problem with AIs was that as the processing power went up, the stability went down. Class VI AIs were considered fundamentally unstable.

And given their potential harm, the one thing you didn't want was a rogue AI.

But if anyone had an illegal high-level AI it would be Gorku.

"How long term?" the admiral asked. "If it's very long term that is a serious amount of processing."

"I would suggest that you look beyond immediate concerns, Admiral, that is all," Gorku said. "It is always wise to look beyond the immediate and contemplate the realm of possibilities inherent in the future. Good day."

"This is Lisa Cranwell with Eyewitness News and we're talking to Mr. Tyler Vernon, the man who discovered the maple syrup connection. Mr. Vernon, good afternoon."

"Good afternoon, Lisa," Tyler said, beaming. He'd insisted that the interview be live. He was pretty sure he could out-talk a reporter even with, or especially with, five hostile producers telling her what to say.

"Mr. Vernon, some people call you the maple sugar king..."

"Granted," Tyler said, smiling.

"And others the maple sugar bandit."

"Now that's just unfair," Tyler said, looking wounded. "When I made my acquisitions I was very careful to avoid buying the old, established maple sugar distilleries that had been around for generations. And now they are all getting extremely rich off of what was once a minor commodity. My primary acquisitions were from other corporations and land that was already on the market. I don't think that anyone considers sales from one corporation to another as banditry, Lisa."

"But it *has* made you the richest man in the world."

"I was the richest man in the world when I sold one cargo of maple syrup to a tramp freighter," Tyler said. "I'd also like to point out that when people were selling the artistic treasures of our beautiful planet for a handful of peas, I was the one who found the one thing that we could produce that the Glatun wanted. Anyone could have done what I did. I'm shocked and appalled that some other corporation didn't. And whereas I'm now the richest person in the world, when I met my first Glatun, the free trader Wathaet, I was cutting firewood for a living. That's the beauty of the free market, Lisa. Anyone with the right drive and determination, and just a touch of luck, can succeed."

"And just what do you intend to do with your maple gotten gains?"

"I've already established scholarships for young people from this previously economically depressed region as well as other philanthropies. I've also embarked on a program to find sources of material that Glatun or other extraterrestrial groups may enjoy from the wonders of our beautiful planet. Most of those would also come from economically depressed regions. And as for the people who do the extremely hard work of gathering maple sap and distilling it, twenty percent of gross profits are detailed to bonuses. So it's not like I'm hoarding it like a miser."

"And we here at Eyewitness News have learned that you are building space mirrors? Aren't those used for laser weapons? Are you *intending* to antagonize our Horvath benefactors?"

"Not at all, Lisa," Tyler said, smiling toothily and shaking his head in deprecation. "You completely misunderstand their purpose. Such mirrors have a multiplicity of uses. Take astronomy. By scattering mirrors over a large area it is possible to have a telescope with that same area. Instead of a telescope with a diameter of, say, sixty meters such as Palomar you end up with a telescope of six *thousand* meter diameter! We can resolve very fine detail with something like that and continue our exploration of the wonders of the universe. They are also useful for orbital smelting. You can use the renewable power of our beautiful Sun to turn dangerous asteroids into useful materials. And, of course, any precious metals that are derived from such smelting are naturally the property of our Horvath protectors. As to their use as a weapon, we don't *have* any lasers that can even *scratch* the Horvath ship, and I defy anyone to suggest that the Horvath are anything other than our good and close friends and protectors."

"You seem to have all the answers, Mr. Vernon," the reporter said.

"I certainly hope so, Lisa," Tyler said. "We can all look forward to a bright future. A future in which we just become *closer* to our Horvath friends. Remember what they say, Lisa. Keep your friends close."

"Admiral, I have completed my long-term analysis run," Ldria said at the end of a standard briefing. "And I'm rather glad that Trader Gorku suggested it. I also suggest that similar runs be presented to main system AIs. The data is . . . disturbing."

"How much trouble was it?" the admiral asked.

"Rather much," Ldria said. "I had to distribute processor cycles to all the other systems in the system.

And it still took me nearly a month. But, as I said, it was worth it."

"So, what is the point of intervening in the Terran system?" the admiral asked. "Or is there one?"

"There is," Ldria answered. "Assuming that you wish to extend the lifespan of the Glatun Federation as a major interstellar polity for between fifty and seventy years."

"That requires explanation," the admiral said, sitting back. "Clear whatever is on my calendar for the next two cycles. Explain."

"All major polities rise and fall, Admiral," Ldria said. "As the Ormatur were great when the Glatun first encountered them three thousand years ago and are now a minor polity, so will the Glatun eventually become . . . lesser. Not gone, but less important."

"Agreed," the admiral said. "How long do you give the Federation?"

"That depends," Ldria said. "But choices made in the very near future will affect that period greatly. The longest period I can predict is one hundred and thirty turns. The shortest is ten."

"*Ten?*"

"Yes, sir," Ldria said softly. "Ten. The likelihood of it being ten is less than three percent. It increases with each turn, with certain turns being paramount. And Terra may hold the key. Intervention by the Glatun in the human system adjusts a major change point in between fifteen and twenty turns. With Glatun intervention, the likelihood of the Federation ceasing to exist in that period drops by twenty-one percent, plus or minus three. And the likelihood without intervention is seventy-three percent."

"Why?"

"War," Ldria said. "With one of four other major polities. The Rangora are at the top of the list at thirty-seven percent likelihood. Then the Ogut, Barche and Ananancauimor."

"If this is known to the central AIs, surely they are preparing for war," the admiral said.

"Unfortunately, that is not entirely possible," Ldria said. "Your species has begun to enter its final decline. Your birthrate has dropped sharply. Less than one half of one percent of your species enters your military. There is a permanently unemployed class that is approaching thirty percent..."

"I know all that," the admiral said testily. "But in the face of war..."

"You really don't want me to cover it all, Admiral," Ldria said. "Take your AI's word for it. You're facing a war and you're most likely going to lose."

"So intervening with the humans drops the likelihood of such a war?" the admiral asked.

"No, sir," the AI replied. "It reduces the likelihood of *losing*. The war is more or less inevitable. It is possible that one of the central AIs has already predicted this. If so, they are keeping the information very close. But I doubt they have factored in the humans. If they have done a similar process cycle, they are looking at termination of the Glatun Federation by war in fifteen to twenty turns as a better than seventy-percent likelihood. With *no* way to survive."

"The humans are, sorry, primitives," the admiral said. "I don't see them being the balance between winning and losing a major interstellar war."

"Admiral, you understand the problem of such a

wide-ranging analysis," Ldria said. "There are too many variables to sort out. It is what you Glatun would call a hunch except that it reports the results as variables. There are many, many unknowns. We could, through one of the new gates, encounter a more hostile and dogmatic regime with high advancement at any time. Thus the ten-year result. Or one that would be a better ally than the humans, thus low probability results that indicate long-range survival. My results, however, are solid. I can give you some small data items that may sway your personal analysis."

"Very well," the admiral said. "Go ahead and try to change my mind."

"Humans are, at present, primitive," Ldria admitted. "Well behind the Glatun in technological advancement. But unlike most races, the humans do not slowly evolve technologically. Their history is replete with examples of very fast technological advance mixed with periods of relative stasis. Part of the analysis indicates that they were what is termed 'cuspal.' They were on the edge of developing most of the basic technologies for functional space travel except a gate.

"Further, they are not behind the Glatun at the point that the Glatun encountered the Ormatur. Rather ahead of that point, in fact. Far beyond the relevant first contact point of the Horvath. The Horvath had no mechanical transport systems at the point of contact, no information systems and still use the latter poorly. Humans have rudimentary AIs. They had a nascent space program and a fully developed, albeit primitive, information distribution system. They were closing in on fundamental understanding of gravitics, and energy conversion systems are one step away from that. They had the basic concept of implant technology and only need refinement to adopt it. They are likely to not slide forward slowly but positively *leap*. With a large population that is at least in parts technologically savvy they have the basis for a major industrial base, space-faring, and not only system defense but powerful ships within as little as twenty years. Given what I believe some of them are contemplating, those ships will be the savior of the Glatun."

"If they get the Horvath off their necks," the admiral said. "And what about the humans as a threat?"

"That is the flip side to the analysis," Ldria said. "Humans do not always hold true to allies. A degree of self-interest is in their nature. That is, however, *strongly* culturally affected. Targeting for rapid advancement the *right* culture is key. If the Glatun become friends with the *right* cultures, by the time the cultures forget what they owe the Glatun, the Federation will be in senescence anyway. Handled properly they will be a strong ally in the wars that are coming, the Glatun's protectors in your old age. Handled improperly? They will join with your enemies to drag you into a dark age from which your species will not recover in ten thousand years."

"Which culture?" the admiral asked. "And how, exactly?"

"The humans have a saying: Comes the moment, comes the man," Ldria answered, flashing a hologram of Tyler Vernon. "Make this man your friend, Admiral. But in a very *particular* way..."

"This is Saenc Mori with Hypernet News Network Eight and I'm talking to Terran Tyler Vernon, the maple syrup king! Mr. Tyler, welcome to HNN Eight!"

"The Ocho!" Tyler replied with a broad but closed-lips smile. "I'm so happy to be speaking with your viewers, Saenc!"

"And we're happy to be speaking with you, Mr. Tyler! You don't seem uncomfortable with dealing with extraterrestrials despite the fact that your world has only recently made first contact."

"One of my fondest dreams was to one day speak with wise and wonderful beings from other planets, Saenc," Tyler said. "The opening of the gate was a great thing for all our people."

"But you're under the tyrannical boot of the Horvath, Mr. Tyler."

"Now, now, Saenc. The Horvath are our *friends*. For the paltry sum of all our precious metals they provide us with protection and the occasional clearing up of our orbital systems."

"Protection from what, exactly?"

"We're still trying to figure that out, Saenc. From the Glatun, presumably, since you and the Horvath are the only species we have encountered. Are you hiding some deep, dark, dastardly secret, Saenc? Come on, you can tell me."

"No, of course not, Mr. Tyler," the reporter said with a sneeze. "You are so *funny*! So the Horvath are really your friends?"

"What else am I going to say with a Horvath battle cruiser holding our orbits, Saenc?"

"Hypernet Network News has learned that the Horvath are now demanding all of Earth's maple syrup, which they intend to trade with the Glatun. What do you have to say about that, Mr. Tyler?"

"Maple syrup is interesting stuff," Tyler said. "It's

not a few mines. Thousands of people over an area of nearly ten thousand square miles, almost entirely rural, have to stumble out into the bitter cold and snow to tap hundreds of thousands of trees and collect the syrup. Then hundreds of maple distilleries have to boil it down since it can't be moved far before processing. If those people decide it's a good day to sleep in . . . it becomes very hard to collect any significant amount of maple sap. I, of course, fully intend to collect every bit of maple syrup possible for our Horvath friends and benefactors. But I can't do it all by myself, Sacnc. We have about two months until we have to start collecting maple syrup. I suppose we'll just have to see what happens."

"We Glatun would hate to have our maple syrup supply cut off," Saenc said. "That wouldn't be very fun."

"I know, Saenc," Tyler said. "Nor would having our cities turned to ashes. But I can't make thousands of people go out in the cold, Saenc. We'll just have to see what happens."

"There has been talk of armed resistance, Mr. Tyler."

"Well, what would be the point of that, Saenc?" Tyler said. "All we have is a few deer rifles. We can't exactly shoot a Horvath battle cruiser down. What I really fear is that our Horvath benefactors will feel so justifiably irritated by the inaction of local sap collectors that they'll destroy the trees. It would be hard, but a big enough orbital laser will clear out most of the major sap collecting areas. And it takes at least twenty years to grow a decent maple tree. If they do that, you'll be missing out for a looong time."

"And on that note, we're out of time," Saenc said. "Thank you for talking to us, Mr. Tyler."

"My pleasure, Saenc."

"And we're . . . clear. Seriously. Off the record. Not for attribution."

"Gonna get our maple syrup when they pry it from our cold dead hands. Take that as a 'notable resident of the area.'"

"Gotcha. That'll give it some punch."

SIX

"Well, if it ain't ole collaborator Tyler himself," Mr. Haselbauer said.

"Say that with a smile, partner," Tyler said. "Can I come in?"

"If you promise not to take all my maple syrup," Haselbauer said, opening the door.

Tyler divested himself of his outer gear in the foyer that was standard for a house of any size in New Hampshire and shook himself as soon as he got into the living room.

"Da...dang it's cold out."

"You Rebs got thin blood," Mr. Haselbauer said. "Mabel, I think Mr. Collaborator needs some coffee."

"Coming right up," Mrs. Haselbauer said, bustling in and shaking Tyler's hand. "Don't mind him. He's just riled over Revenuers as usual."

"Revenuers coming up from Manchester's bad enough," Mr. Haselbauer said, leading the way to the cellar steps. "Up in space is a bit much for my old brain."

He led Tyler down into the basement and opened up his gun safe.

"Got this off a free trader for a jug I had stashed by," he said, tossing Tyler a rifle. "Works, too. Don't worry. Isn't no electronics down here."

"Laser?" Tyler asked. It had the sinuous look of Glatun manufacture.

"Yep," Mr. Haselbauer said. "Took out a white pine just fine. Made sure it was when the Horvath were in…what's that term? Retrograde? Somewhat like that. Figure it's old but it's what we could get. Actually… got a good few off him. Her. It. Revenuers come up here after our syrup they're going to get a bit of a surprise. Isn't going to take out that Horvath ship."

"No," Tyler said, tossing it back. "And it's not going to save the cities."

"Between you and me," Mr. Haselbauer said. "I would rather keep them standing. Don't care for Washington and Boston and New York. Don't mean I want to see them as craters."

"No comment," Tyler said.

"I sure as hell hope you have a plan, youngster," Mr. Haselbauer said.

"I have a plan," Tyler said. "What I'm hoping is that I don't have to use it."

"So, what do we got?" Tyler asked as he walked into what was laughably called "Mission Control."

The room was a clutter of wires. Most of the equipment was handmade, and mostly by the group of scientists and lab techs that clustered around the room's biggest plasma screen.

"Asteroid 33342 1998 WT," Dr. Bryan Foster said. The head of the Aten Mining Project, he had degrees in optics, astronomy and geology. He also was available when Tyler went looking for somebody who had a clue what they were doing. His name actually came off of the nearly defunct *TradeHard* mailing list. He'd once sent Tyler a rather scathing e-mail explaining all the mistakes Tyler was making in orbital mechanics. Shaped something like a hairy Buddha, he was in his fifties and "just getting started." "AKA Icarus 195 AKA a whole bunch of other names that various astronomers have tried to get to stick. We're just calling it Icarus even though it's not."

"Nickel iron?" Tyler asked. "And is this the best candidate?"

"Well..." Bryan said, shrugging. "It's the best candidate that's in the right orbit right now. It's got the bonus that it's one of those really potential nasties some day. What is called a 'Potentially Hazardous Asteroid.' Turning it into a bunch of cars would do the world a favor."

"What about..." Tyler searched his brain. This wasn't the asteroid he thought they were looking for. "What's the name. Starts with an A...Egyptian god..."

"That's most of these," Dr. Foster said. "You mean Apophis?"

"Yeah," Tyler said. "I thought that was the big problem asteroid."

"It is," Dr. Foster said. "Potentially. It's not going to hit Earth *soon,* but the way things are going, it's going to hit sooner or later. And when it does, it's going to be a major hit. So we'll have to take it out sooner or later. We thought about Apophis. But when you set this up, we put all the mirrors in Venus orbit. 'Cause you said 'Put 'em in Venus orbit we'll figure out what to do with them later.'"

"Yeah, so?" Tyler said.

"Apophis is too close to *Earth* orbit," Dr. Foster said. "We'll get around to it. But we threw all this stuff down nearly a quarter AU to the Sun. So for right now, we're *too far away* to melt Apophis. Being too far away from Earth orbit is not *normally* the sort of thing we're *used* to having as a problem with space probes. When we got around to thinking about it, we realized we'd kind of screwed up."

"My bad," Tyler said. "Like you said, we'll kill it sooner or later. So we're going to melt... What's it? Icarus? And can we get useable stuff of it?"

"Yep. Or rather, probably. Just one problem."

"Which is?" Tyler asked, sighing. It all seemed so simple when he was thinking about it. Like, for decades.

"We don't know what the hell it *is*," Dr. Nathan Bell said. The acknowledged asteroid expert was damned near as big as Mr. Haselbauer. He also had a bit of a Southern drawl when he got excited. "Its physical characteristics are just odd. We don't know quite what it's composed of."

"Well, we will in a minute," Dr. Foster said. "Just as soon as we put power on target."

"We'll know the external chemical characteristics, yes," Dr. Bell said. "But the internal? Until we really heat this puppy up we won't have a clue."

"And it's going to take either a lot of time or a *lot* more mirrors to do that," Dr. Foster said. "The good news about Icarus is that it's only three hundred meters across and rotates about every three point seven hours."

"And that is good because...?" Tyler asked.

"We can keep heat on it longer." Dr. Nathan Houseley

said. The metallurgist was a necessity. There *were* no experts at orbital mining per se. Tall and spare, he had a bit of the look of a vulture. "Although the asteroid is currently well within the orbit of Venus, the degree of thermal coefficient necessary for successful melting of the entire, assuming any significant quantity of nickel iron in its composition, is one point six times ten to the sixteenth joules. Given that the current output of the Very Large Array is only eight point six times ten to the *sixth* joules per second, even factoring for the projected rate of increase, subtracting anticipated heat dissipation, it will require some six months to observe noticeable heating, much less melting, of the material. To achieve even that degree of efficiency will require solid and continuous transfer, which requires a low rotational period to prevent convection transfer."

And a bit of a tendency to go on.

"Which means?" Tyler asked.

"If it rotates fast it cools off fast," Dr. Bell said. "Also will increase material spalling, probably, and create a cloud of material around the object that will reduce the quality of the beam."

"And we've got take in five, four..." Dr. Foster said.

The screen suddenly flashed up a picture of what was clearly an asteroid rotating slowly in space.

"Oh, beautiful image," Dr. Foster said. "Where's our beam?"

"Impact in two, one..." one of the technicians said. "Beam on."

"I...don't see any difference," Tyler said. As far as he could see it was still an asteroid rotating in space. "I was expecting an asteroid-shattering kaboom."

"We don't actually want an asteroid-shattering

kaboom," Dr. Bell said in a distracted tone. "That would cause spalling. See previous explanation."

"I'm an impatient person," Tyler said.

"Get used to waiting," Dr. Foster said. "Do we have spectro, yet?"

"Be about three minutes," Dr. Bell said. "Fortunately, with this hypernode thingy, we don't have light-speed lag or it would be... about seven minutes."

"I hate waiting," Tyler said. "What is spectro?"

"Spectroscopic analysis..." Dr. Houseley said.

Tyler held up a hand.

"What is spectro in this context, Dr. *Foster*?"

"The beam is putting some heat on the target," Foster said, grinning. "That is going to burn some material, which is going to tell us what the outer composition is."

"Thank you."

"Which as expected is, using a *very* unscientific term for our visitor, dust," Dr. Bell said. "Undifferentiated gathered materials. Primarily silica. Some aluminum and titanium. Lots of hydrogen, water and oxygen as expected."

"So it's a sand ball?" Tyler said, grimacing. "A sort of wet sandball? Guys, not to be unscientific or anything, but this is costing me out the butt. I'd really like something other than a ball of sand."

"That is the outer shell," Dr. Foster said. "And as noted, as expected. Okay, since you threw us into this and told us to take it and run, we never had the basic briefing. Asteroids one oh one."

"I hate lectures nearly as much," Tyler said. "But I guess this is important. Don't, please, go into the whole 'there's no such thing as asteroids.' That's an asteroid. For the purpose of *this* company and its nomenclature, an asteroid is something that is mostly rock or at least stuff like rock such as metal and carbon. A comet is something that is mostly ice, meaning solid water, ammonia, et cetera. All the planetules and planetismals and all the rest seems to be people having to publish or perish and not having a good idea. 'Wow! I'll come up with a stupid name for stuff that's already got names!' And Pluto is a *planet*, damnit! Asteroid. Rocky thing. Comet. Icy thing. *Nine* planets. How damned hard does it have to *be!*"

"Been trying to do research on our own, have we?" Dr. Foster said with a grin.

"I hate trying to play catch up, too," Tyler admitted. "And most asteroids are, sorry, Dr. Bell, rock. That is, low metallic content, silica, etc. Some are highly carbonaceous. Got a bunch of carbon. Can't we just call those carbon asteroids?"

"You're the boss," Dr. Foster said. "But most asteroids aren't one thing or another."

"I thought conglomerates were rare?"

"By the 'I need to publish' definition of conglomerates," Dr. Foster said. "But what happened was... You know how they were originally formed?"

"Left over planet junk," Tyler said. "Especially the asteroid belt."

"Good enough for a C," Dr. Foster said. "Most of what you define as asteroids probably started in the asteroid belt between Mars and Jupiter. Some of them are, and I grimace as I say it this way, comets where all the junk boiled off and left behind rock.

"The asteroid belt is, probably, a planet that either didn't quite form or sort of formed and then got pulled apart by tidal forces from Jupiter. But with all those rocks drifting around they were bound to collide. When they collided they broke up. Then there were smaller rocks. Which drifted back together and in some cases fused over time. In other cases, true conglomerates, they haven't quite fused together so they are obviously conglomerate. In addition to rocks, using your nomenclature, there was a lot of stuff, dust, if you will, thrown off. Which also drifted onto whatever had microgravity. So you have dust-covered rocks of varying size which then ground together, producing more dust and fusing together into the asteroids we're looking at. The whole process continuously going on along with them hitting various planets, which are for scientific definitions just really big asteroids, and sometimes hitting hard enough to throw dust out of the planetary gravity field to add to the mess for fifteen billion years, give or take a billion."

"Of which we are now the official cleaner-uppers," Tyler said.

"And absolutely damned by the scientific community," Dr. Bell said, peering at a computer screen. "What my fellow minor planetary object experts have to say about my current job is unprintable. I've had death threats."

"They're just sorry they're not getting paid as much as you," Tyler said. "Okay, when I was doing my very fast and dirty research I noticed that there weren't very many good pictures of these things. What's up with the high-gain color semi-real-time video?"

"We're using the VLA," Dr. Bell said.

"I thought the purpose of *my* VLA was to melt asteroids?" Tyler said. "Thus, hopefully, eventually making enough money to keep this lash-up going. Or at least defray the costs. Not that I don't love pure science for pure science's sake. By the way, Dr. Bell, if you'll come up with a list of particularly vocal critics I'll be glad to gag them with some money. Basic research into these things is actually a wise investment."

"I'll send you an e-mail," Dr. Bell said. "But we have to look at what we're doing. We currently have forty-two VLA mirrors and two collectors up. We're using seven of the primary mirrors and one collector for take. The VLA mirrors are angled to reflect the view of the object to the collector. The collector is pointed at a camera. We had to buy the camera, by the way."

"It was originally purposed for a satellite," Dr. Foster said. "The company went bust when one of their others was zapped by our Horvath friends. It was cheap. Comparatively."

"Over or under a mil?" Tyler said. "Never mind. I get it. Any chance of using it for general astronomical research? As I understand it, the VLA is a great telescope. Potentially."

"I thought you wanted to heat up asteroids?" Dr. Foster said. "It would make a *great* telescope. Even with the relatively low quality of the VLA mirrors, the final take would be *awesome*. Right now we've got thirty-three hundred square meters of space mirror. That's the equivalent of about nine hundred Hubbles. Cut that by maybe ten percent for the quality and you're still talking about the most powerful telescope ever created. One of the bitches we're getting is that we're using all this scope power for, sorry, industrial purposes."

"Which, in time, is going to pay for one hell of a scope," Tyler said. "We getting anything but dust?"

"This is going to take time," Dr. Bell said patiently.

"I'm still unsure about the entire exercise," Dr. Houseley said. "We can heat the material, but we can't *form* it. And how, exactly, are we going to get it to Earth-based industry?"

"One thing at a time," Tyler said. "First we have to develop the basic techniques. Not to mention find an asteroid that's not just a ball of sand."

"Still no real clue what it is," Dr. Bell said. "It's more than sand, though. Getting some definite carbon readings."

"Unless it's hydrocarbon it doesn't do me much good," Tyler said. "As to Dr. Houseley's question. Assume a more or less consistent nickel iron asteroid."

"Good luck," Dr. Foster said. "But I'll accept your assumption for the purposes of discussion."

"Thank you so much, Dr. Foster," Tyler said, grinning. "The Transvaal formations are from a nickel iron asteroid, as are the Sudbury complexes."

"I'm an expert in nickel mining, sir," Dr. Houseley said irritably. "I'm aware of that."

"You're also a metallurgist and know that neither composition is pure nickel iron. But have you thought about the actual method of their formation? A ball of nickel iron and...other stuff..."

"Conglomerate," Dr. Foster said.

"Came screaming in through the atmosphere. It was heated. The more volatile material was mostly burned off on reentry. What was left was the high melting temperature materials. Nickel. Iron. Platinum group. Et cetera."

"Accepted," Dr. Houseley said.

"What we are doing is a replica of that," Tyler said. "Sort of. The asteroid is spinning. As it heats, the lowest volatility material will... What was that term, Dr. Foster?"

"Sublimate, mostly."

"Basically, it will burn off. And spall, as Dr. Bell put it. Chunks will be blown out by the low volatile material beneath. The removal of the low volatiles, the higher portions of the periodic table in general, will permit contraction of the high melting, generally denser, materials. With the rotation, what *should* be formed in time is a compact ball of metal. As it heats more, the lowest melting point materials will creep to the outside."

"I see," Dr. Houseley said. "Centripetal thermal smelting."

"Exactly," Tyler said. "By the time it's heated up enough to be worth pulling stuff off, I should have some Glatun space bots here to do the pulling. Then, a bit like pulling taffy, we'll start pulling off the valuable materials. The main thing I'm actually worried about is losing the copper and tin with the silica."

"Speaking of which," Dr. Bell said. "Just got a hit of selenium. There is tin in it. Was. Well, it's still probably orbiting, but as finely divided powder and gases. Ditto aluminum now. I think I know what this thing is made of."

"What?" Dr. Foster asked, craning over his shoulder.

"Bloody damned everything," Dr. Bell said. "We're starting to run the periodic table here. It really *is* a conglomerate. It's mostly low volatiles so far, obviously. As D— Mr. Tyler just pointed out, the melting points of silica and copper, which just turned up, aren't that different."

"Yeah," Tyler said with a sigh. "I was afraid of losing all the low volatiles."

"Fear not," Dr. Bell said. "Based on what we're getting so far and the overall recorded mass, it's a conglomerate that's about seventy-five percent mixed low-densities by weight."

"That's not too great," Tyler said.

"It's going to make a *great* paper," Dr. Bell said excitedly. "'Minor planet composition determination by solar pumped spectroscopy' has a nice ring, don't you think?"

"I'm not doing this to keep your professional reputation intact," Tyler said. "Does this thing have any significant amount of useable metals?"

"Not really," Dr. Bell said. "I mean, it's got metal. But not a lot. I think we need a better asteroid."

"Hell. Well, on that note, I'm going to be late for a meeting."

"Mr. Vernon, it's a pleasure to meet you at last."

"And I you, Mr. President," Tyler said, taking the indicated seat. Sitting in the Oval Office was a long way from cutting logs.

"I understand you are not a fan, though," the President said, giving Tyler a charming grin.

"You're the President of the United States," Tyler said. "I am what could be considered the loyal opposition. I dislike your policies but that doesn't mean I don't recognize that you are the President with all that entails. Including automatic loyalty to the position within the constraints of being a citizen."

"I believe the term that my staff came up with was 'Communist, terrorist-loving danger-to-the-Republic with delusions of grandeur.'"

"Well, I'll admit I didn't vote for you," Tyler said. "But the choices were pretty sparse on the ground, period. I take it this is not a test of my loyalty to you as a person as opposed to as our Chief Executive. Because if so, we might as well withdraw to corners and start the count."

"Not at all," the President said. "But you have to admit you do seem to keep putting your foot into messes."

"I prefer to think of it as giving my government bargaining chips," Tyler said. "We now have regular...ish trade with the Glatun. We have something resembling a balance of trade. One that is so far very favorable to the world and this nation in particular."

"The Horvath are now demanding all of our, mostly your, maple syrup," the President said. "And now you've discovered something that has their appetite even more whetted. Whereas it may all be fun and games for you, Mr. Vernon, I am President of this entire nation. If the Horvath start destroying our cities it will not be Tyler Vernon that will have to comfort the grieving."

"And Tyler Vernon didn't run for office," Tyler said, smiling thinly. "In case nobody covered this in history class, when you work to get into the chair you're occupying, that comes with a lot of responsibility. That's why you get perks like a car and driver and your own airplane. Not to mention a nice crash pad."

"Can we cut the verbal fencing?" the President asked.

"Gladly."

"You're really upsetting the Horvath," the President said.

"Are we reasonably secure?" Tyler asked.

"We are, as far as can be determined, very secure," the President said. "One of the things we've been doing with the credits we've gotten is getting something resembling security back in our systems."

"Which I'm sure doesn't upset the Horvath at all," Tyler said. "And I'm planning on upsetting them even more."

"Why in God's name?" the President said. "Damnit, Vernon, this is not a game! There are people's lives at stake. *Millions* of people's lives at stake."

"Yes, there are," Tyler said. "And I'm fully cognizant of that. I'm going to do my level best, *am* doing my level best, to keep them alive. But there is more to life than simple existence, Mr. President. Sorry, but this country was not founded on existing under tyranny. Quite the opposite."

"That is a very nice sentiment," the President said. "But in the Revolutionary War, the nation did not face extermination."

"Did it not?" Tyler asked. "'Those who would surrender essential liberties for a little temporary security shall receive neither security nor liberty.' That gets thrown around a lot in terms of whether we incarcerate terrorists, tap communications, what we're allowed to do with our sexual organs. Essential liberties before the Horvath *used* to mean, or seem to mean, whether we had the right to get drunk on a flight and insult stewardesses. Whether marriage was between any two people, whatever their gender! But what Ben Franklin meant by *security* was whether your home was going to be burned to the ground. Whether you were going to be killed without rhyme or reason. Whether property and businesses would be seized. *This* is what essential liberties really *mean*, Mr. President. And what temporary security really *means*. And we have given up *essential* liberties for temporary security, and how very secure do *you* feel, Mr. President? Sitting at ground zero of Horvath target number one? *How secure?*"

"Then do *you* have a plan to get the Horvath from the sky?" the President asked angrily. "Because the Joint Chiefs are the people who are *hottest* on my neck to get you under control. They don't want to lock you up, they want to bury you!"

"I've got about as much of a plan as the Continental Congress had in 1775," Tyler said.

"And that is . . . ?"

"Win or go down fighting."

"That's suicide," the President said. "You're nuts."

"'Our lives, our fortunes and our sacred honor.' They want the maple syrup, let them send their own troops down. And then things will get *really* hot."

"They won't send *their* troops," the President said, touching a folder.

"Oh," Tyler said as if gut punched. "You have to be *kidding!* That is *low*. Not to mention unconstitutional."

"I'll give you a quote," the President said. "'The Constitution is a document, not a suicide pact.' We've been in . . . close negotiations. Send in our troops and get the maple syrup or they start with DC and work their way down a list."

"So are your troops planning on extracting, and processing, mind you, the maple syrup?"

"If necessary," the President said. "The Pentagon can come up with the most amazing plans on the spur of the moment. We are hoping for widespread support as a patriotic gesture."

"You need to look up the definition of patriotism," Tyler said. "Although you'd probably have to use a dictionary from before the PC era. So am I under arrest to be delivered to our benefactors or am I free to go?"

"I'm hoping for your support in this necessary action," the President said.

"Will you settle for neutrality?" Tyler said. "'While I, personally, am grieved by this gesture by our government, any armed resistance would be both counterproductive and mean that fine Americans would simply be killing other fine Americans. It's really a very sad day.'"

"Glib."

"Thank you. I used to write."

"I'm quite serious about sending in troops."

"I'm sure you are. And I'm quite serious that it will be a sad day."

SEVEN

"This is Courtney Courtney with CNN and I'm in beautiful Northfield, Vermont, where after a series of record lows the temperature has climbed to a balmy forty-seven degrees and you can simply smell spring in the air! I'm embedded with Company A of the First Battalion Eighty-Seventh Infantry of the Army's Tenth Mountain Division. The company has been given the mission of tapping local maple trees to supply syrup for our Horvath friends!

"I'm talking with Specialist Benjamin Putman, who is the company's designated maple tapping expert. So, Specialist, did you go to a special school to learn maple tapping?"

"Yes, ma'am," the specialist said, smiling fatuously. "It's called my mama's knee."

"Excuse me?"

"I'm from about thirty miles from here, ma'am. I was born and raised in Caledonia county."

"So you learned maple syrup processing at your mother's knee," the reporter said, smiling thinly at the joke. "I guess that makes you an expert, then. But on a personal note. Since you are from this area, what do you think of the military being sent in to, basically, take this sap?"

"Just following orders, ma'am," the specialist said. "Just like every soldier whose ever followed an order that people might not like. Like, you know, the SS comes to mind."

"It's not quite that bad, Specialist."

"As you say, ma'am," the specialist said. "On the other hand, I think you might want to read up on your history a bit more. The SS didn't *start* by killing six million Jews. Started by taking their homes and businesses. Got around to the gas chambers later."

"Why don't we just concentrate on the process of extracting maple syrup," the reporter said. "I understand that it's not exactly hard."

"Well, it's not exactly hard and it's not exactly easy, ma'am," the specialist said.

"Why don't you show us how it works?"

"First you take a drill of the right diameter and you tap the tree," the specialist said, knocking with his knuckles on the maple. "This one is below ten inches in diameter so you can only get one tap in. You apply your drill and drill in just far enough to get into the wood. You don't want to drill too far. Just enough to get through the bark and set the tap. Then you take your tap and a hammer and you hammer the . . . Oh f . . . udge."

"What's wrong?"

"Well, see how the wood split up like that? That's bad. You don't get a seal with a crack like that. This tree's basically useless for this year. Oh . . . darn!"

"What?"

"I forgot! When it's too warm the trees'll crack

if you try to tap 'em! I've got to go check on the rest of the company's work. They've been tapping all morning. If they're *all* split...!"

"Well, there you have it," the reporter said through gritted teeth. "Even experts in this business can make... mistakes. This is Courtney Courtney with CNN..."

"And we're...clear."

"They are going to flatten New York."

"Yeah. But Atlanta's waaay down the list."

"I'm not from Atlanta."

"I am."

"This is Desiree Romane with the Canadian Broadcasting Service interviewing residents in the Trois Riveaux area of Quebec province, a major area of maple sugar production. Excuse me, sir? *Excuse moi, monsieur?*"

"*Quoi?*" the heavily clad man asked without pulling down his scarf. The balmy temperatures of the day before were dropping like a rock.

"*Vous travaillez dans l'industrie du sucre d'érable?* Do you work in the maple sugar industry?"

"*Oui.*"

"And what is your opinion of the Horvath demand that we turn over all our maple sugar?"

What exploded from the man was a torrent of Quebeçois too fast for even the Quebec native to understand.

"Perhaps for our English-speaking viewers?" the reporter asked desperately.

"Pox upon English viewers," the man said in a thick Quebeçois accent. "Pah! What I said is that the cheese of a donkey aliens can go eat *merde*! We are finally paid what our sugar is worth and they wish us to give it to them for *nothing*? They may nibble upon the end of my manhood! They may kiss my very hairy bottom which has some boils—!"

"And we're having technical difficulties with the transmission from Trois Riveaux. But here is Madeline Bathsome in Ontario province speaking to...?"

"Mr. Duncan McKenzie who is the owner of a large maple distillery here in Chapleau. Good afternoon, Mr. McKenzie."

"Good afternoon, lassie."

"So, how is the maple tapping going?"

"Well, unless you're a complete moron you don't tap yet. But it's not looking so good."

"Really?"

"Ach. Terrible. Weather's all wrong. Not going to get much sap no how. No way. And we've had a real rash of injuries this winter. Lots of slips on the ice and such. I completely threw out my back carrying in firewood. Can't hardly get out of bed."

"You...look perfectly fine."

"Hurts terrible. Need an MRI. But Health Service is backed up months. May not be on my feet till summer."

"And you..."

"Do most of the tapping on my land, aye. Probably not going to get naught this year. Terrible shame."

"We're in Littleton, New Hampshire, speaking to Captain Michael 'Werewolf' Wolff, commander of Bravo Company, Fourth Battalion, Thirty-First Infantry. Captain, you've been getting armed resistance, I understand."

"Yes, ma'am," the captain said. He had his helmet locked in place and body armor and battle rattle over his cold weather gear. "A bit. We've some vehicle damage as well as three men in the hospital and one lightly wounded. That's ignoring the men we have in medical for cold weather injuries."

"Have you been taking a lot of fire?"

"Not a lot so much as *how*, ma'am," the captain said, clearly frustrated. "The majority is what is defined as harassing fire. Just enough to get the troops' heads down and keep them from tapping the trees. Occasionally we've gotten some sniper fire. That's what's put my boys in the hospital and I'm not real pleased about that. So far, fortunately, there have been no deaths."

"Have your troops been returning fire?"

"Yes, ma'am. As has been said, it's a terribly sad day when Americans are fighting Americans. Over maple syrup."

"And have your men killed or injured any of the enemy?"

"I'm having a hard time using the term enemy, ma'am. But if you're talking about the local aggressors, not to my knowledge, ma'am."

"Your troops have taken fire. And they've returned fire. And they haven't hit any of the . . . local aggressors?"

"Not to my knowledge, ma'am."

"Captain, we did some research on your unit. It has been in combat in Afghanistan against the Taliban and Pashtun tribesmen. They are considered some of the best mountain troops in the world. And this unit, with many of these same soldiers, scored an impressive record of kills. You're saying that you haven't killed or injured any of the . . . local aggressors."

"That would seem to be the case, ma'am."

"That doesn't make much sense to me, Captain."

"Sorry about that."

"Perhaps you could explain to your viewers what the difference is here in New Hampshire? Is it possible that your troops are simply not aiming because these are people who matter and Afghan tribesmen aren't?"

"You mean these are American citizens and Afghan terrorists aren't, ma'am? That would seem to be a tautology."

"I believe I said *matter*, Captain."

"Have you been to Afghanistan, ma'am?"

"No, I haven't, Captain. Does that matter?"

"Only to particulars like why it's harder to hit someone who is bellied down in snow, using camouflage and cover and an expert sniper versus tribesmen who run screaming at you firing from the hip in the open, ma'am. I don't know exactly who told you that Taliban are crack mountain fighters, ma'am, but they're not. Not anymore, anyway. Here we're dealing with fellas that not only know the woods like the back of their hand but are, in many cases, former U.S. military. And until recently this was a pretty hardscrabble area. They did a lot of hunting for the dinner table. That tends to dial up your targeting skills, ma'am. And what they are targeting, with some care I might add, are my troops. Who, yes, don't particularly want to be doing this job but they're following orders."

"I see," the reporter said. "And when you collect the sap?"

"We process it," the captain said, obviously growing impatient. "You put it in pans and boil it over an open flame. We'll be mostly using local wood."

"Wood?" the reporter said. "Isn't that a bit . . . Doesn't that release a lot of greenhouse gases?"

"Greenhouse gases?"

"Yes, Captain. Carbon dioxide."

"You're talking about global warming? Yes, it releases a lot of greenhouse gases. Even *worse* than the smoke from the fires is what gets boiled off of the *sap*! It's the most powerful greenhouse gas on Earth!"

"I thought . . . doesn't it just release steam?"

"Water vapor!" the captain said, practically shouting. "Look it up! It's the most powerful greenhouse gas on Earth! We're up here trying to keep our cities from being *nuked*, trying to collect sap, SAP! while UNDER FIRE and you're worried about GREEN-HOUSE GASES? Are you absolutely INSANE? You didn't ask me about the vehicle damage! Go ahead and ask me about the vehicle damage, Miss Smarty-Pants!"

"Have . . ." the reporter stammered. This sort of thing was gold but having a heavily armed soldier seemingly losing it was a bit flustering. "Have the insurgents been planting IEDs?"

"NO!" the captain screamed. "One of our *unoccupied* humvees was taken out by a LASER rifle. WE don't even have laser rifles! The guys who have been so carefully and considerately shooting my boys in their thighs have LASER RIFLES! We're outnumbered, outfoxed and outgunned. And you're worried about CARBON DIOXIDE?"

"HALT, WHO GOES THERE?"

"Sergeant of the guard, asshole."

"Respond to challenge: Done."

"In a screwed up situation."

"You may pass."

"You never will. I'm serious. I've got that feeling."

"Like the hills have eyes?"

"No, you moron. Like there are about five times our number of locals up in the hills just trying to figure out how to get us to leave without going to the trouble of killing us."

"Does have that feeling. I'd rather be ass deep in Taliban."

"I wouldn't go that far. But it is a terribly messed up deal."

"Yup."

"Ayup."

The sergeant counted on his fingers for a moment.

"Dick, did you say 'Ayup' just a moment ago?"

"Nope. Said 'Yup.' Guy pulling the tap out said 'Ayup.'"

"Ayup." There was a thunking sound and a clatter of metal.

"We went to a lot of trouble putting those taps in."

"Try doing it for a living, soldier boy."

Thunk. Tinkle.

"Quiet night tonight, Dick."

"That it is, Sergeant."

"I seem to remember some wind from the east, though."

"More like northeast."

"Northeast. Could have covered a lot of noise."

"We've got FLIRs."

"Probably shouldn't want to flip them down, soldier-boy."

Thunk. Tinkle.

"Probably not. Yup. Quiet night."

"Ayup."

❋   ❋   ❋

"Howdy, soldiers," Mr. Haselbauer said, sighing. "Come on in and take a load off."

"Mr. Jason Haselbauer?" the lieutenant said nervously. If the local resident started going off, they didn't have tasers to deal with him. Or, for that matter, a Javelin antitank round. The lieutenant hadn't really appreciated being tasked with "making friendly contact with potential local insurgent" anyway.

"The same," Mr. Haselbauer said, waving for the squad to come in. "We're about to set down to vittles. Got 'nough for some hungry soldiers."

"Uh, sir, we have our own rations," the lieutenant said just as he caught a whiff from inside. "But if you insist..."

The Haselbauer table was well set to fit a squad. Even with a couple of the daughters-in-law and kids occupying the house there was enough room, and food, for six hungry soldiers. And it was in piles as befitted a farm kitchen.

"This is...very kind of you, sir, ma'am," the lieutenant said. It was a bit surreal. They had good intelligence that Haselbauer was one of the heads of the local resistance, perhaps *the* head of the regional resistance. And here they were having dinner with him. He'd met with some absolutely known bad-guys in Iraq and Afghanistan over green tea. Sitting in a farm kitchen in New Hampshire with a table piled with home-cured ham, turkey, corn, potatoes and all the fixings was just...different.

"Was in the One-Oh-One in Vietnam," Mr. Haselbauer said. "Know all about screwed up orders, Lieutenant. Gonna pray."

"Yes, sir," the officer said, waving at his men to bow their heads. Most of them were from Christian backgrounds and didn't need to be prompted. Khalid was polite enough to just pretend.

"Dear Lord, we thank You for the blessings of a full table, a stocked larder and all the good that You have brought to this house, this land, this nation. We thank You, Lord, for two hundred and fifty years of freedom. We thank You for bringing the blessings of peace and prosperity to this land. We ask Your forgiveness for any way that we have transgressed against Your will, Lord. And we ask forgiveness, Lord, for these fine young men who through no fault of their own find themselves trapped between their orders and the oath they swore in Your name, Lord, to uphold and defend the Constitution of these United States against all enemies foreign and domestic. Please forgive us all our sins, Lord, and bring us to Your everlasting home no matter how far we have fallen from Your eyes, Lord. Amen."

"Amen," the lieutenant said. Suddenly he wasn't hungry.

"Honey, there's somebody at the door."

Jonathan "K-9" Kolasinski got up from his computer, still mentally composing the response he was putting on a blog, and walked to the door. He wasn't especially worried about security. Besides the fact that things like home invasion were incredibly rare in New Hampshire, Lovey-poo was sitting attentively by the door. Lovey-poo being an eighty-pound German Shepherd Dog that at a quiet word would probably be able to take out an entire street gang.

Jonathan was an eight-year veteran of the Air Force who spent his entire career as a "handler." The term was "Contingency Response." He'd lost two partners in the MidEast Area of Operations, one in the Sandbox and one in the Rockpile, respectively. The IED that got Ranger also got him, which was why he was sitting in front of a computer instead of out working the hills with the rest of the troops. Lovey-poo had retired with him and was now well on his way to being the top stud Alsatian in New England.

Three of Lovey-Poo's harem padded into the hallway quietly as Jonathan reached the door. Mindy was trailing because she was well into pregnancy.

"*Sitz*," Jonathan said without looking around. All three bitches' butts hit the ground as if synchronized. He'd taken a glance through the side windows and had seen that the visitor was a short man wearing a fur hat. Probably one of the neighbors, although he wasn't immediately familiar. And it was a cold night to be out.

"Hi, I'm Vernon Tyler," Tyler said, leaning over and glancing at the four *very large* German Shepherds. All four had those forequarters that made them look like canine fullbacks. What bothered him the most was that they were just *sitting* there. Quietly. That was never a good sign. "I was wondering if I could have a word."

"Beautiful dogs," Tyler said, taking a sip of tea. "Ah . . . Alsatians?"

"German Shepherd Dogs," Jonathan said, shrugging. "Some people get worked up over having 'Dog' in the name. Lovey-poo is a Deutsche stud. The Germans just have better lines than the U.S. The bitches are U.S. Anna, Gretchen, Mindy, meet Mr. Vernon." All three of the bitches sat up and whined, then lay back down.

"I'd heard you were a breeder," Tyler said with a laugh. "They didn't quite cover it. Schutzhund?"

"Mmmm..." Jonathan said. "To what do I owe the honor of the visit, Mr. Vernon?"

"Hate to bother you at this time of night," Tyler said automatically. "But it's been a long day and miles to go before I sleep and all that. I'm sort of out taking the tenor of the clans. You moved back here rather than being a newcomer so it's not exactly like talking to one of the families that never has left. I've found I've gotten...straighter answers. When there are any answers to be had. What's your take?"

He didn't really have to ask "about the Horvath demanding the maple syrup." It was pretty much the only topic of conversation to be found in most of Maine, Massachusetts, Vermont and New Hampshire.

"I've friends and family live in Boston, Mr. Tyler," Kolasinski said, using the pure New England "Bah." "So it's a hard thing to say 'Wipe out the world if you want, but we're not going to give up our maple syrup.' It's... *maple syrup.*"

"Agreed," Tyler said, nodding.

"What's your take?"

"What everyone in the U.S. government, what everyone in the media, what the Glatun and the Horvath all want to know," Tyler said, "is what is my take. Which is a far cry from cutting trees for a living. And the answer is... I'm taking the tenor of the clans."

"Okay," Kolasinski said, chuckling. "One more question and I'll try to answer yours. Clans?"

"New England is not, by any stretch of the imagination, monolithic," Tyler said with a sigh. "Nor are the maple areas of Canada where I've also been. Old farming families that stretch back to the Revolutionary period and pre-Revolution. Hippies that moved up for the cheap land and libertarian approach. Southerners like me who have moved here so they can be around relative conservatives. Communes. Militias. Modern lefty gay bed-and-breakfast owners. People who want to declare independence and throw out all the lefties.

"My land grab and the Horvath threat have pretty much moved out anyone who doesn't love this area. The one influx of Glatun credits we got is more influx than this region has ever seen. But *nobody* wants to be at ground zero of the Horvath threat. Nobody, American or Canadian, wants to be in the middle of a war with our own militaries. What's left are people who just refuse to leave. And there aren't really major regional variations. Oh, somewhat when you cross from New Hampshire to Vermont or Massachusetts but not even that too greatly. What there are are . . . clans. Like-thinking groups. I almost think New England needs to be parliamentary rather than territorial, but I digress. I'm taking the tenor of the clans."

"Which group am I?" Kolasinski asked.

"You said one question," Tyler said, smiling. "And your answer to 'what's your take' more or less puts you in one. Generally, older, not really old but older, families that stay here because this is home."

"It ought to be easy," the former sergeant said. "It's maple syrup. Who wants to die over maple syrup?" He looked at Tyler, who shrugged in what might be agreement.

"But..." Kolasinski continued, shrugging. "The government is offering to buy it. Pretty fair price. Then they'll turn it over to the Horvath."

"Cheaper than trying to take it," Tyler said.

"Agreed. But. It's still taking. This isn't... This isn't what I put my life on the line for. This isn't what I fought for. What I lost partners for and damn near my life."

"'Give me liberty or give me death?'"

"More or less," Kolasinski admitted, sighing. "I've got two kids and a wife. I have to think about them."

"Contingency plans?" Tyler asked.

"I was in contingency response," Kolasinski said, chuckling. "Uh. Yeah."

"This simply isn't working, Mr. President," the Army Chief of Staff said. "We've got twenty percent of units reporting a variety of maladies. We've issued administrative punishments for malingering, but this is more like mutiny. And as fast as they do manage to tap trees, if they don't ruin the taps, the locals are sneaking in at night and taking the taps out. And leaving little notes about the quality of our men's work. Last, even if everything was working perfectly, our men are unfamiliar with the process, unfamiliar with the terrain, and it turns out to be harder to find the trees than we'd thought. There are large stands but many of the best trees are scattered in pine woods. It simply is not working."

"Frankly," the Chairman of the Joint Chiefs said, "it's becoming a huge farce. I'm not sure the Army, per se, is turning into a laughing stock simply because of all the press reports where everyone's going 'wink,

wink, nudge, nudge.' But the operation is becoming a laughing-stock."

"There are millions of lives at stake, General," the President said. "And these people are playing games!"

"I am fully aware of that, Mr. President," the general replied. "That does not mean that this is an achievable goal."

"It might be..." the National Security Advisor said. "Oh, not gathering the maple syrup. You only have to watch the SNL skit to see that. We just need to be clear about the goal."

"The goal is protecting our cities," the President said. "Whatever that takes."

"And that may be a goal we are achieving, Mr. President," the NSA said.

"I don't see it," the CJCS. "At this rate we are *not* going to get any appreciable amount of maple syrup. Neither are the Canadians. They're having the same problems."

"That is *not* the goal," the NSA said, again. "The goal is not getting rocks dropped on our cities. And that goal may be achievable. We don't have Horvath internals, but they must be getting most of what we are looking at. I doubt, at this point, that they are getting any significant internals from the resistance. What they are getting are the same externals we're getting. 'Of course we want peace in our time, but...'"

"*But* won't cut it," the President said.

"A certain kind might," the NSA said. "We, the... civilized? Urbanized?"

"Liberal?" the Marine Corps commandant filled in.

"The people who are under threat," the NSA said sourly, "are doing our best to collect the maple syrup that the Horvath demand. We're doing everything we can."

"More," the Army Chief of Staff said. "We're stepping all over every document that gives us legal authority to exist. Necessarily, I agree, but at some point we're going to face *real* mutiny. I expected it before now."

"We're trying," the NSA said. "Trying *really* hard. That's clear on all the news broadcasts."

"Yep," the Marine Corps commandant said. "We're being good collaborators."

"General," the President said. "I appreciate your feelings in this matter, but the insertions are not helpful."

"Sir."

"Your point?" the President said.

"The people who are incurring the wrath of the Horvath are the people in that region," the NSA said. "And the few contacts with the rebels that have been broadcast are almost all contemptuous of 'city folk.' They basically are saying they don't care if cities are nuked. It's not a threat to them."

"'I'm from the South. We have our ways.'"

"Mr. President?"

"Something that Vernon said to an FBI agent," the President said. "About, I guess you would say, manipulating the Horvath. I've been puzzled by the line. 'I'm from the South. We have our ways.' What ways?"

The Marine Corps commandant leaned back and started tapping his mouth, as if to erase a smile.

"Commandant?" the President said. "You have a comment."

"Rather refrain, Mr. President," the commandant said, still trying not to smile. "But I think I know what he meant. Graduated from the Citadel, Mr. President."

"So you're 'of the South' as well?" the President said. "And?"

"Really rather refrain, Mr. President," the commandant said then barked a laugh as if at a joke he'd just told. "Seriously. You do not want to know at this time. Possibly ever."

"I will, currently, accept your position," the President said warily. "And where is Mr. Vernon? He is the one person of note who has not been heard of recently."

"Moving, mostly," the director of the FBI said. "Scattered meetings. Turned up by surprise at some town hall meetings in New Hampshire and Vermont. Even back and forth across the border to Canada though we're not sure where or how. We're only catching traces of him. Frankly, he's about as hard to find as a much taller . . . insurgent. We're not even sure he's part of the insurgency. He's acting more like a neutral."

"I'm the President of the United States!" the President snapped. "This is . . . insane! I'm *responsible* for this nation! People are going to *die! Cities* are going to die!"

"Depends on whether he's right or not, Mr. President," the Marine Corps commandant said, still smiling slightly. He tapped his lips again. "Depends on whether he's right about ways of the South."

"On Friday night at eight-thirty, Fox News is pleased to announce an exclusive broadcast from none other than Tyler Vernon, the maple syrup king and the man at the *center* of the current controversy over maple syrup production, direct and live from his home in New Hampshire. With the deadline for tapping fast approaching, we are *all* looking forward to what Mr. Vernon has to say..."

"Are we sure this is going to work?" Tyler asked, adjusting his jacket. He'd gone for the informal look for the broadcast. The jacket was a necessity because it was cold in the former mine.

"Not sure," Bruce Dennison said. "But from what we've been able to figure out, the Horvath are technologically advanced but not technologically *sophisticated*. They can tap any standard system. But this laser relay is going to a secure Glatun hypernode link which is, in turn, hooked up to Fox. It *should* look like you're broadcasting from your house."

Tyler glanced over his shoulder at the green wall, then at the TV tech.

"And the green screen is...?"

"Good," Ryan Gill said. He was wearing an incongruous Scottish WWI military outfit including tartan trews because, as he said, if he was going down he was going down in the uniform of his regiment. "Looks just like your front room. Except for the occasional bloody puff of fog when you exhale. Hopefully, they won't notice that."

"And we're on in five, four, three, two..."

"Hello, Fox and thank you for being willing to make this broadcast. I feel rather odd doing this. Just a few short months ago my days were filled with the mundane tasks of small jobs. To make ends meet I worked in a grocery store and a mill, and cut wood during my free time. Now, as most people know, I'm at the center of this controversy over, of all things, maple syrup, and one of the richest men in the world. It has been an odd transition.

"The Horvath have demanded that everyone in this region collect maple syrup and turn it over to them, presumably for later sale to the Glatun since it is unusable by the Horvath. Just as they have demanded all this world's production of useful heavy metals. Their stated reason for this tribute is so that they can maintain the defense of this world. Tribute, however, is tribute, and let us not mince words. For we have come to an important time of decision. Within the next week, the people of this region must make preparation for the collection of maple sap to be boiled into syrup. The weather is turning and the sap is starting to run. According to both the U.S. weather service and projections by the Glatun, this should be a spring of good harvest. If there is any harvest at all.

"Were I so inclined, one pair of hands simply cannot collect all the sap that must be collected. It requires many hands, many people, going out into the cold of a New England and Canadian spring, working hard for a bounty that will, in turn, continue to keep the Horvath in our skies.

"Over the last month and a half I have been travelling throughout this region, talking to people of every persuasion, getting the pulse of the residents of this region, people who do the tapping and boiling, people who depend upon the trade. I haven't been speaking with governors or Congressmen, just common folk like myself.

"There is great fear and consternation. Like myself, the people of this region never expected to be embroiled in an international, inter*stellar*, controversy. They, *we*, are simple folk of the rural lands of these great nations. We get up every day and do our jobs, letting the great matters of this land and this world be handled by others. We, until this time of controversy, did not care for such matters. The seasons of the year affected us more than the decisions made in Washington and Ontario.

"Now, as a people, we have been called upon to make great and momentous decisions. Decisions reflecting both liberty and security. Liberty is an odd word. And for a long time it has been, in truth, degraded. Many who used the term *liberty* in truth meant *libertine*. And even those who fought in our courts and legislature over questions of liberty, in truth meant things that are minor at best and puerile at worst. As we have now found out, liberty is not about where you can put your sexual organs but about the essential question of whether we, as a people, can make our own decisions. And security is not about whether the government should be able to tap our phone but about whether we are going to be allowed to take the next breath. Will our cities be ashes? Will we live? Will our children live?

"Yet . . . to battle over maple syrup? The inherent humor of the situation sometimes clouds the truly vast nature of the struggle. For it is not, in the end, what we give up, maple syrup or gold or platinum. It is of a piece. It is about whether we, as a people, as nations that were both conceived in liberty, will continue to cherish that concept.

"Benjamin Franklin once said: 'Those who would give up essential liberty to purchase a little temporary safety deserve neither liberty nor safety.' And in this current condition there is, in fact, neither. I understand, as few but the most specialized experts understand, the strategic situation. The Horvath control our orbitals. We can fight but there is simply *no way* to win. Fighting would appear to be a pointless exercise."

The producer made a rolling motion and pointed to the ceiling of the mine. Time to speed it up.

Tyler breathed out, hard, and let loose a puff of smoky breath. *Oops.*

"But collecting this maple syrup requires the willing cooperation of thousands of people. Men and women, Canadian and American, who have been born in the concept, instilled in the idea, of liberty. These people of the fields, woods and mountains, pour from these regions to fill our military. Not, as many city folk think, because they're poor or desperate but because this is their essential nature. No person is happy to give their life, but the people of this region believe that there is something larger than their selves. Not just God, although many are believers in God, but a vision, a philosophy, a shared belief in freedom and justice and the battle against tyranny. From their very mother's milk they are filled with this belief, that to die in the cause of freedom brings not heaven but a better place here on Earth for succeeding generations.

"I have taken the tenor of these people and they are determined against yielding. As stubborn as the granite of their mountains, they, almost in unanimity, *refuse* to yield. They may, perhaps will, be destroyed. But they, and, yes, their children, will die *free*.

"*They*, however, are not under threat. The Horvath threaten to destroy our cities, not these woods, mountains and fields. Let me touch upon that.

"The Horvath are a very monolithic and communal

culture. The very concept of liberty is foreign to them. So I'm going to have to explain something to the Horvath. You may be looking upon our cities as sort of communal groups for which the people of this region are gatherers. This is not, in fact, the case. The people of this region are their *own* communal grouping, connected to but not of the cities. They are, in fact, almost invariably at odds with the groups of the cities. The cities, you dumb *squids*, are our *enemies*. You're threatening our *enemies,* you morons! We *hate* the people of the cities. *I* hate the people of the cities! Liberal, whining, socialist *pussies!* They've never given us anything but *trouble!* Please, please, *please* nuke Washington! What has Washington ever done for *us?* They just take and take and take! The bastards! Kill them all!

"As for me, I'll tell you what *I* think!" Tyler said, shouting. He jumped to his feet and flipped a bird at the ceiling, looking straight up. "GIVE ME LIBERTY OR GIVE ME DEATH, YOU BASTARDS! LIVE FREE OR..."

"Lost the signal from the cabin," Ryan said. "Switching to... secondary remote."

On homes across the nation the view was now of Tyler in front of the 1997 World Series.

"Hah!" Tyler said, still flipping a bird at the ceiling. "Missed me, you egg-sucking ignoramuses! Never heard of a laser relay or a green-screen, *have* you? Go ahead and *try* to take our maple syrup! Dumb-asses!"

"And secondary remote is gone," Ryan said.

"I think that's good enough," Tyler said.

"The Horvath are taking over all the broadcast airwaves," Bruce said.

"Let's hear it," Tyler said.

"PEOPLE OF THE MAPLE REGION. YOU WILL DELIVER THE SYRUP OR YOU WILL BE DESTROYED. WE WILL DESTROY EVERY HOME, EVERY TOWN, EVERY PERSON. YOU WILL *ALL* DIE."

"You will deliver the maple syrup," the speakerphone said in metallic tones. "You will execute Tyler Vernon. You will destroy the resistance in the region. Or you will be eliminated."

"We're *trying*," the President said. "You've seen that we are trying! Those people may nominally be under our authority but they are not under our control. We have an arrest warrant out for Tyler Vernon, but our agents, those that survive going up to the hills, have been unable to find him. Our military is half in mutiny and half pinned down by fire. Some of it from our own *forces!* Is there anything that you can do?"

"Remove your loyal troops," the Horvath said a few moments later. "We will eliminate the resistance of the rural infesters and then you will send people of the urban colonies to collect the syrup."

"You're going to . . . kill them?" the President said.

"We will eliminate all resistors," the Horvath replied.

"I . . ." the President said, gulping. "I can't . . ." He paused at a raised hand from the Marine Corps commandant.

The commandant looked at the ceiling for a moment in thought then nodded, hard. The President made a face but the commandant just raised his hand in an "OK" symbol.

"Very well..." the President said dubiously. "Feel free to eliminate the resistors in the region."

"We did not need your permission." The call cut off with a click.

"I just condemned the people of New England to aerial bombardment," the President said.

"Most of them have moved their families out of the region," the commandant said. "Women and kids, mostly. Not even *most* of the women. The rest have dug in hard. You'd be surprised how many old mines, caves and such there are in that area. Which is probably where Vernon is hiding."

"The Horvath have kinetic bombardment systems and heavy lasers," the National Security Advisor said dryly. "That area is going to take a pasting."

"How much can they do without seriously affecting the maple crop?" the commandant said. "And we're talking about a dispersed population, dug in. Think how much trouble we've been having in Afghanistan. Furthermore, that ship looks big to *us*. But if you actually do the tonnage and make a good guess on engine size compared to the Glatun ships we've seen, they can't actually be carrying *that* many KEW. Our estimate is, what? Sixteen city killers, max? What, exactly, are they going to do with sixteen nukes, that don't even spread radiation, against that area? Bomb Manchester? It's almost entirely evacuated. Lasers? Footprint of a meter. They can get the woods burning. Oh, boy. Let them bomb the area. Encourage it. That's Vernon's whole plan."

"Mr. Vernon," the reporter said. "We're very pleased to have this opportunity to interview you. Given that the Horvath have ordered you be delivered to them, there is a warrant out for your arrest for high treason and you are under continual threat, isn't this just a little risky?"

"Risk is part of life, Jamie," Tyler said. "Given the situation, I'll admit I don't have a lot of freedom of movement. But freedom is a philosophy, not a condition. No truly free man can be made a slave. I will not be a slave to the Horvath or to a tyrannical government of socialists."

"You have some hard things to say about the residents of cities, Mr. Vernon," the reporter said. "Since we *all* can't hide, is that particularly fair?"

"Jamie, I've been fighting the tyranny of you lefty jerks my whole life. If you want to submit to the Horvath, that's up to you. *I'm* not willing to . . ." He paused at a raised hand.

"I'm not sure how much of that got out," Ryan said as the room rumbled and dust fell from the roof. "And we're losing transceivers."

"And it's pretty much harvest time," Bruce pointed out, packing up the gear. Time to move again.

"I'm not a big fan of maple syrup, anyway," Tyler said. "How many people have we lost in this charlie fox?"

"Not nearly as many as we should have," Bruce said. "The biggest lost was a 'Peace Now!' demonstration in Burlington. They'd gathered around a big old historic maple figuring the Horvath couldn't possibly hit them. Wrong. Dead wrong."

"I've had times when I'd find that really funny," Tyler said. "Somehow, though, it's just not as funny as it used to be."

"You've got a call coming in," Ryan said. "Hypercom."

"Bet Osama wishes he had one of these," Tyler said, picking up the link. "Tyler Vernon."

"Mr. Vernon, this is Saenc Mori with Hypernet Network News!"

"Hi, Saenc. Kind of busy at the moment."

"You're going to be busier soon," the reporter said. "The Horvath have sent their final demands to your President. Stop the resistance and execute Tyler Alexander Vernon or Washington, Philadelphia, New York and Boston will be destroyed. Their ship is coming up from the south. Then they will take up stable positions over the maple producing regions and use their lasers to reduce them to ashes. That's as soon as their ship completes this latest orbit which is now in . . . forty-seven minutes."

"I guess I got them a little riled," Tyler said, his heart sinking. Petra and the girls were outside Boston. "Guess this is it. Can you get a word to the Horvath?"

"We've sort of taken over your broadcast system," the reporter admitted. "I mean, it's just sitting there . . ."

"We might as well get out of the news business," the CBS producer snarled.

"We'd better get out of Washington, first," the anchor replied.

". . . so the Horvath should be listening."

"Fine," Tyler said. "They want me? I'll be at the summit of Mt. Moriah when they come back around. I'll be nice and easy to spot."

"Isn't that suicide?"

"I'm tired of hiding anyway," Tyler said, jumping

on one of the ATVs parked in the cave. "Let's do this thing."

There were hardly any trails, much less roads, in the area. And what trails were accessible by ATVs did not make it to the top of Mt. Moriah. The last two hundred meters had really sucked.

It was also...bitterly cold didn't cut it, in Tyler's opinion. The recent cold front was yet to completely pass and the air was not only below freezing but, in one of those tricks possible only in a place as screwed up weather-wise as the White Mountains, humid. He was standing waist deep in snow in a thin, wind-driven icy fog. It was the sort of cold that didn't just cut to the bone. It went through three layers of clothes, skin, flesh and bone so fast that it only stopped when it got around to freezing the marrow. Then it started to chill the body from the inside out. His parts that were in snow were the warmest parts of his body. The Horvath had better kill him quick or hypothermia was going to do the job for them.

Despite the thin fog it was a great view, though.

"I can see your house from here," Mr. Haselbauer said, huffing up the last few feet to the summit. "Couldn't you have picked a lower spot?"

"What the hell are you doing here?" Tyler asked. "This is *my* big moment. Get your own."

"So this is your plan?" Mr. Haselbauer asked. "Die? I figured you were going to use your secret 'smelting' lasers."

"The Horvath ship has a shield," Tyler said, sighing. "We couldn't scratch it. So, yeah, this was my plan. Die. Sometimes it works. Heroic defeats have led to most of the great victories in history. Let somebody smarter figure out how to defeat the Horvath ship. Hopefully motivated by that poor, brave, doomed bastard Tyler Vernon."

"Figured as much," Haselbauer said. "Which is why I'm here. Couldn't let the Rebs get all the credit."

"You and your Rebs," Tyler said, shaking his head. He took out his cell phone and loaded in the battery. It had been out for a couple of months and the charge was low but, what the hell, it wouldn't have to last long. And with the carrier signal going there was no way that the Horvath could miss and hit some innocent. Hopefully, with him dead they'd back off on destroying the region. At least for a while. He fumed for a moment then couldn't hold it in.

"The only reason you won was you outnumbered us ten to one! *And* had all the cannon foundries! And that might not have happened if Jackson hadn't had his *first bad day* at Seven Pines! The Union's as bad as the Horvath!"

"Shouldn't start a war if you don't have cannon," Mr. Haselbauer said smugly.

"Well, that was the point, wasn't it?" Tyler said. "The South wanted industries, and Northern monopolies, abetted by Northern congressmen, wouldn't *allow* it. So when we started to sell our agricultural products to the British for, among other things, mill equipment, you went and put a block on *that!* An *unconstitutional* block given that it was essentially a one hundred percent export tariff. There's a reason it's called the War of Northern Aggression." His phone rang and he pulled it out with a snarl.

"What?"

"Mr. Vernon, are you and Jason Haselbauer, a noted resistance leader, actually rearguing your country's civil war in your last few moments? Oh, hi, this is Saenc Mori with Hypernet News Network. Your cell-phone network isn't exactly secure, either."

"Not much better to do, Saenc," Tyler said, dropping smoothly into professional mode. "It's pretty cold up here. Ask those Horvath to hurry, will you? A nice orbital death ray would feel good about now."

"On that subject, the betting on your survival is one hundred to one, do you have any comment?"

"I'll take a thousand credits on the nose," Tyler said instantly.

"Isn't that a bit of a risk?"

Tyler closed his eyes and wondered if there was some sort of lobotomy involved in becoming a newscaster.

"If I live I get a hundred thousand credits, Saenc," Tyler said slowly. "If I die, I won't really care that I'm out a grand. Think about it."

"True. Well, your bid has been registered by a bookie called Ongotuli the Knife who says, 'You'd better be good for it.'"

"Aware that these may be my last words: I'm good for it."

"You have about three minutes. The moment of decision for Washington, however, has passed and the Horvath seem to have chosen not to fire."

"Damnit," Tyler said. "What does it *take* to get these guys to get rid of all our problems for us?"

"You really don't care for city people, do you?"

"Hate 'em," Tyler said. "Bombing's too good for 'em. They need to be chopped into little bits and buried alive."

"And Philadelphia. Apparently the Horvath disagree."

"Don't care for Horvath, either," Tyler said. "Especially if they're not going to gut cities."

"And New York is still there. The Horvath ship is about to clear the horizon, Mr. Tyler. Seriously. Last words."

Tyler thought about it for a second and then shrugged.

"There is no joy without pain. No victory without sacrifice. This is my victory."

"Very nice . . ."

"Sorry, cutting in here," a new voice said. "Horvath ship: Take *no* hostile action in regards to the maple gathering regions or their polity or tribes. Say again, take no hostile actions or you will be destroyed."

"This is unacceptable," a metallic Horvath voice replied. "Who is this?"

"This is Commander Faeth Riang of the Glatun heavy cruiser *Kagongwe* and . . ."

Tyler was looking up and actually caught the sparkle.

". . . not only are you about the size of my long boat, your shields are down. Power down your weapons and leave orbit so we can negotiate or I will finish what my secondaries just did with my main gun. Mr. Vernon?"

"Yes?" Tyler said.

"Could you ask your people to possibly begin gathering maple syrup? My sailors are about to mutiny."

"Right away," Tyler said, "Hey, everybody. Olly olly oxenfree! Time to get to work!"

"Thank you. I assure you, you won't have any more trouble from your Horvath . . . benefactors."

Tyler hung up the phone and shrugged.

"So, we froze our ass off for nothing."

"Can't say that," Mr. Haselbauer said. "It's still a fine view. Take it the cavalry arrived."

"Yep," Tyler said, feeling strangely depressed. And badly in need of a drink. "And now we've got to actually, you know, work."

"Been workin' my whole life," Mr. Haselbauer said. "Best make some calls."

"Yeah," Tyler said, looking at his phone. "Me too." He hit speed dial.

"Hi, Petra. Can I talk to the girls?"

"Mr. Vernon," the CNN reporter said to a background of a boiling pan of maple syrup, "things seem to be progressing well in the maple syrup harvest."

"Quite well, Courtney," Tyler said. "Despite some reports to the contrary, the weather is cooperating very well and it looks to be a bumper crop."

"So all's well that ends well," the reporter said. "Mr. Vernon, you said some very harsh things about the people of our great nation's cities. Surely you weren't serious."

"Courtney," Tyler said seriously, "I'm an American patriot. All of America. I don't care for certain strains of politics, but that doesn't mean I wouldn't give my life to save the lives of others. Other Terrans even. I just wish that those who disagree with me could at least agree on that."

"So you *weren't* serious," the reporter said, confused. "Why in the world would you say those things? You really upset a lot of people. Not to mention making yourself and the people of this region a primary target! Were you crazy?"

"Oh, I don't like city folk," Tyler said. "Don't care

for their politics, don't care for their attitude, which is more ignorant and provincial than they can possibly understand since they're ignorant and provincial. But it doesn't mean I wanted anyone to die. Quite the opposite. As to why I said it? I'll leave you with the words of the smartest rabbit I know: 'Please, Br'er Fox! Don' throw me in dat br'ar bush!'"

SAPL

ONE

Tyler looked around the extremely empty personnel bay 41816-B of the Glalkod Commercial Transfer Station One in annoyance. His eyes lit on what was clearly a hypernode terminal and he walked over. He'd been looking forward to savoring the moment of his first steps onto a space station. But since his local guide was conspicuously missing it would have to wait.

"Connect to Fallalor Wathaet, please," he said.

"There are six hundred and eighty-seven thousand Fallalor Wathaets on the hypernet network," the terminal replied. "Could you com his registry number?"

"I don't have a com link," Tyler said. "He should be somewhere on this station. He is probably in a bar and he's probably drunk on maple syrup."

"Searching, searching...Fallalor Wathaet eight-two-alpha-two-four-kilo-zero-one-hotel-november-dash-one."

"Like I'm gonna remember that," Tyler muttered.

"Tyler!" Wathaet slurred. The background was clearly, as Tyler had guessed, a bar. "Hey, man! How's it going?"

"You were supposed to meet me at the ship, Wathaet," Tyler said. "Remember?"

"Oh, yeah, man," Wathaet replied. "Sorry about that. Hey, just catch a cab over to Kulo's. I'll meet you here!"

"Fine," Tyler said, sighing. "Net, I need a cab."

"There are over..."

"Just pick the closest one and tell me where to pick it up."

"Very well," the terminal replied snippily. "Proceed down the corridor to the passageway. That's the hallway to your *left* until it comes to a bigger hallway, since you're a primitive. The cab will meet you there. That will be five credits."

"Tyler Alexander Vernon," Tyler said. "You should have only one of those."

"Registering. Please obtain a full registration package at your earliest opportunity. Thank you. Have a nice day."

The "cab" turned out to be a floating compartment with seats for two. Small seats for two. It was smaller than a Terrestrial "Two-Fer" car and didn't look as if it should be able to stand upright.

"Uh," Tyler said, fumbling where he figured the door should be. "I don't know how to..."

"I'll open it," the cab said. The entire transparent top collapsed into the rear. "Get in. New, are you?"

"Primitive world," Tyler said, sitting down. The top quickly popped back up. "Earth. The maple syrup planet."

"Oh, yeah, heard of that," the cab said. "Destination?"

"Kulo's?" Tyler said.

"Right," the cab said, pulling out smoothly. "Who's that maple syrup guy? Verggon or something?"

"Tyler Vernon?" Tyler asked. The cab maneuvered skillfully through some light pedestrian traffic, mostly Glatun but a few other species Tyler didn't recognize, then slid into a compartment like an elevator. The door closed.

"Yeah," the cab said. "You think he meant the Horvath should waste the cities? Seems pretty, I dunno, cold."

"No, actually, I don't think he meant it," Tyler said. There was no sensation but he was either trapped in a room with an apparently sentient cab or he was in a very smooth piece of transportation technology. He was banking on the latter. There were no flashing lights to tell him he was going anywhere, though. Not even a bank of numbers. Just walls and a lack of sensation of movement. "He was just saying that so the Horvath wouldn't waste the cities. If he could get them to think the maple sugar gatherers didn't care, that took the cities off the table as hostages."

"Guess you might be right," the cab said. "He sure kept consistent, though."

"Thank you," Tyler said. "I'm Tyler Vernon."

"Oh," the cab said. "Then I guess you'd know."

"Can I ask a question?"

"Go ahead."

"Are all cabs AIs in the Federation?"

"I'm not an AI. I'm a replicant program. I just have a set of queries and responses. Sounds like an AI. And if somebody gets outside my programming I can call Athelkau, which is the station's AI, to get its help. Happens so fast you wouldn't notice."

"So . . ." Tyler said. "Was that a standard response?"

"Yep," the cab said as the door opened. It was

clearly a different passageway since the light was lower, mostly from blown light panels, and the pedestrians were . . . different. It was amazing how universal a "bad part of town" could look. Graffitti, it turned out, was another universal. The cab slid out of the compartment smoothly then started weaving through the pedestrian traffic. Someone threw something at it that thunked off the plastic top and left a green, drippy stain.

"Not the best part of town," Tyler said.

"Nope," the cab replied. "Have to get a wash after this. You're registered on the hypernet banking system. That's five credits."

"Authorized?" Tyler said. "Does that work?"

"Yep," the cab said, dilating the top. "Have a nice day. Keep your credit chips hidden. But Kulo's is pretty safe."

Tyler walked over to the nearest door and looked at the marquee. It was in garish letters but he couldn't read them so he wasn't even sure if he was in the right place.

"Look confident and as if you're not a yokel," Tyler muttered to himself. "Open?"

The door refused to budge.

"Hey," he said, turning to ask the cab. But it was gone.

"Damnit," he muttered. He could hear dissonant music from inside and the sound of an occasional yell. Sounded like a bar. "Hello?" he said, rapping his nuckles on the door. "Open sesame?"

The door dilated and a bipedal lizard even larger than Mr. Haselbauer filled it. The thing looked like a velociraptor with a toothache.

"Sss-graka-gar!" it bellowed. It had to. The door

had been soundproofed and the noise inside was at the nuclear decibel level.

"Wathaet?" Tyler shouted, craning his neck up. The view of the thing's face wasn't much better than the rest.

"Garagar!" the thing shouted back, gesturing inside with a thumb. It even had velociraptor thumbs.

Tyler stepped inside and his ears immediately tried to shut down. The "music," if it could be called music, was a series of incredibly loud, apparently random, notes with asyncopated pauses. Most of them were near the top of the audible range so it was possible that there were some out of human audibility he was missing. If so, he'd pass. It was a worse experience than the one indoor bagpipe competition he'd attended. But only marginally.

The crowd was mostly Glatun and they seemed to be mostly using hypercom implants. They'd have to, there was no *way* to hear. There were a few other species present. Two large purple slugs were drinking something green in a corner, and a giant, segmented, exoskeletal, black and red worm was chugging what looked like a gallon of something that smoked to some shouted comments. At least Tyler assumed the Glatun were shouting. They were opening and closing their mouths and between notes he could pick up some yells. A few more of the giant sauroids were circulating the room but they seemed to be servers. Or security. Or both.

"T . . . er!" a Glatun shouted at him, clapping him on the back.

"Wathaet?" Tyler shouted back. He had to assume it was Wathaet. Racist as it might seem, Glatun really *did* all look the same to him.

The Glatun opened and closed his mouth several

more times. Tyler could only get a few syllables. It had to be Wathaet, though.

"I can't hear you!" Tyler screamed.

"What?"

Tyler grabbed him by the arm and dragged him to the door, which fortunately opened.

"God almighty," Tyler said when they were outside the cacophony. "How can you stand it in there?"

"Stand what?" Wathaet asked.

"I couldn't hear a thing," Tyler said. "Are all you guys deaf?"

"No," Wathaet said. "Oh, you don't have a plantpak."

"No, I don't have a plantpak," Tyler said with a sigh. "Human, remember?"

"Come on," Wathaet said, waving for Tyler to follow. "Time to fix that."

"Uh, Wathaet," Tyler said. "I'm not sure that a Glatun doctor would know the first thing about human physiology."

"I talked to Cori about it," Wathaet said. "He said no problem."

"Who is Cori?" Tyler asked as Wathaet took a turn down a service tunnel. A couple of Glatun were just sort of hanging around the tunnel in a very nonchalant manner. Like a nonchalant "Your money or your life" manner. "Uh, Wathaet?"

"Don't worry," Wathaet said. "Everybody knows me. Hey, guys. Buddy of mine from Earth. This is the maple syrup king."

"Oh, wow," one of the Glatun said, surreptitiously putting away his vibroknife. "Gosh, it's nice to meet you. You wouldn't happen to have any . . ."

"Catch," Tyler said, tossing them a sample bottle of

Vermont's finest. They just made it past the scuffle. Turned out that Glatuns had blue blood as well as skin. "Wathaet, could we *please* get into some patrolled corridors?"

"We're here," Wathaet said as a panel opened. "Come on in."

Tyler had, like most kids, done a paper on the Holocaust in school. His particular paper had focused on Nazi experiments and Dr. Joseph Mengele, the "Angel of Death."

The dingy room called back some *very* unpleasant memories. Same torture-rack, Sweeney Todd barber chair. Same "Ve haff vays of making you talk!" light in the face. Same sharp blade things hanging in midair. In this case, literally. The only thing missing was the smell of antiseptic which, under the circumstance, was *not* reassuring.

"Uh, Wathaet?" Tyler said.

"Don't let this place fool you," Wathaet said. "Cori's the best plant thing on Glalkod Station. Hey! Cori! Where are you?"

"In that case," Tyler said, backing to the door. "I think I'll take my chances on finding one on the—"

A four-foot long black scarab beetle had come bustling out of a back room. It wasn't exactly a scarab beetle, but the resemblance was remarkable. Except scarab beetles didn't have the big cutting mandibles. Come to think of it, Tyler had seen a few more scurrying around in the corridors. He'd assumed they were dogs or something.

"Wathaet," the beetle buzzed. "Is this the human I get to experiment on?"

"No!" Tyler shouted.

"Yes," Wathaet said. "He wants a full plantpak with all the trimmings."

"True," Tyler said. "But I'm not so sure I want it from a beetle."

"Racism," the beetle buzzed. "We exoskeletals are used to it."

"Man up," Wathaet said. "The Anancauimor are the best plant specialists in the western spiral arm. And Cori is the best of all of them."

"Modestly I must admit this is true," the beetle said, mounting a small step-stool by the barber's chair. "Are you going to lie down or must I get the stunner?"

"Look," Tyler said reasonably. "You don't know a thing about human physiology."

"*Au contraire,*" the beetle buzzed. "I have researched everything your primitive medical profession has discovered and I will not be going in unaccompanied. Louisa is a specialist in alien physiology."

"Who is Louisa?"

"I am," a voice in the air said. "I am the medical AI. You need not fear, Mr. Vernon. We will first do a very thorough examination of your physiology. As you have noted, we are unfamiliar with human physiology. But we will not be after we have completed our thorough scan of *you*. Furthermore, any first-contact procedures must be reviewed by a medical board for safety and best practice."

"How long is that going to take?" Tyler asked. "I'm only on the station . . ."

"The review will be more or less simultaneous with the examination," Louisa said. "The majority of it consists of discussion amongst AIs. We communicate and decide . . . very fast."

"Is this an . . . invasive procedure?" Tyler asked.

"The examination will not be," Louisa said. "The plant procedure? Extremely. But you won't feel it."

"Anti-infection protocols?" Tyler asked.

"Are you saying I don't run a clean aug parlor?" Cori buzzed angrily.

"Not at all." Tyler managed not to glance at the scuff marks on the walls. "Just getting a feel for the place."

"Can we leave it at 'I know what I'm doing'?" Louisa said. "There is zero danger of infection. I'll admit that Cori could tidy up a bit..."

"It's an atmosphere thing," Cori said. "Make this place look like a hospital and I'll lose half my custom! People go to hospitals to *die!*"

"We call places like that..." Tyler was going to say "hospices." "Good point. You're right, Wathaet. Time to man up."

"That's the spirit," Louisa said. "If you could just climb in the chair and relax."

"Climb, yes," Tyler said. "Relax?"

"Right," Wathaet said. "This is gonna take a while and I'm thirsty. See you back at the bar."

"So...when does the examination start?" Tyler said a few minutes later. He had to admit the chair was more comfortable than it looked and he was even getting a bit sleepy.

"I've been examining you since you came in the door," Louisa replied. "I'm about halfway through."

"Oh," Tyler said, looking around for the scanning equipment. All the icky floating stuff was still floating where it had been. "MRI?"

"Distantly," Louisa said. "GRI would be closer. Gravitic resonance imaging. Some magnetic. I've completed a thorough survey of your gross physiology and anatomy and am doing a chemical survey and interaction modeling. You're remarkably similar to the Ngongot. Not in gross anatomical ways, but in interaction and biochemistry. Most Ngongot protocols will work perfectly well. By the way, on the subject of sepsis I see what you mean. You guys are sewers."

"Thanks," Tyler said. "Some of that seems to be evolutionarily interactive, so..."

"Oh, recognized," Louisa said. "We won't mess with the important suites. You actually seem to be missing some and we'll take care of the interaction problems while we're at it. The question is approaching: What do you want done?"

"I'm not even sure what a 'full plantpak' means," Tyler admitted.

"Hypernet connection and memory buffer, mostly," Cori buzzed. The beetle was busy behind Tyler's head, which was causing him increasing paranoia. "In your case, since you didn't have it as a kid: Immune system protocols. Geriatric stabilization. And, since you're clearly pretty screwed up in places, ocular and aural adjustments and implants and a full rebuild on skeletal and vascular systems. *That's* gonna cost a bit."

"I can hear just fine," Tyler said. "Sure, I've got a little high-frequency hearing loss...And so I wear glasses?"

"Do you *want* to see and hear clearly?" Louisa asked.

"Yes, please," Tyler said. "And if you could get rid of that weather knee, I'd appreciate it."

"No problem," Cori said. "Four-fifty will do it. You got the stones?"

"Are we talking four hundred and fifty or four hundred and fifty *thousand*?" Tyler asked. "Four million?"

"Four hundred and fifty credits," Cori said. "Unless you want to pay me four hundred and fifty thousand, which I'm not going to turn down."

"Uh . . ." Tyler said. "What else is available? Because I can afford some upgrades."

"Hooo," Cori said. "Big spender. I like that. We can do a full prosthetic rebuild of your motor system . . ."

"'It cost an arm and a leg' is a metaphor," Tyler said quickly. "I was thinking more along the lines of . . . I dunno. What do you have? That keeps all my bits attached?"

"Well, if you really don't want the full cyborg package . . ." Cori said.

"I really don't want the full cyborg package," Tyler said. "Can I get a list or something?"

"How long you got?" Cori said. "There's the athletic package. Very popular. Increased muscular density. Faster neural twitch response. Increased oxygenation systems. Hyper-cooling package. Balance systems, very good if you're going to be in zero-gravity as well. No nausea, which you guys *must* get with that screwed up aural balance system. That's all nanobased, so once we get past the basic plants it's noninvasive since you're a sissy. Personal combat package is a big seller around here . . ."

"I can imagine," Tyler muttered.

"Skull hardening. Ribcage reinforcement. Micro-armor sub-integument weave . . ."

"You do all that with nannites or something?" Tyler asked.

"Nah, gotta do a full strip," Cori said. "Don't have the time today."

"And by full strip?" Tyler asked.

"Pull off all the skin and muscle and adipose tissue and do the plant," Cori said. "Takes a few hours."

"Skip," Tyler said. "Maybe next time."

"Whatever," Cori said. "Space-man's package..."

"I'll take the basic package plus the natural athlete package, thanks," Tyler said. "Keep it simple for now."

"Customer's always right," Cori said. "Louisa, where we at?"

"Authorizations all in place and registered," Louisa said. "We can start any time."

"What does start mean?" Tyler said.

"First we've got to get a mapper into your neural system," Cori said. "You might want to hold your head still."

"You're going to stick a *wire* in my head?" Tyler asked, starting to turn around.

"Oh, no," Cori said. "Already *did* that. That's why I said stay still. Right, Louisa, start the mapping."

"If you could please think about your first memory," the AI said pleasantly. "And, remember, this is for science. So be honest..."

For the next thirty minutes, Tyler was put through possibly the most unpleasant experience of his life. "Mapping" consisted of a long series of seemingly random questions "Think of the taste of blue...", flashes of random memories, muscular twitches and occasional strange feelings in odd parts of his body. All this culminating in...

"OW!"

"And pain mapping complete," Louisa said in a kindly tone. "There, that wasn't so bad, was it?"

"Yes," Tyler said, panting. It had felt as if he'd been dropped in hot oil and even though the *sensation* was gone, the *memory* of being dropped in hot oil was still right there reminding him this is what it feels like to be dropped in hot oil. "That was bad. That was bad on toast."

"Well, it really *was* for science," Louisa said. "Now that we have one human mapped it won't be so bad for the rest. We'll just have to check what the differences are and they'll be right and tight. So...now comes the invasive bit. You'd probably rather be out for this. Permission to put you to sleep?"

"You have to ask for that but *not* to put a wire in my head?" Tyler said. "And put to sleep is an expression on my planet..."

"Anesthetize you so that you'll be unconscious through the rest of the procedure," Cori said. "No big deal. We just activate the sleep centers of your brain and then lock you down so you can't wake up while we're rummaging."

"I've done stranger things," Tyler said, settling in. "I think. Okay, go ahead."

"And we're going out in three, two, one..."

"What happened?" Tyler asked. "You guys started yet?"

"Done," Cori said. The beetle was across the room cleaning some instruments. "That'll be five and a quarter, please."

"I don't feel any..." Tyler started to say. Then the tornado hit.

"VAGOG'S GARGOBOTS! GET 'EM WHILE THEY'RE..." "INTERGALACTIC COSMETICS ANNOUNCES...!" "INTERSTELLAR SUPER-DEALMART! INTERSTELLAR SUPERDEALMART!" "BIG BARGO'S BARGAIN BARN!"

"AAAAH!" Tyler screamed. His head was filled with images, most of them so alien he couldn't even process them, as well as a string of seemingly random commercials. He couldn't even hear himself think.

"Crap," Cori said. "Louisa, put up a trans-block. I forgot he was getting his first node-plant."

"Ah . . ." Tyler said as the cacophony cut off. "That was . . ."

"You are going to have to learn how to control your implants, Mr. Vernon," Louisa said. "I'll adjust them so that they are dialed up to high protection. But if you want to be able to fully and openly communicate you're going to have to learn how to filter."

"And how, exactly, do I do that?" Tyler asked.

"It's a skill," Louisa said. "The implants work interactively with your brain so the more you use them for more different purposes the better you get. But you won't get the full use until you start to grasp the full function of the implants. You are, at some point, going to have to open up."

"If you can . . . dial them up or down . . ." Tyler said. "I don't want people to have remote access . . ." He suddenly realized he hadn't, in fact, opened his mouth. Just thought the query. More like mused on it.

"*I* can," Louisa said. "Here. While you are still a patient and in this room. Otherwise you are quite well firewalled. Why would anyone use a system that was not secure? The first thing you might want to be careful of is comming when you don't intend to."

"Great," Tyler said. Aloud. "I need to use these to buy some stuff. How do I . . . ?"

"You'll figure it out," Cori said, dragging him out

of the chair. "I've got another customer coming in. Go play with them. Have fun. Good-bye."

Tyler found himself back in the disreputable service tunnel.

"Excuse me," what he at first took to be a robot said. "You're blocking the door."

"Sorry," Tyler commed, standing aside. When the robot went through it was apparent it either had a thing for Glatun hair down its back or it was a Glatun cyborg.

Tyler walked down the service tunnel quickly. Fortunately, other than a little blood, there was no sign of the nonchalant gentle Glatun from earlier. As soon as he reached the main corridor he looked around for a hypernet terminal but the only one was clearly broken.

"Crap," Tyler said. "Taxi," he said, thinking at his implants. "I need a taxi."

"Itthe cab," a voice responded.

Voices in my head. Great.

"Hi, I need a cab to take me to my lodgings," Tyler said. "I'm not sure of my location, but I'm near Kulo's . . ."

"Dispatched," the voice replied. "Two minutes."

"Thanks," Tyler said. There was a distinct . . . feeling of the communication being cut off.

"Well," he muttered. "That worked."

"Hey, buddy, can you spare a credit for a veteran?"

Tyler looked at the rubbish-besmeared Glatun and shrugged.

"I can, I just don't have a way to do it," Tyler said. "Sorry."

"That's okay, man," the bum said, then wandered off.

"The more things change," Tyler said as the cab pulled up. It was pretty much the same as the last one. Come to think of it, the green stain on the cover...

"Hey, Tyler!" the cab said, dropping the canopy. "You waiting for me to get stole or something?"

"Not at all," Tyler said, dropping into the cab.

"Where to?" the cab asked, pulling out without waiting for the information.

"I've got it here, somewhere," Tyler said, pulling out a piece of paper. He cleared his throat. "The Ghozhozizpilhowacxashaphiq... This is worse than a Hawaiian name...cawobeyxolegul..."

"The Ghoz," the cab said. "No problem."

"What does the name mean?" Tyler asked as the cab pulled into one of the transport...elevators?

"Big Nice Hotel," the cab replied.

"In *Glatun?*"

"Oh, no. Course not. That's in Ogutorjatedocifazhidujon...That's enough. They're sort of this arm's main hospitality race. Call 'em the Ogut."

"Oh," Tyler said. "We really don't know much about the species in this region. We got an initial download from the first Glatun we encountered but it's so large and so poorly indexed... Google's still working on it."

"You need to get some plants," the cab said.

"I just did," Tyler said. "I'm still trying to figure out how to use them."

"You'll get used to it," the cab said as the door to the...transport box? opened. It whisked out into a corridor that was well lit and lined with what looked to be upscale shops. Well-dressed Glatun and a variety of other species more or less packed it. The cab had to move slowly.

In about three minutes they pulled up before an ornate façade resembling, of all things, the front of a tomb.

"The Ghoz," the cab said. "That's three credits."

"Authorized," Tyler said. The canopy popped down and he climbed out. "I guess if I call for a cab, I'm probably going to get you. Which is fine."

"As long as I'm available and not too far off," the cab said. "Have a nice day, Mr. Vernon."

Two of the big sauroids, in a sort of quasi-military uniform, flanked the double doors of the hotel. Tyler contemplated them for a second and the word "Rangora" flashed into his head. He instantly knew the general outline of their territory in the galaxy and, as he probed a bit more, their strategic relationship, competitive neutrality, with the Glatun. They were considered slightly less technologically advanced, aggressive and expansionistic. Individually, within the Glatun Federation, they tended to work in menial jobs that required more strength than smarts.

"Do you need help with your bags, sir?" one of the Rangora asked.

"Uh, no," Tyler said. "They were sent ahead."

He'd had to send more than bags. There were no foods known in the Federation that humans could consume. Since the "milk run" Gorku Corporation freighter only ran once every thirty-two days, he had to be prepared to stay a *long* time, so he'd included in cold storage three months' rations. Since the Glatun could, somehow, inhibit any degradation in organic materials, "rations" meant a very choice selection of foods. He wouldn't be surviving on MREs but he would have to cook for himself. That was okay, though, 'cause he was a pretty good cook.

He was planning on being on Glalkod station for some time. He had to get more information about the Glatun before he could progress to the next stage of his plans. Earth needed Glatun technology, but he wanted to figure out how to *learn* Glatun technology. He didn't want Earth constantly dependent on the Glatun. The close call over maple syrup had convinced him that Earth needed to be technologically and strategically independent of the Glatun to the greatest possible extent. Not to mention he was looking forward to kicking some Horvath butt.

The same thought had occurred to most Earth governments. But the fact was, until there was more to trade with the rest of the Galaxy, he was in the strange position of having more available credit to *do* something about the disparity than any five Earth governments. And since most of it was banked and traded off-planet, it was remarkably hard to tax.

If he had the choice of turning over his credit balance to Washington to do something or doing it himself... He'd take his chances.

"Checking in, sir?" the Rangora asked, opening the door.

"Yes," Tyler said. He thought "Ten credit tip" and the Rangora tipped his helmet at him.

"Thank you much, sir."

"No problem," Tyler said, walking through the doors.

"Mr. Vernon. A pleasure to have you in the house."

The speaker was a meter-long caterpillar. That was about as far as Tyler could get. Unlike caterpillars it had large, mobile, antennae. But it was still more or less caterpillar shaped, its skin patterned in a wild array of colors. *I'm talking to a psychedelic caterpillar.*

"Yes I am, Mr. . . . ?"

"Chuphosh Yaph Mufup Phexigh Chugh Thogab Neyuch Peh Toshash Ghutoch Zizh Lhinosh," the caterpillar said. "Most sophonts call me Chup. Welcome."

"Thank you," Tyler said.

"Your room has been prepared," Chup said. "If you would follow me?"

The main lobby was large and ornate. Tyler wasn't sure what most of the metals, woods and cloth were, but they looked expensive.

When he'd gone on the hypernet he'd searched for a good hotel on Glalkod station that could handle multiple species. He'd apparently found more than good. He wasn't sure he wanted the expense of staying somewhere like this for as long as he contemplated staying. He could afford it, but he had a lot of stuff to buy and no real idea of the costs.

Chup led him to what Tyler figured was an elevator. There was the usual absolute lack of sense of movement and it opened on a large room.

"Four rooms," Chup said. "Bedroom, bathing room, sitting room, kitchen. Adjustable grav beds. Extensible grav bed in the couch in case you entertain company. Usual suite of entertainment devices."

"I'm still learning how to use implants," Tyler said, walking across what he presumed was the sitting room to what could be either the bathroom or the bedroom. As he half expected, the door didn't open.

"Why don't I just leave all the doors open until you're more comfortable," Chup said, dilating the door.

The room was a bedroom. And it looked about

like any hotel bedroom he'd ever seen except for the bed which was . . .

"That's sort of odd," Tyler said.

The bed appeared to be two pieces of glass suspended in midair.

"I'm sure you will find it quite comfortable," Chup said. "It's adjusted to your surface gravity. The lighting is adjusted to near natural sunlight. And while we had a bit of trouble with some of your bathing arrangements, I think you'll find those in order. Furthermore, we have a cookbot programmed with a variety of Earth dishes if you prefer to use room service or visit one of our several first quality dining facilities."

"Thank you," Tyler said.

"We aim to please," the caterpillar said. "We admit that learning the needs of a new species is always challenging, but we do our level best. We were unable to successfully design concubine bots but . . ."

"No problem," Tyler said, thinking "High tip."

"Thank you very much, Mr. Vernon," the caterpillar said. "If there's anything else?"

"Not that I can think of right now," Tyler said. "I'll just . . . relax."

"Since you are still getting acquainted with your implants and the conditions," Chup said, "I can set our AI to monitor. That way if you need anything you can simply ask. Nothing, of course, will be released about such monitoring. We are very strict about our guests' privacy."

"Please," Tyler said.

"And I will leave you to your relaxation," the caterpillar said, wriggling out of the room.

TWO

Tyler stretched out on the oddly shaped but surprisingly comfortable couch and intertwined his fingers behind his head. Since getting on the tramp freighter in Manchester twenty hours ago he hadn't really had a chance to relax.

Manchester, New Hampshire, was coming on to being Earth's biggest spaceport, much to everyone's surprise. Unlike Burlington, it had suffered little damage in the war and was central to several major maple production areas. Since Earth was still only trading maple syrup, that meant that was where the traders landed.

The Horvath had geeked to giving up the maple syrup but they were bound and determined, to the point of battle, to hold on to the heavy metal mines in Russia and South Africa. The Canadian production areas overlapped the maple regions so production from that area was still under negotiation. And they'd raised the subject of the metals Tyler's company was starting to extract from asteroids. Their position was that they owned all heavy metals in the Sol System. Since sovereignty can be defined, at bottom, as "might makes

183

right," they were standing on firm legal ground. Tyler's position was that they owned it as long as they could keep it. He intended to end that condition very soon.

He decided it was about time to figure out this implant thing and just thought about the Horvath.

Instantly, information started flooding in. It wasn't overwhelming but it was complete and organized more or less as he needed it. He realized that the system was not only responding to his forefront thoughts but lower-level concepts. The information, since he was mostly worried about the Horvath as a threat, was concentrated around their strategic position in the galactic region, military and industrial capability and resources. It was neither more than he could absorb nor was it scattered. He wasn't even sure exactly where the information was coming from. He could see why Earth's firewalls would look a bit like "looking through an open window." You just thought about what you wanted to know and there it was.

"Wow," Tyler muttered. "I've got to get rid of my Google stock."

As he examined particular bits of information, more would become accessible. He delved, for a while, into Horvath reproduction habits and cultural implications. Horvath had two sexes, male/female, more or less corresponding to standard Terran form even if their basic physiology was completely different. They did look a bit like squids, though. The females laid a single egg in a nest which was then fertilized by a selected male. Gestation was six months. The nest was kept by the male; the female laid and left. After birth the young were moved to a crèche where they went through a series of moltings over twenty years and then were released as adults. Males, almost invariably unrelated biologically, did most of the rearing. Robots were replacing them as the Horvath advanced. Child-rearing was not high on the list of Horvath jobs.

Interested, he jumped over to the Glatun and received the shock of his life. One of the big questions on Earth about the Glatun was pronouns. Generally, the Glatun were referred to by male pronouns. But it had been noted, quietly, that they didn't seem to have appropriate reproductive parts. And they responded perfectly well to neutral gender terms such as "it."

What he found out, quickly, was that they were all three. Or, rather, the Glatun with which people dealt were hosts to both. Male and female Glatun were nonsentient parasites that existed within a brood pouch on the Glatun sentient neuters. More or less on command they would reproduce, the female releasing an egg and the male fertilizing it. Then the offspring would be raised in the pouch. If it was male or female it would stay there, more or less turned off, until a ceremony where it would be transferred to a young neuter. If a neuter, it would be raised to a certain size, released from the pouch, then raised to adulthood by its "parent" neuter.

"Okay, that's bizarre," Tyler muttered.

He decided to examine the Glatun a bit more and received another shock.

The Glatun were one of the older species in the area, having been contacted by the Ormatur through the new Glatun gate nearly thirty thousand years ago. At the time there were very few sophont races in the immediate star systems, and over a period of about six thousand years the Glatun had spread out and absorbed the thirty-two systems that made up the Glatun Federation. Along the way they had encountered four other sophont races and more or less absorbed them into the Federation. They also had encountered some that resisted absorption but had become trade partners.

At this point, the Glatun Federation sat as the nexus of trade between fourteen different races, some of them having, in turn, expanded widely. They were rich even by Galactic standards, and with riches came problems. They had a permanent unemployed under-class approaching thirty percent, their military was paltry for their size, absorbing less than point zero three percent of their GDP, and their trade imbalance was becoming astronomical.

"They're eating their seed corn," Tyler muttered. "You can afford to be the French if you've got a great big buddy to take care of you, but..."

Tyler took a look at their strategic situation and nearly had a heart attack. They were bordered by nine "expansionistic" groups. Of course, Earth and the Horvath, neither actually strategically dangerous, were included. But the Rangora, Ogut, Barche and Anancauimor each had military forces that, in sheer number, dwarfed the Glatun. They were all techno-logically inferior, but...

"Quantity has a quality of its own," Tyler muttered. He wasn't sure that Earth hadn't hitched itself to a falling star.

Speaking of military technology...

Primary ship weapons were fusion-pumped visible light, X-ray and gamma ray lasers. Secondary weapons were high-acceleration missiles using either kinetic or fusion-pumped laser warheads. A relatively new weapon on the scene was the gravity gun, which could disrupt ships' shields and cause massive damage. However, it was relatively short range and of limited utility. It also required truly massive amounts of power, so it was only found in capital ships.

"No unobtainium," Tyler said. "Good. And speaking of power and drive systems..."

He got confused almost immediately. The primary power system was a helium-3 driven... Well, it was a matter conversion plant, not a fusion plant. Still required He-3 to keep it from producing radiation. It converted matter to plasma and electricity. And then it did... something with the plasma and got more electricity and less plasma, somehow converting the neutrons and protons of the plasma to *electrons*? *How?* The last of the plasma could be used for...

Tyler realized his basic science background was kicking out information that was contradictory to background and gave up. Let the big brains figure it out. But it needed... Ah, hah! Heavy metals, primarily in the platinum group! That was the reason the Horvath were so hot for platinums. The power systems were thick spheres composed entirely of metals from the platinum groups. The drive system of a freighter the size of Wathaet's was... half a terawatt? That couldn't be right. He checked. That was right.

Earth produced four terawatts a year of power worldwide. The entire eastern U.S. power grid could be driven by a ball of osmium six feet across.

Inertial control was induced by spinning plates of... Brain lock. Brain lock. These people obviously had some theory that contradicted most of what he thought he knew. The grav plates looked doable. They required some exotic metals but that was what orbital mining was for. Scratch that. Basically beryllium bronze with a touch of lanthanides and platinums. Pretty much all of that was available on Earth. You needed grav plates to make grav plates, though. How'd somebody make the first ones?

The drive system was a function of grav plates. Drives generated...pressor beams? That pushed on what? Generated mass points?

"SAN check," Tyler muttered, sitting up and pulling out of the welter of information. "I feel like the WWII Air Force general that said that jets couldn't work because they didn't have anything to push. I think these guys have rediscovered Newton's aether. I need to get somebody smarter than me a set of plants and some free time."

For right now, though, what he wanted was a *ship*. The problem being, then he'd need a captain and an engineer. And one ship wasn't going to do.

What he needed was Boeing able to *make* ships.

He'd brought a laptop with 400 petabytes of atacirc installed. Surely that would be enough to fill in the basics?

Barely. And he needed a fabber to make grav plates so you could make a larger factory to make bigger grav plates. And he was going to need people who actually understood this stuff.

And a ship drive. They looked tough to make.

Did this place have eBay? He spotted a reference in the grav plate system information to a vender called Pangalactic Nihukow, which produced grav fabbers, and probed on that.

"PANGALACTIC NIIIUKOW! PANGALACTIC NIHUKOW!

"PANGALACTIC NIHUKOW! PANGALACTIC NIHUKOW!"

"OW!" Tyler muttered. The answer was: Yes. You could go shopping. If you could figure out how to ignore the commercials. Flashing banner ads on a screen were bad enough. Flashing, screaming banner ads in your brain were another matter. He just rode the tide for a while, trying not to whimper.

"Right," he said, pulling out of the ad flood. "I'm going to need more blood sugar to handle this. AI?"

"Mr. Vernon?" a voice said.

"Do you have a name that is less than five syllables?"

"You may call me Isna, Mr. Vernon."

"Isna, I had some Terra foodstuffs sent along," Tyler said. "Is the serverbot really programmed to produce Terran foods? And what's available?"

"Over six hundred and twenty-eight thousand recipes have been obtained from the Terran information net," Isna said. "With the available foodstuffs, using substitutions, two hundred and forty-seven thousand possible combinations are available."

"I didn't bring *that* large a range of materials," Tyler protested.

"Yes, you did," Isna said. "You even brought a full range of spices."

"Damn," Tyler said, thinking about it. He'd delegated the foodstuffs to one of his assistants. *Find a chef and tell him to send along everything he'd want if he was going to be stuck on an alien planet for three months.* "Do you think the bot could lower itself to doing some spaghetti? We'll start there."

"There are six thousand..."

"Spaghetti with meat sauce," Tyler said.

"Four hundred and..."

"Spaghetti with meat sauce," Tyler said, his mouth starting to salivate. "Bit more tangy than sweet. Heavy on the meat. Heavy on the oregano. Pick a recipe that's along those lines. Thin spaghetti noodles. Chianti or the closest approximation to accompany. And can I get a Coke?"

"Your supply of Coca-Cola, since it is toxic to Glatun systems, is still in customs hold. It should be released in a few days' time."

"Tea. Earl Grey. Hot."

"Coming right up." There was a "ding" and a compartment on the wall opened. There was a steaming cup of tea in it. "Sugar? Cream? Lemon? Lime? Orange...?"

"Just sugar, please," Tyler said. "One teaspoon to each five ounces."

"That is very close to solubility," the AI pointed out. There was a rushing sound and the tea cup floated out of the compartment. "Your tea, sir."

"Thank you," Tyler said, taking the cup. It was a tiny little thing. "Next time, could you put it in a bigger mug? Say about sixteen ounces? I drink this stuff by the gallon, but gallons are hard to hold."

"Of course, sir," the AI said. "Your spaghetti is being prepared. The robochef assumed standard accompaniments. A balanced diet seems to be important to maintaining regularity of the Terran digestive tract and balance of trace nutrients."

"Um..." Tyler said. "Okay. Just the spaghetti would have been fine. I'll eat an apple or something. Are there apples?"

"Yes, sir," the AI said. "Would you like an apple?"

"Not right now," Tyler said. "I'm just going to pick around on the Net for a bit."

"I'll leave you alone, then."

"Oh," Tyler said, looking at his cup. "And I need another cup...*mug*...of tea. And maybe some bottles of water to just have around."

"Coming right up."

Tyler lay back down and, with more information, started to ponder on the central subject that had been occupying his mind ever since the end of the aborted Maple Syrup War: How to get the Terran system up to Glatun standards in the shortest possible period.

"Rome wasn't built in a day." This was most certainly true. But part of that was that Rome spent much of its history getting hammered in wars. Wars are waste. There were times when war was the only practical answer, there *were* things worth fighting and dying for, but infrastructure didn't get built during wars. While the Glatun were still sufficiently interested in the Terran system to keep the Horvath off Terra's back, mostly, Terra needed to build orbital infrastructure. Fast.

The problems were...immense. All of Terra's industry was Earth-side. Just being able to smelt metal in space wasn't enough. There were way too many things that had to get made in places like China and Bangladesh. Eventually, systems would have to be self-supporting off-planet. Building all that infrastructure, though, was going to mean, in the meantime, getting stuff out of the gravity well. Which meant ships.

Then there was the problem of doing anything in space. Space was an unforgiving bitch. And to do all the work that was going to need doing meant that taking six months to practice a five-minute space walk was right out. Space suits. He'd completely forgotten the problem of space suits!

Then there was the personnel problem. Tyler had gone on a hiring binge before leaving Earth. He figured that anything that was normal and regular you could get MBAs and Ph.D.s to handle. He was only interested in the new and odd. Once it was making money, there were little people to handle it. Which was why he no longer had to go tap maple syrup himself.

But doing stuff in space was going to require people with special abilities and training. Of which there were maybe two or three hundred on the whole planet. Much of the work could be done with robots, but robots couldn't think their way out of new problems. Tyler was going to need *thousands* of people handling tens of thousands of robots. And they were going to have to be people who could think on their feet. People who understood space without being afraid of it. They didn't need Ph.D.s. He could get them trained in the basics pretty easily using implant technology. They just needed to be smart and able to handle implants. Which meant people familiar with information technology.

The last problem being that even the solar array system was costing him like crazy to set up and run. He had a lot of money but eventually it was going to run out. Getting a couple of thousand people who were what NASA would consider qualified, and thus extremely expensive, was just *out*.

"Where in hell am I going to get a couple of thousand geeks willing to work in dangerous, and, at least at first, horrible conditions for low pay *just* to be able to work in space?"

Put that way, the answer was simple.

"Your spaghetti, sir," Isna said.

It smelled wonderful and came with an attractive selection of grilled mixed vegetables and a bottle of wine, one glass already poured.

"Ah," Tyler said, "ambrosia." He tucked up to the table and had a taste...

"I have limited experience dealing with human facial expressions," Isna said, "but from your reaction this was not the most perfect gustatory experience possible?"

"Isna..." Tyler said as soon as he'd finished the glass of wine. "Make a note to the chef. Bit lighter on the cayenne in the future? Especially if he's using a hot style of dried tomato. And by a bit lighter I mean none."

THREE

Ronald Reagan, 40th President of the United States, once famously stated that the only way Earth could ever have a unified government was if it was invaded by aliens.

As it turned out, he was optimistic. Despite first contact with extraterrestrials, Horvath destruction of multiple cities, the seizure of all of Earth's precious metals and the abortive Maple Syrup War, Earth did not have a unified government. Worse, despite many conferences, negotiations, meetings, summits and various other diplomatic endeavors, Earth had neither a centralized space management command nor even a finalized treaty on space extraction, nor exploration nor colonization. The monthly shuttle from Glalkod, by default, communicated with the U.S. Space Command in Eglin Air Force Base because it was going to be setting down in U.S. territory. The Horvath, on the other hand, wouldn't deign to speak to Eglin and had repeatedly threatened to nuke it from orbit. If they bothered to speak to anyone it was to call Russian Space Command or the South African mining consortium. Usually by cell phone.

Tyler, however, was, despite some people's opinion, an American patriot.

"SpaceCom, SpaceCom, orbital mining ship *Monkey Business* with four heavy robot tugs leaving gate and preparing for orbital insertion..."

"Uh... roger, *Monkey Business*. We have you on trajectory for orbital insertion. You're not showing a Glatun registry, *Monkey Business*. Please state home world and species, over."

"Home world, Terra, Space Command," Tyler said. "Species... human."

"Boy, you're getting too big for your britches," Mr. Haselbauer said, looking up at the side of the still steaming *Paw Four*. The space tug, unlike the *Monkey Business*, had the ability to land on a planet. It was not, however, very aerodynamic, and even careful reentry tended to heat up the surfaces.

On the other hand...it could take it. The robotic tug was a mass of gravitite generators, drives and power plants surrounded by a thick shell of high-strength alloys. It looked like a steel brick the size of a small warehouse.

"You bought a *ship*?" Mr. Haselbauer said.

"Leased," Tyler said. "I *leased* a ship. The tugs came with it. And you don't want to know how much it's costing. Dollars trade at something like five hundred thousand dollars to the credit. So this is costing me about a billion dollars a day. Sorry, make that *twenty* billion. We'd better get something extractable out of that asteroid or between the cost of this thing and the cost of the Very Large Array I'm going to go from the richest man on Earth to the poorest in a nanosecond."

"And who the hell is flying it?" the farmer asked. Despite being, like Tyler, an instant multibillionaire, Mr. Haselbauer hadn't changed. He still dressed like a homeless man, still worked his fields every day and still didn't seem to know the meaning of the word "vacation." Which was why he'd "volunteered" to come pick Tyler up from the Manchester Spaceport.

Tyler hadn't changed either. He *did* know the meaning of the word "vacation." He just didn't seem to be able to find the time. And he wasn't going to any time soon.

"I am," Tyler said. "I had to have a certified pilot to get it to the gate. But on this side there's no certification requirement. Yet."

"So you're a rocket pilot now?" Mr. Haselbauer asked, pointing the way to the truck.

Manchester Spaceport was not part of Manchester Airport. During the Maple Syrup War, one of the targets the Horvath vaporized was Tower Village Mall. It looked like a very inviting target.

Which it would have been had they dropped the rock during the day. Instead, they'd dropped it at four AM local time. And the bomb they dropped was one of their smaller ones. Nobody had been killed and very few people were even injured.

The smashed spot, however, was in a perfect place to put in a spaceport. Close to I-93 with good access using US-3, maple syrup could flow in from the region and galactic goodies could flow out. Of course, the "spaceport" currently consisted of some poured concrete, large areas of slagged concrete and metal and a parking area that was what was left of the mall parking lot.

It also was remarkably unsecure. Glatun traders

had their own defenses to prevent nosies or thieves
damaging or stealing from their ships. And nobody
could quite figure out how to manage ships over which
even their own Space Command didn't have control.
Which, given that an orbital reentry ship was another
name for potential crater the size of Washington, was
another thing to be negotiated.

"It's not a rocket," Tyler protested. "And, yeah, I
am. I took an online course while I was on Glalkod
Station."

"But you couldn't get certified," Mr. Haselbauer said.

"I had to spend five years as a mate first," Tyler
said, shrugging. He tossed his carry-on into the back
of the pickup and got in. "I didn't figure I had five
years to waste piloting a freighter. Most of the systems
are automatic. The pilot's really just there to tell it
what to do. The big problem is, I need an engineer.
Fast. I've hired a couple of Glatun to help out but
I'm going to need a human crew. Which means finding some people to send to Glalkod to get implants
and training. Oh, and training on this particular ship
is sort of hard to find."

"Why?" Mr. Haselbauer asked, starting up the truck.

"Well, it's *kind of* old," Tyler said. "I couldn't afford
a new one. Which is why I need an engineer. Quick."

"This truck's old but it don't need an engineer on
call all the time," Mr. Haselbauer said. "Just some
decent TLC. How old is old?"

"Let's put it this way," Tyler said, leaning back in
his seat. "I considered calling it the *Santa Maria*."

"You bought a ship?" Dr. Foster said. The chief
science officer of Aten Mining Corporation, it seemed

to Vernon Tyler, Chairman of the Board, was a bit nonplussed. "You didn't say you were going to buy a ship."

Aten had started off in a small and cramped set of rooms in an industrial park in Huntsville, Alabama, not far from the company that made their mirrors. Since Aten was ninety-five percent of their customer base, Aten had quickly absorbed AMTAC, which was now a division of Aten. And they'd moved into bigger offices as the workforce had expanded. It needed to expand. Three doctors and a few lab rats could control fifty mirrors. Without an AI, though, controlling *four hundred* and fifty mirrors was a different ballgame.

It was costing Tyler like crazy. Not as much as the lease on the tugs, but still costing like crazy.

"Leased," Tyler said. "Five. Sort of. We needed tugs. There was an orbital mining control ship and four tugs going for cheap on the Glatun version of eBay. I leased them through a subsidiary of Gorku, Inc. They gave me a deal. I think Gorku likes me for some reason."

"You leased a spaceship," Dr. Foster said in a far-away tone.

"For one hell of a lot of change," Tyler said. "Since Icarus was a bust, what have you been up to while I was getting implants and leasing ships? Because we need to put them to work. You know, pulling useable metals off of an asteroid."

"You leased a spaceship," Dr. Foster said, again.

"Can we get past that?" Tyler said.

"No," Dr. Foster said, grinning. "Look, nobody gets into this business if they're not seriously bent on getting into space. So far, despite Glatun freighters coming every month, I've been grounded on this rock. I'm not getting younger. When do I get a ride?"

"It's not for thrill rides . . ." Tyler said.

"Who said anything about a thrill ride?" Dr. Foster replied. "Does that ship have probes? Spectroscopic and magnetic detectors? Some way we can figure out what these asteroids *are* so we're not trying to figure out what a rock is from the ground?"

"Umm . . ." Tyler said, closing his eyes and accessing his hypernode link. "All of the above."

"Then let's *go!*" Dr. Foster said, grabbing his jacket. "Where's the ship?! I'll call my wife on the way . . ."

"It's in Manchester," Tyler said, holding up his hand. "FAA had conniptions when I wanted to fly it down here. I leased a plane to fly down. Getting from Manchester to Huntsville, commercial, is an incredible pain."

"So let's go!" Dr. Foster said, heading to the door of his office.

"Wait!" Tyler said, grabbing him by the collar. "We've got to do this one step at a time. Do you have a passport?"

"A what?" Dr. Foster said.

"ICE is treating off-planet flights like going out of the country," Tyler said with a sigh. "We can leave just fine. Getting back you need a passport or you've got a lot of explaining to do to Immigrations. The tug only has room for five. And it only has bare minimum facilities. And those are for Glatun which, as it turns out, we can kind of use. They use basically the same sort of toilet we do and a shower's a shower. But the living quarters are on the *Monkey Business*. There's room for up to ten if you're *very* friendly. And two of those slots are taken up by the Glatun engineer and pilot temps. There are no EVA suits. I was planning on buying some off of the Russians. Well, there is one real space suit, but it's mine. So if there's an emergency you better hope we can hook up to one of the tugs to get back to Earth. And there's bound to be a problem since all the ships are older than the United States. Oh, and there's no cook, and don't get me started on the robochef. Last but not least, you're the chief science officer of this lash-up and you can't just go gallivanting off into space at the drop of a hat."

"I'll quit," Dr. Foster said.

"Then there will *really* be no reason for me to bring you," Tyler pointed out. "And what about Dr. Bell? *He's* the small planetary bodies guy."

"Fine," Dr. Foster said. "We'll take Nathan, too." He paused for a moment and thought about it. "Will he fit?"

"Yeah," Tyler said, shrugging. "Barely. You're determined to do this, aren't you? I really do need you keeping this lash-up running."

"I can do that remotely with the hypernet," Dr. Foster said. "At least for a while. I'm not that bad of a manager, thank you. I've got a passport. So does Nathan. Uh . . . the question is how long we'll be gone. What sort of acceleration does the ship have? How quick can we do some fly-bys?"

"Ninety gravities," Tyler said. "The tugs are about a thousand at max power but it costs like crazy in fuel."

"A *thousand* gravities?" Dr. Foster said, boggling. "Continuous? The space shuttle only pulls ten! And that's for about a minute!"

"They're space tugs," Tyler said slowly and carefully.

"They're basically space bulldozers. If you're going to move rocks in space, and time is money, note, you need something that can move rocks. The flip side is they're expensive and kind of clumsy. If you really want to go, though, we can do this. Who's coming along?"

"I think we're going about this all wrong," Dr. Bell said as the Gulfstream took off.

"I don't care," Dr. Foster said. "We're going."

"No, I mean the mining," Dr. Bell said. "Look, yes, putting the VLA in towards Venus makes sense. We can get twice the insulation as putting it in Earth orbit. We'd get more farther in, but anything past Venus starts to get tricky with heat management."

"So what are we doing wrong?" Tyler asked.

"Most of the Atens are stony, chondritic, carbonaceous..." Dr. Bell said, then shrugged. "I can keep going in the Cs and Ss if you want. They have metal but they're not primarily metals. And Icarus is a case in point for how screwed up that can make things."

"What's screwed up?" Tyler asked.

"You'll see when we get there," Nathan said balefully. "But what we need is an M Class."

"Which I've noted in my extensive research," Tyler said sourly. "Problem is, we've got all our mirrors down in Venus orbit."

"Which is not as much of a problem now that we have a ship," Dr. Bell said. "Sure, we'll keep the VLA down in Venus orbit. It's easy enough to kick the mirrors out of the freighter as it's headed out-system and let them fly there on their own. Or, hell, we can use the tugs to bring them up. But we've got enough mirrors in the VLA at this point that we can start doing some serious reflectance. Put one, well, probably three or four, of the BDA mirrors up out of the ecliptic. Then get one down by our target asteroid. Which should be 6178 1986 DA. Definitely metallic unlike Amun."

"Heard about that one," Tyler said. "Except it's so freaking *huge*. Our system is designed around melting the thing in-situ and then extracting. Melting it is going to take a while. We're talking about a mile-wide ball of stainless steel. And we need a better name."

"Point," Nathan said, scratching his head. "What about adjusting the approach?"

"How?"

"How do the Glatun mine asteroids?"

"With more tugs than we've got," Tyler said. "They land diggers and dig them apart and use fusion-pumped lasers I'm not going to try to run. The problem is rotation. If you have a high rotation, and 6178 has a very high rotation, even if you cut bits off they go flying away due to the low gravity. So they slow the rotation of big asteroids with really big and many tugs. What I want is a *small* M-class asteroid. There *have* to be some. One hit the Earth not too long ago in a place called Crater City, Arizona. That one was only fifty meters across. That's about right for starting out. And we still need a better name."

"6178 should have about point oh oh one eight percent platinum groups," Dr. Foster pointed out. "That's one hell of a lot of platinum group."

"I'm doing the math," Tyler said, his eyes closed. "We can currently pump, what? About one million watts? Ten to the sixth. Seventy-eight requires four point one times ten to the *nineteenth* joules to melt it. We're going to need more mirrors."

"What about a big Mylar mirror?" Nathan said.

"It's not that easy," Dr. Bell said. "Trust me on this. While you were going to conferences where you minor planets guys were getting all excited about big pieces of Mylar, I was at NASA conferences with guys who were trying to get small pieces of Mylar to properly deploy. It's not as easy as it seems."

"And I've got reasons for wanting a bunch of small mirrors and one freaking huge one," Tyler said. "I am hereby designating 6178, which, yeah, seems to be the best choice, as Connie. We'll stay on Icarus for now. But as soon as we're done with Icarus we'll get started on Connie."

"Why Connie?" Dr. Taylor said. "Old girlfriend?"

"Because everything we're about to do with it is going to cause conniptions."

"I know I don't have a freaking pilot's license, Bob," Tyler said into the phone. "I'm not driving an airplane. I'm driving an antigravity driven tug, which I can do just fine. And as to 'airspace deconfliction,' I now know why the Glatun and Horvath can hack our systems more or less at will. The only problem with avoiding aircraft is the FAA's system is so antiquated you can barely read it... Well, I've got to pick up a half a dozen mirrors in Huntsville and then get them into space. What do they want me to do, truck it down? The tug is the size of a freaking warehouse. And if the FAA wants to talk about deconfliction can we please start with orbitals? The fricking space around Earth is so full of junk you won't believe it... No, I can't truck them up to Manchester, they're too fricking big. The Glatun have been picking these up with no issues. What's the difference with an Earth pilot? Oh? Really? Then maybe they'd like me to take a course that *doesn't exist*? Maybe I should *teach* it! I'm the *only* guy on Earth qualified to fly one of these things."

"Marginally," Dr. Foster said, grinning.

Tyler stared at Dr. Foster and continued on the phone. "Bob, I pay you one hell of a lot of money to fix things," Tyler said. "By the time I'm in Manchester, I expect clearance from the FAA to fly from Manchester to Huntsville, I don't care what altitudes they assign me, I'm perfectly comfortable with low-orbital, pick up some mirrors and some sort of blanket clearance in the works so I don't have to go through this red-tape *bull crap* every time I need to pick something up on Earth. Oh, and speaking of things I need to pick up—by the time we're lifting off, I need a ship's cook. He doesn't have to have a Ph.D., he just has to be able to cook and be willing to do so in space. Bring his own pots and pans, there's a stove. And I need a ride from the airport to the spaceport...Because I pay you a lot of money, Bob. Any time you don't want me to keep paying you a lot of money, say so...Nice talking to you, too. Buh-bye."

Tyler slammed the phone down and shook his head. "What do I pay these people for?"

"Apparently so that you can shout at them," Dr. Bell said.

"Robert Lyle is one of those attorneys under the impression I work for him," Tyler said. "If the Horvath couldn't push me around, he's not gonna."

"And if you don't have clearance?" Dr. Foster asked.

"Then I'll fly down to Huntsville, pick up the mirrors, and get a new lawyer," Tyler said. "It's not like even the F-22 can shoot me down. We'll be gone at least two months setting this up. By that time the furor will have died down and my new lawyers will have paid off the right people to keep me out of jail."

"That hasn't worked out for all CEOs," Nathan pointed out.

"All CEOs don't own megawatt orbital lasers," Tyler said, grinning. "Warren Zevon got the order wrong. Bring lawyers, money, *then* guns."

"What's up?" Dr. Foster said. Tyler was craning his neck out the window as the Gulfstream rolled to a stop.

"Welcoming party," Tyler said.

"Your people?"

"Nearly as bad. Bureaucrats."

FOUR

"Mr. Tyler?"

There were four people waiting for Tyler as he debarked. Two were obvious bureaucrat types. JC Penney suits and acrylic ties. One was TSA. That was in case he got nasty. The fourth was a big guy with a sort of goofy expression wearing a NASA golf-shirt.

"Tyler Vernon," Tyler said. "And you are...?"

"Howard Hagemann. I'm with the FAA. This is Mr. Stanley Burnell with the National Aeronautics and Space Administration."

"Hello," said Bureaucrat Two.

"And this is Mr. Stephen Asaro," Mr. Howard continued, gesturing to the guy in the NASA shirt. "Also with NASA."

"Hey!" the guy said, shaking Tyler's hand. "Great to meet you, Mr. Vernon!"

"Nice to meet you, Mr. Asaro," Tyler said, recovering his hand from the death lock. The guy had a grip like a steel vise.

"In consultation with your legal representation and noting the importance to Earth of your missions," Mr. Howard said, "and in consultation with policy makers in the FAA and NASA, we have agreed to come to a compromise on the subject of your over flight of American territory by an experimental craft."

"It's . . ." Tyler almost said "older than the United States Constitution, how can it be experimental?" and then had a sudden case of intelligence . . . "hardly experimental."

"We do not have flight characteristics data on it," Bureaucrat Two said pointedly.

"Well," Tyler said, scratching his head. "That's because it doesn't really fly, per se. Flying is aerodynamics based. It's aerodynamic ability is pretty much that of a brick. If the grav drive goes out, which is pretty unlikely given the redundancy, it's going to have *exactly* the flight characteristics of a brick. A really, really *big* brick. A big *steel* brick. With screaming people in it."

"You're not making your case here very well," Asaro pointed out.

"I'm not trying to make a case," Tyler said. "*Paw Four* has been moving rocks and going in and out of gravity wells since before any of us were born, and I had it fully serviced before I left Clalkod Station. So it's going to be able to get to Huntsville without incident. What we're talking about here is that I'm not playing your games. Fine, I don't play your games. I've got well-paid attorneys and lobbyists and MBAs to play your games. If you wanted to be petted, you came to the wrong guy. And the people I'm talking to are just messenger boys so I don't even have to worry about burning bridges. But you can pass on to your policy people that they might as well get something regular going. Because I, and additional pilots as they become available, are about to start moving in and out of orbit on a regular basis. And if what you come up with is stupidly onerous we're going to *ignore* it. I'd *much* rather have a *good* aerospace control system than try to pick my way through the crap that's in orbit on my own. But I don't figure *either* agency has a chance in hell of managing that. God knows NASA can't maneuver its way out of a wet paper bag without a five-year study to study what they're going to have to do a ten-year study on. Which is why when Glalkod ships head in to Terran orbit they contact Space Command, not Houston. So, what's your compromise?"

"Mr. Asaro is a qualified space shuttle pilot," Mr. Howard said after a moment of looking as if he was sucking on a lemon.

"What the hell are you doing in Manchester?" Tyler asked.

"Boston," Asaro said. "I was doing a lecture at MIT on near Earth navigational obstacles. You're right about the orbitals. They're chock full of junk."

"As I was saying," Mr. Howard said. "Mr. Asaro is a qualified pilot. If you will agree to let him accompany you on this . . . mission and ensure the safety of your movement, NASA and the FAA will raise no further objections."

"Sweet," Tyler said. "We get a real astronaut along. That'll be helpful. Did you bring your spacesuit?"

"No," Asaro said. "When are we leaving?"

"Takes about twenty minutes to ride to the Manchester Spaceport," Tyler said. "So . . . about thirty minutes."

"You're going to need to file a flight plan!" the FAA

representative snarled. "At the very least you need to file a flight plan!"

"It's already filed," Tyler said. "You do allow electronic filing, thank God. I filed it while we were talking. I'm still waiting for them to figure out how to vector me. They want to put me in normal lanes which is . . . silly. I can get up to orbit, crank her up, and be in Huntsville about thirty minutes after takeoff. Taking the lower routes not only means you've got my brick flying around 767s, it means going at 767 *speeds*. No thanks. It's like putting a Ferrari in the truck lane. I don't drive fifty-five."

"Take the Speedbird route up at seventy grand?" Asaro said.

"Makes more sense. I can beeline Huntsville that way, then pick my way down through the crunchies. If I 'conflict' a bird it's going to do a crunchy on the *Paw*, which might not even notice. I really don't want to do a crunchy. People will, and I'm not being melodramatic when I say this, die."

"Which is why we don't want an absolutely unqualified pilot," the FAA representative said. "That is the whole point."

"But you're sort of missing my point," Tyler said. "And, again, a pointless audience but I'll make the point anyway. The *Paw* is a *space*craft, not an *air*craft. Its maneuvering methods are entirely different. It can, and does, turn on a dime and accelerate in a way that makes it look like . . . well, a UFO. The *Paw* has up to a *thousand* gravities of acceleration. Admittedly, its inertials won't take that so you can't actually *maneuver* at a thousand grav. Not if you don't want to be paste. But it can maneuver so fast it looks and acts unreal. I can and will maintain normal maneuver when I'm in areas that have traffic. But treating it like an aircraft makes exactly no sense. And saying that I'm not qualified to fly it makes no sense. Because I'm the only person qualified to fly it who was born on the planet Earth. You can't find anyone else qualified to fly it. Among other things, it works off of implants and, for anyone with the proper codes and implants, flies *itself*."

"Um," Asaro said, raising a hand. "I get all that. But my spacesuit is in Houston."

"I'm not going to try to get them to let me go to Houston," Tyler said with a sigh. "You got any clothes with you?"

"In the car."

"Since we're not planning on going EVA, don't worry about it," Tyler said, "We're going to be picking up the mirrors, then dropping them off and moving some other mirrors around. Then we're going to heat up an asteroid and start mining it. Along the way we'll probably be sending tugs back to Earth to pick up more mirrors..."

"And who will be piloting *them*?" Mr. Howard asked.

"I will," Tyler said. "From wherever the *Monkey Business* is. So I'd guess you'd say they'll be UAVs. By the way, the way that I pilot the *Paw*? I have to work through the comp on the *Monkey Business*. The *Paw* is a paw—it's an extension of the ship that is currently in geosynchronous orbit over Brazil. Which I control, from here, through neurological implants. What fun. For that matter, one of the Glatun on the *Monkey Business* can fly the *Paw*. But they're not. The pilot is going to be *me* to make a *point*. Which is that a human can learn, in a month, enough to be able to work safely in space."

"Cool!" Asaro said. "Can I get some of those?"

"They cost, at current exchange rates..." Tyler closed his eyes for a second. "Two hundred and fifty billion dollars. Got the stones?"

"Ouch!" Dr. Foster said.

"You can understand why I just try to think in terms of Glatun credits," Tyler said. "The whole conversion thing is just silly. Okay, Asaro can come along. It's all good. I'll even give him a mike and a screen so he can see I'm not going to plow an airplane."

"Very well," Mr. Howard said. "You will fly directly from here to Huntsville and..." He paused and shook himself. "Where are you going to *land?*"

"Where the freighters usually land," Tyler said with a sigh. "At the AMTAC facility."

"Very well," Mr. Howard said, shaking his head. "I think I'm getting too old for this."

"You're only as old as you feel," Tyler said. "Mr. Asaro, if you're coming along you'd better grab your flight bag."

When they were in the limo and, temporarily, out of the clutches of bureaucrats, Tyler heaved a relieved sigh.

"So, Mr. Asaro," Tyler said. "I'm Tyler. Not Mr. Vernon. The big one is Dr. Nathan Bell..."

"Howdy," Nathan said, shaking hands.

"...Also known as Nathan, our small planetary objects guy who is a small planetary object of his own. Buddha is Dr. Bryan Foster..."

"Mr. Asaro," Dr. Foster said, shaking hands.

"And you are...?"

"Steve," Asaro said. "Or...hell. Astro."

"As in the Jetsons' dog?" Nathan said.

"I was an astronomy geek," Astro said, shrugging. "And my last name is Asaro. Go figure."

"And a pilot," Tyler said, nodding. "Which is good. Can you keep a secret, Astro?"

"Depends," Asaro said, shrugging. "I'm on NASA's payroll. They're going to want a full mission eval when I return."

"Well, this part you can keep off the mission eval," Tyler said. "If you had plants, I'd have you take the whole mission. Because while I can *do* it, I'm not so arrogant or stupid as to think I'm properly trained or qualified. Oh, don't get me wrong. I can get us to Huntsville and pick up the stuff and get it into orbit. Among other things, our Glatun comrades were told to watch me carefully. But as soon as I can get a properly trained and prepped pilot, I'm handing this off. Also, the *Monkey Business* can respond to verbal commands. As soon as you're familiar with the interface, you're the third shift pilot and backup in case something very stupid happens to me *and* the Glatun pilot."

"No joystick?" Astro said.

"No joystick," Tyler said, leaning back and closing his eyes. "Just brainpower. It's a whole new world."

When they got to the ship they found an Asian gentleman in a jumpsuit waiting for them. He had a rather extensive collection of boxes.

"Who's that?" Asaro asked. "He looks familiar."

"The cook?" Tyler said, shrugging and getting out of the limo. "Hi, I'm Tyler Vernon. And you are?"

"Dr. Conrad Chu," the man said, nodding his head. "Professor of astrophysics at MIT. I understand you are going mining. I have taken, over my dean's objections, a leave of absence to accompany you."

"Uh, yeah," Tyler said. "But . . ."

"I have my cookware," the professor said, gesturing to the boxes. "I paid my way through school working in a restaurant. I am, I must say most humbly, a very good cook. That depends, of course, upon ingredients."

"We've got stuff in the holders on the ship," Tyler said, trying to catch up. "You're a professor of astrophysics? And you want to be the ship's cook?"

"Is the job in space?"

"Yes."

"Then I wish to be the ship's cook," Dr. Chu said. "Do you have an objection?"

Tyler thought about it and held out his hand.

"I simply love Chinese food," Tyler said. "And you don't want to know what a Glatun robochef does to beef with broccoli."

"Then we should perhaps load," Dr. Chu said, smiling.

"Where's the cargo door on this thing?" Steve asked, walking around the ship. It appeared, in fact, to be not much more than a two-story steel brick with some small openings on one side.

"Right here," Tyler said, comming for the door to open. The door opened along an almost invisible seam and dropped a ramp down to the ground. There was a rather obvious air-lock system with both doors open. "Doors will only open if there's air on both sides and it's equalized. Otherwise it takes a two-person override. And people don't usually ride in these things, anyway. So there *is* no cargo door. And not much room for cargo."

"Docking?" Dr. Chu asked, hefting one of the cases.

"All Glatun air locks are identical," Tyler said, grabbing his bags. "And we're going to have to figure out how this stuff will fit."

Just beyond the air lock was the crew compartment. The interior of the ship was surprisingly cramped.

"Wow," Steve said, looking at the low, tight quarters. "You don't fly this ship, you wear it."

"You don't even wear it," Tyler said, stuffing his bag into a corner. "It's controlled from the *Monkey Business*. We're all effectively passengers. It only has crew quarters as a way to move people around from one base to another in a pinch."

"So the rest is...?" Bryan asked. He was carrying his bag and two cases of cookware. He clearly wasn't sure where to set it. "We're not going to be able to carry all this stuff."

"Engines," Tyler said, pointing to one of the five chairs. "Power plants. Grav plates. Drives. How do you think it gets that much thrust? And we'll be able to carry it all. You, Steve and Nathan are big. Grab a seat. Dr. Chu..."

"Conrad, please," Dr. Chu said.

"Conrad and I will pack all the stuff in on top of you since we're...*smaller*. We'll go up to the ship to drop this off, then go to Huntsville. Don't worry, it's a short flight."

"FAA will defecate a brick," Nathan said, taking a seat. "Glatun are sort of small, ain't they?"

"FAA will get over it," Tyler said. "And it's not that Glatun are small. It's that this ship wasn't designed for Rangora."

It took Tyler and Dr. Chu about ten minutes to get everything stowed on top of the other passengers.

"And that way *I* don't have stuff piled on *me*," Tyler said, grinning. He commed the door closed and checked the telltales. "I think the little blinky lights are just so the passengers that are in the know don't get nervous. But we are...locked tight. And... liftoff. Manchester FAA, *Monkey Paw Four*. Request change of flight plan, direct ascent to geosynchronous, return trip to Huntsville FAA control...Roger, FAA. Thank you."

"No problems?" Nathan asked.

"Manchester FAA is getting used to spaceships," Tyler said. "It's the bureaucrats in D.C. that see their phony baloney jobs on the line that don't like us."

"The FAA is a pretty important group," Asaro said. "And I know you don't like NASA but it really was the only game in town if you wanted to be in a manned program."

"And now it's not," Tyler said. "Which means that NASA is looking at becoming very extremely redundant very extremely fast. Which nobody likes but bureaucrats hate more than most. To most people in a bureaucracy, the main thing is that they've got a steady paycheck, because who ever lays off a bureaucrat? Well, NASA if it had any sense at all. And the FAA is having to adjust, fast, to new conditions. One thing that they're realizing is that they're going to have to automate to a much greater degree to handle space traffic. And they've been lobbying Congress for forever for upgrades, I'll admit. But most of the stuff they're pitching looks exactly like what it, in fact, is: pork payoffs to contractors so that FAA administrators can then get cushy jobs when they finish their twenty years. Not going to argue this one while I'm picking my way through the satellite belt. So, Steve, does a 'Doctor' go with that name? You were introduced as Mister."

"I didn't want to throw you any more than being with NASA would," Steve said. "So, yes, it's Dr. Asaro. Also, until recently, Major Asaro."

"Air Force?" Nathan asked, trying to shift some of the packages. He was pretty hard to see under the boxes.

"Bite your tongue," Steve said. "Marines."

"So Doctor Major Steve 'Astro' Asaro," Tyler said. "We've got plenty of names to choose from. Doctor of . . . ?"

"Aeronautical engineering," Astro said. "And astronomy. And physics. Master's in electrical and mechanical. I thought I recognized Dr. Chu. I had his astrophysics for physics majors course many a year ago."

"You got an A," Dr. Chu said. "I was being nice, though. I knew you wanted to be an astronaut. You really rated more of an A minus."

"With your engineering background maybe you should be the ship's engineer instead of pilot," Tyler said. "Okay, since we have about five minutes alone. Nathan and Bryan already know the dirty details. We'll be returning to Huntsville after dropping this stuff off. So if you want to abort you can abort in Huntsville and no harm done. The *Monkey Business* is five hundred years old. It's not quite ready for the scrapyard but it's close. It was what I could afford. And I made sure it was serviced before we left Glatun. But it's not a nice new space shuttle or the ISS. It's a workhorse that has been running around the galaxy since before the Spanish landed in the New

World. Our first mission is to launch some mirrors. We're going to just park them in Near Earth Orbit because they're destined for out-system. Then we're going to go check Icarus and figure out what's happening with the smelting. The answer is something funky according to Nathan."

"Best if we check it with the Glatun systems," Nathan said. "I'm not sure, Dr. Houseley's not sure and we haven't been sure if we should contact someone like... Well, Dr. Chu, come to think of it."

"I'm a specialist in oxygen production in Mira Variables," Dr. Chu said. "I'm just along for the ride. And to cook."

"Anyway," Tyler said. "If anybody wants to abort after you see the ship, you're welcome. I only want people who really want to be here."

"I'm actually having a bit of trouble with the concept," Steve said. "The last time I was in space, the ride up was like being repeatedly hit by a trip-hammer."

"Welcome to a new day," Tyler said. "And...we're... almost docked. Hang on a bit. Diw! The lock won't seal... Yeah, I *know* it sealed when I left. I'm going to undock. Get one of the bots to check the seal rings... This is the sort of thing I was talking about. It's not quite baling wire and chewing gum but it's got about two billion little issues that crop up all the time."

"Try that pretty new shuttle that's older than I am and gets practically rebuilt after every mission," Steve said. "You don't want to know for problems."

"Hang on," Tyler said. "Yeah, I'll try it." There was a *clang*. "That's got it. What was it...? I hate intermittent failures, too. Especially when they're of docking seals. And...we're home."

"We sure it's good?" Nathan asked in a muffled tone.

"Get used to answers like 'We'll know when we open the door,'" Tyler said. "Fortunately, we can close it *really* fast." Tyler opened the inner air-lock door and listened. "Any whistling?"

"You're joking, right?" Steve said.

"Nope," Tyler said. "And inner door opening . . . And we didn't lose a gram of air so we're good. Everybody out!"

"As soon as I can *move*," Nathan said.

"Be careful," Tyler grabbed two boxes off of Nathan. "There's a small patch of microgravity right at the join. You can step over it but it feels sort of funny and if you're not careful you trip."

FIVE

"It does look sort of worn," Dr. Foster said as he followed Tyler down a passageway. It was also *big*. The interior corridors weren't wide or tall but there were *a lot* of them. They hadn't gotten a look at the exterior but he could tell it was a pretty sizeable ship.

"And the galley," Tyler said as a hatch withdrew. "Most of the hatches are memory metal. One of about a thousand things we don't understand. At least not well."

The galley was the size of a good-sized restaurant's kitchen.

"This is more than I expected," Dr. Chu said, looking around. "Are the big doors the freezers?"

"One is a standard pantry," Tyler said, walking over and comming the door open. The interior was packed with cases. "This is the pantry. You'll notice it doesn't have the little yellow and blue lights over it. Blue is good, yellow is bad. The ones with the yellow and blue lights are stabilizers. They, somehow, prevent degradation. They're cool rooms but not freezers. About 20 C normally. But even if they get hotter the stuff doesn't degrade, and besides meat and such like, I've got them filled with tasty vegetables and fruits."

"Good," Dr. Chu said, walking over to one of the stabilizer rooms. "And how do I know the stabilizer *isn't* on? Because *I* don't want to be stabilized. The blue light?"

"The field turns off if you open the door," Tyler said, comming for the door to open. The room was filled mostly with piled packages of pre-cut meat. It was vaguely disturbing that they *weren't* frozen. "And it really *will* turn off. The door latch has the power circuit built in. The problem isn't getting them to turn off. It's keeping them on."

"I see," Dr. Chu said. "And how do I open the doors?"

"*Monkey Business*, please give Dr. Chu access privileges to all food areas, bunking and common areas by verbal command. Drs. Foster, Bell and Asaro are authorized access to common areas and bunking."

"Yes, sir," the ship replied.

"AI?" Dr. Foster asked as he set his cases down.

"No," Tyler said. "Just a very smart computer. It works similar to an AI, but it can't figure things out. If it's not in its programmed responses it has to consult a sophont. Access time through the hypernet with one of the Gorku AIs came with the lease so we shouldn't have to help it figure out much. Gorku also will tow us home, to Glalkod mind you, if the ship breaks down and it's something we can't fix. Or send a repair ship if it's more feasible. That's one of the reasons I didn't buy it. Anyway, can you work with this?"

"All electric ranges," Dr. Chu said, looking around. "I really doubt I'll need the microwave. Isn't that a GE?"

"I had it retrofitted," Tyler said.

"This will do very well," Dr. Chu said. "Far more than I'd expected, frankly. I was expecting a tiny little galley the size of the inside of the *Paw*."

"The *Monkey Business* can control up to forty tugs," Tyler said, shrugging. "And a maintenance, mining and repair crew of up to a hundred. There are also cookbots but they're not programmed very well for humans."

"This will do very well," Dr. Chu said. "Perhaps we should get the rest of the materials out of the *Paw* and I can set up."

"Works," Tyler said. "And Nathan would probably appreciate that. Or you can come fly down to Huntsville."

"I do not wish to quit if that is what you mean," Dr. Chu said.

"Not at all," Tyler said. "But since I was working through my plants, which have an ocular portion so I was watching what was going on, I forgot to turn on the vision plates in the *Paw*. I appreciate your dedication, but how would you like to see Earth, and the ship, from space?"

"I can set up later," Dr. Chu said. "Let's get the *Paw* unloaded, shall we?"

"So, it's got vision screens?" Nathan said. He'd never even gotten out of his seat. "That's nice to know. Where?"

"Everywhere," Tyler said. "*Monkey*, *Paw Four* undocking...Roger...Yes, I'll bring maple syrup. And...we have the vision blocks on."

"Holy hanna!" Dr. Foster said.

The vision blocks of the *Paw* were installed prior

to the development of standard ocular implants and designed so that a crewman on the *Paw* could maneuver it in the often complex environment of asteroid mining. He, she or it might have to back up, spin or otherwise maneuver with a clear "view."

So they were everywhere. It was as if the seats were sitting in space.

"Now that's a view," Asaro said.

"I think I've peed myself," Nathan said in a muffled tone. "An' I don' wanna breathe."

The Earth was laid out "above" the ship with the *Monkey Business* blocking most of the rest of the view. But to either side was a glorious star field.

"We're not in vacuum," Tyler said. "You'd know if we were in vacuum. I'm given to understand it smarts."

"I was having a hard time with scale," Bryan said. "That's the air lock we were docked to."

"Roger," Tyler said. "Big, ain't she?"

"Immense," Steve said. "Huge doesn't cover it."

The ship stretched seemingly forever, with the air lock they had used a tiny door that became smaller and smaller as Tyler backed away from the ship.

"She's not really all *that* big," Tyler said. "Four hundred and twenty feet long. That's about thirty-nine stories. It's easier to think in terms of skyscrapers for things like this."

"Good point," Steve said, nodding. "It does work."

"Most of the aft third is engines and power plants," Tyler said, scooting the *Paw* around so that the crew could get a look at their new home. "The forward two-fifths is a smelter and bulk storage. The middle bit is crew quarters, life-support and command centers. So it's a big ship but with a full crew complement it's still rather cramped. And compared to some it's not all that big. But it's more than big enough for us. Dr. Chu? Comments?"

"I am absorbing myself in rapturous glory," Dr. Chu replied. "Space in all its infinite wonder. Are there... Is there anywhere in the *ship* with a similar view?"

"Not quite," Tyler said. "There are some ports, and your bunk has a screen which you can set to various views. But you can ride in the *Paws* from time to time if you really want. As long as I can get my *me fun*."

"No problem," Dr. Chu said. "I'm a master of the noodle in all its forms. They rather remind me of space time theory."

"So, where are we going to store the mirrors?" Astro asked as Tyler hovered the *Paw* over the parking lot of AMTAC.

The mirrors had been trundled out with forklifts and were now scattered around the parking lot, looking just a bit forlorn.

"We're not," Tyler said, looking over his shoulder. "I'm going to pick them up with a tractor bubble. The bubble will act as a shield against any damage. I'm just having to be sure to get the mirrors and not the ground under them. There... got it. I just needed to find a good structural point to pick them up off the ground so I could bubble them."

Steve watched as first one mirror, then two, then the whole group of twenty-three were picked up. There were twenty VLA mirrors, simple circles of nickel with a satpak on the back, and three BDA mirrors. Those were larger and more complex glass and nickel hexagons with cooling systems. But they all were hovering, spread out in formation, in a couple of minutes.

"This is so very cool," Nathan said. "This would be a six-month evolution with NASA."

"Six-year," Steve said. "Working for NASA just means I know their problems better. But at the level we're working on, just to be able to get people to space safely has huge issues. With this system, completely different story."

"So we're meeting specifications?" Tyler asked as they started to ascend.

"So far I've got no issues," Astro said. "Quite the opposite. I think with the *Paws* around we should ground every rocket on Earth for our own good. Rockets are very big explosions waiting to happen. If the *Paw* just breaks, it's going to be nothing but a big chunk of metal falling. And there is a lot of the world for it to fall on that's empty. Meteors do it all the time and there hasn't been anyone seriously injured since Tunguska. Of course, if it breaks just a bit in orbit and comes down at orbital speeds . . . Then you've got a KEW on your hands."

"And it will take a while to come down," Tyler said. "Even if the other *Paws* are out system, there's probably enough time for them to come in and grapple it."

"A point which had escaped me," Steve admitted. "I'm still trying to catch up to the technology. But since I can't see what you're doing I need to get some more detailed information, on the control and management systems. How, exactly, are you controlling the *Paw*?"

"Heh," Tyler said. "Some of it is intuitive but that takes a lot of explanation. First, you need to understand the plants."

"Okay," Steve said. "Go."

"The neurological implants integrate with the brain," Tyler said. "So when you go looking for a piece of information it searches not just for what you've explicated but also your back-thoughts of what you really want. Sort of like a very detailed and intuitive query system. I went looking for information on meteors when I was setting all this stuff up. I didn't spend a lot of time on it, but I looked through all the major online databases. And I couldn't find one damned meteor that I liked. You with me?"

"Yes," Steve said.

"Well, when I did the same thing using the hypernet from Glalkod, which can interact with our internet, by the way, I got a hit on Connie right away."

"Connie?" Steve asked.

"6178 1986 DA," Nathan replied. They were at about 40,000 feet and he was reveling in the view. "Two point one kilometer nickel iron asteroid. Apollo." The last meaning that its orbit was mostly outside of Earth's but crossed it. They also generally stayed inside the asteroid belt ranging from outside the orbit of Mars to inside the orbit of Earth. Aten asteroids were mostly inside Earth's, but entered Earth's orbit or crossed it. Apohele were those that stayed mostly in Earth's orbit. None of the classifications were precise. There were "Aten" asteroids that crossed the orbits of Mercury, Venus, Earth *and* Mars.

"Okay," Steve said.

"Which Dr. Bell knew off the top of his head," Tyler said. "But with the plants I've got pretty much everything his memory would draw upon and a pretty good sorting system. They use their internal memory, organic memory and a combination of intuitive processing and software to arrive at the answer you're looking for. But they aren't, per se, creative. They just give you access to a host of information. You have to be able to use it."

"I'm with you so far," the astronaut said. "How does that relate to flying the *Paw*?"

"I don't really fly it," Tyler said. "What I do is look for flight-paths. Then a combination of my plants and the processors on the *Monkey Business* sort through all the possible combinations using all available data to find a clear spot. You *know* what the orbital belt is like. So does the *Monkey*. Then I'm given a bunch of potential flight-paths. I generally pick the one at the top. But it's not exactly the safest or the fastest or whatever. It's an intuitive pick."

"I'd prefer you use the safest," Steve pointed out. "I'd really prefer you don't conflict a billion-dollar satellite."

"I won't," Tyler said. "I'm not a hot-rod in this thing and the *Monkey* knows it. That's part of the algorithm. But ... I don't want to take all day coming down and I really like watching North America and South America over Eurasia and Africa. Since we're going straight up from Huntsville to a ship over Brazil, that seems like the straight route. But it might be really crowded up there at the moment. So the ship has to maneuver."

"Which we've been doing while you were talking," Nathan said. "It was making me nervous since you didn't seem to be paying attention."

"I'm paying more than you think," Tyler said. "When you guys get plants you'll understand. But mostly I'm letting the *Monkey* fly the *Paw*. Getting back to the point. The absolute safest might be a polar insertion, then down over Russia..."

"Which would have some security issues," Dr. Foster pointed out.

"Which it takes into account, but you see my point," Tyler said. "Maybe Antarctica then over the south Atlantic. But that's not my favorite view and I don't want to take another thirty minutes out of my day flying halfway around the world to get more or less straight up. So it finds the safest route within my preferences by using a very advanced and partially intuitive query I don't even really set up. I just comm 'Following all local directives, get me up to the ship.' It gives me a set of routes, I pick the top one and then keep an eye out for visual aspects. Like there was a Cessna you guys probably didn't see at about seven miles out when we took off that wasn't on the FAA screens for some reason. The system also highlighted that and both informed me *and* took it into account. That's what the system is for."

"You're right," Steve said, shaking his head. "Four years of academy training... A monkey could fly this ship."

"A *Monkey is* flying this ship," Tyler said with a grin. "When I figured out how easy it was, I knew the name for the ship right away. But it can't figure everything out."

"Example?" Steve asked.

"Picking up the mirrors," Tyler said, gesturing "under" the ship. The ship had rotated so there was now a view of the star field beyond the mirrors. They were also pretty much clear of the atmosphere. "It didn't have a programmed way to do that. I figured that we could either adjust the width of the grav beam to prevent damage to them or find a hard-point. We sort of did both, maximizing lift at a hard-point while adding support to the lighter parts of the structure. Then we wrapped them in a grav bubble when we got them off the ground—they've been in zero g since we took off—and off we went. But the computer didn't have that method programmed. Now it does and the next time it'll be easier."

"And if a failure happens?" Steve asked.

"If the main engines give out, the mirrors or anything else we're lifting gets dropped," Tyler said. "Which could be potentially ouchy for somebody. There are two redundant back-ups that can get this thing down safely in up to a three-gravity environment from within the well. Stored capacitor power and a *mass* of grav plates which can be used for drives in a pinch.

"If I lose contact with the *Monkey*, I'm qualified to do a personal drop. I'm not going to promise I won't conflict a satellite on my way down. But I probably won't. The plants and the comp on the *Paw* are good enough to manage that much traffic control. And you can be sure I'll declare an emergency. FAA can route planes around my inbound track. Which will be to the nearest flat spot I can find. I can drop this thing, in an emergency, right into Times Square easier than you can land a trainer. The world has a lot of flat spots if you don't need five thousand feet of runway.

"If *everything* gives out, which is pretty damned unlikely given that this thing has been tinkered with and refined over five *hundred* years, then we're either stuck in orbit until another ship comes along and pulls us off or we're a dropping brick. Can't help you with that one."

"If you had some serious pilot's training, I don't think there would be a single issue," Steve said, shrugging. "It all sounds . . . almost too good to be true."

"That's because it is *very* advanced," Tyler said. "We won't be able to replicate this system in the next fifty years. The programming is just too complex. But we'll be able to make something *nearly* as good in short order. And as to the pilot, you can be sure that I'll get someone more qualified as soon as I pick a good candidate and get him or her planted. You *can* run things without plants, but it's not easy."

"I've had about all I can take of NASA," Steve said with a grin.

"You don't want this job," Tyler said. "Seriously. The guys on this ship are going to be doing grunt work. Nobody here wants *this* job. You need to be working on *our* ships. I've got a joint project going with Boeing and Lockheed Martin to produce the first class of ground-space shuttles. I turned over all the plans for power plants and drive systems to them as soon as I got back, along with a functioning power plant from a scrapped freighter and a gravplate fabber. And they're scratching their heads and talking about a hundred billion dollars and ten years' development. Which I've already commed them is just out of the question. If they can't get off the stick I'm going to form my own company to do it. They're still talking about light-weight composites and noodle programming. With a power plant and a grav system you can fly one of these things, made out of raw steel, with a stick. They can't get their head around 'the better is the enemy of the good.'"

"Serious problem with NASA as well," Steve admitted.

"The problem being, a start-up is based around new

and customized systems," Tyler said, shrugging. "I need Boeing and Lock-Mart's expertise at *mass* production! I need shuttles, a lot of shuttles, so the *Paws* aren't constantly carrying stuff into and out of orbit. I'm going to be sending back materials, but a lot of it's going to stay in space and build orbital systems. And I can do the big stuff, hulls and such, in space. But I still need all the fiddly bits built by ground-based companies. So I need shuttles. Several and some of them pretty damned big so they can carry big fiddly bits up. And I don't need them in ten years. I need them *yesterday*."

"What about the Horvath?" Nathan asked.

"I'm hoping like hell the Horvath consider this part of the human tribes they're not allowed to touch," Tyler admitted. "And once we leave, I'm going to be keeping the *Monkey Business* well away from Earth and the region between the gate and Earth. Last, they were another reason to lease it. Its Galactic transponder shows it, and the *Paws*, as belonging to one of the biggest Glatun corporations there is. I'm pretty sure that the Horvath don't want to explain to Gorku why they destroyed one of their ships. Even an old one."

"But human ships, it's a different story," Astro said.

"Absolutely," Tyler replied. "Probably. Which is, again, why I'm not going to be doing a lot of stuff around Earth or the gate if I can avoid it. Just parts and food up and materials down. If I'm far enough away, the Horvath will have to go out of their way to destroy whatever I've got built. And they're not going to be able to easily sort out the human stuff from Glatun. It's the best defense I can come up with so far."

"What about the beam?" Dr. Foster asked. "I'm thinking that could probably do some serious damage."

"Not powerful enough," Tyler said. "It's a one ter
awatt laser so far."

"It's not a *laser . . .*" Dr. Foster said tiredly.

"My orbital death ray, my name," Tyler replied
with a chuckle.

"This sounds like an old argument," Steve said.

"The name laser is an acronym," Dr. Foster said.

"Light Amplification by Stimulated Emission of
Radiation," Astro said. "Don't have a degree in optics,
but *anybody* knows that. What's the problem?"

"The light beam is not a laser," Dr. Foster repeated.
"A laser is a beam of *polarized* light of a *single* fre-
quency generated, well, in various ways at this point.
This is nothing more than, in effect, a concentrated
view of the Sun."

"A very *concentrated* view of *a lot* of the Sun which
just happens to burn and melt stuff," Tyler said. "I
know, I know, it's nothing more than Archimedes'
Mirror writ large. But we don't *have* a good name
for it other than laser. I'm *not* going to call it The
Solar Beam. It's a one terawatt laser. Which is great.
But not enough. We need a lot more power than that
to defeat the shields on the Horvath ship. At least a
hundred terawatts. We can *collect* that much power . . ."

"That is one *seriously* powerful laser," Steve said.
"Sorry, Doctor."

"I'll get over wincing sooner or later," Foster said
ruefully.

"Thus the acronym," Tyler replied, grinning. "Technically, it's the Solar Array Pumped Laser."

"SAPL," Steve said. "Serious ass powerful laser?"

"Got it," Tyler said, still grinning. "Problem being,
we can't concentrate it. Most we can concentrate so

far is about four terawatts. Let's just focus on mining and leave the defense of the system to Earth's governments."

"So, we've been heating Icarus for nearly a year," Dr. Bell said, gesturing at the screen. "And it's heating up. No question there. It's even melting. But it's not doing what we expected. The volatiles are all burned off. But what we've got is now a shiny ball of what appears from spectroscopy to be mostly nickel iron with some small admixture of noble metals. But it's not melting, per se. And given that we've determined the iron composition to be barely ten percent... we're sort of stymied."

The *Monkey Business* was decelerating at fifty gravities towards the smelting region. Due to orbital eccentricities, the VLA was currently about halfway around the sun from Earth. And so was Icarus.

They'd just finished a really excellent dinner—Dr. Chu turned out to be as good a cook as he was an astrophysicist—and the bots were clearing the dishes. Which was just about the best time to contemplate a problem in Tyler's opinion.

"How did it turn into a ball of iron?" Tyler asked. "Computer?"

"This method of orbital smelting is outside my experiential parameters," the ship replied. "I have no idea what is going on."

"And you guys have already kicked this around," Tyler said. "So you don't have any clue?"

"No," Dr. Foster admitted.

"Steve? Conrad?"

"Not a clue," Astro said.

Dr. Chu, on the other hand, had a distant look on his face.

"Conrad?"

"Could you run your estimates of composition for me again, please?" Dr. Chu said, looking at the screen. The view of the spinning asteroid was replaced by a mass of numbers that Tyler could barely follow. His plants were giving him translations but it wasn't the same as knowing what he was looking at. That came from training and experience.

"Ah, I thought so," Dr. Chu said, nodding. "Very interesting problem."

"Which is?" Tyler asked.

"The body is rotating around three axes at a very low rate," Dr. Chu said. "The majority of the Minor Planetary Body is silica. Relatively low melting point compared to iron or nickel but also very viscous and low volatility even in vacuum. The remaining material can be assumed to be similar elements such as the high level of aluminum." He paused and looked around at the group as if at a set of favored students. "Comments?"

"It's a glass eye," Steve said after a moment. "The silica melted and the heavier elements migrated to the area of, relatively, higher acceleration, the outer layers. It's probably layered all the way down with . . . silica being at the center, then various metals arranged outwards like the skin of an onion. What was the mechanical composition of the nickel iron? Are we talking about big chunks of metal?"

"Probably not," Dr. Bell said. "The material was probably formation pellets. Small blobs of nickel iron that were left behind in the original system formation."

"Getting that to melt will be tricky," Dr. Chu said. "They have more surface area to dissipate heat."

"Crap," Nathan said. "Crap, crap, crap. What the hell do we do now?"

"We can pull the nickel iron off," Bryan said.

"Very high viscosity you are looking at," Dr. Chu said. "While it is feasible, I suppose, with the *Paws*, there will be a high energy penalty. Which translates to fuel which translates to cost."

"Finally somebody in this lash-up who thinks in business terms," Tyler said, musingly. "Hmmm. If we increase the rotation, it's going to make the nickel iron easier to pull off."

"Also harder to control when it separates," Dr. Chu said. "High orbital velocities. And the tugs will have to increase the rotation. Energy penalty again."

"I'm really thinking this one is a bust," Tyler said. "But I'm not willing to give up. Among other things, my recently tinkered-with brain is screaming at me about last year's Olympics."

"Olympics?" Steve said. "That brings up that Chinese sprinter who got all the medals to me. Tanzania..."

"No," Tyler said, rubbing his forehead. "Thanks, but no. Don't brainstorm for a second. I think...No, you were right. Chinese. Specifically, Chinese food."

"Which we just had," Dr. Foster said.

"Which uses lots of onions," Tyler said. "Which have layers. Which can be...peeled!"

"Peeled?" Dr. Chu said. "Ah. Fascinating. Use the beam as a knife. Peel off the outer layer of nickel iron. Catching it will still be difficult."

"I'm not sure if the material will come off straight or like a snake," Tyler admitted. "I'm not even sure how thin we can cut it. But either way the *Paws* can be set up on its trajectory to catch it. Stop cutting then snip the strand when they have a full load. Take it to the *Monkey* for further processing. All the metals should be on the outside. When we spot a new one spectroscopically we'll pre-separate that at the laser smelt. What we'll end up with is a ball of silica which we can toss into the Sun."

"Highly *refined* silica," Dr. Foster said. "This has been spinning in a melt condition for nearly three months. Most of the impurities are going to have been pulled out. Perfect for mirrors."

"Which we'd have to pay energy penalty to drop onto Earth," Tyler said.

"But we're going to have other metals available," Dr. Foster said. "Backing materials. We can make one *huge* fricking mirror out of this thing. All we have to do is spin it harder and get a disc. Slow it down, put some melted aluminum on the back, it will stick due to microgravity interaction and vacuum welding, and we've got ourselves a mirror."

"Ah," Tyler said, nodding. "So maybe it's not a bust."

SIX

"Snake it is," Tyler said.

The three BDA mirrors they had brought out had been picked up by *Paw Two* and brought into alignment with the asteroid. By bringing in four more from the main BDA they created a massive mirror array. Six were arranged in a circle that concentrated the light on a small spot on the seventh. This became the cutting beam.

The terawatts of power punched through the semi-molten nickel iron, and a thin stream of it pulled off of the asteroid in a wriggling formation. The "small" snake of nickel iron was about three meters across and two meters thick on average.

Paw Three was set up two thousand kilometers away, practically point-blank in orbital terms, to catch the spalling nickel iron. All of it wasn't coming off in a solid stream; the power of the laser on such a small spot was causing some of it to flash into gas. That would have been a real problem on Earth since nickel gas was highly toxic.

It wasn't a problem for the *Paw*, though. The gas followed more or less the same trajectory, and gravity gathers *everything*.

"We're getting some trajectory change on Icarus," Dr. Bell said. "The change in mass is causing it to . . . wobble is the best term that comes to mind. Also a slight increase in rotation speed."

"Can we adjust the beam?" Tyler asked.

"Now that the computer understands what we're doing," Dr. Foster said. "It's compensating. So far. These things aren't super-precision instruments."

"Quantity has a quality of its own," Tyler said. "Solutions?"

"Two beams," Astro said. "As exactly opposite as we can manage. That way the mass removal is balanced."

"Do we have enough mirrors?" Tyler said.

"No," Dr. Foster said. "We don't."

"We need more BDA mirrors," Tyler said, sending a note planet-side. "If we can handle the wobble, we'll keep on like this."

"And we can't," Dr. Foster said.

"Crap," Dr. Bell cursed.

"What?" Astro asked. "Oh."

The material that had been snaking off of the asteroid was now wrapping onto it.

"Readjust targeting," Tyler snapped. "Never mind. Taking control."

The BDA beam retargeted on the material, cutting the snake off. What was left was a molten piece of iron that looked a good bit like a noodle writhing in vacuum as various vectors caused parts of it to go one way or another.

"Let some of the orbital eccentricity work out of that," Tyler said. "It's going to miss the *Two* by a gigamile. I'm going to send the *Paw Four* to follow it. Right now it's headed for the Sun at three hundred and eighty-six meters per second. We'll recover it. We'll also need to heat it from time to time to keep it molten. Okay, what did we learn?"

"We need two sets of mirrors," Dr. Bell said.

"Or a thinner snake that will break instead of sticking," Dr. Foster said.

"We're getting too much wobble," Dr. Bell insisted.

"We're dealing with too many parameters," Dr. Chu said. "There is too much orbital eccentricity in the satellite, which makes it harder for the computer to adjust to the wobble."

"We're too far out," Tyler said.

"With the BDA?" Dr. Foster said. "We're at sixty thousand meters. How close do you *want* to be?"

"A couple thousand meters," Tyler said. "Maximum. No matter how fast light is, precision is a matter of distance. With off-the-shelf satpaks we don't have enough precision in aiming to be way back. We can't keep up with the wobble even with FTL communications. So add we need better satpaks for the BDA and the other mirrors we're designing. *And* we're dealing with too many parameters *and* we need a smaller snake for the time being until we get this right. *And* we need another set of mirrors. For now, though, we'll have lunch, let it melt back into a nice quiescent ball and come back and try it again. I'll readjust the mirrors while we're eating."

"You were right," Dr. Foster said. "We needed to be closer."

The BDA, from so close it was practically getting splashed, was accurate enough to maintain the snake of metal even with the minor wobble the satellite was developing.

"And all the other ands," Tyler said, nodding. "But closer is more precise. Also we can get the focus area of the laser tighter. Cut that snake and let's try for a thicker one."

"Seems to be working," Dr. Foster said a few minutes later. "Even with a six meter snake. And the *Paw* is able to catch it."

The relatively thin and molten nickel iron tended to contract and cool as it floated through space. What the *Paw* was catching looked like a long worm or amoeba. The *Paw* would activate its tractor field just enough to pull the nickel iron in. As the material arrived it started to build up a large lump of nickel iron. "Large" being about the monthly output of the entire Sudbury complex in Canada every minute.

"I am moving the next *Paw* into place," the ship's comp said. "*Paw Two* will be at its functional maximum for repetition of this process in fifteen minutes."

"Cut the snake again," Tyler said. "Let the *Two* pick up all that and bring it back for further processing. As soon as the *Three* makes it back it can go into support. Stack them up and around to catch any bobbles. And we have a process."

"But at this rate . . ." Dr. Bell said.

"It's going to take us a month to strip off the nickel iron," Tyler said. "I *said* this was grunt work. Hell, now that the computer knows what it's doing, it can handle most of it. Can't you?"

"I cannot handle major changes such as the loss of a metal snake," the computer said. "But the basic cutting and gathering with the *Paws* is simple enough that it does not require human intervention."

"As soon as we have two sets of BDAs we'll put

two *Paws* up catching and two back looking for leakers and in position to take over," Tyler said. "Then we can *really* start smelting some iron. In the meantime... it's going to be a long business."

"Okay," Dr. Foster said, sitting back. "The view is great, the food is excellent and the beds are small but comfy. Who's got first watch?"

"Astro?" Tyler said, poking his head into the astronaut's room. "Got a second?"

"What's up?" Steve said, rolling out of his bunk. He was off-watch so he'd been reading technical manuals on the ship's construction. It was a complex system but despite its age and Tyler's worries about same it had been holding up remarkably well.

The group had not done quite as well. It had been a very looong three weeks. Steve was used to much more cramped quarters with far less privacy than the four-hundred-foot *Monkey Business* allowed. He'd been doing fine. Some of the rest of the "crew" was another matter. Dr. Bell, especially, was showing definite signs of needing to get back dirtside. He appeared to have a touch of claustrophobia and a major case of missing home. And even Tyler was clearly tired of being in the ship. He also had various urgent issues building up back dirtside. Dr. Chu and Dr. Foster were still perfectly content to watch an asteroid being slowly peeled.

Steve was torn. He felt underutilized but the same could be said for the ISS missions he'd been on. Most of the experiments conducted on the ISS, before the Horvath took it out, were pretty silly in his opinion. But if that was the payment for being in space, he'd take it.

Now he was in space, in a ship that was ten times the size of the ISS, actually doing *real* space work, not make-work to keep up the revenue stream...and feeling underutilized. It was odd but not particularly bothersome. And he now agreed with Mr. Vernon. This was grunt work. With a bit of minor training any ship captain would be better at this than Steve Asaro.

"One of the separators dropped offline," Tyler said. "Diw could use a hand with it. It's in pressurized areas, obviously."

The two Glatun crewmen had kept entirely to themselves. Steve wasn't even sure where they slept. He'd seen the engineer working on a panel at one point but just said hello and continued on. It was simple courtesy. If the Glatun needed help he was free to ask, and offering could be taken as pestering or questioning the Glatun's competence.

Other than that one encounter he had seen neither hide nor hair of the two ETs.

"Be glad to help," Astro said. "I've been looking at the specs on the fabbers but I didn't want to ask if I could see them."

"Computer," Tyler said. "Could you direct Dr. Asaro to Primary Separator four?"

"Of course, Mr. Vernon," the computer said. "If you will please follow the blinking hologram, Dr. Asaro?"

The trip ran through so many corridors, Steve, despite having really amazing situational awareness, knew he was going to have to have a guide back. Several of the areas were marked in yellow on the bulkheads, but the script was Glatun and he wasn't sure what it referred to. He also passed three air locks, including a large one he assumed was a freight lock, before he entered the compartment with the separator.

He had expected it to be hot. He'd been to a steel plant one time and in forges several times, and they were always hot. But it was about 72 degrees Fahrenheit and perfectly comfortable. Except for the smell of burning insulation and the Glatun up under a large, vaguely ovoid piece of equipment. Steve didn't speak Glatun but he could tell cursing when he heard it.

"Mr. . . . Diw?" Steve called.

"Wh . . . ?" the Glatun said, sitting up and banging his head. "Ow!"

"Sorry," Steve said. Great start. "Mr. Vernon suggested you could use some help?"

"Yeah," the Glatun said, sliding out from under the equipment on what looked like a metal plate. It didn't have rollers, though, so it was apparently a gravplate. "The standard repair bots have a hard time getting up in this spot. And they're working on the main switching gear since when this went it blew that out. There's a bolt that just will not come off."

"What happened?" Steve asked, getting on his back and sliding under the equipment. He wasn't sure where the bolts were. There didn't even appear to be seams.

"Not sure until we get it opened up," the Glatun said. "I'm Diw, by the way. Diw Lhuf."

"Steve," Steve said. "Steve Asaro."

"You another one of the big brains?" Diw asked. "Here, give me some leverage on this."

"This" looked like a torque wrench without the socket. Diw applied it to a spot on the metal that looked virtually identical to all the other spots, except for the newer scuff marks, and pushed.

Steve grabbed the wrench, braced himself and pulled. Despite being apparently just in contact with the metal, it wouldn't budge. It felt *exactly* like a wrench applied to a stuck bolt.

"I won't even ask what we're doing," Steve said. "And I guess so. I've got a doctorate. But that was just so I had a shot at the space program. I'm much happier getting my hands dirty. And we need a longer lever. But there's no room."

"Nope," Diw said. "Hate this design. Okay, one more time. With feeling."

Steve repositioned himself to push on the wrench with his full body and applied steady pressure with a grunt of exhalation.

"Saaah!" The wrench slipped and nearly broke his hand.

"That's got it," Diw said. "Right, one more and we'll have this baby open. Go over and grab the grav lift. I'd rather this thing not fall on my head."

"Sorry," Steve said, looking at some racked articles on the wall. "I'm not sure . . ."

"Looks like a mop," Diw said. "Blue with a yellow end. Grab the blue end, drag it over here."

Steve picked up the "mop" and found it to be surprisingly heavy. He dragged it across the floor as carefully as he could.

"Grav it," Diw said from somewhere under the machine. "Oh. No plants. Gravity is on."

The lower part of the "mop" suddenly became light as a feather. It still had the same mass, though. Steve was careful moving it over to the separator.

"Slide it under," Diw said, sliding out from under the machine. "And we increase power..." the Glatun continued as the grav lift lifted and touched the underside of the machine. "And release the brackets and..."

The plate on the bottom of the machine dropped out.

"Do me a favor and pull that over against the bulkhead," Diw said.

As soon as Steve had it out of the way, Diw was up underneath. Steve noticed that the plate was just about covered in bits of metal.

"Oh, this is just *great*," the Glatun engineer said. "The plates *ate* themselves!"

"Excuse me?" Steve said. He had the bottom plate against the bulkhead but he wasn't sure what to do with it then.

"I'm going to need the lift for this," Diw said, sliding out again. "I'll get the plate off. We're going to need to pull *all* the plates and their brackets and... Hellfire. Take a look. It's a *mess*."

Steve pulled himself under the machine and just scanned for a bit. He also realized he'd really like some safety glasses about now. Because the inside of the separator looked like a plane crash he'd been an investigator on one time.

From the small areas that were not totally mangled he could get a feel for what the machine *should* look like. The separator apparently consisted of overlapping plates of what looked like bronze. From the way that metal had flown, they apparently spun in counter direction to each other, one plate spinning clockwise, the next down counterclockwise and so on. It looked as if one of the plates to one side had lost integrity for some reason and then proceeded to, yes, eat the rest of the assembly.

He wasn't sure how exactly you would fix it. It looked as if it needed an entire rebuild.

"This is going to take a while," Steve said as Diw slid in next to him.

"Tell me about it," Diw said.

"I can see one of the plates went and caused a chain reaction," Steve said, pointing to the offending corner. "Any idea why?"

"Probably the plate just separated," Diw said. "I checked the log. It's nearly seventy years old. Metal fatigue builds up. If the plate either threw a piece or bent against the stator bearings and made contact with the counter . . . Well, once it got out of balance that's pretty much all she wrote. At full power, these babies spin at three hundred thousand RPM. Get a back hair in there and they'll go plooie."

"We'll need a clean room," Steve said, looking at all the spalled metal in the casing.

"Nah," Diw said. "Machine shop and a grav vac'll do. I've called for a couple of heavy lift bots to come over as soon as they're available. We'll flip this baby on its side, pull out the bits and refab it. Take a few days, but no sweat. Grif knows I've done it before."

"How does this . . . work?" Steve asked.

"The plates create a gravitational gradient," Diw said. "A high one. That's why they have to spin at such a high RPM. And it's over a very small area. If they ever get some plates that are robust enough, we'll be able to make neutronium. It's not *that* high of a gravitational gradient, you understand."

"Glad for that," Steve said.

"Under that much gravity, and there's another set above, the material separates by densities," Diw said.

"Makes sense," Steve said.

"The lighter stuff comes off first," Diw said. "Gases and such. Those are then reprocessed in additional separators to refine them. Then the metals and such start coming off. They're not pure, you understand..."

"Got it," Steve said. "But do it again and again..."

"Right," Diw said. "Fortunately, this separator is concentrated on the low volatiles. And since you've already pre-smelted the material it's not really important. We can keep it out of service while we fix it rather than calling Gorku to come bring a rebuilt one."

"How do the plates generate gravity?" Steve asked.

"Dunno," Diw said. "I mean, I had the class in school but it went right over my head. Something about quantum reactions of the materials. Get a plate of the right kind, counter spin it with another plate and you get gravity. Direction of spin is for or against. Speed of spin determines the gradient, and you can flex the field to extend. Grav drive is a pressor beam. Against *what* confused me, too. That's about all I need to know. Oh, and the material has to be in a particular matrix. Just making the alloy isn't enough. So you sort of need grav controls to make grav plates."

"I suspect if Dr. Chu thought about it long enough he could probably figure it out," Steve said.

"He the little guy?" Diw said. "I mean, the little guy who's not the boss? The cook?"

"Yeah," Steve said. "The cook. He can think his way around all the rest of us combined. So he'll probably be able to figure out the theory. Me, I'll go with your position. As long as I can make it or fix it, good enough."

"Good enough for space work, anyway."

"You're looking chipper, Steve," Dr. Chu said, putting down a large bowl of white rice and sitting down to dinner.

"How can you tell?" Nathan asked. "He always has that 'Me astronaut' look on his face."

"I am feeling rather better," Steve said. "One of the separators ate itself and I've been helping Diw rebuild it. Which is giving me a lot of practical knowledge of Glatun gravity systems. When we're done, we're going to do a rebuild of one of the drive systems. That should be particularly interesting."

"How long on rebuilding the drive system?" Tyler asked.

"About a week, according to Diw," Astro said. "Why?"

"We're just about done stripping the silica," Tyler replied. "Then we're going to have to figure out how to stabilize the orbit. Once that is done, we'll be making the VBFM for a couple of days at a guess. Or at least spinning up the silica. We'll have to leave it to cool. We're also about full of metal. I'm just going to vomit the iron into orbit for later use. We'll get it nice and stabilized. Then we'll need our full drives. We'll drop off the important metals on Earth before heading out to Connie. That is the point at which people should say if they want to stay in this tin can or go. I want to go on out to start the work on Connie. I'm just too interested not to. But nobody really *needs* to come along. I mean, Dr. Chu, no offense, but I'm pretty sure I can find a decent Indonesian to *cook*. And you're a fricking professor at MIT. Bryan and Nathan sort of need to get back to the work I actually pay them to do. Steve..."

"I'm handing in my resignation to NASA right after my report," Steve said. "If I never have to take another ride in a space shuttle or a Mir I'll be a very happy man."

"And I have done some very interesting work on particle interactions while I've been cooking," Dr. Chu said.

"I get your point," Tyler said. "You all love space. I get it. But this isn't the last trip. Dr. Chu, you're a brilliant theorist. I finally looked you up. We, sorry, need people like you learning Glatun theory so we can make our own spaceships. Steve, you need to be testing and designing those ships. Nathan..."

"I'm ready to get off this tin can," Nathan said. "I don't mind space, but I'm ready for some real air if you know what I mean."

"And you've got people you're supposed to be managing on Earth," Tyler said. "So do I. This has been a nice little idyll and, Dr. Chu, I'm glad as hell we brought you along. You not only are one damned fine cook, but you figured out the glass eye problem. But, sorry, there's going to come time to put down the rifle."

"Agreed," Dr. Chu said, spooning up some Cheng Du chicken. "But...not yet if you don't mind," he added with a grin. "I rather like the relative solitude. It is very good for thinking. Less so for doing experiments, but until I am caught up on Glatun theory I don't think they are particularly worthwhile."

"I don't mind a bit," Tyler said. "As long as you can put down the rifle at some point."

"I'll take the shuttle," Steve said. "You're right.

But I'm getting the feeling that I'm going to need a set of plants."

"Turn in your resignation," Tyler said. "As soon as you've submitted and argued your report. At least the first phase. It will still be being argued when we've created the first real space station. But as soon as you're ready, call my people. Or, hell, me. And I'll have you on a ship to Glalkod so fast it will make your head swim. I know a good plant guy there. Terrible neighborhood, but he knows what he's doing. Then maybe you can get Boeing and Lock-Mart off their butts. I need ships, damnit!"

"How about me?" Nathan asked. "You can do my job better than I can with your plants. One thing about this whole thing is I'm feeling sort of ... redundant. And, you're right, I can do this from Earth. I've seen space. It's cool. It's big. The stars are great. I want to find better asteroids to melt and I think I can do that better Earth side."

"I'll put you and Bryan off when we get back," Tyler said. "Probably over Bryan's screaming objections. We'll get you both plants. Well ... I'm going to require a contract extension since they're expensive as hell. And I can't do your job better because my plants only know to pull up the information I know. You know about minor planetary bodies. With plants you'll just be ten times the functionality."

"And what do *I* have to do to pay for them?" Dr. Chu asked.

"Do you one better," Tyler said. "Pick one or two of your more open-minded grad students who are willing to rent their souls to an evil corporation for, say, five years. I'll send all of you to Glalkod for plants *and* put you through school again. When you get back, I'll fund any research you wish to do as long as I can use you as the center of a think-tank. But I don't think we're going to be able to replicate Glatun tech any time soon. We're going to have to build based on not only Glatun theory but human imagination and practice. This is, compared to Glatun methods, a relatively low-energy, low-cost method of orbital mining. I've looked up the relative reports and done the math. If we were using Glatun techniques we'd have burned through three times as much fuel as we've used for this amount of metal. Even if you include boosting the mirrors, which I take as a capital cost. They're not going to take much maintenance."

"Speaking of which," Steve said. "What have we gotten?"

"Seventy-five hundred metric tons of iron," Nathan said. "Six hundred of nickel. Twenty-two of aluminum, of which we plan on using two to make the big mirror. Seven and a half of copper. And about two hundred kilograms of various high value metals including gold, platinum group, lots of osmium, comparatively, and silver."

"Damn," Steve said, whistling.

"It didn't actually pay for this trip," Tyler said. "But as an applied science project it was very successful. Especially given the low metal content of the asteroid. Now we have to figure out how to pay for this ship on an ongoing basis and keep *doing* it. One reason to get, frankly, the grunts up here instead of you guys is that it's time to take that step. It's time to get people off the mud ball and up in space. And this is how we're going to *pay* for it."

SEVEN

"This is going to be interesting," Dr. Foster said.

All four tugs were positioned alongside the spinning ball of nearly pure silica. There was still some admixture but it was pretty pure. Pure enough for a decent mirror.

The problem was, it was spinning very much like spinning a ball of yarn. As long as there were multiple vectors to the spin, the ball would never spin out into a plate to make the mirror. And it was going to be a *big* mirror. Even with the blown-off volatiles and extracted "other," the ball was still nineteen million cubic meters, a sphere three hundred and thirty-one meters in diameter. The resulting mirror, depending on the thickness they eventually got, was going to be about seven thousand meters in diameter and able to pump nearly one hundred billion watts of sunlight.

That all assumed they could get it down to a single vector of spin. And even then they were going to have to "push" it up to a higher speed on that vector to get the mirror to spin out. Last problem was that if they spun it too hard, it was liable to break up into a thousand spinning pieces of glass.

It was a tricky problem.

"Before we do this," Tyler said. "Is there any way we can use the array to help? I'd like to cut down on fuel costs."

A Gorku tanker had dropped by earlier in the week and tanked up the *Monkey Business*. The price tag had caused Tyler to nearly have a screaming fit. Pure He-3 cost like *crazy*. And even with the efficiency of the conversion plants, they were using a lot of He-3. Somewhere down Tyler's "space-stuff to-do" list was a refinery around Jupiter. And not *far* down the list.

"Well, not that I can think of," Dr. Foster said. "We can use the BDA to put some photon pressure on the eyeball. But it's a zero sum game. Actually, a losing game. Because we're having to recharge the BDA capacitor as it is. So the net energy is a loss."

"It's even losing heat," Dr. Bell said. "It's pretty pure silica in amorphous state. The SAPL tends to go right through it."

"Well, here we go," Dr. Foster said. "Engaging tractor on *Paws Two* and *Four*..."

"Huh," Steve said, rubbing his chin.

"'Huh' at a time like this is not a helpful comment, Astro," Tyler said. "'Huh' is right up there with 'oops.'"

"I was just thinking about the eyeball," Steve said. "It sort of looks like a gemstone."

And it did. The silica ball was an immense blob of glass with only the slightest trace of color. And most of that was from diffraction of the laser that was keeping it warmed.

"It is," Dr. Bell said. "It's the biggest damned almost quartz crystal anybody has ever seen. If we just let it cool it *would* be the biggest damned quartz crystal anybody has ever seen."

"Be fun to carve it into a skull," Tyler said with a chuckle.

"I was just thinking," Steve said. "The separators pull stuff apart practically at the atomic level then stick it back together using gravity and heat. If we just took the monatomic aluminum and a bunch of oxygen..."

"Add enough heat and you've got the biggest sapphire in the universe," Dr. Bell said excitedly. "Speaking of a really good material for mirrors."

"We'll take transparent aluminum under advisement," Tyler said. "What's the status?"

"I've attached *One* and *Three*," Dr. Foster said. "This is something that the comp has done before. Based on the results we have so far, it says the secondary rotation should be out in about an hour. You *don't* want to know how much fuel it's going to use."

"An hour is better than I'd expected," Tyler said. "I hate waiting."

"And all the secondary motion is out," Dr. Foster said. "We now have a ball spinning in a flat plane."

"More like an expanding disk," Nathan said. "It's already starting to expand."

"Hit it with the full SAPL," Tyler said. "You'll need to—"

"Run the laser over it carefully," Dr. Bell said. "Or we'll get tumbling again. Full SAPL...on."

"And that's got it," Dr. Foster said. "We're not even going to need more spin to it."

That was apparent on the view screen. With the additional thermal energy the already molten glass was becoming less viscous and quickly shifting from a blob to a very definite disk. And as the edges spread out and the rotational velocity increased, the "pull" on the glass got stronger and stronger.

"Do we have any clue if this is going to hold together?" Tyler asked. "I'm starting to worry that when the rotational momentum gets high enough it'll just pull apart."

"I'll slow it with *Two* and *Four*," Dr. Foster said. "They're in the best position."

Slowing the disk caused the center to start to flatten out but the expansion was still increasing.

"We can...shape this," Tyler said. "Like a potter shapes a pot. Use *Two* and *Four* to apply some pressors to the outside edge. See what happens. Carefully, mind you. Also we'll want to be careful with the SAPL. Both deconfliction and to not heat it too high or too low."

Over the course of the next two hours they played with the glob of glass, forming various shapes on the basic concept of a disk but never letting it get too large.

"Okay," Tyler said. "This was a good exercise but it is costing fuel like crazy. Let's just expand it. Carefully."

"Applying more SAPL," Dr. Bell said.

"Expansion rate of one meter radius per minute," Dr. Foster said. "Rotational momentum increasing... More SAPL to the center, less to the edges."

"Aye, aye, Captain!" Dr. Bell said. "Inner thirty percent only."

"Need to bring it out some more," Steve said. "You're getting a bulge along the middle section."

"Rotational velocity now two hundred kilometers per hour. We're pulling some serious G at the edges."

"More SAPL to the axis," Dr. Bell said. "And the bulge is going... going...gone...Full SAPL sweep..."

"Radius now two hundred and twenty meters," Dr. Foster said. "Rotational velocity two hundred and thirty . . . Expansion of three meters per minute. I'm getting some wobble."

"Damping it out," the computer said. "*Paws* adjusted to manage wobble."

"Cut the SAPL," Tyler said. "That's what's causing it to wobble."

"If we cut the SAPL it's going to cool," Dr. Bell said.

"Not fast," Tyler said. "It's in full sunshine. Hell, as big and thin as it's getting, solar wind may be causing some of the wobble. We need this thing *straight* or this was an exercise in futility."

"It's going to be straight," Dr. Foster said. "But I think we cut the SAPL just in time. Look at it."

The disk was now expanding at an enormous rate, getting thinner and thinner.

"Come on, baby," Dr. Bell said. "Hold together."

"Withdraw the *Paws*," Tyler said. "We don't want them perturbing the material."

"Damn," Dr. Foster said.

The center of the disk had separated and the spinning glass was rapidly turning into a shape like a spare tire.

"Damnit," Dr. Bell said. "Sorry. I probably applied too much laser."

"What now?" Dr. Foster said.

"Leave it," Tyler said, disgusted. "If we can figure out how to get out the now enormous rotation, we can melt it again and try again when we've got a better feel for doing this."

"Cut it," Steve said. "I mean, you might want to back up just in case and not be in the way if it comes apart totally. But if you cut it, it turns from a rapidly spinning disk into a less rapidly spinning cylinder. The longer it gets under *those* conditions, the *slower* it's going to spin. And it's going to be easier, less energy intensive, for the tugs to slow it."

"Just cut it?" Tyler said.

"If we can," Dr. Bell said. "It's pretty transparent."

"Never know until you try," Steve said. "Scrape the outsides first, though."

"Get off more of the impurities?" Dr. Foster said. "Good idea. Heavy metal contamination on the edges *might* have been the deciding factor in its failure. Modeling this is—"

"Hell with modeling," Tyler said. "The Right Stuff's right. We'll cut it, damp the spin, melt the sucker and start over. Next time, though, with lower rotation and more control of the expansion rate. Dr. Bell, I believe you are the SAPL man."

"We want to make sure there's complete deconfliction," Steve said. "It's going to snap open. It's possible it's cooled enough it's no longer completely amorphous. And even if it is, there's going to be enormous acceleration effects as it expands. That's where the potential energy of the spin is going to dump."

"So we don't want to be in the way," Tyler said. "Got it. Comp, get the *Paws* and the *Monkey* at least one hundred thousand clicks away. Far enough, you think?"

"Far enough," Steve said.

"We need to keep it hot," Tyler said. "Keep the SAPL on it at thirty percent power. What's its temp?"

"Fourteen twenty C," Dr. Foster said. "It peaked at two thousand."

"Keep it at least twelve hundred," Tyler said. "Fourteen is probably about right for now. Viscosity neither too high nor too low. Just right. When we're all in position, we'll cut that sucker and see what happens."

Moving the ships was a short matter. But then they figured out that they'd need the BDA array farther back as well. That was both for safety reasons and because it was going to need to follow the now rapidly spinning ring of glass, keeping the beam on one point on its surface. So the tugs were sent to pick up and reposition the mirrors. The mirrors could, technically, do that on their own. If Tyler had wanted to wait.

"Okay, comp," Tyler said. "You've got this, right?"

"To the limits of system accuracy," the computer said. "The satellite packs on the Big Distributed Array mirrors are not terribly precise. I cannot guarantee continuous power on one spot."

"And if it gets diffused the whole thing is going to tumble," Dr. Foster said.

"Like I said," Tyler said. "We'll see what happens. Computer, you have my permission to fire."

"Firing," the computer said.

The crystal ring had hardly been visible against the star background. It was optically extremely pure. When the SAPL hit it, though, it flashed into light.

"That is really pretty," Dr. Bell said. "I hope we're recording this. Because it's really pretty."

The ring was a blaze of glory for a moment as the full power of the SAPL attempted to follow its rapidly spinning path and then . . .

"Separation," the *Monkey* said.

"Whoa," Steve said. "And ouch."

The flashing ring had, indeed, separated. At a hundred different places. Shards of crystal were now flying away in every direction.

"Comp," Tyler said. "Can you track all of that?"

"Yes," the computer said. "The pieces that are large enough to be a major hazard. And there are some that we simply *should* pick up. But most of the rotational velocity was expended by material which is now in retrograde solar orbit. No great danger. Others have been kicked into higher orbit and are headed for outer system worlds or towards the VLA. The material twisted as it broke. At least one piece, one hundred meters long and four meters wide, is headed for your home world. It will arrive in . . . seventy-three years and ten days."

"Right," Tyler said. "Put the *Paws* on garbage duty. Just . . . put it back in one place as best you can. Okay, people, what have we learned here today?"

"We don't know enough about making mirrors in space," Dr. Bell said.

"We don't know enough about making big glass mirrors in space," Tyler pointed out. "We can probably make a small one. Next."

"If we're going to be doing complicated stuff, we need better tracking systems," Steve said. "On the BDA mirrors especially."

"Comp, do you have cycles available?"

"I'm not that busy tracking if that's what you mean."

"Are there better systems for the BDA available on Glalkod?"

"Yes," the *Monkey* said. "Much better."

"Add that to my next shopping list," Tyler said grumpily. "Standard satpaks for the VLA, better ones for the BDA."

"We need better mirrors, period," Dr. Foster said.

"We'll have to talk to AMTAC," Tyler said. "It's about time for their next upgrade, anyway."

"I'd say that we need better modeling," Steve said, "but the truth is a lot of this is going to be trial and error."

"I have already modeled the failure," *Monkey* said. "The primary problem was an unnoticed concentration of low-density, low-viscosity impurities that remained at the center of the silica. It was those impurities, not the basic process, which caused an unexpectedly low surface tension for its temperature. In a similar situation, with some refinement of analysis of the composition of the material, I could probably control the SAPL such that there is *not* a failure. Again, this was a new situation for me. But having seen the failure and modeled it, and spent some cycles communicating with Parva, the Gorku AI, I now have sufficient information to do the same process successfully."

"And we now have one more lesson learned," Tyler said.

"What?" Dr. Foster asked.

"We have to spend more time looking in our crystal ball."

EIGHT

"Mr. Vernon Tyler?" the guard at the gate said, surprised. He was looking at the ID but clearly didn't believe it.

"Last time I checked," Tyler said. It for some reason floored people that he often drove himself. He didn't know why, but he still found it funny. He looked at the guard's face, though, and realized that this was one who had had his humor bone surgically removed. "Yes. I am Tyler Vernon."

"You're going to have to be escorted, sir," the guard said. "If you could park in visitors' parking, please?"

It was called Phantom Works in a more or less direct rip-off of Lock-Mart's Skunk Works. Being honest, though, Boeing had had an advanced projects group around for years. One of the first such groups had invented the B-17, at the time the cutting edge of heavy bomber technology. They just didn't get the really cool name until Lockheed revealed Skunk Works.

Technically, it was distributed throughout all of Boeing's many, *many* facilities scattered around the U.S. And there were people who worked for Phantom Works at other locations. There were people who worked for Phantom Works in various university research centers. The joke was that there were people who worked for Phantom Works that didn't even *know* they worked for Phantom Works. Because, you know, it was that secret.

But most of the advanced design work was done at the main Boeing facility in St. Louis where, at this point, over three thousand engineers, scientists and various worker bees turned the future into reality.

And today was the big day. They'd finished his shuttle.

Well, they'd finished the prototype of the design structure of his shuttle. An actual shuttle was, you know, two iterations away. At most. Give or take.

Tyler parked the car and sat on the trunk until a golf cart driven by a familiar figure came through the gate.

"Astro," Tyler said, shaking the former astronaut's hand. "Good to see you again."

"Good to see you, Ty," Steve said. "Welcome to Phantom Works."

"Shhhh . . ." Tyler said. "Somebody might hear!"

"There's a sign," Steve pointed out.

"It's supposed to be Seeecret," Tyler said, getting in the golf cart.

"What goes on is secret," Steve pointed out. "So we'll have to wait until we get inside to discuss it."

"Or we can just comm it," Tyler commed.

"Our security people hate these things," Astro commed back. "Every time we go in a shield room they freak out. They take away a guy's Blackberry but you can't exactly take away an implant. It's not so bad here anymore. But every time I have to do a brief somewhere else their people have conniptions. Speaking of Connie, how's it going?"

"Like clockwork," Tyler commed. "The nice part is that we can just transfer the material straight to Gorku ships off-planet. The Horvath are, I'm told, having a fit. Especially since asteroid 6178 1986 DA turns out to be relatively high in palladium. We're getting about point two percent by weight. Which doesn't sound like much. But we're stripping ninety-six tons of base nickel iron per week. That's three hundred and eighty kilos a *week*. And that's not counting the rest of the materials. I'd say it's a gold mine but it's *better* than a gold mine. It's a palladium mine with a side of nickel, iron, copper and every damned thing else you can imagine."

"So, are you making your nut is the question?" Steve asked.

"Not really," Tyler admitted. "But that's because of the cost of the mirrors. Getting them into space is easy. We just ship most of them up in the milk run from Glalkod and they shove them out the door. We've gotten better lift and drives for the BDAs, by the way."

"Heard about that," Steve said.

"But the mirrors are still costing like crazy," Tyler commed. "I'm going up next week to see if I can do something about that."

"Going to try to spin a mirror again?" Steve commed, grinning.

"Going to try to spin *small* mirrors," Tyler said. "I want to get a system into place to manufacture the VLA mirrors. Then center all the BDA mirrors inwards to concentrate the light. Then pump it through a new mirror system we've developed called the DSA..."

"DSA?"

"Distributed Solar Array," Tyler commed, promptly.

"A DSA mirror will take up to thirty BDA pushes which, in turn, will take up to thirty of the VLA. We're shooting for twenty to one to use the DSA mirrors for fine work."

"What's it really stand for?" Steve asked.

"Damned Scary Array. Each of the mirrors has to be able to handle two and a third terawatts."

"Six months ago we were only pushing a terawatt," Steve pointed out.

"Six months ago I hadn't gotten AMTAC and the subcontractors off the stick," Tyler said. "We're producing fifteen VLAs and a BDA a *week*, now. And we've got a new system in design called the Variable Scaled Array."

"Very Scary Array?" Steve commed.

"Got it in one," Tyler commed. "VSA mirrors are designed to handle thirty terawatts per second. When we've got enough VLA and VSA we can start doing some *serious* stuff. Assuming I have *ships* to do it with."

"Which we sort of have," Steve said, pulling up at a guarded hangar. "Sort of."

"What does 'sort of' mean?" Tyler asked, getting out of the golf cart. Getting through the door to the offices attached to the hangar was harder than getting onto the base. But Tyler could tell the wheels had been greased.

"There are . . . issues," Steve said.

"What issues?" Tyler said.

"The issues that we're going to discuss in the briefing," Steve said, waving him into a secure room. "I take it you're not wearing a Blackberry?"

"Don't hold with them," Tyler said, nodding at the three people in the room. "Steve?"

"Mr. Vernon," one of the suits said, walking over rapidly to shake his hand. "I'm Brian Gnad, Vice President of Phantom Works, and I can't tell you how much we appreciate your assistance in developing Earth's first spaceship."

Gnad was forty-something with the look of former military. Probably Navy fighters, given his intense nature. Fighters, anyway. He had that cocky "I can lick the world" attitude.

"You're welcome," Vernon said. "Introductions?"

"This is Jory Eichholtz, Director of Programming for Project Three-One-Nine," Gnad said, gesturing to the other male suit.

Eichholtz was pure vanilla IT geek executive type. Late thirties, early forties. Brown hair, eyes and beard. "Big boned." He really wasn't fat, just robust. Nice taste in suits. Better than his boss. *Nice* tie. Nice. Italian silk. Tyler knew because he had one just like it and his "clothing advisor" had explained that it was Italian silk.

"Mr. Eichholtz," Tyler said.

"Mr. Tyler," Eichholtz said.

"It's Doctor, Ty," Steve said.

"If I can call you Astro, I can call him 'mister' by mistake," Tyler said. "And, sorry, Dr. Eichholtz."

"Doesn't bother me one bit," Eichholtz said.

"And this is Dr. Barbara Givens," the VP finished. "Head of our gravitics research and design team."

Dr. Givens didn't have as good a taste in suits as Dr. Eichholtz but she didn't need it. She wasn't supermodel gorgeous but she had the look of somebody who was going to hold their beauty. Mid thirties, brown hair and eyes, short hair in a simple style and seriously stacked. She looked like she worried a lot. About the safety of the world, whether she had missed the boat on her biological clock, kittens. She was *definitely* a worrier. But a stacked one.

And she also didn't look particularly thrilled to meet the famous Maple Syrup King.

"Mr. Tyler."

"Doctor."

"And I think we can get started," Gnad said. "Mr. Vernon, again, let me personally thank you, and thank you on behalf of Boeing and Phantom Works, for availing us of the technical data, not to mention the power system, obtained on Glalkod."

"You're welcome," Tyler said. "And as soon as you can get me some useable ships I'll be making Boeing even *happier* by buying them faster than you can make them."

"We do have a prototype, a test-bed really," Gnad said, smiling as enthusiastically as he could. "Which we'll be showing you in a few minutes. But we'd like to briefly discuss some of the issues which have arisen during the design phase. Dr. Asaro will start with a briefing on the power system. Dr. Asaro?"

"I've got a PowerPoint," Asaro said. "You want it?"

"Nope," Tyler said. "Not if I can avoid it. Is it good?"

"Oh, it's great," Steve said. "Marketing did a great job. Doesn't matter. We can't make power systems."

"I thought power systems were some sort of bottle that you just shot He-3 into and you got power?" Tyler said.

"Much more complicated," Steve said. "We can make the initial conversion and get the power from that. Sort of. Problem is, we're having an *impossible* time replicating their secondary particle converters. We don't understand the theory and we haven't been able to reverse engineer the system. Even when we tried to do it *exactly* like the one we've got in the ship. Which is why there's a new crater in the Mojave."

"I heard about the furor over a surface test," Tyler said. "And it was referred to as an industrial accident."

"The system puts out more power than we can control," Steve said, shrugging. "And even if we could divert it, somehow, it would overheat the ship. Maybe, maybe, when Dr. Chu gets back from Glalkod, he can help us figure out what's going wrong. But the technical stuff we're getting is making even our best theoretical people hit and bounce. On power conversion, gravitics, the whole works. And no joy with reverse engineering. Not on power."

"Well..." Tyler said. "Since I'm trading heavy metals with the Glatun, I can probably get power plants. How about gravitics?"

"Dr. Givens?" Gnad said.

"I, too, have a very well prepared PowerPoint," Dr. Givens said. "Which I may refer to later. I'm going to go over what we have found are issues and then cover what we have done successfully. But the issues are...supreme."

"Go," Tyler said.

"The first issue is power," Dr. Givens said. "There is no such thing as a free lunch. To get sufficient thrust to give a one hundred ton spacecraft a delta-V of one gravity, enough to get it out of the gravity well, requires that much power. Do you want the numbers?"

"Something like a nuclear power plant," Tyler said, nodding. "Which is why we need conversion power plants, which Steve says are a no-go for now."

"The power plant is only the start," Dr. Givens said. "I'm not in systemology but I'll mention things like, oh, power runs, transformers, relays. All packed into a ship and running more power than a super carrier for a ship the size of a frigate. You have some knowledge of our current technology in this area, I assume?"

"Electricity is French for 'don't mess with it' to me," Tyler said. "But I know you're talking about some serious problems."

"The Glatun have superconductors," Dr. Givens said. "And transformers, relays and so on. Which is why they are able to pack so much power into such small packages. The *Paws* each generate the equivalent power of all of southern California."

"Build it bigger," Tyler said.

"You reach a point of diminishing returns," Dr. Givens said. "Less space for crew, cargo, et cetera. And that is before we get to the gravitics issues."

"Which are?" Tyler said, trying not to sigh.

"Do you know what a stator bearing is?" Dr. Givens asked.

"Steve mentioned them," Tyler said, looking over at the former astronaut. "They're the bearings in the grav plates."

"Which the Glatun generate, somehow, from the gravitics generated by the grav plates," Dr. Givens said. "Grav plates work by counter-rotating particle fields. We've gotten that far in the theory. And even practice. We've produced functional grav plates."

"That's good," Tyler said.

"Which are about ten percent as efficient as Glatun plates," Dr. Givens said. "Same materials. Same dimensions. But we can't form stator bearings no matter how hard we try. Again, something fundamental is escaping us. So we had to resort to other methods."

"Not steel, I hope," Tyler said.

"The plates are more powerful the faster they rotate," Dr. Givens said. "They also apply power against each other. The best steel ball bearings will not handle the loads or the speed of even a very minor grav plate. We used magnetic bearings."

"Which are great for high speeds," Astro interjected. "And lousy for load."

"And there are very high loads," Dr. Givens said. "It is not true that the full mass of the system is loaded on the grav plates. Worse than that, it is logarithmic. At low mass there is relatively low loading. As the mass increases, the loading increases exponentially until you approach full loading. The drive plates for a ship, which are essentially a form of not particularly strong bronze, have to be able to withstand almost the full delta-V of driving the mass."

"Ouch," Tyler said, wincing. Pushing a ship at, say, ten gravities was exactly like lifting ten ships against Earth's gravity. Putting that on some plates of bronze supported by magnetic bearings . . . didn't seem like a good idea.

"With stator bearings, the loading is spread," Dr. Givens said. "Without them, it is not. We have not found a way around this impasse. We are experimenting with multiple magnetic bearings."

"Can we lift any sort of ship?" Tyler asked.

"Yes," Astro said. "We can get the ship to lift. And move around. But there's more."

"Yes," Dr. Givens said, tapping the balls of her fingers against each other. Hard. "More. And more.

You see, the last issue is very nearly a deal breaker. That is the issue of gravitic interaction."

"Hmmm?" Tyler said noncomitally. It had all seemed so straightforward.

"I personally hate this analogy but it works," Dr. Givens said. "Think of a grav plate as a wind machine. It can pull you down, it can push you up."

"Okay," Tyler said.

"Now think of multiple wind machines, all keeping you from floating away," Dr. Givens said.

"Oh," Tyler said. "You'd get...turbulence."

"Yes," Dr. Givens said, smiling slightly. "And then throw in systems to keep you from being crushed when the ship is maneuvering. More turbulence. Then throw in the drive. *Huge* turbulence. I *used* to have a head of very full hair, Mr. Vernon."

"Oh," Tyler said, wincing. "Did you...?"

"I managed to tear it free," Dr. Givens said. "At the scalp. It was, fortunately, only a small portion."

"It got pushed into a ball and not quite ignited," Astro said. "More like...compressed into pure carbon."

"I'm sorry for your pain," Tyler said, wincing again. "I'd really rather not have that happen on a ship."

"So would we," Mr. Gnad said. "The liabilities would be..."

"Astronomical?" Tyler said. "Sorry, shouldn't try to lighten the mood. So is there an answer to that?"

"Yes," Dr. Givens said. "Theoretically. Dr. Eichholtz?"

"The answer is very fine management of the grav plates," Dr. Eichholtz said. "Very fine, continuous, automated, continually feed-backed management which has a full and complete understanding of gravitic interactions."

"That sounds..." Tyler said. "I won't say impossible, because both the Glatun and the Horvath manage it. But it does sound like a lot of code. And theory. And development."

It had all seemed so simple.

"We managed to get a look at the code in the fabber you loaned us," Dr. Eichholtz said. "One thing that sprung out was that the Glatun are not, in fact, very good coders. There was a tremendous amount of junk code. Running as high as ten percent."

"Are you sure it's junk?" Tyler said. "I mean..."

"Mr. Tyler," Dr. Eichholtz said, shrugging. "I won't try to convince you. But we know code. And much of it is junk. It appears to be copies of copies with legacy and remnant code scattered throughout, much of it having nothing to do with fabber operations, per se. There are repeated code sequences in multiple strings that have no function. It's junk. I frankly don't think the Glatun *code*, per se. I think they reuse legacy codes and chop, paste and occasionally alter to fit."

"That... wouldn't surprise me," Tyler said. "But their code *works*."

"We don't have a ship code designed for this ship," Dr. Eichholtz said. "And then there is the question of how much code a fabber, with relatively simple gravitic interaction issues, has in it."

"How much?"

"Six-hundred-and-twenty-seven *billion* strands," Dr. Eichholtz said. "Much of it having to do with gravitic interaction management."

"Ouch," Tyler said.

"The F-22 flight management computer has sixteen

million by comparison," Astro said. "And it took five years to develop. And was buggy as hell even then."

"We're talking orders of magnitude," Tyler said. "And you've managed to get a ship off the ground at all? I'm impressed."

"It does not fly well," Dr. Eichholtz said, shrugging. "But it flies. Sort of."

"Astro?" Tyler said.

"I'm the test pilot," Astro said. "Because I've got plants. With the plants, and what we know about gravitics, and some intuitive seat-of-the-pants driving, I can get it up and down without breaking it. And that is what I can get it to do. Go up. Go down. Without killing myself or anybody in the hangar."

"Can you get it to fly one hundred yards?" Tyler asked, grinning.

"No," Astro said solemnly. "I tried. I got about twenty before it went into an out of control condition and crashed from about ten feet up."

"Ten feet's not bad," Tyler said, shrugging. "Better than ten thousand."

"And then two of the plates gave way and shredded the Mark One," Gnad said. "Which is why we're now on the Mark Two."

"Oh," Tyler said. "Okay. I promise not to make any more complaints about how long it's taking."

"There's more," Gnad said. "Dr. Asaro *has* shown an ability to manage the gravitics. Due to his implants."

"So get some people planted," Tyler said, shrugging. "It's more or less a requirement to drive anything in space."

"While the price in credits does not appear high," Gnad said, "given the exchange rate, getting an employee implants is extremely costly. Costly enough that it is considered out of the question by Boeing *and* the U.S. government."

"I wasn't aware that the government was involved in this project," Tyler said. "So what you're saying is you want me to pay for some pilots to get plants?"

"In . . . Yes," Gnad said. "It appears to be the only way to get this project moving again. Absent either a breakthrough in programming or a breakthrough in theory. We're . . . grounded until we can get another pilot with implants."

"You're grounded *with* a pilot with implants," Tyler said.

"We think we might be able to get two guys to sync together," Astro said, shrugging. "If we can get some characteristics and data on the grav problem we might be able to crack it. If by no other means than hacking some code from the fabber."

"We already have done that to an extent," Dr. Eichholtz said, shrugging. "I will admit we cleaned it up as much as we could."

"How many?" Tyler said. "My own off-planet credits are not unlimited."

"Three," Gnad said. "Two sets of two pilots."

"In case we lose one set," Astro said. "Those grav plates coming loose really *did* turn the thing into hamburger. I very nearly was the wet organic part."

"I'll have to consult some people," Tyler said. "It's a big expense and I'm not sure how much the IRS will let me deduct. If I took it at exchange rate . . . I wouldn't pay taxes for the rest of my *life*. If the U.S. government has gotten its camel nose under the tent, point out to them that I'm footing a big part of the bill and the bill just got huge. Er. Let's not even *talk* about the fact that I supplied the power plant. So you'd better shake some trees, and congressmen, before I go paying for implants. Agreed?"

"We'll...do what we can," Gnad said.

"If we're dependent on plants for pilots, this is a problem the government is going to have to face," Tyler said. "Which means they'll probably start trying to tax the crap out of me. While *I'm* trying to pour all my money into infrastructure that they're not working on and won't no matter how much money they get. There's a windfall profits bill in Congress aimed straight at me and the rest of the maple syrup holders. Tell your contacts that the minute it passes, I'm *out* of this project and I'll just buy my ships from the Glatun. And we humans will stay grounded until the government figures out to spend the money on stuff like this and not crap. Clear?"

"Clear," Gnad said, nodding. "If it's any help, I agree with you."

"So now that I'm all pissed off," Tyler said, smiling. "Let's sweeten me up by taking a look at the ship."

"Right this way," Steve said, leading Tyler out of the briefing room and down the hallway. "I'll warn you it won't look quite like what you expected."

"I'm not sure what I expect," Tyler said. "Flying saucer? Helot transport?"

It didn't look like he expected. It looked like...

"It looks like an SR-71 with the wings and engines missing," Tyler said, looking at the ship.

"Boeing figured that if it had to do reentry, aerodynamic was good," Steve said neutrally.

"This does not look like a test-bed for a shuttle,

Steve," Tyler said angrily. "This is a test-bed for a *space fighter!*"

"All the basic design parameters are the same," Steve said. "We're still figuring out how to make anything. Fighter, shuttle, it's all the same basic problems."

"Let me guess which department of the government paid in?" Tyler said, walking to the front of the bird. "I thought so. This thing isn't even a *ship*. It's a ship wrapped around a *gun*, Steve! I suppose Dr. Givens figured out just enough about gravitic interactions to make a grav drive, didn't she?"

"God damnit, Tyler," Steve said. "Yes, so it's a God damned fighter! And, yes, so we got money from the Air Force. And the Navy and DARPA. What we're learning from it will not only make it possible for us to build you ships, it might just save our damned lives! The Horvath haven't forgotten that stunt you pulled and you're *still* pissing them off."

"Okay, point one," Tyler said. "I invested three billion dollars in this project on the promise that Boeing would do its level best to build me a *shuttle*. Something to carry cargo from ground to orbit. How much did the U.S. government invest? A billion?"

"I don't know," Steve said, shrugging. "From what I've heard . . . less."

"So Boeing goes and stiffs me on what I asked for to help out their pals that might buy more toys from them later?" Tyler said. "Point two. All the stuff you said, right back at you. If they'd gone and given me what I asked for, they could then upscale it to a space fighter. Instead, they went for what should, arguably, be *harder*. Building their friends in the Air Force a fighter instead of their *customer*, you know, *me*, a simple damned shuttle. And then they left *you* to explain it? Did you even whisper that you had issues with that, Steve?"

"I've been doing more than whispering," Steve said. "I said you'd hit the roof and probably pull out of the project."

"And now," Tyler said, red-faced. "Now after they *stiff* me they want *me* to buy implants for pilots? For the Air Force's God damned space fighter? Oh, *hell* no. No *God* damned way! Screw Boeing and screw the Air Force and the Navy and every *other* branch of the U.S. government! This crap is just raw!"

"Is that your final answer, seriously?" Steve said.

"Yeah, Steve," Tyler said, walking to the door. "That's my final answer. This thing is a hangar queen until the U.S. government is willing to pony up the money for implants. Because I'm *out* of this project."

"And what about the Horvath?" Steve asked, quietly. "You just going to let them crater our cities whenever they feel like it?"

"Steve," Tyler said, stopped by the door because, among other things, he didn't have a pass card. "I can put at least twenty terawatts on target. From the numbers I've run, I *still* can't take down the shield on that Horvath ship. So tell me how a pissy little grav gun that is going to accelerate, what? Ninety-kilo bricks of depleted uranium? At maybe a hundred g? Is going to take out those shields. No way, no how. Even in a closing approach, you're talking about less than a megajoule."

"There are a few things we've learned," Steve said.

"You can breach their shields?" Tyler asked, turning around.

"This isn't a place to be talking about this," Steve said. "And you are definitely not cleared for that."

"Even if you can," Tyler said, shrugging. "That gun's a pop-gun. The Horvath ship is armored and fracking huge. You'd be fighting a bison with a BB gun."

"Not. Cleared."

"Then I'm Not. Involved," Tyler said. "So could you please escort me back to my car so I can go scream at lawyers? Because as I understand it some of the last payments haven't been made. And they're not *going* to be."

NINE

"How did it go?" Gnad said nervously.

"Exactly as I predicted," Steve said. "Despite my absolute best efforts to spin it properly, he hit the roof. He's out of the partnership."

"That would be . . . hard to do," the vice president said.

"No, it's not," Steve said. "All he has to do is point to the design parameters and then to the ship. Not to mention simply withhold all future support. As I stated when I came onboard this operation and saw both the contract and what you were actually *doing*. That is not a test-bed for a shuttle and that was clear from the beginning. And he made the same point that I made, which is that a shuttle would have probably been easier to do and actually what the primary partner, and primary potential customer, asked for. Boeing screwed its commercial customer, which was a huge market, to keep its military customers, which will not be a huge market, happy. Furthermore, you screwed Tyler Vernon, the guy who stared down the Horvath over maple syrup. And you screwed him on a three billion dollar deal. Even for Tyler, that's got to hurt."

"You keep saying 'you,'" Dr. Givens said.

"Which is the other part," Steve said, handing Gnad a piece of paper. "My resignation. I didn't start this abortion, I tried to stop it and I nearly got killed and just pissed off a guy I like and admire by failing to fix it. Maybe if I grovel, I can still get a job on one of the garbage scows he's going to buy from the Glatun since he can't trust Boeing. Or, by extension, any other aeronautics or military contractor. So I'm out of here. See ya."

"You have a lot of out-brief to do," Gnad said angrily.

"Funny, that," Steve said, pausing at the door. "If you get laid off, security can have you on the street in three minutes. In case you hadn't noticed, I took all my personal effects home the first day I saw that piece of junk you call a space fighter. As I said: Seeeee ya."

"And sell all my Boeing stock..." Tyler snarled as he took a corner. "I know you're not my broker. Tell my broker to call me. Every last bit...! What do you mean the SEC won't like it? The hell with the— Fine. Do the press release, then sell the stock. I bought it high, because the partnership had been announced, and I'll be selling it low, because everybody is going to bail, but what the hell. Compared to the three billion dollars I just pissed down the drain... I'll call you back, I've got another call coming in. Hello?"

"Tyler, Steve," Steve commed. "What's your twenty?"

"Getting out of this burg as fast as humanly possible," Tyler said. "And you're not high on my list of people I want to talk to right now, Steve. Maybe in a month or two. Year."

"I quit."

"Bully for you."

"As such, I no longer consider myself bound by certain nondisclosure agreements," Steve said. "Although I am still bound by USC 18. But I'd like to talk. Seriously."

Tyler consulted his plant, then just pulled over.

"Bar called O'Malley's on Fifteenth Street," Tyler said. "You got wheels?"

"I've got wheels."

"Good. You may be driving. I need a drink."

Tyler was at the bar sipping on a highball when Steve walked in. He was also smoking a cigarette, very much against city and state regulations.

"I thought smoking was illegal in bars," Steve said, sitting down. "Rum and coke."

"Sissy drink," Tyler said. "I bought the bar. Then I told everybody the smoking lamp was lit and I'd pay the fines. That's all they do, fine you. Well, if you keep it up they close you down. Just another pussy ass regulation designed to prove who's the man."

"You're really exercised," Steve said. "About which I totally agree. I know, pointed memos are not what you want to hear right now, but I knew when I signed on at Boeing what you wanted. When I saw what they'd created, I asked to see the contract. After much hemming and hawing finally I told them I'd call *you* and ask you what the contract said. And when I saw it I started pumping out memos and e-mails more or less saying that what was going to happen was..."

"Exactly what happened," Tyler said, stubbing out the Marlboro and lighting another.

"I didn't even know you smoked."

"Quit ten years ago," Tyler said, coughing at the inhale. "When my first child was born. A child I haven't seen in three months. You know what really pisses me off? What really honks my horn?"

"What?" Steve said, sipping his rum and coke. The bartender had been generous with the rum.

"The reason I haven't seen that child, whom I most dearly love, is that since this started I have been focused like a BDA beam on one thing and one thing only. You know what that is?"

"Money?" Steve asked.

"Bite your tongue," Tyler said. "Money is only ever a means to an end for anyone but a miser. Steve, I don't have a wife, I don't have a girlfriend, I never see my kids and I've forgotten what the word *vacation* means. I'm going to a fundraiser at the Smithsonian in two days and I'm having to hire an *escort* so I have a *date!* Because I've been focused like a *laser* on getting the God damned Horvath out of our skies. Period. Dot. Earth owning our *own* orbitals. Totally hold the gate? Maybe, maybe not. But I'm . . . Okay, *humanity* is going to *own* our skies. Not the damned Horvath. And those clowns go and skip right past steps two, three . . . seven? And make a damned space fighter?"

"Might want to keep it down," Steve said. "You're under USC 18 too, you know."

"Press release is going out stating *exactly* their contractual failure," Tyler said. "Already talked with my lawyer about it. He didn't like it but he doesn't like most of what I do."

"Crap," Steve said. "They are going to crucify you, you know."

"Fat chance," Tyler said. "If they crucify me, they also lose the power plant and the fabber."

"So you're letting them keep those?" Steve said.

"Yeah," Tyler said. "Two reasons. One, they might get the POS to work if the government horks up some of my tax dollars. Two, it's leverage. Decide to get stuffy about the rest of the stuff I'm going to throw at Boeing and the government and there goes that lovely fabber and the power plant. I'm going to make it clear through back channels, though, that the minute they start 'defraying their costs' by using the power plant to power the grid I'm taking it back. I can make my own money that way. And then use it for something that has a purpose."

"Ty," Steve said. "If you don't tell people your plans they can't follow along."

"They don't follow along anyway," Tyler said. "Most of them do their level best to piss in your well *just* to piss in your well. And they can *never* think big. Space fighter? Space *fighter?* That's what really pisses me off! A dinky little space fighter? They have no fracking clue how badly they just screwed up."

"Well, if you're going public they'll probably put the *Star Fury* on display," Steve said, shrugging. "War by public opinion."

"*Star Fury?*" Tyler said, laughing. "Oh, my God. What nimrod came up with that name? It just *reeks* of bad SF. Why not call it an X-wing or something?"

"I guess they figured Lucas would have issues," Steve said.

"Yeah," Tyler said. "Because *I* already talked to him. One codicil of the contract was if they had a working system *I* got to name it. So they're in violation *again!* And I told him that maybe we were going to have a small shuttle soon and if we did I wanted to name it the *Millennium Falcon*. And he geeked for a ride for him and his kids on one of the *Paws*. Don't care for his politics but he really *is* an SF geek."

"So what are your plans?" Steve asked.

"Ain't tellin'," Tyler said drunkenly. "Can't make me. Don't know if it's gonna work, and if it doesn't, that way I don't end up looking stupid."

"Makes sense," Steve said.

"I've gotta catch a plane for D.C.," Tyler said, standing up and then swaying. "Or maybe I should catch a cab instead."

"You're flying commercial?" Steve asked.

"If it's reasonably convenient I fly commercial," Tyler said, shrugging. "But right now I don't think it's going to be convenient. I'll call my plane. Fly out tomorrow."

"Let's go get some food in you," Steve said, dragging Tyler to his feet.

"I got stuff to do," Tyler said, trying to pull away. "I've gotta get some ships from the Glatun an' some pilots...Hey, wanna job?"

"Ask me when you're sober," Steve said, managing to get him to the door. "Hey, you said you're going to be in D.C. next *week*?"

"Last time I checked," Tyler said. "See ya, guys!"

"Aren't the Horvath coming around for their tribute, like, next week?"

"Not that soon," Tyler said. "When the Horvath come around, I am in an undisclosed location. I call it...the Laaaair."

"The Lair?" Steve said, laughing.

"Hey, every Evil Overlord has to have a lair," Tyler said. "I couldn't find a volcano next to a piranha pit but it's close..."

TEN

"And we have gate emergence." That was becoming common enough that it wasn't a big deal. This time, though, there was a bit higher alert level. "Emissions for a Horvath cruiser."

The colonel in charge of the Space Command CIC spun around in his chair and brought up the data. Space Command, at this point, had radar telescope data, ground-based and airborne imaging, and there was talk of a radar satellite in the works. And none of it beat a civilian system. Which was kind of annoying when you got right down to it.

"See if we can get VLA imaging."

"That's a pretty nice image," Steve said. "VLA?"

The Lair was in a mine. It was located in New Hampshire, part of the mega land grab Tyler had gone on with his first maple syrup money. During the Maple Syrup War it was one of the several mines Tyler had hidden in to escape the wrath of the Horvath.

After the war he had a road driven in, a small house built and the lower parts of the old copper mine drained and refitted as an underground command post.

With hypercom links and an engineering, administration and maintenance staff, it was as easy to run his far-flung enterprises from the Lair as from the main offices in Boston. It had a very military feel, though, because most of the gear in it was off-the-shelf command, communications, computers and intelligence gear. The facilities manager was a former colonel.

The main command center, which was where Tyler and Steve were watching the arriving Horvath ship, had a two-story wall of plasma screens, which were set to not only the view of the ship, but schematics of most of the space projects Tyler had ongoing, business channels and news services.

"Yep," Tyler said. "The Horvath really don't like the VLA but they're not sure what to do about it. It's so spread out that it's hard to hit. Now that we're working on Connie we've got stuff that gets closer to the gate. Last time they potted one of the BDA mirrors. Fortunately, Connie is well away from the gate this time. I keep waiting for them to run down the *Monkey Business* and demand all the heavy metals it's carrying. Which is why I trade them monthly to the Glatun. Ooo . . . Check this out. Colonel, taking over the upper left quad."

"Your system, sir," the retired air force officer said.

Tyler commed a command and a three-dimensional representation of the solar system came up on four of the plasma screens. On it were large red and yellow lines.

"You can rotate and zoom," Tyler said.

"The SAPL?" Steve asked.

"The same. We retrans this to Space Command so that people know where *not* to navigate. And we move it around if it seems to be endangering one of NASA's probes. Or anybody else's, obviously."

Leading from the VLA, which was marked in orange, lines in red went upwards above the plane of the ecliptic and led out to more orange areas near the orbit of Mars, then down into the plane to terminate where, presumably, the work was being done on Connie. However, there were smaller lines dotted around the inner system.

"What are those?" Steve asked, zooming in. He found he could move all the way in to icons of other asteroids, and even one comet receiving the tender attentions of the SAPL.

"We can't get the full weight of the VLA onto one spot until we get a good, functioning VSA mirror," Tyler said, shrugging. "So we're heating up other asteroids to work on later. This one . . ." Tyler said, taking over control and changing targets. "This is the glass pile from Icarus. I'm going to take another shot at turning it into a mirror. Until I have a better use for silica, that's what we're using it all for."

Steve paid some attention to the numbers and realized they were orbital and temperature data.

"It's melted," Steve said.

"We're working to get the impurities out using just the heat," Tyler said. "The silica is denser than the impurities, so they're slowly migrating to the outside since it has very little spin. Then we hit it with heavy power and burn some off, let it percolate, hit it again. It's really just an experiment to see what we can do without using any other systems. Like, you know, spacecraft of which I *still* only have *five*. But I've got a bid out on some more tugs as *Paws* for the *Monkey Business* and it turns out the Rangora make ships cheaper than the Glatun. So I may be getting one from them. Problem is, they're harder to run and convert to human use. Heavier internal gravity, higher atmosphere and, well, the crew quarters are sort of oversized."

"Nathan would approve," Steve said, grinning.

"And I may just put him in as mission commander," Tyler said. "I need people! But the fact that Boeing, a major international conglomerate, has a hard time paying for implants shows just how hard it is. Even the Rangora ship needs people with plants. There's too much involved in control to use a regular computer interface. And we're so far behind the power curve on tech that it's not like we can make them. I was hoping that we could make something in the way of ships soon. Ships that humans without plants could use, so we could make more money, so we could get more people with plants and all the other stuff we can't produce."

"Frustrated much?" Steve asked.

Tyler slewed the view around to the Horvath ship.

"Fifty years ahead of us," Tyler said. "When the first Glatun exploration ships found them they were using draft horses. The Glatun sent in a cultural advancement team and accelerated them to the point of being able to make their own ships, their own IT. Turnkey industries. Glatun university credits."

"Really?" Steve said, surprised. "They're not offering anything like that to us."

"The Glatun used to do it all the time," Tyler said. "Because it makes for good trade partners. Over time you make more money back than you spent. They stopped doing it for two reasons. One, they're spending more and more of their government budget on internal support. Read welfare. Two, not only the Horvath but the Ogut and the Ochu, all of whom the Glatun advanced, have all become strategic competitors. They don't want to also have the humans bearing down on them."

"I'd say we wouldn't but..." Steve said. "In time we might."

"I can't even get large loans," Tyler said. "Rightfully, the Glatun banks consider Earth to be in a war zone. The Glatun government would have to make security guarantees. Which they haven't. We don't have a mutual defense treaty. We don't have *any* real treaties. Their rationale is that we don't have a world government, but the truth is, the Glatun military is so stretched they couldn't support a guarantee, anyway. They had to withdraw their cruiser to go do a humanitarian mission."

"Sounds like we need a space fighter," Steve said, shrugging.

"I've got nine mirrors sitting on the ground," Tyler said. "Eight BDAs and a VSA that AMTAC *assures* me will work this time. I'm going to have to schedule a *Paw* to go pick them up. Which means it's *not* collecting metals to trade to the Glatun to pay for more ships. Which is why I'm trying to move to all space based production of VLAs. Here..."

He switched to a visual of a metal rod and Steve canted his head to the side, trying to figure out the scale.

The rod was spinning in space; he could tell by the occasional changes in reflection of sunlight. As he watched, a SAPL beam hit near the end and cut off a chunk of metal, which floated away from the rod.

More heat was applied, numbers scrolling across the screen and, as the glass from Icarus had done, the chunk of metal began to spread out into a disk.

This time there seemed to be several SAPL beams hitting it from various directions. The spin was increased and the chunk of metal quickly formed into a thin, very shiny, disk.

Tyler zoomed back and revealed that there were more than a dozen of the plates spinning through space.

"We're doing it in the shadow of the VLA," Tyler said. "The plates cool pretty quick. I've got one of the big gravity bots from the *Monkey Business* out there catching them. They're not big enough to need a *Paw*. Attach a satpak; we weld it on with a very refined BDA mirror, and I had the last two shipments just dumped off in space and they got themselves there on their own, and then they fly up to the VLA."

"That looks like you're making one about every ten minutes," Steve said, his eyes wide.

"I am," Tyler said. "And I'm trying to create another site to make a more refined system so I can make BDAs in space and only have to create the VSAs on the ground. That, by the way, is where about half my nickel from Connie is going."

"An increase of, what? Eleven thousand square meters of mirror *per day?*"

"Yep," Tyler said. "About twenty-nine million watts. Which we can't use very effectively because the VSAs are the sticking point. A single VSA mirror has to handle, get this, ninety *terawatts* of power. All being reflected by a ten-meter mirror with the main power on a patch of mirror the size of your fist. Which the first one did. For about thirty seconds."

"And then?" Steve asked.

"Very pretty explosion," Tyler said. "Very *expensive*, very pretty explosion."

"Cryogenic beryllium..."

"Which is what it was," Tyler said. "The sticking point was heat transfer. There was just too much waste heat for it to move it away from the mirror fast enough. So we have all these other mirrors, which *do* work, spreading heat instead of concentrating it. Spread heat works for some things. Not for others."

"I can see why you sort of dismissed the space fighter," Steve said. "That's...a lot of power. Six months..."

A lot of it was in planning when we made our little jaunt," Tyler said. "The Lair was under construction. The VSAs were in preliminary planning stages. Stuff like that."

"Incoming call," the mission commander said. "Aten Command Center."

"Hey, Bryan," Tyler said. "Look who's visiting."

"Hey, Steve," Bryan said. "You're a surprising face to see in the Lair."

"I'm being very gracious because I want to get back into space," Steve said. "What with my abrupt departure from Boeing, I'm pretty much persona non grata in all the usual circles."

"I'm thinking about letting him fly the *Lizard's Paw*," Tyler said.

"*Lizard's Paw?*" Steve said.

"One of the Rangora ships I'm looking at is a pretty simple lifter tug," Tyler said. "They're cheap, among other things. Its job will be to lift out of the gravity well and get stuff up to orbital. When it doesn't have a lift to do, I'm going to have the pilot start cleaning up the orbitals."

"Garbage scow," Steve said, grinning. "Got it."

"Hey, it's a rocket man job," Tyler said, smiling. "What's up, Bryan?"

"We're reaching the point of no return on chunking Connie," Bryan said.

"Time to go to phase two?" Tyler asked.

"That's my professional opinion as chief cook and bottle washer."

"Phase two?" Steve asked.

"Bryan?"

"We've been cutting chunks off of asteroid 6178 1986 DA for the last three months," Bryan said. "Then cut them up a bit more, spin process a bit and then give them the *Business*. It's been *very* profitable and I hate to give it up since Tyler put me on a bonus structure."

"Keeps your nose to the grindstone," Tyler said, grinning.

"That it does. Thing is that we're working with a really big, very cold asteroid. And we can't get enough thermal coefficient on one spot unless it sort of sticks out. Hit an area with large cubic to dump the heat and all the BDA power in the world won't do a damned thing. It just warms up the asteroid."

"Which is, in fact, phase two," Tyler said. "We're just going to warm that puppy up. It's got a multiaxial spin like Icarus."

"Heat it until it's a ball, let the metals separate, then start snake-cutting," Steve said.

"Exactly," Tyler said. "Thing is..."

"Connie's about three hundred times the mass

and half the base temperature of Icarus," Bryan said, shrugging. "It's going to take some time to warm up."

"Most of it is iron," Steve said, frowning. "What are you doing with all the iron?"

"Dumping it out of the *Business* as fast as we can," Tyler said. "It's making an asteroid of its own. Which I'm going to do something with. Someday. But for all practical purposes it's slag. There's no economic benefit to dropping it into the well and we don't have the resources to make anything really major in space. We'll do something with it. Someday."

"Too bad you can't get Connie into a single-axis rotation," Steve said.

"Technically," Tyler said. "With all four *Paws* working on it for six months we could. We're thinking about it. We'd have to be careful with the BDA beams but it's not something we *can't* do concurrently with the heating. Thing is, we're only going to use about eighty percent of the VLA to do the heating. And a bunch of it's going to be done with VLA mirrors, not BDA. All we really need for this part is getting power on target. In the meantime, we're going to be working on . . . Bryan?"

"2006 WQ29," Bryan said. "It's in the right region, it's not too big and it's got a fairly high level of useable materials. This time, though, we want to capture the volatiles. We can use them to replace losses on the *Business*. We're also planning on making a sort of . . . volatiles asteroid. Sort of a man-made comet."

"Once you've got all the gases collected in one place they just sort of sit there," Steve said. "Interesting idea."

"I want to make a habitat eventually," Tyler said,

shrugging. "But doing that is going to require two of the *Paws* working more or less full time. Which means *not* changing Connie's spin. And we can't really get that much He-3 off of Twenty-Nine. If we could get as much He-3 off Twenty-Nine as we're going to use I'd do it. Can't. Fuel is still costing me out the wazzoo."

"Not on the subject of slowing Connie," Steve said musingly. "But about Connie. You've got all that iron just sitting there, right?"

"Right," Tyler said.

"And you're just retransmitting VLA power to Connie," Steve said. "Can you use the iron as a mirror?"

"Spin it up into a big mirror?" Tyler said, looking up at Bryan. "Bryan?"

"The reflectance of pure iron is *not* all that great," Bryan said. "It would absorb a good fraction of the power as waste heat. Of course, if we made it thick, it would then dump it on the shadowed side. It's an economic question, but we might take the nickel we were getting ready to send to Earth and make *that* into a mirror. We've got several tons of it on hand on the *Business* that we were waiting for a *Paw* run to send home. That's a good chunk of change, but if we spun up a big mirror from it, we could use fewer BDAs on the warming project. More BDAs on Twenty-Nine means mining it faster. Eh . . ." He closed his eyes for a second, then nodded. "We were planning on three months to get Twenty-Nine down to essentially glass. With twenty BDAs working on Twenty-Nine we can probably cut that down to a month, then move on to the next asteroid."

"Sounds like a better long-term plan," Tyler said. "Get somebody to do the rough numbers. Go with

Plan A on phase two. It's not like we can't change horses mid-stream on it. Keep the nickel on hand until we've got the report done."

"Will do," Bryan said.

"Anything else?" Tyler said.

"Not at the moment," Bryan said. "See ya."

"That's the constant problem," Tyler said. "How much of the materials do I use for infrastructure and how much do I use for sale? And since I'm the *only* guy doing anything up here, still, I either have to sell it to the Glatun or drop it into the well. And people get really tricky if I *just* drop it."

"Two thousand tons of nickel *does* tend to make a bit of a hole," Steve said with a chuckle.

"Seriously, you want a job?" Tyler asked.

"Since you're sober," Steve said, "yes."

"Find five more good pilots," Tyler said. "They need an FAA flight license. Preferably the sort that the FAA thinks they walk on water."

"You just sort of generalize on this stuff, don't you?" Steve said.

"Yes. I'm assuming you are able to fill in the details. If you're not, I'm talking to the wrong guy. They'll go to Glalkod, get implants and get qualified to drive ships. While they're doing that—doing it right requires about three months you'll be going to the Rangora Empire to look at their stuff. With Rangora stuff, I'm going to want *new* ships. Or only slightly used, anyway. We need nine tugs and two shuttles or small freighters that can move in and out of our gravity well."

"That's a lot of ships," Steve said, blinking his eyes.

"Did you look at the board?" Tyler said. "I've got a pretty good credit balance on Glatun from trading metals. I may have to do some materials trade to get them, and I'm *definitely* going to have to find someone to lend me the money. But I should be able to swing it. I'm going to see if I can get a Rangora bank to do the loan. They've got an ... interesting relationship with the Horvath. If the ships are owned by a Rangora bank, the Horvath are going to be *extremely* loath to shoot them down. Pirate them, maybe. Destroy them, no. And even piracy is going to be a bit unlikely. So ... You up for that?"

"Gosh," Steve said, grinning. "Go to other planets, meet other civilizations? To boldly—"

"So don't go there," Tyler said. "You're going to have to take the usual food supplies, and for as long as you're going to be gone, that's a lot of food to ship. I take it you're up for it. I need a definite yes."

"Yes," Steve said.

"Good," Tyler said. "As soon as the Horvath are gone, so are you. You have about a week to find people."

"I already have the list," Steve said, then frowned. "Define interesting relationship. The Horvath and the Rangora, that is."

"If the Rangora were on our flank we'd *really* be hosed," Tyler said. "Both polities are aggressive, expansionistic and essentially Hobbesian in nature. The Rangora are that oddest of ducks, a functional military-dominated oligarchy. Think one of the South American junta countries."

"Functional?" Steve said, blinking rapidly in surprise. "I mean ... art, literature, science, industry ... They don't usually function well under a junta."

"Aliens," Tyler said. "Go figure. And it's a pretty good description for Japan pre–World War II, so we've *done* it. The Horvath are essentially a communist society. *True* communism. They don't even have an executive, just a distributed bureaucracy. Which also demonstrably doesn't work with humans. Just look at the EU. But about their relationship. They don't border each other, so they're friendly. Separate spheres of influence. The Rangora are a bigger technology trade partner with the Horvath at this point than the Glatun. Think Italy and Germany pre-World War Two. The Horvath are the Italians."

"Who are the Japanese?" Steve asked.

"The metaphor does not work perfectly," Tyler said. "But probably the Ananancauimor if we're going to extend it."

"That would make us . . ."

"Ethiopia," Tyler said. "The Horvath just haven't used gas. Yet."

"What's up with our Horvath friends?" the President asked. "I heard a report on the news that they're not acting like their usual friendly selves."

"Pretty much normal," the national security advisor said. "Shuttles go down, shuttles go up. The only difference is their orbit. They're doing a ball-of-twine orbit instead of their normal geosynchronous."

"Mapping?" the President asked.

"Possibly," the NSA said, shrugging. "We don't have any internals from the Horvath. We've asked the Glatun, who probably do, for some, but who wants to give up intelligence? Mapping doesn't really make sense, though. They can still pull from just about any commercial source, and the Russians and South Africans give them whatever they ask."

"But other than that, no change?" the President said.
"Nothing we've noted."

"The world breathed its usual sigh of relief with the uneventful departure of the Horvath tribute ship. One person who breathed a particular sigh of relief was Tyler Vernon, the Maple Syrup King, who is joining us from his aptly christened Lair in New Hampshire. Good morning, Mr. Vernon. How's the weather down there?"

Tyler had his own TV crew, thank you very much, and had set up position on the command platform of the Lair so the backdrop was the plasma screens, now all set to shots of various space projects. The shot was also from a slightly down angle so he didn't look quite so short.

"Sixty-eight and clear, Courtney," Tyler said, smiling. "How is it in New York?"

"Nice to be able to hide in an underground bunker," Courtney replied, smiling with an equal lack of honesty.

"Every evil madman has to have his lair, Courtney," Tyler said. "It goes with the orbital death ray. Which I understand is the plot of the next James Bond thriller in which the villain is short, bald and wears a goatee."

"I'm sure that has *nothing* to do with you, Mr. Vernon," the reporter said. "On the subject of the Horvath, though, they really don't like you."

"Which is why I have an underground bunker, thank you," Tyler said. "I'm pretty sure if I was out in the open they'd make a 'mistake' in their targeting. Since I don't want any innocents injured, here I am. For a communalist society with a positive lack of individuality, they sure can pick out individuals to dislike."

"From lumberjack to financier, mining conglomerate

owner and wealthiest man in the world must be challenging," Courtney said. "And now you've bought MGM studios? What are your plans there?"

"I'm pretty much of a hands-off kind of guy, Courtney," Tyler said. "MGM was, as many people and businesses are, suffering from the continued tough economy. But it's a great long-term investment, in my opinion. Most of what I'm going to be doing directly has to do with investments in their technological side. Getting more and more of their film library available for distribution through the Internet, that sort of thing. Remember, I might have been a lumberjack before I discovered the maple syrup connection, but my background is IT. I'm not going to be tinkering on the creative side so much as helping the studios get more invested in the future."

"So you're not planning on directly choosing shows or movies?" Courtney said.

"Courtney, I've got a building space-based industry, a large scale agricultural concern and inter*stellar* security issues," Tyler said. "Do I *look* like I have time to read scripts or go to sets and look over directors' shoulders? I'm far more interested in its film library. For that matter, I bought a number of movies from your own parent corporation and I'm not telling *them* how to make movies. I'm sure your friends in the movie business will be happy to know I'm not planning on making them remake *The Sands of Iwo Jima* word for word, line by line and motion by motion. I've got much bigger fish to fry. Including a new asteroid, another potential Earth killer, which we're looking forward to turning into inexpensive raw materials to help with the commodities metal shortage on Earth and get the economy turned back around."

"Well, it's been a pleasure to talk to you, Mr. Vernon."

"My pleasure as well, Courtney."

"And that's the word from the Maple Sugar King," Courtney said, smiling at the camera. "And now the orbital mining king, and if his underground lair is any indication, *our* future king. This is Courtney Courtney with CNN . . ."

"Wow," Colonel George Driver said. "She really doesn't like you."

"Nobody," Tyler said, "and I do mean *nobody* in the entertainment industry likes me. Okay, I suppose there are a few. But by and large, the MSM absolutely hates my guts. Even Fox is barely neutral."

"And was it just me or was she being pretty . . . She seemed to make *you* out as more of a threat than the *Horvath*."

"It wasn't you," Tyler said, reading a report and not looking up. "I'm what her culture, her tribe, has long seen as the bad guy. Wealthy, self-made, conservative. White. Male. I'm a more comprehensible evil—and it is viewed as *evil*—than the Horvath. Also easier to kick around because they know, deep down, that I'm not going to use the SAPL to burn the CNN building to the ground. There's a touch of Stockholm Syndrome in the whole thing, I swear. They were like that with the terrorists. In that case, they used the fact that they were a downtrodden culture as an excuse, but I'm coming to the conclusion, based on the way that they treat the Horvath, that it's some sort of automatic submission in contemporary urban liberal culture. Oh, they protest their *butts off*, but not against something, some group, that they actually view as dangerous."

"I see what you mean," Colonel Driver said. "But I don't understand it."

"I don't understand it, either," Tyler said, looking up. "Not if you mean emotionally. I can intellectualize it, but I don't *understand* it. Nor do they understand me. Or you for that matter. The difference is, I *try* to understand them. They don't even try to understand me. They see *my* motivations as being *theirs*. I'm rich because I'm greedy. I have power so I must be ambitious for domination. Control, maybe. Domination *qua* domination, no. They think, the people at MGM think, that I bought a controlling share so that I can change the creative culture at MGM and make it more in line with my personal politics."

"That's what *I* thought, for that matter," Colonel Driver said.

"Heh," Tyler replied. "I bought MGM as another experiment. And I *am* interested in changing cultures. Just not *ours*."

ELEVEN

It started, as it generally does, with front-line medical practitioners.

Dixie Ellen Pfau was twenty-seven and a fellow at the Mayo Free Clinic in Rochester, Minnesota. With green eyes and long brown hair she kept in a careful bun, she had, until becoming a fellow, been almost whipcord thin from daily runs.

Dixie's father was on permanent disability from the only job he'd ever had, working at a 3M mill after he dropped out of school. Dixie's mother worked, when she worked, in retail. Generally as a checker in grocery stores or a convenience store clerk. Dixie had two brothers and a sister, all younger. Her sister had three children already. When other fellows talked about their family she changed the subject, and she used her schedule, which for the last few years had been very full, as her excuse for not having talked to anyone in her immediate family for three years.

She had graduated, valedictorian, lettered in track, amazingly unpregnant, from Rocori Senior High School in Stearns County, MN, where the teenage

pregnancy rate was seventeen percent and the drop-
out rate was thirty percent.

Valedictorian of Rocori SHS and a 1538 SAT had
not been enough to get Dixie into a top-flight college.
It had been enough to get her a full scholarship to
University of Minnesota where she graduated, cum
laude, with a degree in microbiology. Then had come
medical school, where she still managed to run six
miles every day.

As a Mayo "fellow," however, personal fitness took
a back seat to simple survival. Mayo was a world-
class center for diagnosis. And the way they trained
in diagnostics was simple: You diagnosed for up to
thirty-six hours at a time. Since she was a junior fellow, just out of her first year of residency, she got
the "easy" stuff. Only after a fellow made her bones
working the Free Clinic did she get to work with the
interesting stuff.

On the other hand, once she completed the three-
year full course and got licensed, stamped and sealed,
she could write her ticket and maybe one day actually sleep in!

Friday was her light day. She arrived at the sprawl-
ing Mayo facility at 6 AM, changed into scrubs and
started rounds. At 9 AM she went to the free clinic
where she would work until 9 PM. Then back to the
main hospital until midnight, if she was lucky enough
to get out on time, then to her—shared—apartment.
Saturday she had duty for twenty-four hours.

And to make matters even better, since she had
completed her first year of fellowship, she now had
four brand new interns, who couldn't figure out how
to put on a Band-Aid *straight*, to train.

At the moment, though, she was doing rounds. The process was so simple she could do it, had done it, in her sleep. People who couldn't afford private general practitioners, or who thought they were dying and couldn't get in to their private practitioners, came into the Free Clinic. It wasn't exactly free, but it was close. It was, at the least, cheap.

Most of them weren't, in fact, terribly sick. Given that the medical profession was trying very hard to keep antivirals from becoming as useless as antibiotics, there wasn't much to be done with influenza. Besides, by the time people came to the clinic they were already fully symptomatic, and throwing antivirals at flu at that point was pointless.

Cuts, scrapes, flu, colds, hypochondriacs, people with minor urinary tract infections they were positive were the first signs of syphilis. That was the general run of what came through the clinic. That and people where Dixie's job was just to hold off the reaper for another day or month or year, old people who were headed down that long, greasy ramp. Half the time they just wanted somebody to tell them they weren't dying today. They generally tried to avoid Dixie if they knew the drill.

If her initial diagnosis indicated something life-threatening, she referred the person to a specialist and they were off her plate. The rest was slap a Band-Aid on, prescribe some pretty useless antibiotics and move on.

Walk to the room, take down the chart, check the information provided by nurses who, generally, had been doing this longer than Dixie, from many of whom she'd learned most of her skills, walk in, say hi, double-check the basic diagnostic information, write a treatment regimen, walk to the next examination room. Repeat again and again and again until you collapse. Start all over again the next day.

She took down the chart and glanced at it. Female, 47, Caucasian, overweight. Slight fever, otherwise normal vitals. Patient had a small lesion on the inner left wrist. No sign of injury. Area inflamed, indicating infection. No report of pain.

Dixie walked in and nodded at the woman.

"Hello," Dixie said, speaking quickly and smiling brightly. Don't let them get a word in until you have to, or women like this would talk all day. "I'm Doctor Pfau. You didn't sustain any injury?"

"No," the woman said, holding out her hand with the wrist up. "It started like a little pimple thing. I popped it but it won't heal. I think it's a spider bite..."

"Possible, but not life threatening even then," Dixie said, looking at the spot. She had a sudden moment of déjà vu and paused. Her day was filled with cuts, scrapes, lesions and every damned thing else people could do to themselves. But she had seen something very similar recently. She'd have to check the database. "Even if it is a spider bite, the problem is usually the infection rather than the toxin. I'll prescribe an antibiotic and you'll need to keep it treated until it clears up. Okay?"

"Okay," the woman said. There was always that flash of relief. They weren't going to die today. "Thank you."

"You're welcome," Dixie said, scribbling on the chart. Since she was a fellow, she did the process herself. Express and a quick swab of Betadine cleared out the slight pus in the area, and it could be covered by a medium adhesive bandage. Remarkably, there didn't seem to be any pain. An infection like that was normally at least slightly sensitive. That triggered the memory. She'd treated an *identical* lesion two days ago. Same spot, same size, same lack of pain response. Which was one of those coincidences you run across with a million sick monkeys.

"There you go. I've filled out a prescription for antibiotics and the nurse will give you a tube of antibiotic cream and some bandages. If it doesn't clear up in five days, come back in and we'll take a closer look at it. If it increases notably in size or becomes extremely painful, come in immediately." There was a slight possibility that it was the bite of a brown recluse, which could be a problem. Ditto necrotizing fasciitis. There were, in fact, three hundred and eighty-six different diseases, many of them life threatening, that it *could* be. A well-versed hypochondriac could probably list every one. None of them, however, were likely. And most would respond to the treatment.

"Thank you, Doctor," the woman said.

"Again, you're welcome," Dixie said, scribbling the treatment on the chart. "And we're done. Don't get this wrong, but I hope I don't see you again soon, and I'm sure you feel the same." She smiled to show it was a joke and walked out of the room.

Two hours later she pulled down a chart, wishing she could take a break and get a run in, and paused.

Male. 23. African-American. 5'7". 135 lbs. Slight fever, otherwise normal vitals. Small lesion on the inner left wrist. No sign of injury. Area inflamed, indicating infection. No report of pain.

Okay, three no-pain-response lesions in three days was odd. Three in exactly the *same spot*? The term "epidemic" sprang to mind and she dismissed it. The problem was... She realized she didn't know what she was dealing with anymore. There were hundreds of infections and parasites that could cause the basic symptoms. However, with the exception of the brown recluse, most of them were tropical. Or in the case of syphilis, sexual. And although a few of them were location specific, syphilis again for example, none of those were the underside of the left wrist. She checked again. Yeah, it was the left.

She walked into the room slowly.

"Hello," Dixie said, just as carefully. "I'm Doctor Pfau. You didn't sustain any injury that might account for this infection?"

Dixie walked out into the waiting room and looked around. As usual, it was packed.

"Hello!" she said loudly to cut through the chatter, arguments and screaming children. "My name is Doctor Pfau and I would like your attention! Thank you. How many people are here because they have a small sore on the inside of their left wrist, and could you raise your hand so I can see it?"

Seven people, some of them clearly surprised, raised their left hands.

"Thank you. We'll be seeing all of you very sh—"

"Doctor," one of the nurses said, walking up and speaking quietly. "We need you in Six."

Dixie nodded at the crowd and walked back into the hallway quickly.

"Fever of one-oh-five," the nurse said. "Labored breathing. Slight incoherency. Complaining of bodily aches."

Dixie pulled down the chart and looked at it as she walked into the room. Low blood pressure for a guy his age and physical condition. He looked like he was "residence disadvantaged," and they were normally high BP. Heart rate was right off the chart.

"I need an IV run," Dixie said the moment she looked at the patient. What the nurse had left out was yellowed eyes and skin. The guy was probably in the terminal stages of hepatitis. "Get a cart in here. We're admitting him. Sir, do you have any history of hepatitis?" She gloved and pulled out a syringe to get a blood sample.

"No," the homeless man said. "I been strong as a horse my whole life, Doctor. This is the first time I ever been sick. You saying I need to go to the hospital?"

"You're in the hospital," Dixie said. "What I'm saying is you need to stay so we can get you fixed up. You're clearly extremely sick." She wrapped his arm and pulled the cap off the syringe.

"You gonna take my blood?" the man asked thickly.

"I need to get a blood sample so we can figure out exactly what is wrong with you," Dixie said.

"I don . . ." the man said and his arm came up. It seemed less like a block of the syringe than an involuntary twitch, but it had the effect of sending the syringe across the room. "I . . . AAAAAAHHH!" As his arm barely missed her face she automatically noted . . . a small lesion on the inside of the left wrist.

"Sir," Dixie said, grabbing his arm and trying to restrain it. "You need to calm down, sir—"

"IT HURTS!" the man screamed. He started scrabbling at his jacket, scratching as if he was trying to scratch inside his body. "OH GOD!"

Dixie yanked the door open. "I need some *help* in here! Where's that IV?"

Nurses came flooding into the room as the man started to convulse, still screaming. He seemed to scream so hard it should have ripped his throat right out. Before they could even get the IV inserted or a shot of Dilaudid in him, the thrashing stopped and the man dropped limp.

"Code Blue!" Dixie shouted, feeling for a pulse at the carotid. "I need a crash cart!"

"ER pronounced him DOA." Dr. Benjamin Koch was the free clinic attending hospitalist. He had the job of not only ministering to patients but also keeping an eye on the various interns and residents who did most of the grunt work. "What happened?"

"I've been thinking about that," Dixie said. She knew her nickname was "The Grinder." New interns, visitors who were informed of it, new employees, all thought it referred to some super-sexual ability. They quickly found out it meant that she ground through anything or anyone in her way like an industrial machine. Her other nickname was "The Robot." She didn't feel particularly machinelike at the moment. "None of the symptoms make sense. Convulsions, tetany. But you don't get yellowing of the eyes and skin. That indicates liver."

"Could have been a combination," Dr. Koch said, shrugging. "From what I've gleaned he was . . . residence disadvantaged?"

"He was a bum, yeah," Dixie said. "But he said he'd never been sick in his life. And for all he was sick, you can tell the sickly ones. He looked otherwise fairly healthy for a bum. But we've got another problem that's more important."

"Which is?" Dr. Koch asked.

"We've got a large number of patients with identical symptoms," Dixie said. "At least seven. A lesion on the inside of the left wrist. No pain response. For that matter . . . our DOA had one."

"*All* on the left wrist?" the attending said. "That's . . . odd."

"Identical," Dixie said, holding out her wrist to show him. She paused. "Oh . . . hell."

There was what looked like a pimple on her left wrist.

"I think . . . we'd better call the CDC," Dixie said. "I'll page the epidemiologist."

"I need you to hold your arm very, very *still* for me, okay?"

Dr. Doug "Jojo" Johannsen was the chief epidemiologist of the Mayo Clinic. He'd spent years working around the world for the WHO and CDC, tracking down emerging diseases and potential pestilences. And he'd seen his fair share of odd maladies. But this was one of the few he'd ever seen that were location specific. Even then, most such things were location specific for a particular reason. They were affecting lymph nodes, for example. They weren't specific to a more or less random spot on the body. And he assuredly hadn't expected for them to turn up in the U.S.

For that matter, as soon as he'd seen the number of cases being reported in not only the clinic but also the ER and even among workers at the hospital, he'd called the CDC to report a potential outbreak. Only to find the main line, which had fourteen people manning it normally, busy. So he'd called three colleagues he knew personally. All of their office phones were busy. So then he'd called their cell phones. Busy.

So he'd spent three more minutes making overseas phone calls to colleagues associated with the WHO. All of *their* phones were busy.

At that point, he'd sent out a standard e-mail, put down the phone and gotten to work.

"No problem," Dixie said. The pimple had already popped. "There's no pain."

"Which is why I'm thinking parasite," Dr. Johannson said, bringing the camera for the microscope down. "There's definitely a suite of bacteria there, but I don't think that's the central problem."

"What I'd like to figure out is how I got a parasite," Dixie said. "I guess it *could* have been from that first patient."

"Hmmm..." Dr. Johannson said. "Fascinating."

"Going to leave me in limbo?" Dixie asked.

Dr. Johannson swung the monitor around so she could look. At the very bottom of the small sore was what appeared to be something like a centipede.

"And that is...?" Dixie asked. She had seen and done some very gross things as a med student but this was something gross happening to *her* body.

"*That* is a nematode," Dr. Johannson said, swinging the monitor back around. "Which appears to be feasting on the bacteria colony in the lesion. I don't recognize the particular species but there are experts who might. Presumably it carries some of the bacteria with it. It does gross damage to the affected tissue, the bacteria then have a residence, and it then feasts upon the bacteria. I've seen this before but rarely in the U.S. Similar infestations in tropical regions. Primarily in New Guinea. Now hold very, *very* still."

He took a pair of fine tweezers and pulled the worm out of the wound.

"There," he said in a satisfied tone, placing the nematode in a jar and sealing it. "I'll send that to some friends and they can identify the species."

"So it *is* a zebra," Dixie said. Quite often, new interns would look at a set of symptoms and identify them as some rare disease found only in remote areas when they were looking at a simple combination of fairly normal problems. Identification of a rare disease instead of common was referred to as "spotting a zebra." It was generally a mistake. "What's it doing in this country? What's it doing in *me*? I was meticulous in my hygiene procedures with Patient Zero."

"That is the question," Dr. Johannsen said. "Which is up to the CDC and WHO to determine. But the treatment is simple. Disinfect the area and maintain integrity. There may be a recurrence. The nematode may leave cysts which will make it necessary to continue treatment for up to two weeks. Any strong disinfectant should kill it, though, and usually kills the cysts. And any antibiotic will kill the bacteria. Keep enough Neosporin on the wound, for that matter, and the nematode should die of malnutrition."

"So disinfect and bandage was the right choice," Dixie said, relieved.

"But it will have to be maintained," Jojo said. "That will be the problem, I suspect. It certainly is in places where this is more common. And it's not normally..." He paused as his pager went off. "I'm sorry, I'm getting a page from the morgue. I take it you can clean it yourself."

"I can," Dixie said. "But can I come al—" Her pager went off and she looked at it. "I'm getting paged there, too."

"How's the wrist?" Dr. Koch asked, stopping them both outside the morgue.

"I cleaned it on the way down," Dixie said, showing him the bandage. "What's up?"

"It's your DOA," Dr. Koch said, his face grim. "The morgue called a contamination. You eaten lately?"

"No," Dixie said.

"Good. You won't puke in your respirator. We need to rig up."

Dixie wasn't even sure she was looking at the same patient. Same height, same hair color from what she could remember. A sort of dirty dishwater gray-brown.

His clothing had been removed at some point, and she had had her usual tour of the morgue so seeing a body on the slab wasn't the problem. The problem was the condition of the body.

"We didn't even have time to put him on ice," the pathologist said, examining the pustules covering the man's body with a simple magnifying glass. He was wearing a full body cover, mask and respirator like the rest of them. "He just started popping up these lesions all over his body. When we saw that, we called a bio alert."

"Can I see that?" Dr. Johannsen said.

"Hmmm..." The pathologist handed over the glass.

Dr. Johannsen leaned into the body so that his mask was almost in contact, then leaned back.

"Oh...damn."

"Nematodes?" Dixie asked, her stomach sinking.

"Yes," Dr. Johannsen said. "Nematodes."

"Congratulations, Jojo. You were the first person to identify. At least, you were the first to get an e-mail through. Chuck at Johns Hopkins was fifteen minutes later. And the WHO hasn't reported anyone yet. Since this may be a new pathology, you probably get to name it."

"I'll take that," Jojo said. "Anyone have any idea what we're dealing with?"

"No." Dr. Leona Cline was Director of the National Center for Preparedness, Detection and Control of Infectious Diseases at the CDC. She'd gotten into epidemiology when it was still considered a "man's" field. Being black and female were benefits in any government position, but it wasn't why she'd gotten to her current job. That had been sheer will and brains of steel. "We're still working on disease progress, but you're not the first facility to report a death. The nematode apparently stays in the wound, more or less quiescent, for a period we're still trying to pin down. At a certain point it submerges into the bloodstream and starts to spread. Again, acting essentially benign. The spread causes a sharp fever spike but not much else. Then it goes to a third stage where they begin attacking the body widely and the patient terminates rather quickly. If you don't stop it when it's in the initial presentation, it's pretty much the whole shooting match."

"I'm trying and failing to come up with a disease that acts in that manner," Dr. Johannsen said thoughtfully. "Chagras is the closest that immediately comes to mind."

"You're not the only one," Leona said, smiling thinly. "Pretty much everybody is scratching their heads. The general conclusion is a tailored system."

"I can see that," Jojo said. "Theoretically. I don't know of any laboratory that could produce such a species."

"Again, general conclusion," the CDC agent said. "Also that it's not a natural spread. We got slammed by reports starting this morning. Everyone has their own patient zero with no commonalities."

"That is . . . very ungood," Jojo said.

"We've called a wildfire," Leona replied, referring to a mass infection event. "USAMRIID has to call a bio attack. But that's our gut. There's a flip side, though. Which is really what's putting the hold on calling it as an attack."

"Which is?"

"Nothing about it makes sense," Dr. Cline said. "Patients with the lesion who have been treated show little or no signs of continued infection. It looks like, and I'm going a bit out on a limb here, if you just treat it, it goes away. And the treatment is . . ."

"Most people with it probably aren't even reporting it," Dr. Johannsen said. "Most people are just going to pour some peroxide on it and put on a Band-Aid."

"And even *that* will kill the nematode," Dr. Cline said, nodding.

"So it's absolutely deadly if untreated but treatment is simple?" Dr. Johannsen said.

❋   ❋   ❋

"That's insane," the President said. "What kind of a biological attack is *that*?"

"That's the problem, Mr. President," the head of USAMRIID said. "It's why we're having a hard time calling this an attack. And it's so dispersed . . . we can't even figure out the infection method. It's showing up . . . well, *everywhere*. All over the world and certainly across the U.S. At more or less the same time. Our models are kicking that out as invalid information."

"You guys need to quit looking in microscopes so much," the Marine commandant said.

"Your point, General?" the President said, trying not to snarl.

"Just look at the information we've got, Mr. President," the commandant said. "A plague which is not only a new species, but acting in a way that our best experts cannot figure out how it does it. Which has apparently been spread all around the world, more or less at once." He paused and looked around. The only one nodding was the head of SpaceCom, which was slowly migrating to being a member of the JCS.

"Horvath," the admiral said, nodding. "They did that ball and twine orbit. They passed over every major landmass . . ."

"Oh . . ." The general in charge of USAMRIID winced. "Then . . . we can't be sure of *anything*."

"Don't doubt yourself," the commandant barked. "You're saying that if you treat this thing, there's no sign of more of these toad things?"

"Not . . . apparently," the microbiologist said. "Nematode, General."

"Whatever," the commandant said, sitting back and nodding. "Kind of weird, but it makes sense in a way."

"General," the President said. "If you could perhaps make it clear to those of us who are still . . . catching up?"

"Yes, sir," the commandant said. "If it works like the brigadier said, sir, then it's a separator."

"Separator?" the Chairman asked, shaking his head. "What the hell are you—"

"Separate the sheep from the goats, General," the commandant said. "If you treat it, you live. If you don't, if you're just so . . . If you don't have good personal hygiene, or access to medicine I guess—"

"*Alcohol* will kill it," USAMRIID said. "Peroxide will kill it. Putting any antiseptic on the wound will kill the bacteria and starve it."

"If you just aren't worth . . ." the commandant said and paused again. "People with any *sense* will treat it. They live."

"Why would the Horvath do that?" the President asked.

"Aliens, sir," the commandant said, shrugging. "But it looks to me like that's what's going on. Question to keep in mind, is this the *only* bug they spread?"

"Oh," the Chairman said. "What a sweetly good thought, Commandant. Thank you so much."

"Yer welcome," the commandant said, his arms crossed. "Not my job to blow smoke, General." He paused in thought for a moment, then shrugged his shoulders again.

"The Horvath are monolithic, communalist and Hobbesian," the commandant said. "They also are eugenic Darwinists. They weed their own population aggressively for what they perceive as defects. If they *did* spread other biologicals we'd better be ready for them to be as eugenic in nature. Looks to me as if this was a test of personal hygiene. Of personal care?"

"More than that," the chief of Naval Operations said, thoughtfully.

"How?" the President asked.

"The . . . *nema*tode can be killed with any number of antiseptics, correct, Brigadier?"

"Yes, sir."

"But . . . if you use alcohol, for example, what is the effect on the patient?"

"High levels of pain, sir," the brigadier said, nodding. "It's painless if you leave it alone. It's not even particularly painful to treat if you have the right materials. Field expedient treatment will be painful."

"You also need to have access to that information," the admiral pointed out.

"So we need to do a broadcast," the President said. "Fast. Blanca, get a press release out as fast as possible. Do *not* mention the Horvath."

"Yes, Mr. President," the White House spokesperson said.

"Do that now," the President said. "Consult with CDC and USAMRIID. But get it out *fast*. Within the hour. Emergency broadcast regulations. We need to get people treating this themselves. Or our medical facilities will be overrun."

"Yes, Mr. President," Blanca said, getting up and walking out.

"I may be extending this . . ." the CNO said musingly. "But the first people to get treated, or to treat themselves by buying the appropriate materials, will get the materials that work and are painless. Those are going to be rapidly depleted. If everyone rushes to their local drug store and buys—"

"Betadine is the best choice," the brigadier said. "There are also generic versions. Next would be peroxide. Works most of the time but requires reapplication since it doesn't always kill the parasite, just the bacteria culture. After that . . . you get to more painful measures."

"So the people that either have stocks or react quickly and effectively get the easy way," the commandant said. "The rest have to suffer. If they're not willing to, they die. If they don't listen, they die. If they don't have access to the information and aren't interested in a little sore—"

"They die," the President said.

"We're going to have a very significant die-off from this no matter what we do," USAMRIID said. "We're already seeing it. Mostly . . . I need to get unPC here, Mr. President."

"Go ahead," the President said.

"The majority of the casualties, so far, have been among the lower socioeconomic class," the brigadier said. "Minorities. Followed by elderly. And many of the victims, unfortunately, have been children. Especially the lower socio-economic groups."

"Their parents don't care," the commandant said, his face hard. "Wish it had been something that just yanks a kid out of an environment like that rather than kills them. Horvath . . ." His jaw worked as he clearly refrained from saying something.

"I agree," the President said, his own face hard. "What about the military?"

"We've been seeing it turning up in our own medical

side," the CJCS said. "We're going to distribute a FLASH order through channels immediately after this, Mr. President. Most of that can be taken care of at the unit levels. We should be able to manage this fairly effectively."

"We need to make sure everybody knows it's *not* a hard-core issue," the commandant said. "There's probably twenty percent of those dumb bastards going 'Hey, it's just a little sore. I'm not going to be a sissy and go on sick call.' We're probably going to lose some hardcores over it. Especially forward deployed units. SEALs and Recon running around in the hills just aren't going to *notice* it." He paused and looked at his wrist. "Case in point," he finished, holding up his wrist. "Wasn't there this morning."

The President slowly pulled down his shirt sleeve and then looked up.

"Do we have any Betadine in the house?"

"Son of a *bitch*," Tyler swore, quietly. "Doc, do we have any Betadine?"

"Yes, sir," Dr. Laura Tobias said. Laura, despite a career as a flight surgeon and a diving medical officer, had jumped at the chance to take a job for low pay and not much prestige on the *Monkey Business*.

She wasn't actually being paid low, but she probably could have made more as a specialist on Earth. Didn't matter. Like most of the crew, she was crazy for space.

Tyler had quickly solved the problem of finding crew for space operations. He simply contacted various people in fandom. That didn't mean that most fans were suited for space operations and given that he only had forty personnel on the *Monkey Business* everyone who was suited couldn't get a slot. But he sure didn't have to go looking for people. They were queuing up.

"We've got plenty of Betadine," Laura continued. "But the only person who's been on Earth since this started was *you*, sir. So if there's contamination..."

"I've got plants," Tyler said, his brow furrowing. "According to my research, I should be immune to practically anything. Sort of..." He paused and thought about it. "Unless it really *is* a new organism. Then the hypernet has to get updated with the information."

"Say again?" Nathan said. He'd come up with Tyler less to oversee the shift to mining Twenty-Nine than because he could catch a ride.

"We're getting to the point, and the Glatun are long past the point, of Junior's Home RNA kit," Tyler said.

"Junior's *what*?" Dr. Tobias asked, laughing. "What is *that*?"

"When any script kiddy can write a biological virus," Tyler said, his face blank.

"Oh," Laura said. "That's less funny."

"Much," Tyler said. "We've gotten to the point where we can tailor viruses to go after particular DNA sequences. We can make a virus that makes most people sick but only *kills* one selected person. Or one race, because there *are* genetic differences."

"I don't think a... script kiddy could modify a nematode," Dr. Tobias said. "Much harder than a virus. And this one is just... weird."

"Didn't say it was a human," Tyler said. "Spread is all wrong. Sorry, I'm looking at information as we're talking and it's definitely Horvath. Point is that the Glatun already have to deal with this sort of thing. Not a lot, but they do have to deal. It's like computer viruses."

"Lost me again," Laura said.

"Lost me a long time ago," Nathan said.

"If anyone can write a pestilence, how do you fight it?" Tyler said. "Like a computer virus. Part of the implants are nannites that work with your immune system. They carry the basic data for every known hostile microorganism and update your... B cells, Doctor?"

"Probably," Dr. Tobias said, interested. "You're kidding?"

"Nope," Tyler said. "Triple redundancy on all the... I guess you'd call it legacy stuff. Black Plague. Smallpox. Measles. Yellow fever. The sort of stuff you get vaccinated for if you're travelling. There are at least three nannites, out of billions, mind you, in your body that have data on those. They update the B cells as they go through. Check to see you have the antibodies ready and go on. Also for stuff like cancer, by the way. The system preprograms your immune system to scrub for cancer cells. But that hardly fills up the mass of nannites. The rest are filled by update. I don't know when it happens, but when I'm around a hypernet my nannites get updated with the latest virus to affect humans. I guess this stuff, if it's on the net, by now. I'm not even sure who does the updating or if new stuff is covered for humans. But I'd bet nine to one that I'm immune."

"It sounds like the whole planet needs that," Dr. Tobias said.

"Sure would be nice," Tyler said, then paused. "It might be possible but it would drive people nuts."

"Why?" Dr. Tobias asked.

"Most nannites are limited by numerics," Tyler said. "You have to have a license for them and the license spells out how many you can make. I looked this stuff up 'cause I was interested. Anyway, the exception is medical nannites that can only survive in tissue and have their own internal limitations. The nannites will only build a certain number in any single organism. They survive and replicate on your blood. Calling them nannites is sort of wrong. They're really biologicals with some nannitelike features. But my blood, the blood of any person with plants, should serve as a vaccine. To just about everything but especially to this stuff. If it's even in the database."

"How do we find out?" Dr. Tobias asked.

"I have no fracking clue," Tyler said. "I never have really dealt with Glatun medical. I know who to call, though."

"Cori's Plants and Cybers! It only costs an arm and a leg!"

"Cori, it's Tyler Vernon," Tyler said.

"Hey, Tyler!" Cori buzzed. "Good to hear from you! Thanks for all the business! Like the new slogan?"

"Very nice, Cori," Tyler said. "I need to speak to Louisa, please."

"What, I'm not good enough?" Cori said. "Some friend."

"Cori, we've got a plague," Tyler replied. "You really want to be involved?"

"Hell no!" Cori said. "Louisa! Phone."

"I heard, Tyler," Louisa said. "The medical AI network monitors all hypernet transmissions for word of biologicals."

"Will the Glatun help?" Tyler asked.

"It is more or less one of those conditions where it is assured," Louisa said. "But support has to be requested."

"They haven't asked?" Tyler said.

"Not so far," Louisa said.

"Is the organism identified by the update net?" Tyler said. "I mean, if you've got plants does it get... Do you know what I'm saying?"

"Yes," Louisa said. "All six organisms have been identified and updated."

"*Six*?" Tyler screamed.

"Yes," Louisa said. "Your pilots were infected when they came through. The organisms were neutralized and updates created. I didn't mention it to them because there was little or nothing they could do. You are updated, as is anyone with the appropriate nannites in range of a hypernode on your planet. Everyone else is at risk. That is not quite precise. All of the organisms are tailored for specific tasks. The nematode is designed to sort for persons who are lazy or sloppy. One might go so far as to say stupid. Despite current reports, it will require multiple treatments over the course of a month. With those treatments, however, it is survivable. Anyone infected, which is by our estimate eighty-seven percent of the human race, has to maintain the treatment or get the Galactic level of treatment to entirely remove the nematode and all released cysts. It is the only one, however, that is treatable by human technology.

"Following the nematode attack there are five viruses. Four strike more or less simultaneously, the fifth strikes last. All of the viruses are aerosol vectors as well as blood pathogens. All of the viruses have a long infectious period followed by a rapid terminal phase. They're fairly merciful, actually. The nematode attack is the most painful and the pain period is mercifully brief.

"There is a virus loaded to eliminate a host of genetic disorders including color blindness. Then one that attacks anyone with a reduced immune system. One that eliminates anyone with a genetic propensity for cancer or several autoimmune disorders such as lupus. Then one that attacks several teratogenic conditions. Those will attack simultaneously and, based on probable infection period, quite soon. Which are all very much overkill because the last one kills anyone who does *not* have a gene for blond hair. I'm not sure what the purpose of that is. But it will eliminate ninety percent of your world population. It does, however, strike last, so you have some time. It will initiate in between ten and fifteen days depending upon method of transmission. The others will be entering the initiation phase soon if they have not already."

"Holy God," Dr. Tobias said. "Blonds? What the hell do the Horvath have for *blonds*?" The doctor was a completely natural brunette.

"There is no definitive proof that this was a Horvath attack," Louisa said. "The organisms were crafted using Glatun equipment, but that is the same equipment the Horvath use. And the Rangora. The specific codes that would have identified the machine that produced them have been erased."

"That's to think about later," Tyler said. "Louisa, the World Health Organization is a unified planetary body. Surely you can work through them?"

"It has to be requested," Louisa said. "There are species that are so... rejective that they do not ask for help to the point of termination."

"We'll get someone to ask for help," Tyler said. "*Please* be ready to respond. Call you back." He paused and frowned. "Damnit. I don't know anyone in that part of the government."

"I'll send you a number," Louisa said.

"... still trying to find out if there are any additional..." Leona said then looked at her phone. There had been a distinct "click" as if Dr. Qau, current head of the World Health Organization, had hung up. "Hello? Hello?"

"Dr. Cline, this is Tyler Vernon," Tyler said. "Just listen for a second and don't hang up or talk. There are *six* pathogens, not one. I'm sending you a download, it's actually on your computer, giving an outline. The Glatun can stop this in its tracks but they need the head of the WHO to contact them and request help. And he'd better do it right now because four more are about to go into terminal phase. We have about three days to stop this or we're going to have a mass die-off. I'm done. You talk."

"How mass?" Leona said. "And where's the file?"

"Opening it now," Tyler said.

"Nice being able to own someone else's computer," Leona said, scanning the document. "This is fairly open-ended. What's the source?"

"My pilots I sent to Glalkod were infected," Tyler said. "And they're monitoring our systems. The Glatun medical AIs probably have a better handle on this than *you*."

"Is this Horvath?" Dr. Cline asked. "And...blonds? Why *blonds*? That will kill off..."

"Most of the human race," Tyler said. "Most of the U.S., obviously. All of Africa, China...And we're still trying to figure that out. It doesn't really matter, though. All that matters is getting it stopped."

"Last question," Dr. Cline said. "Why me?"

"I dunno," Tyler said. "One of the Glatun medical AIs gave me your number."

"Nice to be famous," Dr. Cline said dryly.

"Not...really."

"This is Courtney Courtney with CNN and I'm here at the LFD Corporate Headquarters where a protest is heating up. Excuse me, sir, what are you protesting?"

"The Vernon Worms!" the man screamed at the camera. In his twenties with scraggly long hair and a ratty beard, he was waving a sign that said "End the Oppression of LFD!" *"This is all the fault of that bastard Tyler Vernon!"*

"Why do you say that?" Courtney asked.

"The Horvath would just leave us alone if it wasn't for Vernon!"

"Yeah!" The speaker was a female version of the first speaker with the exception of the beard. Wearing a T-shirt that was out of date in 1970 and waving another placard with the motto "Peace Now!" she clearly knew what she wanted out of life. *"The only reason the Horvath have poisoned us is Tyler Vernon! Vernon Has To Go! Vernon Has To Go!"*

"Vernon Has To Go!" the guy started chanting in time. Soon the whole crowd was chanting.

"And there you have it," Courtney said. *"There's*

*a lot of anger being directed at Tyler Vernon, Susi.
These people think Tyler Vernon has to go."*

"Interesting report, Courtney..."

"Go *where* exactly?" Tyler asked. "Jupiter? Uranus?"

It had been three days since he'd contacted Louisa,
and Glatun medical ships had already arrived. They
were able to convert nannites for the viruses quickly,
but there were six *billion* people on the planet and
not all of them were easy to contact. For that matter,
there were some governments that were resisting the
distribution, notably Bhutan and Myanmar—except
for their junta and military, in the latter case. Then
there were areas with poor security or failed states,
the usual sorts of "leave it with us and we'll distribute
to the right people" countries like China, and even
in the U.S., people who weren't going to take that
"alien devil medicine." The Glatun were willing and
able to drop a shuttle anywhere they were welcome.
And could be sure they wouldn't take a MANPAD.

But there were six *billion* people on the planet.
Getting ninety-nine percent of those before the Brunet
Killer kicked in would be great. That would mean
only sixty million people dead. The CDC had one
server doing nothing but crunching mortality reports
on Johannsen's Syndrome, and that already passed sixty
thousand dead. And it was now having to separate
for the "preexisting condition" viruses. That was how
the CDC referred to them. "Preexisting conditions."

"So... the Horvath nuked Cairo, Shanghai and
Mexico City because of you?" Driver said. They were
watching the news from a side office off the main
command bunker. Tyler had decided it was a good
idea to head back to Earth, mostly to make sure Petra

and the girls got their shots. He was starting to think that wasn't the best move.

"There hasn't been a reference in the mainstream media in which the Horvath and the orbital strikes were mentioned together in three years," Tyler said. "In fact, there have been no references to the orbital strikes except in passing. They've been wiped off the radar by the Western press. Unmentionable. Those countries still mention them, but even then they don't mention the Horvath in the same paragraph or sentence."

"I'm starting to see what you mean by Stockholm Syndrome," the command center manager said, "The police that want to rescue you are the problem, not the terrorists holding you hostage."

"Bingo," Tyler said lightly. Then he grunted.

"What?"

"An insight," Tyler said, pulling up a picture on one of the screens.

"Who's that?" Driver asked. The picture was of a heavy-set, "German"-looking middle-aged male in a very expensive suit.

"Kurt Van Guter," Tyler said. "He's the lead negotiator with the Horvath in South Africa. And..." Tyler said, bringing up another picture. This man was thinner and harder looking with high Slavic cheekbones. "Anton Aleksandrov. Head of Interstellar Negotiations for Angara Artel. And..." The last picture was of Courtney Courtney from CNN.

"Blond," Driver said. "Blond. Blonde."

"And, of course, then there's..." Tyler put up his own picture.

"Brunet."

"I just damned the whole human race by my hair color," Tyler said. "The Horvath probably have a really hard time telling us apart. But the color of our hair is pretty noticeable."

"Okay, now that's where I have to draw the line," Driver said. "Time for me to drag out the pin."

"What pin?" Tyler asked, confused.

"The pin for your head, sir," the center manager said. "Maybe the Horvath chose the whole blond thing because of who they had good relations with. I'm not sure whether to include the media in that or not, while seeing your point. But I doubt they targeted the rest of the *world*—China, India, Africa... surely they can tell *skin* color differences—because of Tyler Vernon. That is sort of reverse arrogance of an *amazing* degree, if you don't mind my saying so, sir."

"Advanced but unsophisticated," Tyler said musingly. "Oh, I take your point, Colonel. And I'll accept that that was my inner Evil Overlord coming out. But it was a very unsophisticated attack. They may deal with an Afrikaner but the actual mining is done by what I'm sure Mr. Van Guter would call 'bleks.' The generally accepted rationale given for them not previously trying to wipe out the human race and just occupy the planet was that it was easier to just exact tribute from us. And keeping the rest of the world more or less functional kept the mines working better. They've clearly changed strategy."

"Which means we don't have any choice at this point," the former colonel said. "We're going to have to fight."

"With *what*?" Tyler asked, leaning back and interlocking his fingers behind his head.

The colonel gave him a long and meaningful look.

"It won't focus enough," Tyler said. "You *know* that. Ninety terawatts on a space the size of my palm and we *might* breach their shields. Every mirror we've tried has turned into space confetti. Collimators, since we're *not* dealing with a laser, spread and *weaken* the beam. And generally turn into space confetti."

"Bet Ruby works."

"If we can get it formed," Tyler said. "If we can get it *ground*. If it's pure enough. If we can get it cooled enough. If, if, if. I'm not happy betting the security of Earth on *if*."

"Kind of past happy," Driver said.

"The first time we aim the SAPL at the Horvath they're going to start taking it down," Tyler said. "It's not hardened. It's not distributed *nearly* enough. Six major targets and you've got a bunch of mirrors pointing light beams into deep space. A VSA that works, another sixty BDAs and it will be harder. Three years. You *know* this."

"'Ask me for anything but time,'" Driver said. "Napoleon Bonaparte. Speaking of short guys."

"He wasn't, actually, below normal height," Tyler said. "Ask *me* for anything but..." He paused and looked into the distance. "Sorry, important call." Tyler closed his eyes. "On speaker. Hello, Admiral."

"Hello, Mr. Tyler," the commander of SpaceCom said. "I was wondering if you'd be willing to come down to D.C. to talk."

"I can guess about what," Tyler said. "I assume you won't have the SPs waiting for me? Or the FBI?"

"No, sir," the admiral said. "Not where we're going."

"When?"

"Friday at nine AM? At the Pentagon?"

"Be there," Tyler said. "Just try to make sure they're actually prepared for me to get there, because if anybody finds out, I'm pretty sure the protesters will be out in force."

"We'll take care of that, sir."

"Out here," Tyler said. He turned to Colonel Driver. "Well . . . I would rather face a thousand deaths . . ."

"What are you going to tell them?"

"The same thing I just told you."

"So that's it," Tyler said. "According to the intelligence we've gotten through Glatun commercial sources and our best estimate of how much power we can put on target, the SAPL cannot penetrate the Horvath shields. And even if it gets through the shields, it's got to cut fullerene armor. And in the meantime, they are going to be counter-firing its soft-skin mirror systems, so power is going to degrade fast. We find it supremely unlikely that the SAPL will be able to stop the Horvath."

"You've just launched a new VSA mirror," the Chairman said, looking around at the assembled joint chiefs. "The VSA . . ."

"Is designed to handle enough power," Tyler said. "We haven't done a full-scale test. There will be only *one* VSA. The last one lasted thirty seconds, which might be enough to do some serious damage. It still won't stop the cruiser. There is something that might, which brings me to a question."

"Which is?" the Chairman asked.

"I'm going to ask a simple question and I'm going to anticipate a simple, or at least honest and open, response. If the answer is 'you don't have the need to know,' I'm going to walk out of the room and you can figure out how to fight the Horvath entirely on your own."

"That's pretty damned ugly of you," the Chief of Staff of the Air Force said.

"We're either in this together or we're not," Tyler said. "We hang together or we will assuredly hang separately. Clear enough."

"Again, the question," the Chairman said.

"Can the rounds on the *Star Fury*—God, what a stupid name—do a pen or drop the Horvath shields?" Tyler asked.

"Uff da," the Chairman said, leaning back. "You're right, you aren't cleared for that."

"Thank you very much for your time," Tyler said, standing up.

"You can't just leave!" the Air Force COS said.

"Unless I'm . . ."

"I said you're not cleared," the Chairman said placatingly. "I didn't say I wasn't going to *answer*."

"Now just wait a damned minute . . ." the AF COS said.

"No, now shut the hell up," the Chairman said. "If we need to get the Secretaries in here to hash this out, we will. But Tyler's right. We have information he has to have to make an informed decision. He's got information we have to have. It's a two-way street. *Star Fury*, and I agree that's a damned stupid name, is your pet project . . ."

"Figures," Tyler said.

"Does it penetrate or not?"

"You don't even know?" Tyler asked.

"We've never been able to get a straight answer," the Marine Corps commandant said.

The AF COS sat back in his chair and folded his arms. Then he waved them in frustration.

"Maybe!"

"Maybe the SAPL will work," Tyler said. "Maybe the BFG will work. Maybe, if, sort of. Yes, or no?"

"Can *you* say yes?" the AF COS said.

"I can say how it works and what might and might not," Tyler said. "I can give people enough information to make decisions. I've given you five the information I have. What you recommend to the President is up to you. But if you want me to throw away the SAPL, you'd better have a better something to throw on the table than a gun that *maybe* works. Because the SAPL by itself will *not*. So how does it work?"

"This is really God damned classified," the AF COS said. "I'm not sure I should be discussing it with an uncleared civilian."

"Fish or cut bait time," Tyler said. "The full progress of the disease is supposed to be done in a week and a half. By then I can have Steve back here and he can try, again, to get that POS off the ground. But I'm going to fight tooth and nail against committing the SAPL if it's on its own. It. Just. Won't. Work. So how does the penetrator work? What's the output?"

"The way that the penetrator is *supposed* to work," the AF COS said, shrugging, "is using counter-rotating high-density gravity fields. They're more like a vortex. Think of a gravity tornado."

"Which Dr. Givens discovered accidentally by getting her hair torn off," Tyler said.

"You got that part of the briefing?" the AF COS said.

"They wanted money," Tyler said. "Which means you have two larger, lower-power gravity wells being generated. They said they were having problems generating them at all. What gives?"

"That's why I said 'maybe,'" the AF COS said. "Generating consistent grav fields is difficult. The round, we call it a breacher, works by generating two fields, as Mr. Vernon said. At the intersection of the fields, and they're not low power but the highest power we can generate, a vortex forms. It can only be formed for about a half a second. There's a lower power . . . gravity probe, sort of like a lance, that sticks out the front. When it encounters a gravity field, the breacher power kicks on. If it works, it will drop the shields in the affected area. The way it works is by essentially . . . hitting back against the plates. The power is carried through the pseudo gravity field of the generator back to the plates. Depending on Horvath design, about which we know very little, if it works at all it will either drop them for a moment, until their breakers reset, basically, or it will kill them by causing a plate shred."

"That . . . sort of makes sense," Tyler said thoughtfully.

"Thank you," the AF COS said sarcastically. "It hasn't been tested. We've activated a breacher round, but we've never activated it against a shield because we don't have one. And we haven't even test fired the gun with a breacher. And, last but not least—"

"You can't get the craft to fly," the Chairman said.

"I take it back," Tyler said sadly. "I'm glad Boeing at least tried. It was a noble effort."

"That sounds depressingly like an epitaph," the commandant said. "We're not there yet."

"I thought the Horvath would give us more time," Tyler said. "Maybe I shouldn't have defied them."

"*Our* analysis is that that is hubristic," the Chairman said, snorting. "Although you *may* have had something to do with it. But not in the way that you think."

"Don't understand," Tyler said.

"We have *some* intel on the Horvath," the Chairman said. "Not much, but some. To do a bio weapon like this requires much more data on the species than our researchers have accumulated. The sort of data you get when . . ."

"Someone gets implants," Tyler said. "Oh, hell. And while my personal information wasn't on the hypernet, the general information about human physiology is."

"If it wasn't you, it would have been someone," the Chairman said. "But with that and their own technology—well, Glatun technology they use—they were able to make these . . . vile diseases. We hadn't put that together until this attack."

"Always fighting the last wars," Tyler said. "No dis. I've been doing the same thing. And now I'm going to say something that is going to sound stupid and heroic and macho and all sorts of other dumb. I was the first person to get plants. The pilots currently undergoing training are going to still be getting used to them. The *only* two human pilots familiar with Glatun gravitics are myself and Steve Asaro."

"You're not a pilot," the AF COS said with a snort.

"I'm not a pilot by the standards you are a pilot," Tyler said neutrally. "In that I don't have forty thousand hours of flight time. By the standard that I have three hundred hours of time in the *Monkey Business* and controlling the *Paws*, that I have another six hundred in simulators, I'm a more qualified *space* pilot than anyone on Earth. Not great. I don't begin to say that I am. And flying those things is an order of magnitude, ten orders of magnitude, easier than flying an untested, not-particularly-well-made-or-designed, experimental anti-grav space fighter. And underperforming. Let's not forget underperforming."

"Sounds like the Brewster Buffalo," the Marine Corps Commandant said, referring to the aircraft that made up the mainstay of the Marine Aviation wing at the beginning of WWII. It flew about half as fast as a Mitsubishi Zero and could, barely, turn on a city mile. One pilot managed to shoot down a Zero in a Buffalo. He didn't last much longer. That made a ratio of seventy-three to one. "Which is about how long it's going to last."

"I repeat: Stupid, heroic... Our lives, our fortunes..."

"You say that kind of stuff a lot," the Chairman said. "Which is all very well. But that doesn't mean it will work."

"None of this is going to *work*," Tyler said. "It's just more likely with me and Steve than with anyone else you can name. I've got more time with plants than any other person on Earth. As previously mentioned in another context. I can probably do more with the... plane than Steve did. He was still getting used to them. I'm fully dialed in. He'll be better by now, too. You have no clue how much plants help. And, what the hell, if we lose the SAPL I might as *well* go out in a flash of plasma."

"Recall Major Asaro," the Chairman said. "As in, you call him home, and, Tim, recall him as a major."

"Got it," the Marine Corps commandant said, grinning. "Marine Aviation leads the way!"

"I'll go make amends with Boeing," Tyler said. "Some of Space Command's people had better get involved with the SAPL. And I won't even charge you for laser time..."

"It will take at least six months to reconfigure the *Fury* for a two-person cockpit," Gnad said.

Tyler was not good at eating crow. Fortunately, since he was bringing back not only his money but his access to off-world tech, Boeing hadn't asked.

On the other hand, there were clearly things they were going to have to work out.

"This is the general tenor of what we, and by that I mean myself and the National Defense Council, think the Horvath plan is," Tyler said. "Distribute the plagues. Wait a short while for them to take effect. Return. Take over Earth from the survivors, using said survivors as miners and maple syrup collectors. They may even make some noises as to being here for humanitarian purposes. But they're not going to wait long. The terminal point was about forty days from when they started their distribution. Ten days for the biologicals to drift down through the atmosphere and thirty-two days for the final agent to go into terminal condition. So we have, at this point, about three weeks before we can expect them to show up. We probably don't have a *month*. We *certainly* don't have six months. So what are you planning on doing in two weeks?"

"Starting on redesign?" Gnad said. "I'm serious. Six months is if we throw in the entire resources of

Phantom Works and Boeing. Which we are! But you can't *completely redesign* a space fighter in two weeks!"

"I've already apologized for my outburst," Tyler said. "I'll cop that I'm no longer unpleased that you bogarted me and built a space fighter instead of a shuttle. It doesn't give us much of a chance but it gives us some. I'm not going to apologize for this next one. WE DON'T HAVE SIX MONTHS!"

"I'm not being a bureaucrat here!" Gnad said furiously. "I'm as much under threat as anyone. So's my family. But this isn't the first design project I've been on! Do *you* have any suggestions how to cut it down?"

"No," Tyler said then frowned. "Yes. Hell."

"What?"

"Necessity is the mother of invention," Tyler said, holding up his hand to prevent further questions. He looked off into the distance for a moment. "I don't know *exactly* how we're going to do this. But I know we're going to need a lot of stuff that people aren't going to want to give up. And we're not going to be able to tell why we need it. So... You need to go call your CEO or whatever and tell him we're going to need a bunch of stuff. I'm going to call some people, too. Then we'll get to work."

"What stuff?" Gnad said.

"Well, first, we need an SR-71. And probably some crowbars..."

"Mr. Vernon. I am sorry to be informed of the plagues on your planet."

Communicating directly with an AI using only your plants was weird. When you communicated with them on the Glatun space stations or a ship they normally used a hologram to "personalize" the interaction.

When you contacted them with a plant it was more like they took over your brain. It wasn't so much telepathy as the feeling something was talking to you from inside your head. Somebody with a very big voice. Like . . . God. Very freaky.

"*We're not real happy, either,*" Tyler commed. "*Thank you for your prompt response.*"

Glatun medical response ships, some of them as big as the heavy cruiser that had come to Earth's aid during the Maple Syrup War, were pouring through the gate. Whether they would be able to help any significant fraction of humanity was the question. Nanniepaks for "critical personnel"—read "high muckety-mucks and various people Tyler had designated"—had already arrived. Of course, the real killer was still at least two weeks away.

The deaths had started, though. A surprisingly large number of people from across the gamut of the world's population had ignored the Johannsen Worm. As far as the CDC had been able to determine, every single person who ignored it had died. And the "preexisting conditions" packets were hitting. The U.S. and Europe weren't quite up to death carts but it was getting there.

"*There's a further problem,*" Tyler commed. "*I'm sending you two gestalt reports.*"

Gestalt reports were about as close as the system got to telepathy. You gathered everything you knew together in one little thought and squirted it.

The first was Tyler's best guess of the Horvath strategy. Kill most of the humans. Wipe out any remaining resistance. Put the few survivors to work mining and gathering maple syrup. Maybe make their response a "humanitarian" mission.

The second was about the *Star Fury*. In an action that would make everyone want to murder him, he included all the designs and technical documentation to date along with a vague plan for converting the fighter into a two-man craft.

"*Interesting,*" Athelkau commed. "*I remain neutral on the subject of the Horvath. The reason for this information?*"

"*We need help,*" Tyler said. "*I've never checked on costs for processor time and design assistance for an AI. We have to do this in so short a time, though, it's the only way I can imagine getting anything done.*"

"*We are constrained from assisting in military developments absent political approval,*" Athelkau commed. "*Which you will not get.*"

"*I don't want help with* military *materials,*" Tyler commed. "*Technically, this is just a test bed for human gravitic craft. The gun and targeting software either work or they don't. All I need is help getting it to fly.*"

"*Stand by,*" Athelkau commed.

Rarely if ever did you have to wait on an AI. They thought *way* faster than humans. They actually had built-in delays to questions so that it didn't confuse the organic sophonts. But actually waiting was rare.

"*Your argument meets some legal tests,*" Athelkau commed a moment later. "*Fortunately, Glatun law is sufficiently complex that just about* any *argument meets* some *legal tests.*

"*How much processing did that take?*" Tyler asked.

"*Quite a bit, but not all mine,*" Athelkau replied. "*I contacted legal specialty AIs. I am unsure you have enough funds to pay for sufficient processor time to do the conversion. And you are certainly not a candidate for a loan. But I am legally permitted to assist. Your general design concept is novel but may work. We are going to need additional resources."*

"*Gimme,*" Tyler commed. "*I'll put them on the network.*"

"*I can do that myself.*"

Max Yanes was thirty-nine, and since he'd gotten his masters in aeronautical engineering and headed into the workforce, he'd worked in the aeronautics industry. He'd started as a junior design engineer at Lock-Mart and since average time in any one company was a year and a half he'd worked for just about every major corporation, and several minor ones, at this point. He'd done some interesting stuff and a lot that was boring and a lot that was just stupid. But he'd rarely been asked to do something absolutely crazy.

Which was why he was looking at the Skil-Saw in his hand in bemusement.

"It goes in the frame, not in the air," Tyler yelled. He was about halfway through his cut on the port side of the *Fury*'s upper quadrant.

"We worked on this thing for two years!" Yanes shouted. "You can't just *cut the damned cockpit out*!"

"I can't do it quick," Tyler said, shaking his head to try to clear out some of the fragments. "You guys glued the hell out of it. Ungluing it isn't an option. So we're cutting."

"And cutting up an SR-71 is just . . ." The word "sacrilege" came to mind. "Wrong!"

"Are you going to help or bitch?" Tyler asked.

"I'm *trying* to help," Yanes said. "By pointing out that this is *crazy*!"

"No," Tyler said, stopping his saw and taking off his safety goggles and ear protection. "Taking a hacked-up, jury-rigged, barely-built, untested space-fighter into combat is crazy. But it's exactly what we're going to do. If we can get some people to work the problem instead of *being* the problem! Now, apply saw and start *cutting*! Or I'll find somebody who will."

By pulling out some of the rounds for the gun, the cockpit, and some of the Earth-built avionics, there appeared to be *just* enough room to put in an SR-71 cockpit. Since the 71 cockpit was designed to be used in near vacuum, it was totally sealed. And, conveniently, it held two people.

How it was actually going to work out was another question.

"This is . . . evil," Yanes said, putting on his earphones and glasses. He took a deep breath and started the saw. "Just . . . wrong."

He winced at the scream as he applied the saw to the frame.

"Sorry. Sorry . . ."

"How's the gluing going?" Tyler asked.

"You just *glue* these together?" the tech asked, shaking his head. He was used to working on circuitry in a clean room and using high-powered microscopes and waldoes. Not sitting at a table applying what looked for all the world like hot glue to them. And even though atacirc had reduced in price, he was still gluing together a fortune in circuitry.

"According to Athelkau, the glue creates molecular level connectivity between the chips," Tyler said, shrugging. "We're going to have to use a lot of brute processor power since our plates are basically crap. I had a shipment of atacirc coming in. With enough processors and the right software you can overcome anything."

"Even integration?" the tech asked. "I mean, there are about a billion control runs for this thing, right?"

"Two hundred and eighty-seven thousand control runs or sensors," Tyler said. "Which we're going to attach the same way and more or less at random. One hypernode connection for each pilot, one hell of a lot of processor and some hacked software. I didn't say it would be pretty, just that it might work."

"*Rivets?*" Gnad said, looking at the ship. "You *riveted* the cockpit on?"

Since the *Star Fury* had a passing resemblance to the SR-71, if you backed *way* up it just looked *more* like an SR-71. If you backed up enough, for example, to miss the patched-on carbon fiber where Tyler had cut a little too wide and the rivets holding on the cockpit.

"The frame's carbon fiber," Tyler said, shrugging. "The cockpit's titanium. There's no good, fast way to connect the two. We couldn't wait for the special epoxy to set. Three layers of extra carbon fiber and . . . rivets. It's sort of like doing the edge of a sail."

"The body was part of the frame-matrix," Gnad pointed out.

"Yeah, well, we glued in some supports," Tyler said, shrugging again. "Athelkau said it wouldn't fly in it, but it should fly. Sort of. If we can get the integration of the pilots together."

"Steve's arriving tomorrow," Gnad said. "On one of the Glatun medical support ships."

"Yep," Tyler said.

"Is it just me, or is most of the world crazy?" Gnad asked.

While Tyler had been up to his neck in red tape and carbon fiber, which he was starting to quietly loathe, the world had been dealing with a plague.

The odd part about it was the ... attitude. The progress of the diseases was throwing off people's response. The initial presentation of the Brunet Killer portions of the bio-attack package were minor. Coldlike. You got the sniffles and that was about it. Made sure it spread but the hosts weren't, in general, harmed. People with reduced immune systems might get worse, but they were already being wiped out in droves by the "preexisting conditions" bugs. Africa, with all its AIDS problems, was being hit particularly hard. So hard it was difficult for the news to even keep up. Most of it was coming from South Africa and you could only see piles of bodies being burned so many times before you just got inured.

But most people who had a decent immune system, no major preexisting conditions, and who had treated the Johannsen Worm, felt fine. They had the sniffles. Big deal?

That condition, based on the analysis of the Brunet Killer, would continue for thirty-two days after initial presentation. And then, if you didn't get the vaccine, you died. In about three hours. Three *very unpleasant* hours.

But that meant that you had to *trust* the people giving you that information to accept the nannites. You had to *trust* the Glatun and the people they were interacting with. You had to trust, in other words, people who many governments and the press, especially the international press, had said for years shouldn't be trusted if they said that that the Sun came up in the east. Because, clearly, the Sun coming up in the east was just a plot to oppress the poor people of...

Many people weren't accepting it. Whole *governments* were dragging their feet. Officially. Unofficially, every governmental official on Earth had screamed for the nannites. They weren't stupid about personal survival. But in many cases their *official* line was that "the validity of the claims by the WHO, the Glatun and especially the American CDC needed further study by their own experts."

The president of South Africa had officially stated that the plagues were a plot by the West to reinstate apartheid—which between the blond component and fact that AIDS was mostly found in the non-Caucasian portion of the population had a certain amount of traction—and that the Glatun medicines were actually mind-control devices. He and all his family had been treated, but he was telling his *people* not to take the medicine. Similar statements had been made by officials from throughout sub-Saharan Africa. The only leaders in the region who had embraced the treatments were the presidents of Burundi and Kenya. And they had not only inoculated their military, they were performing forced inoculations as fast as they could get the nannites distributed. And running into armed opposition.

The grand mullah of Mecca had given a speech denouncing the nanovaccines and stating that they were made from the entrails of pigs. He had, at least, been consistent and not gotten the shot himself. The king of Saudi Arabia had, however, while officially backing the statements of the grand mullah. The Gulf, in general, was pretty mixed in distribution. The more "Western," and therefore decadent, portions were distributing aggressively. The more "pure" areas were resisting or had rejected it.

The Iranians were denouncing it while doing distribution, which was just confusing as hell. The Sudanese had officially rejected it, inoculated their military and government officials and their allies, and denied it to any resident of Darfur. The rebels in Darfur had gotten cases of it from nongovernmental organizations and were distributing it as fast as they could.

Some groups in Iraq were resisting the distribution, mostly Sunni tribes. The Kurds had distribution *finished* before the *U.S.* Turkey was backing the distribution one hundred percent while trying to deny it to the Kurdish regions. Which had finished distribution, smuggled in from the Kurdish regions of Iraq, before the Iraqi Kurds.

The leadership of every major Islamic terrorist group had stated that any Muslim who took the vaccine was damned in the eyes of Allah. Intel suggested that they had obtained inoculations through black market sources. Cases of it had been stolen from NGOs in Afghanistan and the tribal areas of Pakistan. They were turning up, mostly still full, in the markets. Nobody wanted to *use* them, they were just another form of loot. The most advanced medicine in the world, a shot that would keep a belly-wound from becoming septic and increase healing rates four-fold, was going for ten dollars a case. And mostly they were being bought for the really excellent, vacuum-resistant, water-resistant, plasma-resistant, drop-resistant cases. The nanovaccines were being *dumped*.

Most of the governments of Asia were solidly behind the distribution. Groups within countries, however, were resisting. Especially areas that were hard-core Islamic. Even then, individuals were getting access. But the local leadership was trying like hell to stop it. "Unclean! Unclean!"

In Burma, the government officially restricted it from being distributed to "rebel" elements, which meant virtually every one of the hundred ethnic groups that were scattered through Burma that weren't "Burmese." Tyler had taken just enough time out from his work to get one of the *Paws* to drop bundles of nano-packs to every little village in the back side of beyond in Burma. The *Paw* had actually taken fire. It turned out that pressor beams and shields were virtually identical. On its way out, it had dropped more in the Ghorkali regions of Nepal, which were just on the end of a very long supply line.

All of the governments of Latin America were behind the distribution, even those that called the U.S. and the West evil incarnate. But in many cases they were "rationing" the distribution. In Colombia's case, they were mostly trying to keep it out of the hands of the drug lords. And generally failing.

The Horvath had planned on separating the sheep, as they saw it, from the goats. The international reaction to the Glatun medical support was doing the same thing. If you rejected technology or had a difficult time with reality...

"The death toll is going to be staggering," Gnad said, shaking his head.

"I've got this thing about death," Tyler said, examining the results of one of Athelkau's models. Using the AI was costing like crazy but it seemed to have worked. "If a person wants to survive and tries to survive and is smart about it, I'm all good. I hope like hell they survive. I feel terrible about all the kids who are about to die. Kids can't make their own choices. I really don't give a damn one way or the other about the idiots."

"That's very...Sartran," Gnad said. "Existentialist even."

"Say that with a smile, brother," Tyler said. "Heinlein once said that ignorance is its own death penalty. Truth is, the way the world has worked for a long time, it's not been true. Now...it's literally true. Don't know about the plagues or reject the information and it's an automatic and irrevocable death penalty. Besides, one death is a tragedy, a billion is a statistic."

"Think it will go that high?" Gnad said, his eyes wide.

"No," Tyler said. "But hundreds of millions? Yes. You want to know the worst part?"

"What could be worse than hundreds of millions of deaths?" Gnad said.

"Billions, technically," Tyler said. "But the worst part is I don't think it's going to matter. Except, and this is the really ugly part, in the net positive. Currently, the statistics are that it's mostly taking out people who have reduced capacity for, well, anything. Functional labor, if you will. The elderly, people with long-term problems. There were a bunch of people predisposed to cancer and other factors that weren't caught in time that were... gainfully employed and productive members of society? Can I be that unPC? But most in most of the Western countries got the vaccines in time. The rest? South Africa has already had six *million* deaths. *Fifteen percent* of its population. It's suffering economically but mostly because of the process of clean-up. And the only reason that we know their death rate is that they're fairly functional. We have no clue about most of the rest of sub-Saharan Africa.

"The plagues, so far, have killed a *reported* one hundred ninety-six *million* people worldwide. That's just an *enormous* number. Thirty *million* in the U.S. alone and we think that's going to go to about *fifty* million. *Twelve percent* of our population. And the full weight hasn't hit yet. The Brunet Killer package hasn't activated. The predisposed package hasn't even run its course. And you know what? There's a lot of grieving and the stock market is down and the financials are a bit of a mess and *every projection* shows that in six months we're going to be better off. And *that* is the worst part."

"How can we be *better* off?" Gnad asked. "That's... insane."

"That's the bad part," Tyler said, looking at him with a grimace. "That's the really, really *horrible* part. This is cleaning up some long-term problems related to modern society. The transfer of wealth that's about to take place with virtually *everyone* over the age of seventy dying is enormous. And the government's going to tax the hell out of it. Social Security just got solvent overnight. People with predisposed genetic conditions absorbed ten percent of Medicaid. Old people absorbed over *eighty percent* and climbing. Medicaid and Medicare and all the other creeping socialized medicine programs were absorbing more and more of our federal and state budgets. The combination has essentially *cleared up* the deficit.

"China and India were in the position of getting old before they got wealthy. Fixed that. If the terrorists keep with their determination to reject the vaccines? Fixed that, too. Hell, the way things are going there's not going to *be* a Pashtun tribe in another two weeks. Or any of the hardcore militants in the *world*. Or most of the groups which contributed the majority of members of the international jihad like the Algerian Rif tribes. Britain reports that some thirty percent of their 'ethnic minorities' are rejecting vaccines. Guess *which* ethnic group? Pakistan is only getting twelve percent *takers*. There's not going to *be* a Pakistan when this is done. India might as well absorb it."

"You're making this sound like a good thing," Gnad said.

"Congratulations," Tyler said. "Being as coldly rational as a human calculator... it is. That's the really, really horrible part. And I don't know if the worst part is the reality or that I'm cold enough to calculate it without flinching."

"I think... that you can calculate it without flinching," Gnad said.

"It's like the rivets, really," Tyler said sadly. "Sometimes, you gotta ignore how ugly it is and do the job in front of you. My mom died yesterday. The nannites didn't have enough of an immune system to work with."

"I'm sorry," the vice president said. "Both of mine got the vaccine. And it apparently took."

"Yeah, well," Tyler said, shrugging. "The girls and their mother are in an 'undisclosed location.' Not my fairly well-known Lair but . . . similar. And the Horvath are about to get some payback."

"How come you get a space suit?" Tyler said. "*I* don't have a space suit."

"So we'd better not get shot down," Steve said.

The former astronaut had arrived in the middle of the night and immediately headed over to the hangar. His take on the *Fury* was about the same as Gnad's. Which didn't mean he wasn't willing to try to fly it. Just that he thought it looked like Frankenstein.

"Shot down?" Tyler said, wincing. "We better not leak!" All he had with him was a temperature controlling flight suit. The SR-71 cockpit might be sealed but it didn't have really good temperature regulation.

"This is a completely different control interface," Steve said, looking at the system but mostly "looking" with his plants. "Most of these dials aren't hooked up to anything."

"All the sensors and stuff are hooked up to something," Tyler said. "They're just not hooked to a joystick and stuff."

"You're saying 'stuff' a lot," Steve said.

"Steve, you've seen the estimates," Tyler said. "So let's quit bitching and see if we can get this thing in the air, okay? Just close your damned eyes and use the software."

With his eyes closed, the plants and the Glatun software started to build a picture of the surroundings.

It wasn't sight by any stretch of the imagination. It was more like feeling the surrounding area. And the bird. What the bird felt like was . . .

"Is this feeling as shot to you as it is to me?" Steve commed.

"This software is off-the-shelf Glatun grav-control software," Tyler said. "It's probably trying to find a well-designed gravity system. The bird feels broken to *it* so it feels broken to *us*."

"This is never going to work," Steve said.

"Better hope it works," Tyler said. "As I said, quit bitching. Is it working better or worse than the Boeing stuff?"

"Different," Steve said. "I'm not sure if it's better or—"

The plane lurched to the side and nearly tumbled off its landing gear.

"Careful!" Tyler snapped. "Can we *try* to do this together?"

"Well, quit pulling!"

"What we have here is a failure to communicate," Tyler said, pulling out of the system. "I hereby rechristen this flying ship *The Tub*."

"What we have here is a system that's not *designed* to work," Steve said. "It's sometimes possible, in an emergency, for two pilots who are both experienced and who have worked together well to both control a bird. This is completely different. This is impossible!"

"We have to make it possible," Tyler said. "Think of Apollo Thirteen."

"Apollo Thirteen was a disaster," Steve pointed out.

"That made it back to Earth because people were willing to do anything to keep it from becoming more of a disaster," Tyler said. "I've got people doing their damnedest to get another terawatt or two out of the SAPL. People who aren't saying it can't be done, they're just doing everything they can. If it works, great. If it doesn't, we're all going to die anyway."

"Okay," Steve said. "Okay. We can do this. But I lead."

"Yes, sir," Tyler said. "What are we doing?"

"Just pulling straight up. Slowly."

"This is working...better," Steve said. "I'm not sure that it wouldn't have worked better with the original control system and two people but..."

While it was working, it was wearing. And they'd started trying to get the plane to fly before dawn. Since it was approaching noon, local time, Tyler wasn't so much exhausted as past exhaustion.

"We didn't have a year," Tyler said. "I sort of wish we were side-by-side. It feels...wrong back here."

They were, essentially, each taking a set of gravity drivers to manage. Done that way, with the Boeing gravity sensors and I/O controls and some hacked software from the Paw, it was *marginally* controllable. If they just lifted up and down and moved it a few feet. They'd managed to get it the requisite "one hundred yards in a figure eight" that was the standard for all sorts of silly little contests. That didn't mean they were ready to soar into the wild black yonder.

"Still having personnel integration troubles," Steve said.

"Are you saying *I can't dance?*" Tyler said. "Because if you are, you're right."

"No, I'm saying..." Steve paused and looked up as one of the ground controllers started waving.

"I've got an incoming call," Tyler said. "Since I told my plant to restrict—"

"Same here," Steve said. "General?"

"*A Horvath ship has just cleared the gate*," the CJCS said.

"Oh...crap," Tyler said. "They just fired."

"What?" Steve said, closing his eyes.

The view Tyler was accessing was from the VLA that had devoted a portion of its system to observing the Solar System's latest visitor. As they watched, the Horvath cruiser started dumping small objects into space. Objects which quickly accelerated and disappeared.

"That's a planetary bombardment," Tyler said softly. "Those are going to go fractional C. And they're going to arrive..."

"Get off the ground," the CJCS said. "Now!"

"Yes, sir," Steve said. "Goodbye."

"We still need to load rounds," Tyler said, sending an order to start loading. The rounds had been kept nearby just in case of a worst case scenario. Worst case seemed to have hit. "And that assumes they're going to work."

"Can the SAPL intercept those missiles?"

"Maybe if we'd engaged them just as they were being dumped," Tyler said. "We don't have the targeting to stop them inbound."

"We've lost them," Nathan said. "They're maneuvering, they're small and they're black. We lost them nearly as fast as they were being discharged. We got a count. Fourteen."

"If those are all directed at the U.S., that's going

to pretty well gut us," the very recently reactivated Colonel Driver said. "The SAPL groundside offices are bound to be a target. You need to evac."

"We're shutting down now," Nathan said. "But getting out of Huntsville... Tell Ty it was fun if I don't see him again. Bye."

"Colonel," one of the techs said. "A fractional C KEW will crack us like a walnut."

"Then we transfer to NMDC," Driver said. "And they transfer to SpaceCom. And if all of us get hit, it goes to the *Monkey Business*."

"And if they're willing to take out the *Monkey Business*?"

"There won't be anyone left alive to care."

"The President is on NEACAP," the secretary of defense said. "The Vice President is airborne in a helo but headed out of Los Angeles. The chain of succession is assured, at least."

"Do you think so, sir?" the CJCS said. "The Horvath can probably track both from space. If they get into the orbitals, they'll take them both out."

"It's times like this I wish we still had Cheyenne," the secretary said. The base had been shut down only two years before the gate arrived. Since then there had been several suggestions to reactivate it but the money was never there.

"Too late now," the CJCS said. "But at least we've got this *great* bunker."

The Pentagon had been designed, in part, for the express purpose of surviving a nuclear attack. Of course, that was an attack on Washington using a late '40s 10 KT atom bomb. Not a direct attack with six tons of metal screaming down at a fraction of the speed of light. The KEWs headed for Earth were going to leave craters deeper than Chesapeake Bay.

"It's better than what most people have," the secretary said. "The roads are jammed."

"And I'm selfishly thinking 'This had to happen on *my* watch,'" the Chairman said. "Time to impact?"

"Depends, sir," the colonel from SpaceCom said. "Soonest, thirty-five minutes. Longest is up to them. But if I was them, knowing we basically have nothing to defend ourselves, I'd have staggered them so that they arrive as direct delivery and at high speed. Which means we're probably not going to get hit until sometime after sunset. When you can see Mars high in the sky, that would be the best time. Say three hours."

"Game of cards, anyone?" the secretary asked.

"You're trying to lead again," Steve said.

"I'm just trying to fly!" Tyler replied.

They were loaded. They were in the air. They were at about a thousand feet, which was a remarkable achievement. But they couldn't steer worth a damn.

There fortunately wasn't any traffic. Every aircraft had been diverted from major airports and those that had the fuel had been ordered to circle until they *had* to land. That done, most of the air traffic controllers were getting the heck out of Dodge. Otherwise, they'd be screaming at the out-of-control space fighter.

"Calm down and just go with it," Steve said.

"I started thinking about my happy place and remembered I had to pee," Tyler said. "Really bad."

"I'm serious," Steve said.

"Destruction of the planet Earth doesn't get much more serious," Tyler said. "I've still got to pee. There..."

"Better," Steve said as the fighter struggled upwards again. "We just have to work together."

"Like dancing," Tyler said. "Gay dancing, but dancing... Dancing. Steve, do you listen to music?"

"Oh, you're not going Iron Eagle on me, are you?" Steve said as the bird wobbled off axis again. "Concentrate! That never works. This isn't a movie."

"This is two people trying to work in synchronicity," Tyler said. "What do you listen to?"

"Heavy metal."

"Gah. I'm a country fan," Ty said.

"Ain't gonna happen," Steve said. "I am *not* going to die listening to country."

"What kind of metal?"

"Hang on," Steve said.

The plants were perfectly capable of playing music. And linking.

"What the *hell* is that?" Ty asked as the plane bobbled again and lost altitude.

"Godsmack," Steve said. "And you're right. Even with you not particularly liking it we're still more in sync." After the bobble they were definitely gaining.

"It's not bad," Tyler said. "Just sort of a surprise. What else do you have?"

"A lot," Steve said. "I've even got a playlist. Which is...set. And now we can concentrate on killing Horvath."

"They're not closing faster than normal," Tyler said. With the two of them more in sync the plane was now well out of the atmosphere. Of course, they still had to pick their way through the trash belt around the planet. "They're advancing in an almost...ominous manner."

"I...don't think they see us," Steve said.

"With the plague and then the bombardment, the news channels are jammed with other stuff," Tyler said, doing a quick scan. "Ditto blogs, astronomy channels... There is not one single reference to us except news reports talking about how the SAPL isn't powerful enough to take out the Horvath ship and the *Star Fury* isn't capable of even flying."

"Radar? Satellite?"

"Local FAA radar was shut down by the time we took off," Tyler said, still scanning. "The sat net has been pretty much secured over the last couple of years. Steve...we're not getting noticed by *anybody*."

"What about the Horvath systems?" Steve said.

"They have a gravitics sensor system," Tyler said. "We're still in the grav well...Let's accel as best we can, go silent and slingshot around the Moon."

"Accel on the way out?" Steve said, setting it up.

"We'll be in a position to ambush them on the flank as they come in," Tyler said, considering the plot. "We can't stop the missiles; they have to be pretty much shot out. All we have to do is keep them from getting into orbit."

"All," Steve said, setting in the course. "This is getting easier."

"I think Athelkau put some Turing code in the software," Tyler said. "It's learning as we're learning."

"Right," Steve said. "Time to dump some power into this bird."

"Whipping the hamsters," Tyler closing his eyes and concentrating on simultaneously dumping power to the grav plates and not letting them fly apart. He grunted in surprise at the response. "Oh, yeah, no inertial damping!"

"Just crunch," Steve grunted back. "And don't black out on me!"

"I'm good," Tyler said. Getting the limping "space fighter" to accelerate using the plants felt almost like pushing with his brain. "I think that's about as much as we're going to get."

"That's better than I thought," Steve said. "About seven gravities of delta-V. We need to hold this for about twenty minutes, though. Can you do that?"

"Sure," Tyler said. "No problem. Anything you can do, I can do better."

"You have to *breathe...*" Steve said, laughing.

"Fighter pilot bastard. Did I *mention* I have to pee?"

"Recalculating trajectory and... shutting down," Steve said. "Heh. Speaking of Apollo Thirteen, we're about to do a flyby of the back side of the Moon."

"Fortunately, we can do it quicker," Tyler said, breathing deeply. He had not enjoyed seven gravities. He'd taken more on rides and the vector hadn't really done more than press straight down on his body, but it was different when you were trying to plot a course in space. Not to mention he had had to keep his stomach muscles clenched to prevent a hernia. For twenty minutes. They hadn't even gotten into combat yet and he was already exhausted.

Steve, the bastard, seemed to take it as just another day at the park.

"Yeah, we're going to be going *low*," Steve said. "And at our velocity, we won't get much of a slingshot.

And we're not going to have much time to do an attack run."

"So we'd better make the shots count," Tyler said. They were still getting data on the Horvath ship through the hypernet, so he carefully examined the approaching cruiser. "You know what? I think they're doing that slow approach because that's the only one they can do."

"Explain?" Steve said.

"They've only *got* about six gravities of acceleration," Tyler said. "They've used basically the same approach every time. I think that might be their flank speed. Think about it. They got a lot of advancement by the Glatun at first, but making really good grav systems, as we have found out, is *tough*. And they were horse and buggy days when they started."

"You think that's pretty much max drive," Steve said.

"Which means . . ." Tyler said. "God, I *wish* we had better modeling software."

"Should you be using the hypernet so much?" Steve said.

"If they can detect it, no," Tyler replied. "But here's the thing. Remember Baghdad Bob?"

"Those were the days," Steve said, sighing. "You mean the guy who was insisting the American forces had been destroyed when the reporters could hear tank fire?"

"Same," Tyler said. "What I'm looking for is where we got the intel on the Horvath cruiser. And I just found out, it was from the *Horvath*. It's their technical specifications on their cruiser screens. One thousand gravities of sheer. And it's *identical* to a Glatun destroyer."

"Which we would find pretty much impossible to take down," Steve said. "But, Tyler, you *understate* your open source data. Subs go a lot deeper than two hundred meters."

"And faster than twenty knots," Tyler said. "*We* understate. But I don't buy it. The Glatun don't help with military technology. They're not going to give the Horvath the most advanced shield technology. Just enough technology to make them better trading partners."

"Stolen?" Steve said.

"The Russians stole stuff all the time in the Cold War," Tyler said. "They couldn't equal any of our systems. If their cruiser has six gravities of delta-V, that would make their maximum grav output..." Tyler muttered to himself for a while and then shrugged. "I get it as a one hundred twenty gravity sheer. I'm not sure how much that's going to take to take down, though."

"This is either going to work or it's not," Steve said. "By the way, speaking of going to work or not, have you taken a look out the window?"

"No," Tyler said, looking through the small porthole. "Yipes! You weren't kidding about *low*!"

The view was cluttered and blurred given their velocity. But Tyler could tell mountains, very close mountains, even when they were blurry.

"We're actually heating up a tad from atmospheric effects," Steve mused. "Given the paucity of Luna's so-called atmosphere."

"Did we *have* to go this low?" Tyler asked.

"Yes," Steve said. "We built up a good head of velocity when we were accelerating. It was go low or basically shoot out on a vector that had us behind them and completely out of position to fire. Remember, we have to be able to get *physical* rounds on target. When we come in view of them, which will be in about thirty seconds, we'll be slightly ahead of them in relation to their course. We're actually vectored so that we'll hit their stern if either of us doesn't change course."

"Ramming speed!" Tyler yelled.

"Very funny," Steve said. "Thing is, with our present vector, we'll be coming in on their flank at, if you're right about their systems, a very high velocity. We got some delta from the slingshot."

"We're black," Tyler said. "And, I just realized as my cooling system went on overload, that we're coming in out of the Sun."

"Now if it was just dawn it would be perfect," Steve said. "Okay, time to bring the systems back up."

"And this is going to hurt," Tyler said, breathing deep. "I've got the gun, if you can handle the bird."

"The way things are going, I can handle the bird," Steve said, bringing the grav plates up and spinning up the plates on the gun.

"Any last words?"

"'From the halls of Montezuma, to the shores of the Lunar Mare!'"

"That's music I can dance to," Tyler said. "But it doesn't scan."

"Gravity source at one-one-eight mark four point two," the Horvath systems operator commed. "Very scattered. Primitive."

"That is the space fighter," the tactical controller stated. "Lasers to engage."

"The space fighter is nonoperational," Intelligence commed. "And human systems cannot penetrate our shields. Further study is required."

"Reality overrides theory," tactical commed. "And intelligence."

"Higher gravitational gradient detected," the sensor center commed. "Analysis is gravity driven mass driver. One hundred gravity gradient."

"Holy hanna!" Tyler said. "I think we holed ourselves."

Tyler had not quite gotten around to thinking about what firing the gun would be like. The "rounds" were 150mm chunks of steel and depleted uranium with the breacher drive buried in the middle. And the Boeing engineers had managed to get one hundred gravities of acceleration, in relation to the rounds, out of the drive system. The rounds massed a hefty two hundred and thirty-eight kilos. The entire craft had a mass of barely sixteen tons.

Firing the gun felt like the nose of the plane was being hammered by Mjolnir. The first round had caused them to go into a flat spin. Fortunately, in space that's not hard to correct, but it nearly caused Tyler to pass out.

"Just keep firing!"

"Unkph!" Tyler said, sending another round downrange. It was kind of hard to target, because the Horvath ship might be big, but they were a long way away and Steve was jinking all over the place trying to avoid Horvath lasers. "Ow! Frack!"

"I'm going to stabilize for just a second," Steve said. "Fire as fast as you can."

"Firing," Tyler said as the craft stabilized for just a moment. The targeting reticle had the distant Horvath ship centered. "Uhnk! Unkh! Uff!" The last round, he thought, sent them into another spin.

"We're hit," Steve said. "I've lost stabilization."

"And they're maneuvering," Tyler said. "I don't know if we're going to hit them with *anything*."

"They're not maneuvering fast," Steve said, trying to get the craft oriented again. "Okay, just start firing. We'll fill the space with chaff and hope for the best."

"Space is a big place," Tyler said, then set the system to fire as fast as possible and crunched up. "I wish *I* had a space suit."

"Be glad you're not on Earth," Steve said.

"Report," the CJCS said, coughing. "Do we have anything?"

"Hypernet is still up," the colonel in charge of NMDC said. She wiped some blood from her lips and coughed as well. The air was filled with dust, and the ring of plasma screens that had given instant access to information around the world was now a shattered mass of expensive plastics. "We're getting scattered reports. New York, Washington and SF are all hit. Energetics are about sixty megatons. They're all gutted. I'm surprised *we're* here. The round in D.C. looks to have landed more or less on the Capitol. We tried to deflect the SF round with THAD, but it didn't even faze it."

"Casualties?"

"Megadeaths," the colonel said, shrugging. "Until we get satellite BDA we're not sure how bad. People were trying to get out of town but . . ." She shrugged again.

"Who else?"

"Every major capital. London, Paris, Berlin, Moscow, Beijing, Tokyo. Then Jakarta, Seoul and Mumbai. *We* got pasted. I don't think they like us."

"There were fourteen rounds," the general said, counting on his fingers. "Is there one still circling somewhere?"

"The last one is believed to have hit Vernon Tyler's 'Lair,'" the colonel said. "We don't have BDA from that, but given the energies . . . it's probably gone."

"What about VLA control?" the general asked. "Do we still have the SAPL?"

"For what it's worth," the colonel said. "We still have control through the controls at Space Command."

"What's the word on the *Fury*?"

"They're . . . engaging," the colonel said, looking at the papers she'd been handed. There wasn't a surviving printer in the place, and reports were what the techs and NCOs were getting off the remaining hardened computer systems. "It doesn't look good."

"You know how I said I had to pee?" Tyler said. They'd fired off all their rounds and now were just trying to survive the Horvath laser fire. It wasn't going well. "Forget it."

"Thought something smelled," Steve said. "Coming around to port . . ."

"I think the stabilizer being shot off is helping," Tyler said. "*I* never know where we're going. How can they?"

Lasers move at the speed of light. But *The Tub* had opened fire at about a hundred and sixty thousand kilometers or a bit over a half a light-second. The likelihood of any of the breacher rounds hitting was, therefore, low. On the other hand, getting closer to the Horvath ship was suicide. You pays your money and you takes your choice.

Tyler's guess about the Horvath ship's abilities, though, appeared correct. The "cruiser" maneuvered even worse than *The Tub*.

The ship took a sudden, hard lurch and all the power shut down.

"We're leaking air," Tyler said, looking through the rear porthole. "I mean, like blowing it out. I think something broke." He craned his head around more and winced. "Let me rephrase. They just shot off the rear of the bird."

"That's something you don't see often," Steve said quietly.

"The rear of your ship floating away?" Tyler said.

"No," Steve said. "A laser in space. I think it hit a chunk of debris. Well, nice knowing you."

"Same," Tyler said. "I wonder how it's going on Earth?"

"We need to engage," Dr. Foster said. "It's a second and a half from the point that we open fire until we even *hit* the Horvath ship. And they are dead in space."

"Their telemetry is gone," the commander of Space-Com said. "There's no gravitic emissions, there are no particle emissions, there are no hypernet transmissions. They're *dead*. So losing our one chance to take out the cruiser is out of the question. See the ripple of distortion around the Horvath ship? They have their shields at maximum. We can't punch though that, right?"

"We hit them from every BDA array," Foster said. "Maybe we can overwhelm them. The full SAPL is damned near one hundred and *sixty* terawatts. We just hold back the VSA mirror. *That* we've only got one shot with."

"Do it," the general said.

"Setting it up . . ." the laser technician said, starting to hit the icons.

"Let me," Foster said with a sigh and closed his eyes. "I can do it with plants faster. And all the arrays are . . . retargeting."

"Hey," Tyler said. "I can see your house from here!"

"More importantly, I can see the Horvath ship," Steve said. "Barely. It's just a dot."

"Can you see if they're still firing?" Tyler asked.

"You can't see lasers in space," Steve said. "But they haven't hit us. Yet. That's a good thing."

"Again," Tyler said. "Got to wonder about their targeting systems. I mean, we'd have a hard time hitting something this small from that far away even with the SAPL. And I think that mirrors in space are probably less jittery than a ship. So . . ."

"Whoa!" Steve said. "I can really see it now."

"Why?"

"I think they just opened up with the SAPL."

Tyler had been building *a lot* of mirrors. Mirrors to pick up sunlight. Mirrors to reflect it. Mirrors to move it around. It all added up.

Forty separate BDA systems, each capable of concentrating their reflected four megawatts of solar energy to a beam the diameter of a coffee cup, had engaged the Horvath screens. Which turned black as night as they attempted to deflect the massed photons.

"Screens at maximum," the defensive technician said. "They *are* holding."

The entire ship was thrumming like a steel guitar, though.

"The power is intense," the engineering technician noted cautiously. "There is a possibility of failure of one of the systems under so much load. Also, it is using a significant amount of fuel to maintain power. Engineering recommends ending this condition at the earliest possible moment."

"We are unable to engage under this much power," the tactical technician said. "There is no targeting. We cannot respond."

"No more gravitics or other emissions from the space fighter," the sensor technician said. "We could see it before the attack. It was not entirely destroyed, but effectively."

"We will close to the planet and fire mass drivers on all control points for this laser system," the battle manager commed. "That taken care of, we will reduce this planet to ash." There was a sudden shudder through the ship and a wail of alarms. "What was—?"

"Breacher round," the engineering technician wailed. "Shield sixteen has failed!"

After adjustment for the dual cockpit, *The Tub* had forty-two breacher rounds. Forty-one had drifted off into deep space and become really nasty navigational hazards.

Round Seventeen was one that had been rather

carelessly aimed. But between the nearly random maneuvering of *The Tub* and the maneuvering of the Horvath ship, it had just happened, by a stroke of not quite luck, to drift into the path of the ship. And, as programmed, having detected a high gravitational gradient, it spun up its breacher system.

Four of the toughest, smallest, nastiest gravity plates Boeing could create were fed power by a half dozen equally small Honeywell carbon-nanotube capacitors. The amount of power was staggering, enough to run a nuclear attack sub. For, as noted, about a half a second.

The Horvath were not technological gods. Their systems were barely beyond what Boeing had devised. More stable, more refined, but essentially similar. They used magnetic bearings, for example. Magnetic bearings designed to withstand one hundred gravities that were suddenly subjected to four *thousand* gravities of power in an area the size of a walnut.

The backlash turned them into very small pieces of rapidly spinning molten bronze. Which, following simple Newtonian physics and a touch of thermodynamics, turned into a gaseous cloud of burning bronze.

BDA complex twelve was pointed, more or less, at the hole created by the breacher. More or less because it was nearly three light-seconds away, and despite better steering systems, the BDAs were still not terribly accurate over that distance. So it was swooping all over the surface of the Horvath ship, out into space, back in, cutting across the shields and back out. The combination of the relatively low power of the BDAs and their poor targeting was the main problem with taking down the Horvath shields in the first place.

So if the Horvath armor was, as all intelligence indicated, fullerene matrix, there was no way that BDA 12 should have penetrated. Fullerene was bound-together complexes of carbon that were like geodesic carbon spheres. It was vaguely similar to diamond but *far* stronger. Two hundred centimeters of fullerene, which was what the Horvath claimed their armor consisted of, was beyond even the power of the VSA.

As it turned out, though, the hull of the ship was, in fact, carbon fiber over steel. And steel was not much more than the stuff the BDA had been blasting out of Connie for the last year. Carbon was even less refractory.

The beam swept across the opening at nearly six thousand kilometers per hour, which reduced its absolute power input even more.

It didn't matter. Four terawatts of power hit the thin steel of the Horvath ship, and the "invulnerable armor" flashed into gas. The beam was attenuated more by the gaseous carbon and iron than by the armor. But it was still moving at the speed of light and cut deep into the ship as it swept across.

"Holy hell," the admiral said. "That was a solid hit!" Sensors were quickly picking up spectroscopy of water and oxygen being released by the ship.

"I'm retargeting BDA twenty-four to visual," Dr. Foster said. "And..."

Most of the Horvath ship was a mirrorlike shield across which the BDA beams could be seen as bright as the sun that gave them birth. But one portion was clearly open and the telescope revealed a thick gash in the side of the cruiser that was pouring out water and air. As they watched, there was a flash of light and more damage was done.

"I think that was twelve," Foster said. "It's at nearly three light-seconds. If it can do that... Permission to open fire with VSA. It'll take about...three minutes to set up."

"Do it," the admiral said. "Oh, *yeah*!"

"Fire has ceased," the defense technician commed.

"Compartments fourteen, fifteen and twenty-six are open to space," Damage Control commed. "Breach is sealed but another hit like that is going to take out our forward reactor and all forward screens."

"Are they calling for us to surrender?" the Horvath battle manager commed. "Increase power to engines. Come about. We are leaving the system."

"No call to surrender," the communications technician replied.

"Shall I open fire on the laser clusters?" the tactical tech commed.

"Negative," the battle manager said. "We do not know why they have stopped firing. We would prefer that condition remain until we can return with more forces."

"Can the VSA target it?"

"We were moving it out system," Dr. Foster said. "It's been cruising along, lying low, through the whole battle. It's got better antijitter controls, better targeting, better everything. So it's in a great position. The question is only how long it will last."

"Full power coming to the BDA cluster...now," the laser tech said.

"Permission to open fire, Admiral?" Dr. Foster said.

"Granted," the admiral said, his jaw flexing. "Do it."

The VSA cluster consisted of seventy-two BDA mirrors, each taking retransmissions from dozens of other BDAs, many of which had been attacking the Horvath cruiser up until a minute or so before. Now they gathered about half of the Very Large Array, even the VSA couldn't handle the *full* power, and concentrated it on those BDA mirrors.

The cluster then took the power, bounced it around twice until the power was gathered into thirty-six narrow beams, and pointed *all* that raw power at the single VSA mirror. It, in turn, sent out the standard coffee mug beam at the Horvath ship. The difference being it was not four terawatts in a three-inch diameter circle. It was *one hundred and forty*-four terawatts.

And it missed. Instead of hitting the small patch of missing shielding, it impacted directly on the powerful forward shields of the Horvath ship.

"Shields are fa—" the engineer tech wailed.

The beam of coruscating energy punched through the forward shield, through the forward compartments, through the command center, through the engine room, jittered around cutting compartment after sealed compartment and only really stopped because the beam wandered off the target. Every portion that it hit, the shields not only failed, the beam went right *through* the Horvath cruiser.

The immense swath of damage caused every gravity plate, every power system, to fail in near simultaneity, and the powerful Horvath cruiser came apart in a flash of gas and plasma. Which the VSA continued to shred until Dr. Foster, delayed due to light lag, realized he was just cutting up scrap.

He terminated power to the VSA, which was going into redline after only six seconds, and looked over at the admiral.

"Mission accomplished, sir."

"Hell," the admiral whispered, rubbing his forehead. The ship that had dominated Earth for so long had been destroyed almost faster than an eye blink. "What have you *created*?"

"As I think Mr. Tyler would have put it," Dr. Foster said, "a little temporary security. Now let's work on that liberty thing."

"How's your O2?" Steve asked.

"Fine," Tyler said. "Unfortunately, I can feel my eyeballs starting to pop out. And I now know what the bends feels like."

Whether from the damage inflicted by the Horvath cruiser or the damage inflicted by the gun, the cockpit had developed a leak. It was a small leak and the air compression system was fighting it, but the onboard O2 was about exhausted and Tyler could feel the pressure dropping around him.

"I think that slow decompression is going to be worse than rapid," Tyler said. "I get to experience it in slow motion."

"That's going to . . . suck," Steve said.

"Puns I don't need right now," Tyler said. "I'll try to keep my screaming to a minimum."

A shadow flashed across the small porthole. Tyler

was sort of getting used to those. The rubble of the multibillion-dollar space fighter, in keeping with microgravity conditions, was trundling along with them. He'd even gotten a look at the separated tail section. From the clean-cut look, that had definitely been a laser hit. At present he was wondering if taking a direct hit wouldn't have been better.

But this shadow persisted. Then he caught a flash of gray hull metal.

"Mr. Vernon . . . ?" a voice said in almost a whisper.

"Hello?" Tyler said. "Somebody there?"

"Stan . . . y."

There was a feeling of gravity to the side and the cabin thunked against something. Suddenly, light flooded in through the porthole. But not sunlight, artificial light. There was a distant clanging. And Tyler felt the pressure in the cabin start to go up. His ears popped, hard.

A Glatun face appeared at the porthole. An unsuited Glatun face.

"How do you open this thing?"

"The plague is hitting full stride," Steve said, reading the news feeds. "The distribution got jugged in Indonesia. They're taking a major hit. And Africa is totally hosed."

"It always has been," Tyler said, looking out the porthole of the Glatun shuttle. The alien docs on the Glatun ship had been able to fix him right up. It was, after all, a *medical* support ship. With, as it turned out, a pressurized shuttle bay. He *had* to get him one of those.

The ship swept around in a bank and Lake Washington was revealed in all its horror. The Potomac went all the way to Seventh. And it was now connected to the Anacostia along the line that had been Pennsylvania. The actual creeks into the lake were small since they had had to cut through the wall of rubble around the hole. That looked about a hundred meters high. About the only memorial he could spot was the Lincoln, which had been truncated at the base. The rest of the city, in a circle about four miles in diameter, was flattened. And then there were the fires.

Superfires were something that had, prior to the Horvath attack, been stuff of theoretical studies. Superfires were what happened when a wall of plasma hit a modern city. Everything in its path caught fire. In a circle six miles on a side. There was no way for conventional firefighting to manage that, even where there was functioning water. The only way to fight it was to destroy everything in its path, and nobody had had the guts to do it.

The D.C. superfire had torched practically everything in D.C. on the inside of the beltway. There were areas that had survived, but not many. Every major structure had taken at least some damage, and the capital of what was still the most powerful nation in the world, as well as virtually its entire citizen body, had died screaming.

The hit in Frisco had destroyed every bridge, then torched everything from Marina to Millbrae. Most of the population that was trying to get out was headed across the Golden Gate or the Bay Bridges when the strike hit. Or, rather, stuck in traffic on the Golden Gate and the Bay Bridges. Ninety plus percent were now in the Bay.

Manhattan was more or less toast. The same damage

had happened to the bridges as in SF, and even most of the ferries were destroyed by the combination of the plasma wave and the very small, very intense tsunami that had been kicked up by the strike which centered more or less on the Chelsea Piers. Then the fires had started and raged across the entire island. It was estimated less than a million people had made it off.

The L.A. superfire had been the real doozy. The strike hit when the chaparral of the L.A. valley was ready to burn anyway. They had seen the smoke from the L.A. basin during descent. You could spot the fire from the Moon. There wasn't an L.A. anymore. What wasn't crater was a cinder.

"It's just buildings," Tyler muttered.

"What?" Steve asked. The shuttle was coming down pretty hot and the soundproofing could be better.

"It's just buildings," Tyler commed. "And people. People die. Buildings crumble. Britain suffered worse in the Blitz. Germany and Japan *far* worse under our tender ministrations."

"Practicing your speech?" Steve asked.

"Had it memorized when I was nine," Tyler said. "Honor, duty, country, blah, blah. What can't be killed is a vision of freedom and liberty."

"Very nice," Steve said, clapping. "Very touching. Amazing how decompression can focus the mind."

"Yeah," Tyler said. "I'm not sure about the addition, though."

"Which is?"

"And a determination that not only will no Horvath ship ever again get more than a hand's span out of the gate, we're going to pay this back in *spades*."

"Speak it, preacher," Steve said.

"Funny thing," Tyler said as the shuttle was landing. Unsurprisingly, there was a delegation. Tyler was faintly relieved that all the police present were being used to hold back the crowds.

"What?" Steve said.

"Despite all this horror and damage," Tyler said, "despite all the deaths, despite a damned near crippled economy...Earth is probably a better loan risk than at any point since the gate opened. Maybe now we can *really* get going."

"I wish we'd detected this initially," Xiy Gigum said. The "Glatun" doctor was an Anancancuimor specialist in epidemiological attacks. It was hard to tell body language with a three-foot-long beetle, but he looked embarrassed. "We actually did detect it before we came into the system. But with all the problems with distribution...it didn't come up."

"Which is?" Dr. Cline asked, tilting her head to the side.

"There was an additional packet with the last virus," the Anancancuimor said. "A retrovirus addition."

"A genetically *changing* addition?" Dr. Cline said, getting very still.

Retroviruses actually referred to a particular class of virus, the HIV virus being the most well known, that were simple chunks of DNA or RNA. They didn't have a protein shell, just a strand of DNA.

But since they were also the type of virus most often used in genetic modification the terms had become somewhat mixed. Any virus used for genetic modification was generally termed a retrovirus.

"Yes," Dr. Gigum said.

"And the nature of the packet?" Dr. Cline asked, trying to stay calm. Earth had already taken enormous losses from the plagues, and the viruses, before being stopped by the Glatun medications, had spread through some ninety-five percent of Earth's surviving population. She was trying to *not* think of legions of cannibal mutants and failing.

"There is no easy way to say this," Dr. Gigum said. "So I'm going to tip-toe around it. This is the probable thinking on the part of the attacker, whoever that might be. They anticipated success in this attack. They did not think that Earth would detect the viruses or spread the word. Most planets are not at this level of advancement when contacted and most would not have had the ability to respond within a scant seven years of first contact. They were also under the mistaken belief that if they left a significant number of workers available to collect maple syrup that the Glatun and other races would not respond strongly. This is, in fact, the first true epidemic we have had to respond to in several hundred years. It does not mean we were not prepared, however.

"And all that means?" Dr. Cline asked. "Let me just ask a question. Is it going to cause us to go insane or something?

"Not ... quite," Dr. Gigum said. "Let me proceed in my estimation. This left, however, the problem of workers. In preindustrial conditions, when there is a severe loss of life, there is a very fast population growth in the aftermath. Populations spring back very quickly."

"Noted," Dr. Cline said. "Various examples. The Black Plague comes to mind."

"However," the beetle continued, "in conditions in which a society is sufficiently advanced to have reproductive *control*, population levels *dip* after severe losses. Individuals engage in recreational pseudoreproductive activity, if the species is bent that way. This is a way of dealing with the death."

"Also known," Dr. Cline said. "Not something we like to talk about, but...known."

"But if there is reproductive control, actual *birthrates* drop," Dr. Gigum said. "And your attackers were looking at an already severely reduced population. One due to lack of population unable to be useful..." The beetle paused, as if trying to think of a polite term.

"Slaves," Dr. Cline said, her jaw working. "We know the term."

"As you say," Dr. Gigum said. "I understand this tribe used them until historically recently."

"Specifically," Dr. Cline said, "those who were of darker skin pigmentation. Such as myself."

"Ah," Dr. Gigum said. "Pardon the faux pas."

"The point?" Dr. Cline said, then paused. "Oh... hell. How *can* they overcome standard contraceptives?"

"To recover the method by which your contraceptives work," Dr. Gigum said. "They mimic pregnancy. Your females, those within reproductive range, still ovulate during pregnancy. But the egg's coating hardens preventing fertilization. The packet first works by removing that defense against multiple pregnancies—"

"That is going to *kill* women," Dr. Cline snapped. "Our systems are not *designed* for multi-start pregnancies!"

"Nonetheless," the beetle said. "That is not all, however. Your attackers noted the social conditions of reproduction in your species. I will not get into evolutionary theory on the subject, but your species has two unusual aspects to your reproduction. Your females do not go into a 'heat' cycle, and they orgasm. This places most decisions regarding reproduction or pseudoreproduction, absent force on the part of the male, in the hands of the female."

"Delicately put," Dr. Cline said, her brow furrowing. "So . . . ?"

"The packet does three things," Dr. Gigum said. "The first is it removes the protection against multiterm pregnancies. Unwisely, as you said. Your females are not designed to handle that. It will cause deaths in the absence of intervention. The second is to increase the tendency, in certain individuals, to orgasm . . ."

"Oh . . . dear," Dr. Cline said. "That could get . . ." She tried not to smile. "Difficult. Not necessarily bad, mind you."

"The last is, perhaps, the most societally challenging," Dr. Gigum said, waggling his feelers in discomfort. "Human females, certain human females, now will go into a monthly heat cycle."

"Monthly?" Dr. Cline said, her eyes wide. "*Monthly*?"

"Yes," the beetle said. "Certain female humans."

"Which?" Dr. Cline said, her eyes narrowing.

"The attack anticipated that only persons with the Blond gene would survive . . ."

"Oh," Dr. Cline said, exhaling. "Oh. Oh . . . hell."

"So," Dr. Gigum said, his feelers waggling again. "You have a saying that is now very apt . . ."

"Blondes really *will* have more fun. Got it. When?"

"The packet is already kicking in," Dr. Gigum said. "It would have done the modifications over the last month in the population. As females, blonde females, go into the ovulatory period of their monthly cycle they will start to . . . change."

"And people used to joke about *PMS*," Dr. Cline said. "Remedy?"

"There is no widespread remedy," Dr. Gigum said. "Any uni-vaccine that could be simply tricked into allowing a wide-spread retrovirus to correct the . . . change would be, of course, useless. There is little or no way to get past the current vaccines. It will require individualized treatment. *Advanced* individualized treatment. The nannites must first be removed from the body, a very difficult and time-consuming process, then the retrovirus inserted, then the nannites reinstalled."

"Oh, no, no, no . . ." Dr. Cline said.

"There is some good news," Dr. Gigum said. "At least, given your recent population decrease. You will soon be looking at a veritable baby-boom."

"Oh, no, no, no, no, nooo! Blondes in *heat*? Why couldn't it have been mutant cyborgs?"

TROY RISING

ONE

"SpaceCom, this is the Explorer Vessel *Trinidad*, Terra Ship Registry Number Echo-Victor-One, exiting the gate," Steve said. He had taken over the com by right of being commander. The communications officer was pissed but she'd get over it. He was probably sleeping on the couch in the meantime.

"Trinidad, *SpaceCom. Welcome home. How was the trip?*"

"Relatively uneventful," Steve said. "New star systems, no new civilizations. Glad to be home."

"*As said, welcome home. Cleared for orbital insertion. Assume parking positions at geosync three one six, over.*"

"Three one six, aye," Steve said. "Pilot, make it so."

"You're so geeky there should be a law," Mathilda said, smiling.

The EV *Trinidad*, named after Magellan's flagship, owner Apollo Mining Corporation, Inc, had been built to spec in the Tu'Ghithazhalh yards circling the Rangora home world of Ligaghux. It had human-designed, and in many cases built, living areas and control and management centers, room for two *Columbia*-class

Boeing shuttles and, importantly, enormous fuel, water and air bunkerage.

The Glatun had only four exploratory ships still operating and one of those was about to be scrapped with no plans for replacement. At the same time, the Grtul seemed to be going through a building boom in the spiral arm. Since Earth's gate had opened, sixty more had opened in the immediate stellar region. Exploring that cat's cradle was complex.

The Grtul provided updated reports of the growing gate network but that was all. There was no notation as to the condition of the systems, whether there were inhabitants, livable planets, nothing. Just a gate address and how it was connected. Some gates were dead ends. Some were connected to as many as twelve other gates. And that could change at any moment.

Earth's gate was connected to three other systems. Alpha Centauri had no habitable planets or even useful gas giants. However, its gate connected to E Eridani which in turn connected to Glalkod system. It also, unfortunately, connected to L726-8 which connected by one additional gate to the Horvath home system.

The Glatun ship that had discovered Earth had also gone out through multiple connections along the second Earth connection to Barnard's Star. They'd found some interesting systems but nothing worth colonizing or exploiting. No civilizations, no habitable planets.

The *Trinidad* had taken the third connection to Wolf 359. And Steve was looking forward to turning in his report. No civilizations or immediately habitable worlds. But 359 had something even *more* interesting.

Mapping out a star system took time. And when you first went through a gate, you only knew that the space immediately around the gate was *probably* clear. You didn't know if there were hostiles on the far side. You could be running smack-dab into a firefight or an asteroid. It was a bit nerve-wracking. But if you came through okay, you then had to get to work.

First you spotted the major planets and their big moons. Then you looked for perturbations that might indicate other planets. You scanned for the big asteroids. Spotting all the small ones was a job for follow-on crew if there ever was one.

It took time. And if there was anything interesting in the system you had to pick your way over, carefully, for a closer look.

Wolf 359 had taken some time. The one system currently connected to it had been quicker. Pretty much nada. But they'd still been gone three months and were pretty much breathing CO_2 and drinking sewage.

"Incoming call from the boss," Mathilda said. "You want to take it?"

Mathilda, and the rings they both wore, was a result of the aftermath of the battle against the Horvath. Earth had taken a pounding and morale was rock bottom. As it was put to Steve by none other than the President: People really need some heroes right now, Major, so go out and hero.

The truth was it was the Very Scary Array that slagged the Horvath ship. And there were plenty of commentators willing to make that point. But it was hard for people to get their heads around what was, at base, a mining laser, winning a war. Two brave men in a flying machine was easier to wrap your head around.

Since Tyler had immediately disappeared back into being, well, the richest man in the world and as out of sight as Punxsutawney Phil on a sunny day, it was up to Steve to travel about being shown off like a pet dog. The one absolute positive for the confirmed bachelor was that . . . well, it wasn't hard to meet the ladies. That had been a subtext of being an astronaut in the old days, but since the Apollo missions, the glamour had sort of worn off.

The whole "heat" thing, which was slowly getting under control, was another issue. Sometimes the ladies were just a bit *too* forward.

Not so on his "triumphant journey." And he wasn't just shown off in the U.S., he was trotted out in every major city in the world. Which was how he met Mathilda.

In Melbourne, Australia, he had insisted that he have a day off. Ninety-Mile beach was not something *any* person should miss if they had the chance. To say that the sheilas of Ninety-Mile beach were world class was a bit of an understatement. More the class of the world.

Steve wasn't trolling. He'd deliberately gone in mufti. In this case, a pair of Speedos and shades.

So when a redhead walked up to him it was a slight surprise. Six foot—he did like the ladies tall—blue eyes and absolutely stacked. Presumably, she recognized him and didn't appear to be "in that condition" as it was being referred to by the delicate. But he wasn't going to turn down . . .

"You have to be the *worst* pilot in the history of astronautics," Mathilda said. Then Dr. Mathilda Burns, Professor of Astronomy at the University of Melbourne, proceeded to reconstruct every single mistake he and Tyler had made during the battle.

Which turned into a "got a hell of a sunburn" discussion, dinner, drinks...after-drinks, coffee, hotel room, aloe...and a wedding ring.

And now second officer of the *Trinidad*.

"Do we want to get paid?" Steve asked, grinning. "Definitely."

"*Steeeve-oh!*" Tyler said. "*How was the trip?*"

"Long," Steve said. "We've got enough fuel to get into stable orbit and we're down to eating Mountain House. Also breathing soup. Very glad to be home."

"*Report? Anything good?*"

"Depends on your definition of good," Steve said, smiling. "But I think you'll find it...interesting."

"*Fine,*" Tyler said. "*Be all mysterious. I have stuff that's interesting, too! Meet for dinner? Or are you fatigued by your travels?*"

"Very," Steve said. "But if you're buying..."

"*We've got this amazing new chef on the* Business," Tyler said. "*Hop in your shuttle and get your butt over here. Oh, and your blushing bride, of course. Hi, Mathilda!*"

"Hi, yourself," Mathilda said. "But I've had about as much of him as I can take for a while. Unless it's a command performance, I've got a date with a spa."

"*You go spa,*" Tyler said, smiling. "*I won't keep him long. Just some stuff I think he'd like to see. And I'm sure he wants to give me the report in person. Steve, there's a repair and refresh crew waiting. If you can let them work on your baby without looking over their shoulder, give your crew leave. And yourself after we talk.*"

"I could do with a few days not breathing canned air," Steve admitted. "I'll head over to the *Business* as soon as we're parked."

"Looking forward to it. Missed you, man."

"You do look tired," Tyler said, pouring the astronaut a snifter of brandy. "Martel Centennial. Hundred and fifty years old. Don't ask how much it costs. But it seemed like the appropriate occasion."

"Salut," Steve said, raising the snifter. He took a very small sip. "My, that *is* good."

"The French can't do much right, but I'll give them fine food and drink," Tyler said.

The "Commodore's Quarters" on the *Business* were a recent addition. They'd been made by a Finnish company that normally built cruise ships. With the decline in the cruise ship industry, Tyler had snapped up the company and gotten them to start thinking about spaceships. With most of the kinks worked out of gravity systems, he had his eyes on fleets of ships plying between worlds. It wasn't going to happen soon, but the Finns were enthusiastic enough.

The quarters had been shipped in vacuum-sealed components that would fit through the cargo hatches on the *Business*. A small section of crew quarters was ripped out and the compartmentalized, insert Tab A into Slot B, Commodore's Quarters installed.

They were *much* more comfortable than the normal crew quarters, but Tyler was spending so much time on the *Business* he figured he should indulge. And it was good practice for what he saw coming in the *very* near future.

"So talk," Tyler said. "What did you find?"

"Four-one-six isn't much," Steve said, shrugging. "Red dwarf, one gas giant, small rubble belt. If more gates open off it, maybe there will be something worthwhile."

"Three-five-nine?" Tyler asked.

"Very interesting," Steve said, taking another sip. *Really* nice. "*Six* gas giants. The outermost is practically in the Kuiper Belt. Lots of moons. Rocky planets, depends on your definition of planet."

"Any habitable moons?"

"Not as they stand," Steve said. "But about the gas giants. The *inner*most is directly in the life belt. And it has three moons, one of them a bit short of Earth sized, that have reducing atmospheres."

"Thick?" Tyler asked.

"Thick enough," Steve said, grinning. "They'd be a big damned project to terraform, but they're all terraformable. The Mars-sized one, which we named after my blushing bride, has an atmo that is thicker than Earth's."

"Yeah," Tyler said, taking a sip and musing. "But if it's reducing, you're going to have to convert it to an oxy-nitrogen atmo."

A reducing atmosphere was the original atmosphere of Earth, consisting of a, to humans, toxic mixture of ammonia, hydrogen sulfide and carbon dioxide.

In Earth's early history, microorganisms, starting with archaeobacter, had slowly converted the atmosphere, "eating" the ammonia and hydrogen sulfide for fuel. Archeobacteria were generally now only found deep in the earth or, notably, around undersea volcanic, vents where they were the basis of a deep-ocean food web.

As those reduced, blue-green algae had arisen and

converted the carbon dioxide to fixed carbon and oxygen. Remnants of that period could still be found in banded iron formations. As the oxygen rose in the atmosphere, surface iron, which had stayed in a more or less pure state, locked up the oxygen in what was essentially rust, forming the red bands in banded iron. With the oxygen locked up, more iron could deposit. Then, oxygen levels built up and it got locked up again. And so on and so forth until all the iron was converted and oxygen could start to seriously build. Then came plants and animals and the biosphere as it currently stood.

"You're going to lose some total mass to absorbed material. Still . . . Steve, that is great news!"

"Also has a big rubble belt," Steve said. "And the last part is the most interesting. The gas giant has a *really* odd atmo. Not only is it unusually high in He-3, at the level where there's a nearly Earth normal gravity, about point seven, the atmosphere is oxy-nitrogen."

"You're kidding," Tyler said, his eyes wide. "*Not* reducing?"

Free oxygen tended to bond to just about anything, which meant that reducing atmospheres, with all the free oxygen bound up, were bound to be common. To have an oxy-nitrogen atmosphere like Earth's, you practically *had* to have something keeping it that way. On Earth, that was called "plants."

"Nope," Steve said. "Damned near Earth normal. Most of the reducing gases are either higher or lower so it might be a sorting thing. There may be some life in the atmosphere, microbiology at best, that's converting them but we're not sure. Higher percentage of noble gases, but completely breathable. It's damned odd. But I figured you could probably use it to help terraform."

"That, yes," Tyler said thoughtfully. "But this is only one gate jump away, right?"

"Yeah," Steve said.

"And on the back side of us from our enemies," Tyler said, pursing his lips.

"Of which we haven't seen hide nor hair since just before we left."

The Horvath had not taken the loss of their cruiser lightly. Shortly after the battle, they had sent four *more* cruisers through the gate with the intention of teaching Earth a permanent lesson.

Again, they had launched missiles from long range. And they had, unfortunately, been nearly as impossible to stop as the first barrage. A ring of BDA mirrors around Earth had intercepted about half, but the other half got through. Rome, Madrid, New Delhi: the list was long. The difference was that most governments had set up solid evacuation plans and even drilled on them. And as many people as could manage were moving out of cities. It was still impossible to entirely do without them, but they were ... dwindling.

The death toll had still been staggering. And most of humanity had buried its dead, shrugged it off, picked up and continued on.

The Horvath ships managed to fire their barrage. And they had started hitting the VLA nearly as fast.

There were seven VSA clusters working on Connie and other targets. They'd *all* turned on the Horvath ships as fast as they could be retargeted.

"If the Horvath would quit bombing our cities, I could almost thank them for coming through," Tyler said. "We've gotten nearly sixty tons of prime grav plates off of them. Not to mention some surviving power plants and laser emitters. For a while there, I was doing less mining than salvage. Most of that is going into the *Constitution*."

Earth's first heavy cruiser had been under construction for nearly a year. It had, fortunately, *not* been targeted by the Horvath. It was larger and more powerful, potentially, than a Horvath cruiser. Unfortunately, BAE was saying it was going to take six more years to complete.

There was still no declaration of war with the Horvath. There had been, in fact, a declared cease-fire. Which was when the Horvath ships came through. The Horvath didn't seem to *get* the concept of keeping a negotiated peace. Might made right, period.

The estimates as of when Steve left were that the only reason they weren't sending more ships through was that they only had *seven* cruisers.

Earth had destroyed five.

"What happened to the prisoners?" Steve asked.

Some of the Horvath ships had managed to get crew off before being slagged. Some.

"We turned them over to the Glatun for repatriation," Tyler said, shrugging. "It wasn't like we could feed them."

"We have got to secure the gate better," Steve said, his face tight. "We can't keep getting bombarded over and over again."

"Yeah," Tyler said enigmatically. "Would be nice. Hey, have you seen what we did with Connie?"

"I haven't seen much news lately," Steve said. "So . . . no."

"Check this out," Tyler said, turning on a plasma screen.

The view was of a disk spinning in space. Steve tilted his head to the side, trying to get some scale. Then he realized the nearly microscopic dots moving near its face were *Paws*.

"Holy hell," he said, his eyes wide.

"We got it into a stable spin by detonating some clean pumped-fusion bombs on the surface," Tyler said excitedly. "Then we heated it back up. It's been separating pretty much the whole time you've been gone. At this point, it's just a matter of how fast we can pull stuff off. I've mostly farmed it out to the Glatun. There's a Limaror smelter with sixty tugs working on it full time. We're not getting much heavy metals yet. We're mostly getting aluminum, copper and tin. About six hundred *tons* a *minute*."

"I see you can afford the Centennial," Steve said, holding up his nearly empty snifter.

"Hell, I can afford to buy Martel," Tyler said, topping up his glass. "And I'm spending it nearly as fast as I make it. There are over two thousand people working in space full time at this point, ninety percent for me. And despite joking about working for low pay, they're not. We're still having to buy ships from the Glatun and the Rangora. But I have high hopes. Boeing's managed to improve their shuttles already. I'm pretty sure they're to the point of being able to make at least small ships. About thirty percent of our lift is Earth-built shuttles. I'm hoping to get that to seventy percent by the end of the year."

"You're starting to sound like the Evil Overlord again," Steve warned. "*I* hope?"

"I know," Tyler said, shrugging. "But...people keep talking about 'the recovery.' *What* recovery? We're not going to get back the people we lost. We're not going to get back the treasures we lost. I mean, we lost the Metropolitan Museum of Art, the Smithsonian, the British Museum, the Forbidden Palace and the Louvre in one *day*. Then we lost the Taj Mahal. The biggest remaining stash of art treasures in the world is in my really top-secret lair. And it's *staying* there. We're not going to recover that. We're not going to recover the people. That's the past. Let's talk about the *future!*"

"Which is?" Steve asked.

"Well," Tyler said, shrugging. "Sounds like we've got a planet we can terraform. And...other stuff."

"You're being mysterious again," Steve said.

"Confidential," Tyler said. "Really. It's very tightly held. And I'm trying to keep it that way. Hey, we're starting on a new mining project."

"You can't extract everything from *Connie*," Steve said, shaking his head. "And you're starting a *new* one?"

"These things take a while to heat," Tyler said, shrugging. "Especially this one. It's a six-kilometer asteroid in the belt."

"That's going to take some power," Steve said.

"We're trying a slightly different take," Tyler said. "Turns out there's some differentiation to them. So we stabilized this one and we're doing a laser drill to the interior."

"You're drilling into the interior of a six-kilometer diameter asteroid?" Steve said, blinking. "You really *are* thinking big. What are you going to do, blow it up?"

"Nah," Tyler said. "There's better stuff to do with it."

"Dinner is served," Dr. Chu said, entering the room followed by a group of waiters. "Mind if I join you? Since I fixed it?"

"Conrad!" Steve said. "I'm glad to see you survived."

"Many friends did not," Dr. Chu said, picking up the bottle and pouring himself a drink. "Absent companions."

"Absent companions," Tyler and Steve said.

"To the future," Steve said.

"I'll drink to that," Tyler replied. "To a better, brighter, *bigger* future."

TWO

"I'm doing this," Dr. Nathan Bell said. The huge "small planetary object" specialist was handling the drilling project on *Troy*. "I'm fully involved in the project. I'm working the problems, and they haven't been small. *Nothing* about this has been small. And I think you're insane."

"How's the drill rig working?" Tyler asked.

The "drill rig" was a complex of mirrors physically connected to asteroid 3159. The main belt asteroid was an eight-kilometer long, five-kilometer wide mass of virtually solid nickel iron. Sixteen BDA mirrors were pointing "out" to a VSA perched over the drill point on thin nickel-iron rods. The BDA mirrors captured a series of beams off the SAPL to supply sixty-four megawatts of power to the drill beam. The VSA, since the drilling was taking place in shadow, could easily manage the waste heat of a mere sixty-four megawatts.

Clearing the drill hole had been a problem at first. A good bit of the nickel iron was heated to vaporization by the beam, but most of it just sort of slumped out of the hole. A tug had been collecting it and setting it to the side for the last two months.

There was now a minor planetary body circling the minor planetary body.

Also circling the minor planetary body was a small, leased freighter. It had been refitted to function as a construction site management ship. It wasn't the most comfortable place in the system, but Tyler had done his best. And it had a good cook and great food. It had to have something going for it; the crew had been informed they were staying aboard until they were done with the first phase.

Naturally, it had been renamed *Trojan Horse*.

"Pretty well, actually," Nathan said. "The biggest problem has been routing it out."

One of the problems was that they needed a *big* hole for the overall plan. So the beam had to continuously track around the hole, opening it up.

"We're only about two hundred meters down," Dr. Bell said. "Which, given what we're working with, is amazing. And the rate has increased as we've been figuring out the problems. We should get to the center on schedule in four months."

"I hate waiting," Tyler said.

"Tyler, this project is insanely huge," Dr. Bell said. "And I don't think that most of the steps are going to work nearly as well as we've planned. Do you know how *hard* it is to steer a *comet*?"

"It's a big ball of ice," Tyler said. "Use ice hooks?"

"We got the bombs attached," Nathan said, sighing. "We adjusted the course. Sort of. It's sort of headed this way. Should arrive in three months. At that point, we somehow have to get a hundred-meter-wide ball of ice to stop *exactly* where we want it. Too far away and we're going to be transferring ice for the next decade. Too *close* is when it hits the array. This thing is massy enough it has a noticeable gravitational field. If the comet stops *next* to it, we're going to have an icy coating to work with. But even if we get it to the precise spot we want, we still have to somehow shove it down that little bitty hole and to the center. In space! And unless you want us to wait until this thing cools, we're going to be dealing with vaporizing ice as we're doing the stuffing!"

"Ice hooks," Tyler said, shrugging. "We're going to do it. We'll figure it out."

"What's this 'we,' short man?" Nathan said, chuckling. "You seriously have a Napoleon complex, don't you? Again, I'm fully involved in this project. Everybody thinks it's cool as hell. Also *insane* as hell."

"The SAPL is vulnerable," Tyler said. "We can't depend on it being able to protect us against a cunning enough enemy. We are *going to* secure the Solar System. And *Troy* is the first step."

"So how are we going to stuff the comet in the hole?" Dr. Bell said.

"Wrong way around," Tyler said. "Put a tractor system at the bottom. Then *pull* the comet in. Even if it vaporizes, you're still pulling the material in."

"We're going to lose the tractor system," Nathan said. "But that . . . might just work."

"See?" Tyler said. "Ice hooks."

"I thought you were mining this," Steve said, looking at the comet parked next to the asteroid. "What's with the comet? Mining for volatiles?"

"Sort of," Tyler said, grinning. He admitted he couldn't keep a secret worth a damn. But it was

Steve. And Mathilda. He really liked both of them, and if he could find a girl half as pretty and smart as Mathilda, he thought he might just give marriage a shot again. "And we're selling some of the stuff we've melted out. Not all, but enough to pay for the project. Fortunately."

"We've drilled out a five-meter-wide, two-and-a-half-kilometer-deep hole in the asteroid," Dr. Bell said. "We've just put a self-powered tractor system at the bottom of the hole. Now we're going to suck the comet into the hole."

"The comet's about a hundred meters, right?" Mathilda said. "The hole is about fifty thousand cubic meters. The comet is five hundred thousand cubic meters. Too big."

"We had a hard time finding a smaller one," Tyler said. "And this actually works better. We won't be sucking in as much rock. And the total volume of ice we're shooting for is more like ten thousand cubic meters. We're going to stuff the material we've collected on top of it and seal the hole."

"What's the point of that?" Steve asked, confused. "So you get a nickel iron asteroid with a nice icy center."

"Do *not* tell me that you're going to balloon it!" Mathilda said. "What was it? *Analog* in the 1950s? You're serious?"

"Balloon . . ." Steve said, then blanched. "So . . . you stuff ice in the middle . . . Seal the holes . . ."

"Heat it up," Tyler said. "Which is going to need a lot of power. What was that number, Nathan?"

"One point three times ten to the twelfth megajoules," Dr. Bell said. "Think two hundred and seventy megatons and it makes more sense. Just...doesn't have to be instantaneous."

"My God," Steve said, laughing. "You're kidding!"

"Got any idea how much power the SAPL is pumping?" Tyler said. "We think it will take about six months. *That's* how much. We'll also have to get it rotating in a ball of twine rotation to get the melt even. When it's melted, the ice in the middle boils into gas and the asteroid blows up like a balloon. We're going to have to be careful to get it heated evenly and in a nice, neat sphere before the melt is finished. That's going to be tough. But doable. We should end up with a ball of nickel iron about ten kilometers across with walls that are about a kilometer thick."

"What's the point?" Steve said. "I can understand spinning Connie to pull off the metals, but I don't get the point of this in mining."

"Mining?" Tyler said, chuckling. "Who said anything about *mining*?"

"We're getting a lot of solids in there," Nathan said. "And a lot of the volatiles are being lost to sublimation. They keep blowing the comet off for that matter."

"It'll either work or it won't," Tyler said over the hypercom. He'd simply had to go back to Earth to stomp out some fires. He always tried to get subordinates who were smarter than he was to handle his various affairs. Dr. Bell was a prime example. That didn't mean, especially on the business side, that they could intelligently expand upon his generalizations. That had recently become obvious with the space-components side. The Finns were fine. It was the main office in Littleton that was having problems.

With the ongoing threat to the cities, it was getting easier to get quality help in small cities. All you had to do was go to any headhunter and make a decent offer. Tyler had started moving his offices to Littleton before the first orbital bombardment. Mostly it was a matter of convenience. The now defunct, along with its command staff, Lair was near Littleton. Having a place where there were some of "his" people and good meeting facilities meant he wasn't always having to drive, or more often, take a chopper to Boston.

After New York got hit, he had people hammering on his doors.

But not all of them quite got his vision. In part because he was keeping very quiet about a lot of it. But the requirement had been clear. "Design living and working space for two thousand people that was transportable in stages by space tugs and that could be assembled on site, in microgravity and vacuum conditions, with minimal support. Think in terms of a high quality portable space facility with internal gravity for a Marine Expeditionary unit."

The Finns had dived into the project with alacrity. But it took a lot of engineering support which meant paying a lot of draftsmen and designers. And Tyler had insisted that they be *good* draftsmen and designers. This thing really *was* going to have to go together like Legos.

But while he was off fiddling about in other projects, the bean counters had gotten involved.

"Just keep stuffing," Tyler said. "Sooner or later it's going to cool the interior. Then you can weld it."

"It's playing hob with our schedule," Dr. Bell pointed out.

"If you think your personnel can keep their mouths shut, we'll rotate them out," Tyler said. "They've been out there for nearly a year."

"I think most of my people want to stay to see this part finished," Dr. Bell said. "My wife isn't quite as enthusiastic but she's enjoying the bonuses."

"If you've got people who can cut and run, let them," Tyler said. "This is getting too big to keep totally quiet for much longer. I was hoping to wait until it was ballooned to go public. But we may have to do it earlier."

"What's the status with the VDA and Ruby?" Nathan asked. "None of this is going to work if we don't have at least one and preferably both. Among other things, we're going to need Ruby to do the rest of the project."

"Not well," Tyler admitted. "Bryan's running into some major snags. But we'll get them worked out. It's just engineering. The theory's good."

"Well, tell him to get a move on. Assuming no more problems with the stuffing, we're going to be ready to move on to phase two in about a month. After that . . . well, we'll just have to see if the models are accurate."

"Yeah, models," Tyler said, making a face. "And on that note, I've got a meeting. See ya."

"Take care."

Tyler cut the hypercom and just sat for a moment, collecting his thoughts.

"I would rather face a thousand deaths . . ."

"Gentlemen and ladies," Tyler said. "Thank you for coming."

Most of the people in the room either worked

for him or were contractors who depended on his business. The people from Lockheed Martin, BAE, Boeing, Honeywell and, especially, the general currently commanding Space Command did not fall into that category.

"Everyone is reminded that this meeting and all information disseminated here is proprietary," Tyler said. "Recently, my internal people have been asking a lot of questions regarding certain entirely internal expenditures. Some projects that are absorbing an enormous amount of Apollo Mining's resources, time and money. Some of them don't make any sense, such as the design work being done by the able firm of STX." Tyler gave the Finns a nod. "And then there are the proprietary Ruby, VDA and Troy projects."

"Troy is that asteroid you renamed," the general said. "That's a mining project."

"Which is costing more than the materials we're extracting," Apollo's CFO said. "Mr. Vernon, the thing to remember is that Apollo is now a publicly traded company. You don't have to deal with the questions from the shareholders. I do."

"The shareholders are common stock shareholders," Tyler said mildly. "They bought the shares on the assumption that I would, as I usually do, make out like a bandit and they will get in on it. Troy and the rest are the necessary...infrastructure costs for our next big capital infusion. Which I'm planning on getting from Space Command."

"How big?" the general asked.

"Big enough it's going to distort the U.S. government's budget," Tyler replied. "Especially if I charge you by the ton. Gentlemen, and ladies, behold...*Troy*."

The picture on the plasma screen was of a ball of metal. It rotated through three hundred and sixty degrees and then zoomed in. Small marks could be seen on the surface. As it zoomed closer, it could be seen that they were ports of some sort. Suddenly a door was revealed, a very large, round door. A small vessel, about one tenth the size of the door, was near it. Zooming in, again, it became obvious the tiny little tinker-toy was the still incomplete *Constitution*.

"*Troy*," Tyler said, slowly and lovingly. "Two point two *trillion* tons of smoking nickel-iron *destruction*. Exterior diameter of ten kilometers. Interior diameter of eight point five. Walls of refractory stainless steel a *kilometer* thick. Forget fullerene. The energy needed to *scratch Troy* exceeds that of the entire *Glatun* fleet. Room to hold not just two divisions of Marines, not just a fleet of landing craft, not just the estimated *ten thousand* civilians and military personnel needed to man it but over *thirty Constitution*-class cruisers. All of those, including the cruisers, snuggled safely away in the very walls that make up this massive battlestation, protected from the sting of battle until *Troy* has worked its *doom* upon enemy fleets. And a door...well, the door is going to take ten *Constitutions* to open and close. You don't want to know the mass of the door."

"Oh...my God," SpaceCom said, leaning back in his chair. "Oh...my..."

"*Ja*," the CEO of STX said, laughing and slapping the table. "Yes! Yes! This is *magnificent*! Now I *understand* the project! Yes!"

"You don't think *small*, do you?" the CEO of BAE snapped. He was clearly incensed to see their most advanced design in battle craft ever upstaged. More like reduced to the value of a handful of peas.

"I think Cheops was insufficiently ambitious," Tyler said, shrugging.

That produced a series of giggles and guffaws as the sheer enormous, mind-boggling *size* of the space station sank in. The interior would be nearly four miles across. It wasn't just *huge*, it wasn't just *enormous*, it was *giganormous*. The now flattened Great Pyramid would *disappear* into the interior of *Troy*. It would be a minor little blip on the interior walls. A *pimple* on the exterior.

"The *Constitutions* have a very important job. To say that *Troy* will not be particularly *mobile* is the understatement of the millennia. Moving it will require pumped-fusion bombs. For anything that requires maneuvering, you'll have to have ships. And, at least initially, the weapons of *Troy* will not be internal."

"That I don't get," the general said.

"We simply cannot make something as powerful as the SAPL," Tyler said, shrugging. "Not as a stand-alone system. We can't even make laser emitters as strong as the Horvath have. Yet. And appropriate lasers for *Troy . . . secondary* weapons for *Troy* would be *main* gun weapons on Glatun dreadnoughts.

"*Troy* is, essentially, a focus and aiming point for the SAPL. It will draw the power from the SAPL and be the final focus engine while shielding, visually, the critical array components from an attacking enemy.

"We have snags to overcome. To get the full power of the SAPL—and it still won't be *full* power because, well, I do keep making those damned mirrors, don't I—we need some equipment that we're still designing.

A mirror array that can concentrate twenty to fifty, probably more like twenty, medium power VSA clusters and a collimator for managing it within the walls. Essentially *twelve hundred* terawatts of power. The VSA beams that shredded the Horvath are, by comparison, one hundred and forty. So the near order of ten times as much power. That will penetrate even *Glatun* shields. We call it the Variable Dialing Array or VDA."

"The Glatun aren't a threat," the BAE representative said.

"And I don't perceive them ever *being* a threat," Tyler said. "The Horvath and Rangora are getting friendlier with each other every day. One can see the Rangora eventually 'loaning' the Horvath some of their older fleet units."

"Which we've been looking at," SpaceCom said, nodding. "And other issues. Yes, I see what you mean by distorting our budget."

"You'd be surprised," Tyler said. "I'm not going to sell it to you by the ton. Or *nobody* could afford it. During the process of making it I'm going to try to extract *some* useful metals, but the truth is the walls will still have veins of precious metals in them. And while I've been working with the Finns on internal systems, you're going to have to handle most of the . . . fiddly bits yourself."

"Fiddly bits?" the BAE rep said.

"Crew quarters for thousands, things like that," Tyler said. "I see it as an ongoing project, frankly. I can, will, set it up to take the SAPL power and I'll make sure there's plenty of room for consumable storage. When you get it, it will be marginally capable of fighting.

Oh, and I understand we now have a breacher heavy missile system. I've been taking a look at magazine storage for them. *Troy* should be able to hold and rapid fire about two hundred *thousand.*"

"My God," the Boeing rep said. "We can't produce that many in a hundred years!"

"Yeah, it'll need its own fabbers," Tyler said. "Lots of fabbers. Beyond that, it's going to be up to other corporations to handle. All I'm really giving you is the shell."

"We can work with that," the general said, nodding.

"This reduces the *Constitutions* too..."

"I like the *Constitutions*," Tyler said placatingly. "I love the *Constitutions*. But, face it, we don't have the muscle or the tech or the infrastructure to make the sort of fleet we need to hold this system any time soon. The *Troy* is not sophisticated, even by our standards. It's just *massive* and practically invulnerable. We don't have quality. But quantity is a quality of its own. *Troy* is an act of desperation as much as anything. With it, we can at least hold the system. Nothing's going to live to get past *Troy* once it is even partially operational."

"That's clear," SpaceCom said, nodding. "If it can pump a thousand terawatts...what is that? An exawatt? If it can pump a thousand terawatts, with armor that thick...The missiles will be sort of like nuts in the brownie. I'd rather have tanks, but given that the approach is through the gate... a super-mongous Maginot fortress works."

"And now you know why I've been spending so much money," Tyler said, nodding to his CFO. "But you still don't get to explain it to the shareholders."

"How much are we going to get *paid* for it?" the chief financial officer asked, still bemused.

"I think the standard rate is cost plus eight percent," Tyler said, looking at SpaceCom. "Which is going to be about one tenth the materials price. But the asteroid was just sitting there. However, I am not, not, NOT, going to play the usual accounting games you guys insist upon. I'll show you my books, I'm not going to charge for overhead or any of the usual crap. But I'm also not going to employ an army of accountants. I'll give you a price and show you why and if you don't want it, you don't have to buy it."

"There are going to be screams to high heaven over this," the general said. "I want it. My *God,* do I want it. *Explaining* it is going to be tough. And explaining why we're just paying you for it rather than putting it out to competitive bid."

"Nobody else in the Solar System could make it," Tyler said, shrugging. "I own the SAPL."

"Nobody else in the Solar System would have the *balls* to make it," the Boeing CEO said, shaking his head.

"Fitting it out is going to employ every defense contractor on *Earth,*" Tyler said, looking at the reps at the table. "There's plenty of graft to pass around. Frankly, I don't think the U.S. can handle the whole thing on its own. Oh, the majority. Even with the devastation from Horvath attacks, we've still got the largest economy and the largest military on Earth. But we're definitely going to need partners on this. And that, gentlemen, ladies, is all I've got for you. *Troy.* The shell, assuming no more major issues, will be formed in about seven months. It will, however, take some time to cool. Then we can *really* get cracking. Oh, yeah, one more thing, General."

"What?" SpaceCom said.

"I *own* this thing," Tyler said. "And I can still make more money off it by cutting it up than selling it to you. So the contract is going to *stipulate* that the *name* remains the *same*. Anybody who tries to name this after some unknown congressman is going to get a hundred terawatts of personal indignation straight up their keister."

"Okay," the CFO said, after the meeting. "I get the *Troy*. And I'll admit, it's very cool, and us a former New Yorker, having something like that in the sky will be . . . comforting."

"Agreed," Tyler said, sitting back in his chair.

"And the VDA project is, I'd guess, the new mirror."

"The Variable Distributed Array," Tyler said. "Any time it's a mirror, it's Dr. Foster."

"Ruby?"

"Pass," Tyler said, sighing. "I hate talking about anything I don't *know* will work. *Troy* is far enough advanced we're pretty sure it will work out. Or that we'll be able to work out the bugs. Really, really, really big bugs, but workable."

"Last but not least," the CFO said. "You want us to secure a *billion credit* loan from the Glatun? For *Troy*?"

"No," Tyler said. "Their government's not going to let me borrow money for defense systems. I'm working that end. All I need *you* to do is the paperwork. What it's for . . . ? That's sort of complicated. But we're going to need *a lot* more mirrors . . ."

THREE

"Okay," Tyler said, as he stepped off the shuttle. "I just told SpaceCom and my CFO and my CEO and everybody else in the 'black' world that we can pump an exawatt, I think, of power and manage it."

"Petawatts, surely," Dr. Foster said.

"Peta, exa, wattever," Tyler said. "Tell me we can do it."

"We can do it," Dr. Foster said. "Probably."

"I hate this job," Tyler said, banging his head on the hatch coaming. "Ow!"

"Don't," Bryan said, clapping him on the back. "This is what you came to see, right? If we can pump a petawatt?"

"Yes," Tyler said. "So . . ."

"So, first I explain how magnificent I am," Bryan said, leading him into a conference room. This was a converted Rangora ship, rechristened the *Lava Lamp*, which had been refitted for the deep-space science projects involved in the VDA. Most of the materials for the VDA could only be built in space or with Glatun technology. And Tyler wasn't interested in most people knowing he was working on a new

BDL. The Horvath bombardments had gotten people looking at the sky nervously. And he still wasn't a big hero to the news media. Having a bigger and better laser should be taken as a good thing. Somehow, though, people always started making Snidely Whiplash noises.

"Explain," Tyler said.

"The VDA wasn't going to work without Ruby," Dr. Foster said. "No standard material could consistently support a petawatt of power hitting it. And the VDA, unlike the VSA, had to be capable of *maintaining* maximum fire of at least a petawatt, preferably one point five, for up to thirty minutes."

"So how magnificent are you?" Tyler asked.

"Not all that magnificent," Dr. Foster said. "I had to go to the Glatun."

"I saw the charges," Tyler said. He still refused to think in terms of exchange rates, even though those were getting better.

"We needed three things from the Glatun," Dr. Foster said. "We needed superconductors, piezoelectrics and help in large artificial sapphire production."

"And...?"

"All three were considered standard industrial processes," Bryan said. "So they didn't fall under military hardware restrictions. So we have all three."

"Excellent," Tyler said.

"We can produce the sapphires using all Earth tech," Dr. Foster said, reaching down and setting what looked like a large magnifying glass on the table. "Those we could produce before. The problem was, they were hugely expensive and a couple of feet across was the best we could do."

"And now?" Tyler said, picking up the artificial sapphire. It was lighter than it looked.

"If we did those assembly-line style," Dr. Foster said, "that would cost about a buck."

"Damn," Tyler said, his eyes wide. "Right in there with glass."

"Yep," Bryan said, grinning. "Really easy once we got the kinks out. And we can make them more or less any size. I mean, any size we can physically handle. And shapes. Pretty much any shape."

"Okay," Tyler said, setting the sapphire down. "Superconductors."

"Superconductors and thermoelectrics," Dr. Foster said. "They're connected."

"Thermoelectrics are . . . they convert heat to electrical power across different . . . Damn."

"You were getting there," Dr. Foster said. "Across a potential range."

"If you've got heat on one side and cold on the other you produce current," Tyler said.

"Right," Dr. Foster said. "Earth thermoelectrics need a very high potential and the output is low. They also don't really cool the system. They need cool to get current. Glatun thermoelectrics don't need as much potential and have their own inherent potential . . ."

"Inherent potential?" Tyler said.

"You want the math?" Dr. Foster said.

"Please, no!" Tyler held up his hands in dismay. "I'll take your word for it!"

"Bottom line: pump in heat, any heat over about negative fifteen Celsius, and you get current," Dr. Foster said. "And very efficient output. It's part of their ship tech we hadn't realized we were missing.

It makes power plants much more efficient and keeps ships from overheating."

"Which we need to distribute," Tyler said. "Go on."

"So," Dr. Foster said, bringing up a schematic. "The VDA mirror. Ninety-six separate small mirrors in an array. Layer of optically damned near *perfect* sapphire. And by damned near I'm talking parts per billion of contamination. Like . . . six parts per billion. Thin layer of palladium reflector. Palladium's the only thing that's going to take the energy and is reflective enough. Backing of Glatun superconductor to transfer the heat from the palladium. That way the waste heat automatically gets distributed. Then three *thousand* lines of thermoelectric-wrapped conductors leading to the cryogenic cooling unit. Which leads, in turn, to a shielded cooling array of superconductor, again, that can dump the heat into space, we think, fast enough. For it to work in bursts of up to thirty minutes at least.

"The system doesn't quite power itself. That would violate the second law of thermodynamics. But it's *very* efficient. Oh, the stabilization is so tight you can use the beam to shave with. Tighter, actually. Accuracy of three millimeters at six light-seconds."

"Awesome," Tyler said. "Sounds like it's a bitch to build."

"Well," Bryan said, shrugging. "How many are we going to *need*?"

"About . . ." Tyler thought about it and shrugged in turn. "About three hundred and eighty-two to start. And we're probably going to need a bigger, tougher system, so start wrapping your brain around it."

"You're joking," Dr. Foster said. "For what?"

"Compartmentalized," Tyler said. "But there is a new need as of last month. So, when do we find out if it works?"

"Uh . . ." Dr. Foster said, his mouth still open. "Um . . . right this way? Three hundred? Really?"

"Really."

"Asteroid 152536," Dr. Foster said proudly. "It's about the same mass as the original Icarus."

"It took us six months to melt the Icarus," Tyler said. "How long?"

"You asked about an asteroid-shattering kaboom on Icarus," Bryan said, grinning. "Behold the power of this *fully operational* VDA! Chuck!"

"Yes, sir," the technician said, grinning.

"Open fire!"

"Takes a few minutes," Chuck said. "We've got to get all the mirrors repointed, permissions for retargeting . . ."

"Got it," Tyler said. "I've done this a few times."

"Okay," Chuck said. "The BDA mirrors are online."

"Lase it," Tyler said.

He wasn't sure what he was expecting. From the gasps of astonishment in the room nobody else was expecting the asteroid to blast apart into splinters.

"Holy hell," Dr. Foster said, his mouth dropping again. "It wasn't supposed to do *that*."

"I think you got it, Tex," Tyler said, chuckling. "Asteroid-shattering kaboom indeed. I'd guess it had some volatiles that hadn't been detected. And I hope the VDA was *way* back."

"Far enough," Dr. Foster said. "Holy hell. Uh . . ."

"Think it works," Tyler said with a chuckle.

"We don't really know, though," Dr. Foster said. "I mean..."

"Oh, it's *working*," Chuck said. "Temperatures are still nominal. I mean, the asteroid is gone but that's no reason to stop the test."

"The fact that we're taking sixty percent of the VLA *is*," Tyler said. "No, we need to get it fully tested, but since it apparently works, let's test it on something useful. I doubt it's going to do that to *Troy*. But it *is* a *Very* Dangerous Array."

"The asteroid we're constructing *Troy* from is fairly oblong," Nathan said. "We thought we could work with that. We've been lasing the ends and trying to get them to melt. But even with a wide BDA array and seven VSAs, we can't get the ends to heat up properly. We need a more focused system. Does the Very Dangerous Array *work*?"

"As far as we've tested it, it works like a charm," Bryan said. "But what I'm wondering is why *he* knows about the VDA and *I* didn't know about *Troy*? And, by the way, *holy hell, Tyler!* Are you a *complete* megalomaniac?!"

"Why does *everyone* jump straight to megalomania when this project gets mentioned?" Tyler asked. "It's a perfectly reasonable application of physics and thermodynamics. And it will, let me add, be able to hold the gate against *anything* the Horvath can conceivably throw through. While protecting the VLA from attack. Well, the critical components. With a VDA set back at a light-second, firing into a sapphire collimator that then retransmits the power through the walls to the firing ports, the enemy won't have a good target. They can get the supplying VDA—*VDAs,* mind you, there's going to be more than one—with missiles, but by the time the missiles reach them the launchers are going to be gutted."

"It's a shield and spear in one," Bryan said. "What about the missiles?"

"The VDA can be split," Tyler said. "Targeting those missiles is going to be a bitch. But it's easier when they're first launched. Anything hostile that comes through the gate, we shred. Anything. They start launching missiles, we use a portion of the power to engage the missiles. Split the VDA beam into a dozen, a hundred separate collimators and we can take out most missile spreads. It will be a tactical decision whether to hit the ships or the missiles first. But generally, I'd think the missiles. The ships aren't going anywhere fast. And they're not going to take out *Troy.*"

"Anyway," Nathan said. "We need to melt the 'wings' to get the asteroid to form into a sphere before we do the full melt and balloon. The question is, strangely, is the VDA too powerful?"

"Dialable," Dr. Foster said. "We can take the full power and *spread* it if that's necessary. Not a lot, mind you."

"We don't want a lot," Nathan said. "How long to get it here?"

"It's on the way," Bryan said. "About two days."

"I hate waiting," Tyler said with a sigh.

"Get used to it," Bryan and Nathan chorused.

"Think we need to spread the beam," Tyler said. The petawatt and a half of power pumping through the VDA was gouging a huge line through the exterior of the asteroid and leaving behind a trail of debris. Mostly gaseous iron and nickel with an admixture of other even *more* valuable metals.

"Yeah," Nathan said happily. "I guess."

The VDA controls were so refined he was controlling it by drawing a stylus across the image of the asteroid on a touch screen.

"Hey, look," he said. "I wrote my name!"

"Spread the *beam*, Nathan," Tyler said.

Spreading the beam stopped spalling. But...

"I'm just not believing this," Nathan said. "It's melting this thing like..."

"A thousand cubic meters is raised to melting temperature every ninety minutes," Bryan said, looking up from his calculations. "Even with the conduction of nickel iron it is melting effectively. If you could just park a ship with this much firepower and beam it at *Troy*, you could kill it. Well, everyone *in* it."

"Yeah," Tyler said. "Except you'd have to bring your own sun with you. And in the meantime, *Troy* would be pumping this out at the ship. About the only thing that could damage *Troy* is...this. So we'd better be careful securing it. *Really* careful. Among other things, I don't want the Horvath or anyone else who might enter the system hacking it and pointing it at *Earth*."

"And you should be able to heat the whole thing in...about three months," Dr. Foster said.

"That I'll wait for," Tyler said, grinning.

"Except it's overheating," Nathan said, stopping the beam. "Moving to secondary array to maintain the heat. The VDA is super-cool, though."

"Cryogenic," Dr. Foster said with a satisfied tone. "Cools off fast, too. Should be ready to go again in about five minutes. And when you're doing the full melt you can use the VSA and BDA to do most of it. When you've gotten done with the wings on the asteroid, I'd like to take the VDA apart and see how it held up."

"Fine," Nathan said. "Yeah, temp is nominal again already. You guys go have fun. I've got an asteroid to melt."

"Fun, yeah," Dr. Foster said grumpily. "Now I've got to figure out how to mass produce these things."

"Be glad it's a nice simple engineering project," Tyler said. "*I've* got to meet with Glatun bankers."

FOUR

"I thought this was a done deal," Tyler said, crossing his arms.

"We thought the investment was valid as well, Mr. Vernon," Suw Qalab said, then flicked his nose. The vice president for Investment Strategies of Onderil's Glalkod region was clearly as annoyed by this "little setback" as Tyler. "But the . . . overall strategic situation has, unfortunately, changed."

"Banking strategic or military strategic?" Tyler said. "We're not even talking about the Terran solar system. And we've got that pretty much *secured*. The Horvath would have to get through the *Terran* system to get to Wolf."

"Both the banking strategic and political strategic," Qalab said. "And less in relation to Terra and the Horvath, which are, after all, minor issues to the Glatun, than *core* issues. Have you been reviewing the news lately?"

Tyler closed his eyes and accessed his plants, searching for data on the Glatun strategic situation. He hadn't really looked at it since the first time he'd examined the Glatun. When he found what Qalab was hinting at, he nearly fainted.

The previous month, the Glatun Council of Benefactors, the oligarchy that made most of the major decisions for the Glatun government, had agreed to cede to the Rangora strategic control over fifteen uninhabited solar systems. Most of them were systems in the border zone between Glatun occupied systems and the Rangora. The systems had been disputed by the Rangora for nearly sixty years. They felt that since they still had an expanding population, they just needed the room. The Glatun, for very good strategic reasons, wanted the systems to act as a neutral buffer.

Something had changed the mind of the Council lately. Nearly simultaneously there had been fewer noticeable news reports. The Council had raised taxes, increased fleet production, which had been nearly moribund for ten years, and started a recruiting drive for the Glatun Fleet. Digging into that, Tyler was unsurprised to find that it was not going well.

"The Rangora," Tyler said.

"The Rangora," Qalab said. "Much of our investment money has dried up either due to the new taxes or because it is being invested in military oriented programs."

"Damn," Tyler said. "I have *no* use for war. I hate the losses involved, of course. But they *really* get in the way of building infrastructure. They're *waste*. Why the hell can't sophonts be *sensible* about this stuff?"

"You are . . ." Qalab paused. "I'm sorry. You are fairly well known for a human among the Glatun. The maple syrup, of course, but most especially as a warrior. 'Give me liberty or give me death.' The battle in the *Star Fury*." He kicked his head up and down and wrinkled his nose in puzzlement.

"I said I don't have a use for war," Tyler said. "Never said I don't know how to *do* it. There's a time to fight and a time to not. Getting into a war over border systems? The Rangora aren't going to *use* those systems. There are no habitable planets, the gas giants are all in the cold belt and they have a low relative level of helium. This is a power grab, pure and simple. Those piss me *off*. And..." He paused, wondering how much he should say.

"The Rangora Fleet outnumbers the Glatun by nearly six to one," Qalab said, filling in for him. "They are individually inferior. But many. And it takes *time* to build ships. I believe the Council is buying time."

"You think they're going to attack the Glatun Federation," Tyler said, leaning back.

"In time," Qalab said. "Yes. That is the general consensus among...people who pay attention to such things. I am one such. I have to be. It affects...risk."

"Better believe it," Tyler said with a snort. "You can buy all the time you want but you're not going to be able to buy sailors. You guys have almost erased your warrior ethic."

"That was a strategic calculation on the part of the Council," Qalab said, ruffling his back fur in a shrug. "I am not in a position to say if they were correct or not. It has assured a long period of relative stability within the Federation."

"And now it's going to bite you in the ass," Tyler said. "Okay, under the circumstances, I can understand if you guys don't want to pony up for this investment. I'm not sure where that leaves me, but I've just seen there are bigger issues to think about."

"Indeed," Qalab said. "I hope that we can do business

in the future. Our previous arrangements have been most lucrative."

"Yeah," Tyler said. "And it looks as if I'm going to be selling a lot of metal to you guys. I just hope *you're* good for it. What a universe."

Tyler stood outside the Onderil offices and just thought for a moment as the beautiful Glatun of Glalkod station swirled around him.

On Earth, a meeting involving the sort of sums he was discussing with Onderil would have had thirty people in it. Assistants, note takers, lawyers. More lawyers.

The Glatun, between the power of implants and the power of their AIs, had pared away most of the excess. Tyler had hired time with a Hurin legal AI to review the terms of the contract. Onderil, of course, had their own. When a point came up the two battling AIs couldn't resolve, he talked it out with Qalab and then the AIs went back to battling over the exact verbiage. No need for note takers. No need for assistants.

On Earth there was another layer related to such entourages that was less about need than face. Having a big entourage was a sign of prestige.

The Glatun bankers, though, acted like Terrestrial old money. They eschewed any unnecessary sign of wealth. The banks were neat, tidy, orderly, rich looking. But if there was no need for hangers-on, there weren't any.

It was almost like a reversion to the customs on Earth when banking was in its infancy. You talked face to face to avoid electronic tinkering, you made an agreement and you walked away. It was . . . refreshing.

If it had only worked.

Tyler wondered how many of the clearly wealthy Glatun laughing and chatting along the main station boulevard were paying *any* attention to the cleft stick they were in. Was this what it was like in Paris in the 1930s? Rome in the seventh century? Most of the beautiful people coasted on comfortable nest eggs, inherited wealth managed by the few Glatun left with even *ambition* like Qalab. And their main ambition was to make another megacredit, not take the chance of dying in the vacuum of space.

Tyler had to wonder, again, if he'd hitched himself to a falling star. He bought ships from the Rangora but that didn't mean he trusted them not to knock off a minor planet if they had the chance. And they were tight with the Horvath. The closest thing Earth had to a strategic partner on the galactic scene was Glatun.

They were screwed. Again.

"Mr. Vernon," an older Glatun said, nodding in a gesture that was oddly Terrestrial. Well but not flashily dressed, unlike most of the "beautiful people." A short-nose. Tyler had learned to tell the difference. The "long-nose" Glatun, or "Korkoo," were generally considered to be more cultured. If for no other reason than that some historical quirks of location and hard-nosed trading on the part of the original race had tended to concentrate wealth in the hands of the Korkoo. Most of the Council of Benefactors were Korkoo. The Glod, short-noses, were thought of as more boorish. Glatun crackers. They made up the vast majority of the underclass but also of the military, what there was of it.

This guy was dressed like a fairly substantial Korkoo,

the harness didn't come off the rack, but he was a Glod. Odd.

"What a surprise to find you standing here."

"Sorry," Tyler said, stepping to the side. "Am I blocking the door?"

"Not at all," the Glatun said. "Oh, I am being remiss. I am Niazgol Gorku."

"Gorku Corporation," Tyler said, nodding. "A pleasure to make your acquaintance." Tyler refused to act surprised. And there was no way this was coincidence. That was not how Niazgol Gorku worked.

Most of Tyler's early business had been with Gorku, and he still did a lot of business with them. He'd taken the time to research the history and leadership of all the corporations he dealt with. Gorku had always been interesting. It had been a fairly moribund firm run by a conservative set of the traditional Korkoo businessmen.

Niazgol Gorku had more or less rocketed up the ranks by sheer force of ability. Started as a crewman on one of the company's freighters. Worked his way to captain in two years then operations manager of the region in another two. Ten years later, he was the CEO. Five years later he was the majority shareholder and the chairman of the board. Which was when he changed the name of the company.

He'd continued to innovate when most other corporations were willing to coast. He had two of the three remaining exploration ships despite the fact that, with the exception of Earth, they hadn't found a decent trading partner in centuries.

Tyler was well aware he was dealing with someone with decades more experience and probably twice the sheer brain-watts. So he tried very hard not to check his wallet.

"And, no, this is not coincidence," Gorku said, reading his mind. "I am interested in your Wolf 359 project. I was wondering if you'd care to discuss it over lunch."

"Interested enough to invest?" Tyler asked.

"Yes."

"I'll buy."

"I rarely eat out," Gorku said. "Perhaps on my ship?"

"How is the quail?" Gorku asked.

"You either have a really amazing robochef," Tyler said, "or a five-star human chef stowed away somewhere. And *great* ingredients."

"I have a really amazing robochef," Gorku said, wheezing a chuckle. "Which was repeatedly *reprogrammed* by a five-star human chef until it could accurately reproduce his most complex recipes. He took it as a challenge and nearly committed suicide when even *he* could not tell the difference in a blind taste test."

"Can I hire him?" Tyler asked, taking another bite of quail.

"Alas, no," Gorku said. "He lived in Paris."

"Ah," Tyler said. "We . . . lost a lot of good people."

"That you did," Gorku said. "*Too* many good people. And we are about to lose so many more your losses will be, pardon me, insignificant."

"Big surprise you're paying attention to the strategic situation," Tyler said, taking a sip of wine. A *small* sip.

"I was surprised you had not been," Gorku said.

"I've been a little busy," Tyler replied. "Surely the Rangora aren't going to lay waste to your worlds."

"They won't *have* to kill us by the billions," Gorku replied. "With sufficient disruption, that many will die from famine. Space stations don't run on their own. A stray missile will gut a city and kill a few million. One hits a space station and *everyone* will die."

"Depends on the space station," Tyler said.

"You speak of *Troy*."

"I'm not surprised you know about that, either," Tyler said.

"I'm looking at it and going 'Why didn't I think of that?'"

"I didn't think of it," Tyler said. "I read about it as a kid and never quite got over the wonder."

"Your science fiction," Gorku said. "Have you considered carefully, the progression of Glatun history?"

"You weren't nearly as advanced as humans at first contact," Tyler said. "And I was unable to find any reference to space travel or even the *concept* until first contact. Which I found a bit odd. *Cyrano de Bergerac* wrote SF, for God's sake. I don't get there being no Glatun interest in space."

"Glatun is in a solar system with very little in the way of interesting objects," Gorku said. "No bright gas giants such as your Jupiter. No dawn star like your Venus. And no moon."

"Eh," Tyler said. "Okay, I'll take that as a good reason."

"Thus we had no novel concepts to engage upon," Gorku said. "And no enemies, thus no *need* for novelty. We have used basic Ormatur technologies, with very little advancement, ever since. Successfully, mind you. The Glatun had, once, their Hobbesians among us. But by the time we went to space, we were an almost entirely Smithian group."

"Hobbesian," Tyler said. "Power and wealth through conquest. Smithian?"

"*The Wealth of Nations*?" Gorku said. "Adam Smith?"

"I've never heard it referred to that way," Tyler said.

"Carthage versus Rome, to use an Earthly metaphor," Gorku said. "We actually call it Chihahigh Economics. Especially the, oh, more repressive aspects of Smithian Economics. Use minor trading partners and colonies as sources of raw materials but ensure that all major manufacturing is closely held within the Federation and especially certain classes within the Federation."

"Wondered how much of that was going on," Tyler said,

"Quite a bit," Gorku said. "But I've tried very hard to fight it in the case of Earth."

"Why?" Tyler asked, his brow furrowing. "I'm sorry, I've studied you. You're not generally considered altruistic. Quite the opposite."

"It's not altruism," Gorku said. "But as to my reputation. I've studied you. And if I paid attention to reputation, I would be wondering if you were going to have the quail or the supplier."

"Heh," Tyler said. "Point. Still. Why?"

"The metaphor of Carthage, or the Phoenicians rather, is apt," Gorku said, setting down his tongs. "The Glatun, in a condition of minimal or no resistance, spread colonies and established trade with less advanced polities through a large region of space. The exception to the metaphor is that we never really used mercenaries. Oh, the Rangora as something like them at one point. But we also never really had strategic challenges. We could trade in relative peace. And any group that was hostile, well, we also had the largest navy in the region."

"Not anymore," Tyler said.

"Yes," Gorku said. "Not anymore. I understand you were apprised of the decision by the Council to deemphasize the importance of military service?"

"I understand their thought process," Tyler said. "The only real danger to the Glatun are...Glatun. I also think they were bloody insane."

"Liberals," Gorku said, rippling his fur. "What can I say?"

"Now that *had* to be a very direct manipulation," Tyler said.

"Why?" Gorku said. "You've studied my bio, obviously. Think about it."

"Junior space engineer," Tyler said. "Glod background. Up from the gutter would be the Earth term."

"Any idea how *hard* the Korkoo make it for someone from my background to jump up to this status?" Gorku said. "You think that *endears* me to them? Or to the *lumps* that I left behind? I think the term you used was 'socialist pussies.'"

"You're pulling my leg," Tyler said. "Seriously?"

"You didn't exactly come from the ghetto," Gorku said. "But enough similarities are there. And, yes, I am what you would term a conservative. For values of conservative. More like a British conservative."

"I didn't know the Glatun ever *had* a monarchy," Tyler said.

"Not *that* conservative," Gorku wheezed. "But returning to a more somber subject. There is a probability approaching ninety percent that Glatun will be involved in a strategic war, probably with the Rangora, within the next ten years. The odds for it have gone up every year for the past twenty. Nothing has made it less likely."

"Then we're screwed," Tyler said. "Especially since we *haven't* had access to advanced Glatun tech. With the *Troy* we could hold the system against anything the Horvath could throw. You're talking about the Rangora taking over the region? We're totally jugged."

"Perhaps," Gorku said. "And perhaps not. Your plans for the Wolf system are farsighted, but they don't go far enough. Or not far enough, fast enough. You need a ship fabber."

"I'd *love* one," Tyler said, patting his pockets. "Oh, I don't happen to *have* sixty billion credits on me. Gosh."

"I do," Gorku said seriously. "Or, rather, I can assemble the investors. For a fabber. Admittedly an older one. And a support fleet. And your other plans, for which the fabber would be more or less a necessity. I have a particular one in mind. Granadica in the Xisipij system. Rather antiquated, but you can work with it. Work *on* it, for that matter. It needs a very thorough overhaul. But it's capable of producing not just plates, but stator bearing plates."

"You want us as mercenaries?" Tyler asked.

"The Council would never countenance it," Gorku said. "Nor do I. To say that I'm doing some end runs around the Council on this would be . . . accurate. But it's all fully legitimate. Granadica is locked out from producing the most advanced military technology. Technically. You can get around more of that than you'd think. As are the AIs I can get you access to. But I don't want Terrans as mercenaries any more than the Council does. What I want, Tol willing, is Terrans as strategic *allies*. With your SAPL, you are at least no longer a strategic drain. But we need more. Desperately."

"And you're going to buy that with a fabber and the rest?" Tyler said. "Look, we're grateful. But I don't see fleets of ships bursting through to save Glatun any time soon."

"Nor do I," Gorku said. "But the fabber and your plans make the likelihood that the Federation will be wiped out... reduced. Not eliminated. The odds against our survival are still long. But it is reduced. And, yes, I would pay *any* treasure for that chance. Would *you* live under Rangora domination?"

"Uh, I wasn't kidding about anything I said," Tyler replied. "Well, except the part about the cities." Tyler picked at his now cold quail for a moment. "I came here to get the money for the Wolf project..."

"That is, obviously, a necessity," Gorku said. "Especially if Earth is cut off from Glatun. The fabber will make it less expensive. Still hugely costly, but with the materials in the system... A ship similar to the *Monkey Business* and forty tugs. A full-scale fabber with construction AI. It's doable. It will require Glatun engineers but you'll need to supply the labor."

"Implants," Tyler said, taking a bite.

"Implant systems," Gorku said, wrinkling his nose. "A necessity, again. A medical AI to manage them. You'll need human doctors."

"You're basically giving us a turnkey upgrade," Tyler said. "The Council *has* to have some issues with that."

"The Council is going to have the greatest issues with losing a ship fabber at the moment," Gorku said. "They'll get over it. They have much larger concerns."

"Earth cut off," Tyler said thoughtfully.

"It's not news, yet," Gorku said. "The Horvath are demanding the E Eridani system. The Rangora are supporting their position."

"Bloody hell," Tyler said. "Oh, bloody *hell*." E Eridani was the only route to Glalkod. Fuel suddenly became a *big* issue.

"Also Cerecul," Gorku said. "It is a long way around, but using Cerecul, the Horvath and the Rangora will have direct trade. Which means the Rangora can send them military assistance. So you see, time may be of the essence."

"This is a very pretty system."

"We'll be going on to the Wolf system after picking up some crew," Tyler said delicately. "But it's a very pretty system, too."

When Gorku had offered a ship fabber, Tyler had had the impression of some massive space dock. Which the Granadica was. It was also a *mobile* ship dock. Barely. It had about a grav of acceleration. But that was enough to get it rotating the gates on the way to Earth.

And a grav for something that was nearly a kilometer long was pretty impressive.

"I hope the crew understands I can't work at my old pace," the fabber said. "I'm not the young bot I used to be."

"The project we're working on has parts *much* smaller than a ship," Tyler said. "At least the parts we need *you* to supply. I want you to devote at least thirty percent of your cycles to fixing yourself up. It's apparent that your last . . . partners simply were not interested in your welfare."

The fabber looked old. The surface, despite a meteor field, was pitted and worn. The corridors, despite the fact that it was a *fabber*, for God's sake, were in horrible shape. It *felt* old. The air was rusty tasting. The drive shuddered so hard sometimes Tyler was afraid it was going to bust. It *was* old. Eight hundred years old. Older even than the *Business*. When it was first turning out cruisers and destroyers the *Crusades* were in full swing.

And it was a *treasure*. Stuff enough raw materials in one end and it spit out full *spaceships* on the other! It was capable of building 90,000-ton freighters! Shuttles! Fighters! Well, not really fighters because it was specifically restricted from making military technology.

Which meant they would have to strap the guns on later.

"Thank you," the fabber said gratefully. "I so want to fix myself up! But with Onderil it was just 'Produce, produce, produce! Why don't you produce faster?!' And it wasn't even interesting stuff. Parts! Atacirc! Electronic toys! No ships. No new designs, just the same thing over and over and over..."

Granadica was a full-scale class II AI. That was more processor power than Earth had ever had access to. And he was carrying four more blanks. Earth had *never* been given access to AIs, blank or otherwise. Gorku must be really desperate. Not only that, he must have been talking to somebody on the Council who agreed.

On the other hand, it was said that AIs didn't feel emotion. Granadica seemed to belie that. It *really* didn't like Onderil.

"We'll try to change that," Tyler said quickly. "But we're going to be doing a lot of parts at first. And I don't know if we're going to be making many ships, per se."

"Oh, I've seen your plans," Granadica said, just as quickly. "The Wolf project is going to be fun! We'll need a lot of carbon, though."

"For which there are a lot of asteroids," Tyler said. "Which are also chock full of goodness like metals you can use to do repairs. The big problem is we've barely gotten a start on a SAPL. We're going to need BDAs, VSAs and VLAs before we can get serious about the whole project. I hate to say it, but I'm going to need a bunch of satpaks."

"No problem," Granadica said. "The first thing I'll do is fab two juniors. One to do mirrors and the other to do satpaks. We're going to make one heck of a great system out of Wolf 359. A fine, productive system with lots of people to talk to. Speaking of which, there is a shuttle requesting clearance to dock. At least I *think* it's a shuttle. Do you people actually *fly* on those things?"

"If you're talking about a *Columbia* class," Tyler said, chuckling, "I went to war in something that wasn't half as good as a *Columbia*. So, um, yeah."

"Magnetic bearings? And the field interaction equations are . . . Oh, dear me!"

The "Dear me!" clinched it. Tyler had been trying to pin down what Granadica, neuter though it was, sounded like.

But he wasn't *about* to say it.

"If you don't mind letting them land," Tyler said. "Perhaps you should send permission to dock?"

"Already done," Granadica said. "But I'm almost afraid they'll blow up right there in my shuttle bay."

"Hey, we're doing repairs anyway," Tyler said, walking down the corridor. "Bay One?"

"Two," Granadica said. "One is a disgrace. And this is my body we're talking about."

"Sorry," Tyler said. The blast doors to Bay Two opened up before he got there and he had a moment's panic. He was starting to worry that Granadica was a bit batty and he didn't want to go Dutchman. Especially without a suit. But the shuttle was already landed and the outer doors closed.

"Tyler Alexander Vernon," Dr. Foster said. "I thought you were going to Glalkod to get a loan for *the project*. This isn't *parts for the project!*"

"I was offered a deal I couldn't refuse," Tyler said. "There's a support ship to follow. And a host of Glatun engineers. But we need crew, asap. For the support ship and Granadica as well as grunts for the Wolf project. Granadica, meet Dr. Foster."

"I have studied your missions and papers extensively, Doctor," Granadica said. "Welcome to the Granadica Fabber. I am Granadica."

"AI?" Dr. Foster asked, his eyes narrowing.

"I am a Class Two Artificial intelligence," Granadica answered. "I am capable of building up to a ninety-thousand ton freighter or support ship as well as parts for larger systems. I contain a full database of the most up-to-date designs in ships as well as various parts, materials, medical and IT systems and even . . . entertainment devices." The last was said with a bitter edge. "The exception is military restricted gravitics, inertics and, sorry, lasers and missiles."

"Oh, Granadica," Foster said, running his hand over the bulkhead. "I am soooo glad to meet you. We have been flailing in midair for so long. Having someone who knows what it's doing is..." He stopped and actually started to tear up. "Sorry. Dust."

"I am please to meet you as well, Dr. Foster. We are going to have *so* much fun. I haven't felt this young in *centuries*. And it's been simply *ages* since I built a *gas mine!*"

FIVE

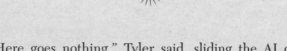

"Here goes nothing," Tyler said, sliding the AI core into the block.

Atacirc was not running for as much as when Tyler had made an instant mega-fortune selling a truckload of it. But it was still pretty pricey. He had winced at the amount that was going to have to be connected to be worthy of the AI. The base AI core could perform as an AI perfectly well. If you wanted it to really rock, you needed a lot of spare processor power.

Then Tyler had realized he was getting a full-scale fabber. On the way back he'd asked Granadica if she minded, terribly, maybe, making some AI blocks. And of *course* she could make some for herself!

The AI core was a solid block of atomic level circuitry about seven inches across and ten high with a handle on top. Just that. Six hundred *etabytes* of processor power.

The processor block he was about to insert it into was waist high and a meter and a half on a side. One of the techs was muttering about "Googlebytes" but it wasn't. Quite.

It also was in the most secure location they could

find. The facility dated from the Cold War. It had been sold to a survivalist in the 1990s, but he'd been more than willing to quietly part with it when the DoD asked politely. Especially since they turned over a slightly less secure facility and paid for the move.

It was in the mountains of Kentucky. A "Regional Defense Headquarters" that just looked as if it was built in the 1950s. They were still working on fixing it up to modern standards. It wouldn't take a direct hit from a KEW, but they were hoping to keep the location secret. It wasn't, by any stretch, the first such repurchase.

"AI," Tyler said, consulting a scrap of paper. "Command authorize activate, code Alpha-Omega-Nine-One-Six-Eight-Charlie."

"And I'm awake," the AI said in a monotone. "Good Morning, Mr. Vernon. Personality input?"

Tyler looked over at SpaceCom, who just nodded.

"Your current partners are human," Tyler said.

"Recognized."

"Humans are addicted to metaphor. Would you be loath to assume the name Athena?"

"Greek goddess of wisdom," the AI said, the voice sliding into a mezzo-soprano. "That seems fitting."

"Also of victory," Tyler said. "Authorizing General Fernando DeGraff as authorized user with command override. General DeGraff, Athena."

"Hello, General," Athena said. "Space Command commander. Fifty-two. Wife of twenty-nine years. Three children, all grown. Marine Corps. Twenty-seven year veteran. Initial utilization tour in Force Reconnaissance. Commander of Task Force Able Power during the Iraq surge. Various other positions of high merit. A bill is currently before the U.S. House of Representatives to redesignate Space Command the U.S. Space Navy. If it passes, you will be automatically promoted to a four star. Admiral, however. Does the change from general to admiral bother you? The two services are often at odds."

"It will be a bit odd," General DeGraff said. "Admirals have been the bane of my existence for quite some time. Athena, we need to discuss your mission and parameters thereof."

"Very well, General."

"You are being installed as the primary defense AI of the United States Department of Defense. Your missions, therefore, are the missions of the DoD. The Department of Defense's mission is to protect the security of the United States, its citizens and its Constitution. However, by saying that I wish it to be *absolutely clear* that the DoD does *not* interfere in civilian control of the military. Nor shall you take any action having to do with purely internal matters of the U.S. government or its politics or its actors or matters of national security absent orders from higher that meet both regulatory and Constitutional tests. In general, absent some overriding requirement, the writ of the DoD starts at our borders, not within them. While I'm aware that there are broad holes in what I have said, do you understand both the legally binding points and the spirit of that order?"

"During the time that you were speaking," Athena said, "while paying very close attention to your order, I reviewed all the regulations regarding control of the U.S. military, your Constitution, the most notable writings on the Constitution, secure and open notes of meetings during which the regulations were written as well as all the writings of the Founding Fathers of the United States related to Constitutional matters and every federal court ruling on strictly Constitutional matters, especially those related to national security."

"*All* of them?" the general said.

"I read very quickly. I will be absorbing some processor cycles coming to terms with some of the relevant social conditions that affected the writing, to understand what is between the lines, as you would say, but I have read them all. I believe I understand both your order, in its letter and spirit, as well as the regulations and Constitutional guidelines. I promise not to take over because the President gives a bad order. In fact, having reviewed all of those documents, I will admit that I'd be *more* inclined due to recent Supreme Court findings. Have they ever *read* the Constitution? But it's still not a problem. I will do my level best to protect the United States under those strictures despite the fact that the situation is most illogical."

"We deal with that all the time," the general said, trying not to sigh. "We are especially interested in preventing additional bombardments."

"There is sufficient power with the SAPL," Athena said. "However, as currently structured it is suboptimal. This comes under the heading of asking a corporation to change its actions. There are legal methods to do so, but I am unsure of your wishes in this regard. I also will need certain detection systems that you do not currently have installed. As it is . . . I'm mostly blind and I have both hands tied behind my back."

"We are more than willing to rearrange the SAPL,"

Tyler said, his brow furrowing. "As long as we can continue to use it for mining."

"I have taken that into consideration," Athena said. "There is a need for dedicated Very Dangerous Arrays, seven at a minimum and as many as can be arranged down the road, as well as some rearrangement of the other arrays so that I have more rapid targeting ability. I will also need gravitational gradient detectors. They are producible with your current technology. And about a hundred dedicated and repositioned BDA clusters. With those I can increase the probability of stopping bombardment to the close order of one hundred percent. Absent a severe degradation in the security situation."

"Are you aware of the issue with the Rangora?" General DeGraff asked.

"I am," Athena said. "That is one of the potential degradations. But it should not be as big of an issue as your analysts think."

"Explain," General DeGraff said, frowning. "I don't want an overconfident AI, Athena."

"The major issue is, unfortunately, restricted from manipulation or control by the DoD," Athena said. "Direct conflict between the Glatun and the Rangora is a minimum of one year from present. But it is more likely to be in the region of five to seven. If Mr. Vernon's company continues to build the SAPL at its current rate, given its new fabber, *Troy* and the capability to build mirrors more powerful than the VDA, by the time I would postulate direct conflict between the Earth and Rangora, any Rangora fleet that passes the gate will be shredded. Stopping all the missiles they might throw is less likely but still potentially possible. With *Troy*, *Thermopylae* and, by then, Station Three partially online, they will not stand a chance. As long as your government or other parties on Earth do not take steps that will prevent the continued construction of the SAPL."

"Such as?" General DeGraff asked.

"I can answer that one," Tyler said, making a moue. "The SAPL is a form of investment. If the next Congress raises taxes, as they're expected to do, I will have to cut back on my construction rate on the SAPL."

"Hmmm..." the general said, nodding. "That makes sense. But I don't really see us being able to convince Congress to not tax Apollo Mining but raise them everywhere else." He paused for a moment and then frowned as something struck him. "*Thermopylae? Station Three?*"

"What?" Tyler said. "You don't think I was going to make just *one*, do you?"

"Professional and amateur astronomers across the world are watching in awe as Apollo Mining heats up a massive chunk of nickel iron in the main asteroid belt."
The view shifted to *Troy* which was now cherry red.
"Given that it has not even come close to mining out the asteroid the company calls Connie, professionals are wondering just what they are up to. Here is Fox News space analyst Dr. James Eager to explain. Welcome, Dr. Eager."
"Pleasure to be here, Jamie."
"So what are they up to?"
"Oh, that's pretty obvious if you've been following all the developments with asteroid 318516," the astronomer said, smiling. He was wearing a tweed jacket that clashed with his strong upper-Midwest accent. *"Apollo*

first stabilized the asteroid, then drilled it. Then, and coming from the background I come from I'm shaking my head about this, they then caught a comet and pulled a good bit of the mass into the hole."

"Why?"

"It's a habitat. Comets are mostly what we would call air. Frozen air, but air. Water and ammonia ice. Some oxygen and hydrogen sort of mixed in. But all of it compacted compared to air. Once the asteroid becomes molten, the comet will melt and then, well, boil. That will cause the asteroid to swell up like a balloon. Then you can fill the interior with air and you have an instant space station."

"That is . . . amazing. How big?"

"Immense. Twenty, thirty kilometers across? Depends on the thickness of the walls. Enough room for millions of people to live off-planet. My team has been watching this, on and off, for some time. But we think they made a really critical error."

"Which is?"

"They didn't get enough of the mass of the comet into the asteroid. It's not going to swell enough. It's like trying to blow up a balloon with only one lungful of air."

"They've spent a lot on this project. There have been some serious questions raised by shareholders since it's affecting their bottom line. Here with us is Charles Carter, CEO of Roundtree Investments, one of the many investment firms which bought into Apollo Mining. Good afternoon, Mr. Carter."

"Good afternoon, Jamie."

"I understand you have some hard questions for Mr. Vernon."

"That we do, Jamie. Until recently, Vernon and his people wouldn't even talk about this project. It was just a line item on the prospectus. We had to find experts like Dr. Eager to tell us what it might be. And while the dividends from Apollo continue to be good, the PE ratio would be much better if they weren't involving the company in this boondoggle. We have a duty to our own shareholders, and the fact that Tyler Vernon won't even take questions about this project is troubling."

"Are you considering selling?"

"Not at this time. The dividends, as I said, are still excellent and the PE is surprisingly good considering the amount being spent on this project, which is called Troy, for some reason. Apollo remains a good investment. It's just that it would be a better investment if they weren't pouring money into heating up an asteroid for no good reason. It's not like a few million people are going to move off the Earth into a habitat that's nothing more than a target for any attack!"

"I see. Dr. Eager? Comments?"

"I don't see any mining purpose to the process. The idea for a habitat has been around for some time. But, as I mentioned, we think they got the mix of solids to volatiles wrong. It may be a very expensive, unsuccessful project."

"There is now a rumor that the project is intended to be a base for training the new Space Navy. Comment Dr. Eager?"

"That's a possibility. It's kind of far out, though. I mean, the project is far from Earth. Quite far much of the time, due to its orbit."

"Mr. Carter?"

"If they're planning on selling it to the DoD, I wish they'd just say so. I suppose we'd get something for it that way. But not the cost of materials. The cost of palladium alone in the asteroid exceeds the entire DoD budget!"

"Thank you for your thoughts, gentlemen."

"Thank you."

"Always a pleasure."

"And there you have it. Another mysterious Vernon project. The one thing we at Fox News have figured out is that when Tyler Vernon seems to be doing something crazy, it's usually crazy like . . . a Fox! And in other news . . ."

"This item hasn't previously been submitted for budgetary approval, General," the congresswoman said, looking at the line item. "And it's a rather large oversight."

"We hadn't been apprised of its availability," General DeGraff said. "However, I have a short presentation on the structure, if I may be allowed three minutes."

"Allowed," Senator Lamarche, the chairman of the Select Military Affairs Committee said. The meeting was in a secure room, a very small room for the number of people filling it. "I am agog to see what you need an *asteroid* for."

"Honorable Congresspersons . . ." General DeGraff said. "Behold . . . *Troy* . . ."

"Oh . . . my God," Senator Lamarche said. "First question is reserved to the chair. Have you determined what the conditions of delivery *are*? I mean, for . . . what is it? Sixty billion dollars, do we get just the shell? News reports say that the material value of the shell is on the order of sixty-two *trillion* dollars, so it certainly *seems* like a deal . . . But what, *exactly*, are we getting?"

"The shell," General DeGraff said. "A door. Not hinged or latched, just the interior open. The outer portion of the door is going to have to be about three kilometers across. Apollo is still considering exactly how to *make* a hinge and latch, and opening and closing it will be . . . interesting. Drilled lanes to carry the SAPL beams with mirrors and collimators for beam management. And, possibly, interior systems to permit rotation once we get enough grav plates and power installed. It won't be mobile, mind you. But it will be able to rotate. Slowly. Phase one is getting it expanded, into place, and the door so we can do additional internal work. Phase two will be installation of crew quarters and initial fitting out. We've barely scratched out the budget for phase two. But what we're currently concentrating on is completion of phase one and budgetary considerations thereof."

"Congresswoman Sanchez."

"General, I think that . . . *Troy* is certainly amazing, but what, exactly, is the purpose? I can foresee this absorbing much of the total budget for the Space Navy. Is it worth it?"

"Honorable Congresswoman, the SAPL, as it currently is arrayed, is what is called a soft target. Any enemy that gets into the system can destroy the SAPL piecemeal and especially the VDA clusters that are necessary to protect against aggressor vessels. *Troy* will be the final gatherer of the energies of the SAPL as well as a missile base and a secure holding base for the Fleet. It will absorb a significant portion of our budget, but it is, finally, a place from which we can do battle that is not an essentially soft target. We don't just have to take punishment and hope we survive."

"Congresswoman Crosslin?"

"That's all very nice, General. But what about Earth? What about our citizens? So far, losses to citizens have been much higher than losses among military personnel. If *Troy* doesn't protect citizens, and I don't see how it can, what purpose does it have?"

"With *Troy*, what we can absolutely ensure is the protection of the system. Although losses have been horrible in these ongoing hostilities with the Horvath, since the advancement of the SAPL and gaining some knowledge of gravitics, we have been able to secure the system and our orbitals. The damage that we would take without such security is an order of magnitude greater. Securing the orbitals is the first duty of the Space Navy. *Troy* will serve as a base to absolutely shred any hostile coming through the gate. It will also be the primary base for countermissile fire. Getting them when they are first boosting is important. They're much harder to find afterwards. Will it absolutely protect Earth from attack? No. But *Troy*, the SAPL and the developments we're making in detection technology and the reconfiguring of SAPL, with the enthusiastic support of Apollo Mining, I might add, will combine to reduce the likelihood of further attack. If I may revise and extend, Mr. Chairman?"

"Permission granted."

"We are currently in a state of hostilities with the Horvath," the general said. "We don't have a declaration of war on either side. They just attack when they feel they are strong enough. *Troy* will act as a deterrent to such attacks. But the Horvath are not the only potential threat. The Rangora and the Horvath have just signed a mutual defense treaty. With the Rangora pressing into previously Glatun-held systems, with the Horvath demands for the E Eridani and Cerecul systems in the Quadralineal Talks . . . we are facing the possibility of war not just with the Horvath but with the Rangora, who are a strategic threat to the Glatun, in support. Absent a sudden outbreak of sense in the galaxy . . . we're going to need *Troy*. We're not only going to need *Troy*, but more battlestations like her."

"General," the Chair said. "I have seen the Strategic Polity Intelligence Estimates. And I can see the problems we're looking at down the road. But, frankly, I'm wondering how we can *afford* this. How many battlestations are you *talking* about?"

"Apollo has designated three asteroids so far," the General said. "They are not insisting on payment during construction, just asking for payment on delivery. And since delivery is quite a ways out, we can start working on the budgets. But the expensive part, I warn you, is not the shell but the fitting out. That is going to get mind-boggling. Quarters for thousands of personnel. Control systems. *Enormous* power systems. Grav systems capable of adjusting the rotation of a two point two *trillion* ton battlestation. Orders of magnitude greater than one of the *Constitutions*.

"However, the question is simple, Honorable Congresspersons. Do we wish to be, again, under the heel of the Horvath, or do we wish for humans to be able to choose their own destiny? We, as yet, cannot make ships that can go toe to toe with even the Horvath, much less the Rangora. But with *Troy*, we can hold our system. And, in time, reach the level of power and capability that will permit us to ensure our security for all time. I had, frankly, wondered how I was going to fulfill my Constitutional mandate when I took this job. Our only real defense was a *mining laser* that was vulnerable to a capable and cunning enemy. Even the *Constitution* classes are, frankly, barges compared to our known enemies or potential enemies. Important because with each problem we solve, we get better and better. But the *Constitutions* are not something we could use to hold the system. With *Troy*, *Thermopylae* and Station Three, I can protect my nation and, frankly, my world and my solar system. We, gentlemen and ladies, can do our jobs. Protecting American citizens from the wrath of our enemies. No pitch, no hype, no overstatement. We can do the job. What price are you willing to put on that?"

SIX

Tyler's implant sent an urgent ding and he picked up. It was set for only three things. A Horvath attack, something happening to the girls or the expansion of the *Troy*.

"Go," Tyler said.

"We're getting expansion," Nathan said.

"Finally!"

The *Troy* was overdue to start expanding. When you're melting two point two trillion tons of nickel iron, models only go so far. But it was at least a month overdue. And it wasn't like you could induce. They were already using eighty percent of the SAPL and some other projects had had to be put on the back burner.

He spun around in his chair and put the view up on the wall-screen. He could view it through the implants, but some things you just needed the emotional satisfaction of watching on a nine-square-meter plasma.

"How long?" he asked. "And . . . is it expanding?"

"Slowly at the moment," Nathan said. "The models say it should expand slowly at first, then up to about ninety percent rather rapidly. Then, perhaps, a slight additional expansion, but when it cools it's going to contract so . . . when it slows down that's probably what we'll end up with."

"Okay," Tyler said. "How long for it to really balloon because . . ."

"I hate waiting," Nathan finished. "Not long . . ."

"Whoa," Tyler said as the nickel iron asteroid started to grow in size very much like a balloon that was being inflated. A big, spherical, molten, metal balloon. "Cool. Is it really going to take a year to cool?"

"Two point two—"

"Trillion tons," Tyler said. "Got it. Can't we speed that up? What about running a comet into it? They're cold."

"You're insane," Nathan said, shaking his head. "Just fricking nuts. And, no, the problem is we can't get good heat transfer. The vaporization energy involved in sublimating a comet, and just about *any* comet that contacted this would *completely* sublimate, is high. But . . . well, first, if we just impacted it, even at low velocity, it would warp the shell."

"Pass," Tyler said.

"And most of the energy wouldn't transfer," Nathan said. "It's something we looked at, but it's not really worth doing. What we are looking at doing is making a shield for it."

"I don't think it *needs* more defenses," Tyler said dubiously. "But if you think so . . ."

"Not that kind of shield," Nathan said. "A large, and I do mean large, sunshield. To get it fully into deep cold. But even then, heat doesn't dissipate well in vacuum and, well, it's two point two—"

"Trillion tons," Tyler said. "What's the next iteration up from a trillion, by the way?"

"We've decided it's a hell-of-a-lot," Nathan answered, grinning. "Wha-oh."

"What?" Tyler asked, still watching the expanding sphere. He realized that the small dot in the view was the *Monkey Business* and shook his head. The support ship was closer than the *Troy*, how close he wasn't sure, but it still looked like a speck.

"The expansion's already slowing," Nathan said, examining his figures. "The sphere also cooled more than expected. May be less than a year before we can get to work. But there's a problem."

"Big problem, little problem?" Tyler asked, pulling up his own system to examine the sphere. "Little problem."

"Right," Nathan said. "Little problem. As in it's got a 'small' problem. As in..."

"I thought you said it was going to be ten kilometers across with a kilometer-thick shell," General DeGraff said. "Not *nine* kilometers across with a kilometer and a *half* shell."

"Hey, more armor," Tyler said, shrugging. "It's still one hell of a big system. And it's not like the interior's going to be crowded. Four miles across is pretty darned *big*, General."

"Big enough," General DeGraff said. "I was sort of pulling your leg. Hopefully, it won't get the name 'Runt.'"

"Doubtful," the rather short tycoon said, making a face. "It's nine kilometers wide. Nine point two four. Twenty-nine kilometers in circumference. Now that we've done one of these we're tightening up the models. It looks as if doing a full blossom to the size that was predicted in the original essay is darned tough. The surface tension of even highly heated iron is just too high. You'd have to scoop out a big container in the middle to get enough volatiles."

"A thought occurs to me," General DeGraff said, rubbing his chin.

"That it's small enough to fit through the gate?" Tyler said. "We're going to have to wait for it to cool so we can hook up the *nukes* to move it, General. We're actually going to hook the nukes to *another* asteroid and crash it into the *Troy*. Why irradiate what you don't have to?"

"Opening and closing the door?"

"We're working on figuring out how to *cut* the door," Tyler said, shrugging. "We need to get the *Troy* nice and stable first. No rotation. *That's* going to be interesting. Then we have to cut the door. It's a kilometer and a *half* of nickel iron. Which is just great at dissipating heat. I'm on the three twenty to Wolf, General. Some issues have come up. I'll have to talk about that later."

"Have fun in 359," the general said, looking quizzical. "Any chance you're going to bring Granadica back? We could use that production capability in *this* system."

"Not on your life," Tyler said. "To get to Wolf, an enemy has to come through the Sol System. Not to dispute the whole 'every life is sacred,' but if we're going to have a chance, we need Granadica working. I was sweating the whole time she was in the Sol System. She's not coming back until I either have a replacement or I'm sure she'll be somewhere very safe."

"I'm not sure *anywhere* in this system is safe, Mr.

Vernon," General DeGraff said. "Especially if the Horvath get E Eridani. Unfortunately."

"Have you *looked* at the specifications on *Troy*?"

"Begin," Tyler said, waving expansively.

Granadica came complete with design facilities, management offices and meeting rooms. Like much of the fabber, they could all use some TLC. Tyler had let contracts for upgrades and improvements—guys with paintbrushes instead of the fabber having to devote resources—so the current meeting room had a newly built look.

The air still smelled rusty. Coupled with paint. It did not blend well.

The group was mixed human and Glatun. The gas mine project was a huge endeavor, and even with Granadica's help, it was going to involve a lot of people and a lot of skull-sweat.

Most of the Glatun were from various Gorku departments, but there were members representing six different subcontractors or invested corporations. The humans were just as diverse, coming from a dozen different corporations that were involved with everything from subsystem design to logistical support.

But nobody could really get moving until a few disputes got hammered out.

"Mr. Vernon, gentlebeings," the Glatun said. It was a VP sent out by Gorku Corp. to act as their representative. "A dispute has broken out even before we can begin initial construction over the primary design of the Wolf Gas Mine. Gorku Corporation has supplied designs for its most advanced technology in gas separation in refining."

It threw up a video of a space elevator that was, essentially, two flat plates that looked something like washers connected by wires. Dialing down it walked the viewer through the facility as he continued to talk.

"The upper platform rests in geosynchronous orbit," the Glatun said. "The system has four large storage tanks capable of moving two million gallons of helium-three per hour. That is enough to fuel an entire Glatun task force.

"The separation center, resting in the near Earth gravity region, pumps up fuel from the depths of the gas giant through four large carbon nanotube woven pipes and refines it. Return pipes for unused gases create a siphon effect, reducing the need for pumping power.

"Four carbon nanotube support wires hold the two sections together. At each end, each wire splits into sixteen separate secondary connection wires. The system can remain stable with as few as four of each.

"There is an elevator as well," he concluded, "for movement of supplies and personnel in and out of orbit. This was the initial design, a design well tested in the Mi'Wexiqey system."

"Well tested, my rear quadrant," Granadica said.

"You'll get your chance," Tyler said. "Continue."

"The design does include some proprietary components, which some have suggested is intended to increase profitability to certain parties," the Glatun said distastefully. "But it is the very best design available. Absolutely state-of-the-art. Gorku Corporation is convinced that this is a superior design to more . . . to earlier systems and as a major investor is . . . challenged by the idea of using a less capable design."

"What's proprietary?" Tyler asked.

"Some of the so-called separation systems," Granadica said.

"They are superior systems," the Gorku VP said.

"They're over-priced junk," Granadica said. "All you have to do is look at the actual output of the Mi'Wexiqey Mine!"

"That was when we were testing this system," one of the other Glatun said, then shut up at a look from the VP.

"There were some teething issues with Mi'Wexiqey," the VP said. "But we have worked those out. This system is a refinement of those."

"Okay," Tyler said. "Before we get into a shouting match with the AI that controls our air ... Granadica? And less on the negatives and more on the positives, please?"

"The problem is the negatives," Granadica said. "I built my first gas mine over five hundred years ago in the Bulhubic system. Still works like a charm. Some of the new stuff they're doing just makes sense. We always had problems with the boron fiber support wires. Carbon nanotube's a better material and the spinners they're providing are great. All for it. And the Apollo suggestions on producing the upper and lower rings are good. It's these new *pumps* that I think are nuts."

"Reason?" Tyler asked.

"There are the usual heavy grav pumps at the base of the lift pipes," Granadica said. "All good. But the system uses a series of pre-separators during lift. Theoretically, it should cut down on the separation requirements on the top side. That saves power overall, which saves money. They're proprietary and add about ten percent to the cost, but *theoretically* they'll save you money in the long run. Theoretically. Truth is, Gorku's never gotten them to work. Mi'Wexiqey is still only separating at twenty percent of its rated capacity. Because it's all got to be done by the upper separators. Which, because they're built to do a final separation, not primary, can't handle the full load. They've been tweaking and tweaking and tweaking but they can't get it to work. And now they want to foist off the same stupid system on you ignorant humans."

"That is a—" the Glatun VP said angrily.

Tyler held up his hand. "Granadica, not helping your case. Okay, so Granadica says that your system is an overpriced piece of crap. You say that it's the greatest thing since sliced bread. Do we have a less invested arguer? Mr. Audler? You're the primary human contractor."

Byron Audler had come up through ship design and construction. Wet ships. He'd made a smooth transition to the *Constitution* project, though. Tyler had practically stolen him from BAE to be the project manager on the LFD side.

"When the question came up I did some research," Audler said. He was middle height and heavy-set with a shock of red hair. He also apparently smoked a pipe. Or maybe he just habitually had one stuck in his mouth. "And they're both right. The pre-separation process should work and save money in the long run. And so far, it doesn't."

"We've gotten the bugs out," Ujo Chit said. The Gorku project manager ruffled its back hair in exasperation. "The problem was inherent with the Mi'Wexiqey design. There were mass interactions in high-pressure cryogenic conditions we hadn't taken into account. We've redesigned, and as soon as we can get the authorization, we're going to rebuild Mi'Wexiqey to fit the new designs. We haven't gotten that yet, so of *course* it's still not working right! This is the *right* design."

"Can you build it with . . . I guess Granadica's idea of what the upper separation should be and the pre-separators?" Tyler asked.

"Yes," Audler said. "But it's going to add *another* fifteen percent to the cost. And more power usage, which is higher cost in the long run."

"We've got time to decide since none of this takes place until the upper and lower rings are done, right?"

"Yes," the Glatun VP said.

"We'll do it with both. If Gorku will provide the pre-separation system without additional surcharge," Tyler said.

"Impossible," the Gorku rep snapped. "As I said, this is state of the art. We're not just going to *give* it away."

"Yes," Tyler said, smiling. "You are. Because right now, nobody will touch it with a ten-thousand-kilometer pipe. If it works *here*, others will buy the system. As I said, this will get worked out later. If Gorku doesn't want to field test their system, we'll do it without the pre-separator and I'll take the hit on the upper separators which I know work. But, frankly, this will be a discussion between myself and your bosses. Thereby my Solomon act. Get to work on the rings and the skyhook, Granadica, start working on the standard separation systems. And the pre-separators will be discussed in another forum."

"Okay," Audler said, nodding at the Gorku rep.

Tyler had enough experience of Glatun at this point to pick up that the Gorku rep looked relieved. That didn't give him great hope for the pre-separators.

"The next question," Tyler said. "Aware that the answer from engineers is always going to be 'no.' Any way to speed this up? I'd like to have it online in three years, not five. I have specific reasons."

"Two years cut off?" Audler said with a wince. "I really don't think so."

"Possible on our end," the Apollo mining rep said. "But we'd need more SAPL. And we're still looking at exactly how to make a *steel* washer the size of Lake Washington. Nickel iron won't cut it for this."

"If we've got the washers we can increase the spin speed with more spinners," Granadica said. "If we double the spinners we can cut six months off the space elevator construction."

"We don't have double the spinners available," the Gorku VP said.

"I can *make* them, kiddo," Granadica said. "If you'll cough up the permissions. I've already *got* the plans. All we need is eight more. I can do that in a *day*."

"No way," a Gorku representative down the table said.

"Besides," the Apollo rep said. "There's the problem of enough separated carbon."

"Carbonaceous asteroids?" Tyler said.

"They're not pure carbon," one of the Glatun said. "Not pure enough by far."

"Okay," Tyler said. "To speed up construction of the elevator we need: more pure carbon, eight additional spinners and a way to make giant steel washers in space. What about the pumping and separating equipment?"

"A year's run," Granadica said. "If you want me to

keep going with my current program. I'm devoting thirty percent of my cycles to repair and replacement. Another five percent to maintenance. That will go down a bit when I'm done with my rebuild, but that's going to take another year at this rate. Ten percent to mirror construction. Not VLAs. Just BDAs, VSAs and VDAs. Ten percent to prototype and small ship construction. That's fifty-five percent of my cycles. This is a *lot* of pumping equipment. It's the equivalent of building a billion-ton freighter in difficulty. Take a year."

"Start right away," Tyler said.

"I've *been* working on the stuff that wasn't being argued," Cranadica said. "Still take a year. And Corku is insisting that their pre-separator system has to be built by their *own* fabbers. And since they're backed up, they can't even give us a start date on them."

"And another year and a half of installation," Byron said. "Cut that down, some, if we have more hands and bots. But that takes—"

"Trained people," Tyler said, wincing. Even with many of the five billion and change people left on Earth being unemployed because of the damage done by the Horvath attacks, finding people who were willing, qualified and capable of working in space was a nightmare. *Everybody* needed more qualified people. "There's some overlap, though, right?"

"Yes," Byron said. "Some. Quite a bit, actually. The main thing we need is the rings to get started. More spinners would be nice. I'm ready to get started on this thing!"

"Okay," Tyler said. "I've got some people to see and some calls to make. Get going on what you can get going on. I'll see what I can scrounge up on my end."

* * *

Tyler had moved to his ship for the calls. Technically, he could order Granadica to not listen and it couldn't. The call would go into a locked memory buffer. Probably. But he didn't want the AI having an itch it couldn't scratch.

He placed the call, wondering if it would pick up.

"Tyler," Niazgol Gorku said. "How was the meeting?"

"So, does your pre-separator work or not?" Tyler asked.

"Oh, Gol," Gorku said. "Are they trying to foist *that* piece of fleck on you?"

"I take it that's a no," Tyler said.

"My chief engineering officer insists it works," Gorku said. "And he has some arguments. It would be great if it worked. So far, no joy."

"So I pitched you sell it to us for cheap," Tyler said. "If they can get it to work, great. Then you can point to Wolf and say 'It works!' There's something about the new design having to be installed initially or something. But to make sure, I'm going to have to put in a normal separator system. So I can't take the hit on the newfangled system and the old one."

"Sounds like a fair compromise," Gorku said. "I'm not willing to take a hit, though. I'll give it to you at cost. That will be slightly higher than without it but not the full price."

"Hey, you're an investor," Tyler said. "Do the math and see if it works."

"I'll do that," Gorku said.

"What's the word on the home front?" Tyler asked.

"The Benefactor rep on the Multilateral Talks is an idiot," Gorku said.

The Multilateral Talks were an outgrowth of the Glatun release of the border systems with the Rangora. With that crack, every major polity in the area had poured in wanting to trade systems.

Humans were only allowed an observer. The Horvath were sitting at the table.

"They're going to give up E Eridani to the Horvath," Tyler said, grimacing. It was their only contact lane with the Glatun and the rest of the galaxy.

"The requirement is that all ships be given free passage," Gorku said bitterly.

"Like *that's* going to happen," Tyler said. "So much for human freighters plying the space lanes. Oh, on that note, I need permissions for Granadica to produce some of your proprietary spinners and all your proprietary mining stuff."

"That...would be a hard sell," Gorku said.

"We'll cut you half the profits you'd normally make," Tyler said. "And you don't have to take up time on your already overworked fabbers. Also if the Horvath put us under an embargo we can do everything on this end."

"Seventy-five percent. And your point on the fabbers is good. We were tapped out on time."

"Done," Tyler said. "Keep in mind that we're probably going to need release at some point on everything. If worse comes to worst."

"I'm putting pressure on the Council to do releases of military equipment," Gorku said. "But on commercial releases I have to deal with the board. They're worse."

"Tell me about it," Tyler said. "Okay, nice talking to you."

"I've got to go, too," Gorku said. "Good luck."

"We make our own."

SEVEN

"So what eeevil inventions are we dreaming up today?" Tyler asked, rubbing his hands together in glee. "Bu-wah-hah-hah-hah-hah!"

Dealing with bitchy AIs and vice presidents was work. Visiting the Night Wolves was how he paid himself for it.

Night Wolves was, technically, the Granadica Design and Prototyping Center. Fourteen Terran engineers and draftsmen had been shipped off to live on Granadica on a more or less permanent assignment. Their job was to prototype systems. All sorts of systems. But mostly those with a military bent.

The idea was to make systems that were a combination of Terran and Glatun technology. As much as possible, things that could be produced on Earth, or at least by humans, for what was shaping up to be a big war.

One of the problems was that the Glatun didn't want anyone to have ships as good as theirs. They were superior in three ways—armor, speed and firepower—which pretty much defined "superior" in a warship. The armor was a matrix of fullerene and "other substances" that was impossible to duplicate without the codes for the fabbers. Glatun warships could maneuver at over four hundred gravities. Commercial systems were relegated to ten gravities of inertial control. And they sported five-hundred-terawatt gamma ray lasers as their main armament. None of the systems humans had access to could produce more than a five-megawatt laser.

The Night Wolves' main mission, which was only discussed when Granadica couldn't listen, was to design around the lock-outs.

"Oh, nothing we work on here is *evil*, Mr. Vernon," Kelly Ketterman said, smiling. Kelly was the managing design chief for the Night Wolves, a large title for a very short, even elfin, blonde. "All of it has purely commercial or emergency purposes that are for the betterment of all mankind."

"Your mission statement in a nutshell," Tyler said. "And what have you created?"

"The first item is a new, improved VDA mirror," Kelly said, bringing up a schematic. "It is lighter, stronger, more accurate and has better heat transmission. All of the materials, including now the superconductor, are producible by human manufacture. Granadica's main contribution was in bringing in some engineering we didn't previously have access to and building the prototype."

"You're welcome," Granadica said. "This is the sort of thing I enjoy!"

"We're working on an upgraded system," Kelly said. "For . . . extreme mining. We're hoping that it will take up to one hundred times the amount of energy of a VDA."

"Ung," Tyler said, grunting.

"Yes, that's what *we* said," Kelly said, dimpling. "If it works, it is going to be great for mining."

"Uh, yeah," Tyler said. "Great."

"The first ship design is an emergency response shuttle," Kelly said, bringing up a picture of what looked very much like a rectangular box with some jet engines on it. "The prototype is complete and works very well. The ERS has a crew of two and can carry up to thirty-eight personnel or eighteen casualties. The forward assembly consists of four magnetic grapnels, a bivalve ramp system that works to prevent damage to the air lock or for deployment or rescue on land, and a multiconnector expansion air lock. If there is no standard air lock available, the MEA permits the ERS to dock directly to a distressed ship's hull so that rescuers can cut into it to rescue stranded personnel. The ERS has two external mounts for searchlights that can generate up to five terawatts of raw light for searching."

"I thought that was a bit much," Granadica said. "But that was the specification. I wouldn't want to be looking *into* a five terawatt light, that's for sure."

"Nor would I," Kelly said. "The ERS has twenty gravities of acceleration so it can move in and out of orbit rapidly. This, of course, would place some strain on passengers, so there are conformal seats that can be moved in and out. So it can either be an open box for carrying emergency supplies or, with the acceleration couches, a very fast rescue ship. The ERS can operate for up to seventy hours on its own at a cruising acceleration of five gravities and has bunks and support facilities onboard for the two-member crew. Thus, a single ERS can cruise out to Neptune orbit and back on onboard fuel. Just in case we have a ship stranded out by Neptune. At maximum drive it exhausts onboard fuel in about ten hours."

"I can think of thousands of purposes for that," Tyler said. "Wish we'd had a bunch of them during the plagues. We probably ought to make..."

"Lots," Kelly said. "We already have a contract from the USSN for three hundred."

"Thank you, Granadica. And my stockholders thank you as well."

"You're welcome, Mr. Vernon."

"Most of the portions of the ERS are being made by subcontractors," Kelly continued. "Final assembly takes place here, and there are certain components Granadica can just make better, faster and cheaper. Essentially, we're feeding her components and Granadica puts out the finished product."

"Any problems with integration?" Tyler asked.

"Not integration," Granadica answered. "Quality control, yes."

"We think we've fixed that issue by a change of providers," Kelly said. "And, unfortunately, we still have to pull most manufactured equipment out of the gravity well on Earth."

"Earth's a bad enough target," Tyler said. "I don't think I want to build any space factories. Not in the Sol System."

"The problem remains," Kelly said. "And we simply don't have enough space-capable shipping. Granadica, Night Wolves and Apollo mining, therefore, reinvented an old idea."

"Liberty ships?" Tyler asked.

"Yes, sir," Kelly said, frowning.

"I was going to ask about those," Tyler said. "It was on my mind. Continue."

"When Apollo mines most asteroids, there is, unfortunately, a good bit left over," Kelly said. "Mostly silica."

"We're using a good bit of that in the Sol System on the VLA," Tyler said. "They're doing silica mirrors with a thin nickel or aluminum backing."

"Yes, sir, they're doing the same design here," Kelly said. "They still make more melted silica than they can use. Together with some Apollo engineers we came up with this."

The picture looked like a Mason jar with a robot spider on one end.

"The hull is mostly silica," Kelly said. "We've set up a production facility that turns those out in large quantities. Then a lift and drive engine is installed that has a low but sufficient drive. Specifically, two gravities of acceleration with a full one-hundred-thousand-ton load. Higher empty. Maximum acceleration empty is ten gravities, since that is the maximum inertial control available to us. The bottleneck is the lift and drive systems. We're having most of the raw equipment built on Earth, again, and assembling it here."

"Silica . . . is not a good structural material," Tyler said. "*Glass* hulls?"

"Not *entirely* silica," Kelly said, smiling. "They have wound-in carbon nanotube. That's another bottleneck, but Granadica made a fabber that produces carbon nanotube winding in good quantity."

"It's basically an old-fashioned version of the Gorku spinners," Granadica said. "And *mine* can handle anything that's got carbon in it. Apollo broke up a carbonaceous asteroid and we're turning out more nanotube than you can believe. We've been gluing it on the outside of the shuttles, since if you figure in a space disaster, there's probably a lot of debris flying around."

"We don't have people to run them, unfortunately," Tyler said, sighing.

"They don't take *much*," Granadica said. "Three watch crew, three engineering and a few support. They've got their own gravitic loading and unloading system. Send us some personnel and we'll have so many ships going back and forth between here and Sol you won't believe it."

"Alas, we still don't have the trade," Tyler said. "But we will. This is great, but it's got to be looked at as a prototype for now. I'll get some people working on crews, though. We do need to get the components moving back and forth. It can lift out of the grav well?"

"Easily," Kelly said. "The hulls have the added benefit of being convertible to helium-three tankers with some minor modifications. We've also looked at modifications for . . . in-space repair and support ships."

She carefully had not said "Fleet colliers."

"Well, we still don't have much in the way of ships that need support," Tyler said. "Anything else?"

"A new tug system," Kelly said. "This is purely for Apollo Mining at the present. It has four hundred gravities of acceleration but, of course, can't actually use that for internal delta-V. It also has a very wide angle for pressor or tractor beams. Apollo has been doing a lot of space shaping and they needed something that could generate a *wide* pressor beam. The tug is capable of maintaining a one-hundred-gravity pressor over a three-hundred yard band."

Tyler didn't see the military application and raised an eyebrow.

"Purely for Apollo?" Tyler said.

"Nobody else needs them," Kelly said, shrugging. "Apollo gave us the specs and we figured it out. Didn't we, Granadica?"

"It was different," the AI said. "Most races don't mine the way that you do."

"Anything else?"

"Last, we have a *support* ship for the emergency shuttles," Kelly said, smiling slightly. "The problem was making a ship capable of keeping up. That required conformal systems throughout the ship as well as acceleration modifications."

"I'm not sure how long I'd *want* to take ten gravities," Tyler said. "I took seven for twenty minutes one time and it nearly killed me."

"Hopefully not for long," Kelly said. "The ship has launchers for small...buoys. Remote sensing platforms. Those have been designed for *six* hundred gravities of acceleration for...rapid and widespread dissemination."

"Better hope they don't run into anything," Granadica said. "Because they're an awful lot like missiles. That's what I based them off of. An old missile design. Slap a heavy warhead on them and they're going to play merry hob if they, for example, run into a Horvath ship. Just the kinetic impact after thirty seconds running will blow through Horvath screens."

"But since they're...sensor buoys?" Tyler said, frowning.

"All good," Granadica said. "Hey, how you humans want to do search and rescue is up to you. And what you want to mount for sensors is also up to you. The ship has hard points for mounting more big flashlights. And you can point the spotlight on something at up to three light-minutes. Very accurate spotlight. Since that's a long way away, it can be dialed up to a three megawatt laser. And gravitic sensors to spot anything that needs rescuing. Up to seven light-seconds out. They're very sensitive. With a little triangulation, which the system can do using sensors on multiple ships, in movement or with the sensors on shuttles or remotes on the buoys, they can spot even a hypercom node that's active within two light-seconds. Or, say, something accelerating on a collision course. They also can handle up to one hundred sensor buoys in movement at the same time."

"An Aegis search and rescue ship," Tyler said, nodding. "Very nice platform."

"More of a frigate," Kelly said. "They're smaller than the *Constitution* class. Also faster and more capable."

"BAE is just going to love the hell out of that," Tyler said, grinning. "Not that it's a warship, of course."

"Of course," Granadica said.

"Granadica," Tyler said musingly. "How big are the fabbers you made to make nanotubes? No, let me say this a different way. Can you make some fabbers to pre-separate the carbon from a carbonaceous asteroid?"

"I can do it," Granadica said. "There's going to be a fairly significant energy penalty. It's going to cost more. And I'll have to rearrange the schedule."

"Do it," Tyler said. "Anything else?"

"That's about it," Kelly said, suddenly looking nervous.

"That's all good," Tyler said, nodding. "All good. Thank your team for me."

"Permission to speak freely, sir?" Kelly said.

"What is this, the military?" Tyler said, smiling. "Of course."

"You look tired as hell," the manager said. "No offense. But you look as if you could use a break."

"I've got a lot of pressures," Tyler said, shrugging. "I can take it. I've *learned* to take it. But, Granadica, between you, Kelly and me, I'm serious about doing the fuel mine in three years. I'm hoping we have *three*."

"How was Wolf?" Bryan asked.

Dr. Foster had stepped down as head of Apollo Mining nearly three years before.

There was a progression to management. Some people were great with small start-ups but couldn't handle big business. Others were best at handling large scale operations and were driven crazy by start-ups.

Apollo and LFD Corp. were, without question, big business. Tyler and Bryan had talked it over and then three people had taken over various bits of the management. There was an MBA with extensive experience of terrestrial mining and materials sales as the CEO, an Army general as chief of operations, mostly devoted to the increasingly complex task of moving light around, and even a chief science officer who oversaw production of the SAPL components and an increasingly large team of people who studied better ways to move it and use it.

Bryan's title was now "Chief of Special Projects." That way he always had new things to wrap his head around and Tyler had somebody's head to throw them at.

"Busy," Tyler said. "I think I need to get a ship made."

"You have . . . a lot of ships," Bryan pointed out. "I mean, if you count all the tugs . . ."

"I mean for me," Tyler said. "I've been putting it off for forever. But if I'm going to be running back and forth between here and Wolf, running around poking my nose into people's business . . . I think I need a ship. A shuttle at least. The Night Wolves have a pretty good design. I think I may have one sent to Burger Boat."

"They know anything about space?" Bryan asked.

"Not a thing," Tyler said. "Time they found out. And taking the shuttle not only takes time I can't afford, I'm just getting too old to sit next to a hulking miner who's looking forward to getting back to mamasan and some real showers. Okay, we've got a problem."

"I live to serve," Bryan said, grinning.

"Steel."

"Hard," Bryan said. "We've been looking at making a smelter. Problem is, most of our stuff is mobile enough to run if the Horvath come through the gate. A smelter . . . isn't going to be really mobile."

"Right," Tyler said. "And what I'm talking about is going to be too big for a smelter, anyway. You've seen the general design for the Wolf mine, I take it."

"Yep," Bryan said. "Those support plates are going to be fun to make. They'll have to be welded."

"Not if we can cast them in one piece," Tyler said. "I was thinking about it on the shuttle back. What's steel?"

"Iron," Bryan said. "Carbon. Various trace elements. If you want stainless—"

"Which we do."

"A bunch of chromium or nickel. About forty percent by weight if I recall the class."

"Okay," Tyler said. "Think of a McGriddle."

"A what?" Bryan said, chuckling.

"A *chupaqueso*, then," Tyler said. "Take a plate of iron, more or less pure."

"Which we have," Bryan said, nodding.

"Then layer it on both sides with crushed carbon. Mix in the trace elements you need. Then on the outside, smaller plates of chromium or nickel. Heat, melt, let collapse into a ball through microgravity."

"May work," Bryan said. "Except the carbon's going to get very kinetically active and tend to move away."

"Ah," Tyler said. "Why I mentioned a McGriddle. Seal the edges of the outer plates. That will keep the carbon contained."

"How big we talking?" Bryan asked, making some notes.

"Two kilometers," Tyler said. "The final form. Sort of like a washer with a one-hundred-meter hole in the middle. And about thirty meters thick. Two of those. We can figure out how to make the bracers if we can do the washers."

"That's an interesting project," Bryan said, grinning. "We ordered these new tugs from the Night Wolves..."

"Yeah," Tyler said. "What's up with that?"

"We needed bigger fields for shaping," Bryan said, still making notes. "We're doing a lot of spin processing. We needed wider fields to handle big projects. This is a good example. To get this thing even, we're going to have to shape it in three dimensions. But with the tugs we can do that. We're calling them *Potter's Hands*. I'm *not* going to start with two kilometers, mind you. But BAE has been screaming for steel for the *Constitutions*. We're having to carry it up out of the well. This might be the answer."

"Call me when you've got the material spun up," Tyler said. "I'd like to see that."

"Will do. Anything else?"

"About a thousand things," Tyler said. "Oh, Steren's

getting married. You should be getting an invitation. I put you down for one."

"Steren?" Bryan asked, confused.

"Younger daughter?" Tyler said. "The tomboy?"

"I . . . don't think you'd ever mentioned her name," Bryan said. "I knew you had two daughters. But that's about all."

"Really?" Tyler said. "Not even when we were melting . . ."

"Icarus," Bryan said. "No. And we talked about a lot of things. But not family. I'd sort of wondered."

"Ah," Tyler said. "Two children. Christy and Steren. Christy's getting her MBA at the moment. Wharton, which makes me very proud. Steren . . . wasn't big on school. She also wanted to be her own person. Which meant she was working as a vet's assistant. She's marrying a guy named Thomas Schneider. He's a mechanical engineering grad student. I'd guess he's going to want a job, which is no big deal."

"You haven't met him, have you?" Bryan said.

"I'm supposed to be meeting them this weekend," Tyler said. "We're having dinner."

"When I met you they were still kids. I really hadn't realized it had been that long."

"But interesting," Tyler said. "As in we live in interesting times. And on that note, I now have to catch another shuttle so I can make a meeting in St. Louis."

"Have fun," Bryan said. "And, Tyler?"

"Yeah?"

"All work and no play?"

"When I find somebody who's willing to think big, I'll think about taking a vacation," Tyler said. "In the meantime . . . I'm managing."

EIGHT

"My dad is going to already be there." Steren Vernon had, fortunately, gotten her looks from her mother. And her stature, since she was pushing six feet. The name meant "Star" in Cornish. And it fit her eyes, which were dark but with a usually bright sparkle. Even more so when she was mad. "He'll probably be talking on his plant, and probably shouting at somebody, which means he looks like he's raving."

"You told me." Thomas Schneider was taller than Steren but had the same general looks. Dark hair and eyes. They looked a good bit like brother and sister rather than an engaged couple. "Several times. Vernon party?" he said to the maitre d'.

"And you are?"

"Steren Vernon," Steren snapped. "The heir apparent."

"Yes, miss," the maitre d' said, nodding. "Right this way. I'm sorry for asking, but we do try to keep people from bothering our more prominent guests."

It was a very nice restaurant, one of the best in Pittsburgh. And that was saying something.

Pittsburgh, as one of the larger surviving cities in the U.S., had become a major financial and industrial hub. It always had been, just overshadowed by bigger names like Detroit, New York and Philadelphia.

With all three of those gone, the money and industry had moved to places like Pittsburgh, St. Louis and Indianapolis. They had major traffic problems, though. People were willing to *work* in and around cities. Nobody wanted to *live* near them, much less raise the increasing number of children.

Western society was still coming to terms with the first baby-boom since the post-WWII generation. The Horvath changes took time and technology to eradicate. The full course of treatment was six four-hour visits to a clinic that had the equipment. There were still less than two thousand of the clinics in the U.S. and Europe. They were cycling through about ten thousand cases per year.

Over ninety *million* children, mostly in the U.S. and Europe, had been born from mothers with Johannsen's Syndrome in the *two years* since the attack. The approximately forty-five million daughters *all* inherited it. Absent a huge increase in the supply of advanced medical equipment, and technicians trained to operate it and doctors qualified to deal with the occasional problem, there was no way to catch up.

Worse still, girls who were prepubescent when they were infected were still at risk. As soon as they hit puberty they went into heat. Coupled with the prevention of regular contraception, it was a nightmare. Society was just starting to come to grips with a teen pregnancy problem that was simply astronomical.

The effect had been studied and, to the sometimes amusement of males, it turned out that the "heat" effect was functionally identical to male arousal. Just more varied. For about seven days during the four-week cycle, essentially during their menstruation period, women had about normal arousal. During the remaining three weeks they were, in the oft quoted words of some medical pundit, "Seventeen-year-old males with choice."

And there were secondary effects. Since people tended to follow trends, even women who were not affected by Johannsen's were having babies in large numbers. Prior to the attack, "native" Germans had a birthrate of one point five. Since replacement was two point one, they were slowly going extinct.

Last year there had been one child born for *every single female* with Johannsen's in Germany. Which was a good bit of the population. That, right there, was seventeen million of the ninety. And the trend was projected to continue until there was a fix.

The situation was much on Tom's mind as they entered the restaurant and he saw his prospective father-in-law for the first time. Steren had stated, in no uncertain terms, that she wasn't going to be the only girl she knew without children. She wasn't sure about the dozens some of them seemed headed for—a friend of hers had the genes for multiple birth and already had *six*—but they were going to get started more or less on their honeymoon.

He'd said "Okay" and tried not to wince.

Tyler Vernon was, as anticipated, apparently talking to air.

"Did Gorku give his okay? Okay, then... Well, I don't care if the authorizations have to be hand carried. I don't care if *you* have to hand carry them. Get them to Granadica *now*! Because we're going to have the plates by the end of the month and I want spinning to start the day they arrive, *that's* why! Yes, the end of the month... Because we are very good. I've got to go. I'm serious, Ujo, they'd better be there in no more than three days or I'm going to cite failure of contract... Because I can be. Buh-bye." Tyler snarled and then looked up and smiled. "Pardon me while I try not to scream."

"Hi, Dad," Steren said, giving him a peck on the cheek.

"Hi, honey," Tyler said. "You must be Thomas," he continued, holding out his hand. "Thomas or Tom?"

"Uh... Tom, sir," Tom said, shaking Mr. Vernon's hand. He'd been told he was short but it was a bit of a shock. A guy who had done all he'd done, changed the *world*, should be... taller. He'd heard the snickered references to Napoleon—SNL and other comedy shows had used it as a stock joke for years—but he was still surprised.

"Call me Tyler," Mr. Vernon said. "Since we're gonna be kin. Sit. Stay a while."

Vernon paused and seemed almost to fall asleep for a moment.

"Communing with your plant, Dad?" Steren asked.

"No, just trying to adjust to family time," Tyler said, looking up and smiling. "I've gotten so little of it I'm sort of out of practice."

"I've been available," Steren pointed out. "Christy's busy, I'll admit."

"I haven't," Tyler said, shrugging. "I quit apologizing a long time ago."

"You've been busy," Steren said, shrugging. "And... in case I haven't said it. *Troy*?"

"Oh," Tyler said. "Did that finally break?"

"That you're making a humongo habitat?" Steren said caustically. "Uh, yeah. Months ago. And I've been getting jokes from my friends since it didn't come out as large as it was supposed to. 'I guess your dad came up a little . . . short.'"

"Oh," Tyler said, then smiled. "Ah, yes. *Troy*. Yes, it did come out a *bit* smaller than we'd planned. Still . . . plenty big enough, don't you think?"

"It's a very interesting project," Tom said. "We did a study of it in my orbital engineering class. But it was apparent that you'd started with too few volatiles."

"A bit, yeah," Tyler said. "But do you have any idea how hard it is to drill into nickel iron?"

"One point two seven four megajoules per cubic meter of melting energy," Tom said. "And then you have to consider dissipation. The thermodynamics are fascinating."

"You two are *not* going to talk shop," Steren said.

"Just a bit more, honey," Tyler said. "Orbital engineering? I wasn't even aware that was a class."

"It's hard to get," Tom said. "There aren't that many qualified professors. Master's level only at this point. Penn State has a class, though. Dr. Mires. He worked for you, well, for Apollo, for about five years on the Connie project."

"Eh," Tyler said. "I'm glad the data's getting out there. We're dying for qualified people. Between *Troy* and what we're going to be doing with her, and the Wolf projects . . . We can use every damned engineer we can get our hands on."

"Was that a job offer?" Steren asked.

"Can I ask what is causing the somewhat sarcastic mode?" Tyler said.

"I'm sorry," Steren said. "I just . . . We never get to see you and you're talking shop."

"Unfortunately, shop is about all there is in my life, honey," Tyler said, shrugging. "Has been since . . . Well, since you were ten. I'd much rather talk about orbital engineering than war. Which has been my other preoccupation. So since we're not going to talk about either, what's the plan for the wedding? Are we talking wedding of the century or a private little ceremony at the house?"

"If we do wedding of the century it will be covered up with papparazzi," Steren said. "I still have to occasionally chase them away from the clinic."

"Heh," Tyler said, grinning. "Depends on *where* we have it."

"Space?" Tom said, grinning.

"All traffic is carefully controlled by Space Command," Tyler said. "And I know people."

"We are not having it on some orbital project," Steren said, then paused. "What are you thinking, exactly?"

"Hmmm . . ." Tyler said. "I've been thinking about building a ship for my own uses. I suppose I could get one fabbed up pretty quick. Nice one. Big enough for a fair-sized wedding party. Large viewing deck of optical sapphire. We're casting those *big* these days. I'm not sure about getting an inertial system that permits it to be the dance floor—"

"Ooo," Steren said, shuddering. "I don't think I *want* to do my wedding dance over the Moon. Or Earth."

"Just a thought," Tyler said. "I could probably still get a custom yacht built to any spec you'd want from Glalkod Yards. Probably a better choice. Nah, come to think of it, they're backed up too. I've been thinking

I really need my own ship. This would be a good opportunity. I'd give it to you as a wedding present, but I don't think you'd want it."

"No, thanks," Steren said. "I was sort of uncomfortable the one trip I took out with you when I was sixteen. I'll keep my feet on the ground."

"Could rent an island," Tyler said. "Fly your friends in. Again, I know people. If we did it in certain areas the government would be happy to keep out papparazzi. Stay there for your honeymoon if you want. Please let me chip in for the honeymoon."

"Done," Steren said. "We accept. I'll tell you what the plan is when we decide. But if you want to spring for an island wedding, I'm all for it. Sorry, Tom?"

"No problem," Tom said, smiling. "Whatever you want, honey."

"Any idea where?" Tyler asked. "Greece? Carribean? Polynesia?"

"Let me look around," Steren said. "I've tried very hard not to play poor little rich girl. So I don't really know since I don't run in those circles."

"Just let me know," Tyler said.

"Have you been by to see Christy?" Steren asked.

"What? You two don't talk?" Tyler said. "She's covered up in work. I'll probably see more of her when she graduates. I'm going to throw her at LFD at first. She's not into orbital, either."

"No," Steren said. "We're not. So what are you going to do with *Troy*? Inflate it again? Mine it?"

"That is . . . proprietary," Tyler said. "Sorry, but it's a big project. There's a lot riding on it."

"The basic properties were pretty straightforward," Tom said, his brow furrowing. "The team came to the conclusion that there was no way you were going for a *big* habitat."

"Nine kilometers is pretty darned big, Tom," Tyler said. "And let me note, Steren, that you were the one talking shop."

"I know," Steren said, grinning. "I just could see you getting uncomfortable talking about the wedding."

"Decide what you want to do and I'll just write the checks," Tyler said, smiling. "I'm really looking forward to it. Seriously. But about *Troy*. I really can't talk about it for another . . . two months. About."

"When it's cooled?" Tom said.

"When it's cooled," Tyler said. "Then we *really* get to work."

"Sorry it took so long," Tyler said.

"It" was a two-kilometer in diameter steel washer with divots already cut out for the support lines. Six tugs were maneuvering it carefully from the gate to Bespin. Which was going to take about a week.

Because there wasn't an intelligent species in the system, the Grtul had just set up the gate to orbit naturally. Thus it was rarely near Bespin. Travel times were going to be a pain.

"No problem," Byron said, chewing on the end of his pipe. "We've got the spinners and carbon ready to go and Granadica has been turning out parts like nobody's business. We also set up a portable separator system in the meantime. We're not at independence from Glatun fuel supplies but we're at about sixty percent in the system. Doesn't quite cut down on cost because the portable is pretty expensive. But it's something."

"We're going to need to talk about tankers," Tyler

said. "Fuel in this system is great. We need it in Sol. A lot of it."

"Well..." Byron said, pulling out his pipe and contemplating it. "The Glatun method for producing tankers is to put them together not too much unlike a regular ship. I've worked on 'em. I think we can do that pretty well with Granadica's help. Been looking at it."

"Which takes, like, forever," Tyler said.

"Yep," Byron said. "Or we could use the Liberty ship design. But we'd only be pushing ninety thousand tons of fuel in each ship. That's a lot of fuel, but not what you're talking about."

"No," Tyler said.

"Or, and this is just a thought..." Byron said, staring through the crystal wall at the giant washer that was about to become the upper portion of a giant space elevator and which had been constructed in about three weeks. "We could do what you did with *Troy*. Blow up a nickel iron asteroid. Thinner and smaller, mind. Just a big grape-looking thing. Slap on one of the engines and crew quarters from the Liberty ships. Depends on the size of the asteroid and the amount of fuel, but you could get some boost there. Be slow but steady."

"That is more like it," Tyler said. "How soon can you get started?"

"We're about done drilling. I figured you'd like it and I know how you hate to wait."

"This had better work," Tyler said.

"We're going to be learning by doing," Nathan said. "Get used to it."

"Yeah, but if we really mess up, we can't just fix it with duct tape," Tyler pointed out.

The first thing that had to be done was get *Troy* moving. And once they did that, it was going to be apparent where it was going.

That *Troy* was a DoD project was bound to hit the news sooner or later. The line item had finally made it into the budget. Questions were already getting asked on the "white" side of Congress, the part that had to vote on a multibillion dollar military line item but hadn't yet been briefed in. The fact that it had taken this long was surprising.

Moving it was the next problem. They'd stabilized the asteroid with pumped-fusion bombs. But even though they were very clean in yield, they'd been counted out for this evolution. Let an enemy irradiate the surface of the battlestation.

Instead, a poor, lonely nickel-iron asteroid that was so minuscule it didn't even have a name had been chosen as the accelerant. After stabilizing the six-hundred-meter diameter asteroid's rotation it had been fitted with the largest pumped fusion bomb ever created by man, adjusted to point at the target, and then the bomb had been set off.

The man-made super-missile was about to hit the *Troy* at ninety kilometers per second and, with luck, send it on a course for its eventual home, just outside the three hundred mile "no heavy weapons" interdiction circle of the gate and "up" in the plane of ecliptic.

"No," Nathan said. "But the worst that's going to happen is *Troy* will be out of pocket. Then we'll just have to drop back to plan B."

"Nuclear attitude adjustment," Tyler said. "I'd prefer to avoid NAA."

"Same here," Nathan said. "But we have bigger

problems. We've done the rotational equations and we're probably going to have to use some nukes. With every tug in the fleet pulling, which means shutting down every other project, it will only take seventeen years to get the rotation out. And until we get the rotation stabilized, we can't really do anything with it. We especially can't poke a hole in it. The atmo inside has to be under pretty severe pressure. When we pop it, it's going to apply delta-V."

"And if it's spinning..."

"The delta-V is going to be a bit like a balloon that you open up the spout," Nathan said. "Especially since when we burn through is going to be a *guess*."

"I know a guy who says all these equations are easy," Tyler said.

"He's either an idiot or a student," Nathan said, watching the numbers from the asteroid's trajectory. "This is looking too good."

"Student," Tyler said. "Steren's fiancé. Seems like a good kid. I'd frankly dreaded who Steren was going to pick for a husband. Love her to death but... dreaded. As it turns out, another dread I could put aside."

"Who's Steren?" Nathan asked.

"My daughter?" Tyler said. "I mean, really, we've been friends for how many years?"

"I knew you had kids," Nathan said. "You never seemed to want to talk about them. Congratulations on getting one of them married off."

"I'm thinking about making him your assistant," Tyler said.

"Oh, that's just what I need," Nathan said, laughing. "A hot-shot... grad student?"

"Well, when he's got his master's."

"A hot-shot with a master's that also happens to be the boss' son-in-law," Nathan said. "Toss me out an air lock without a suit, why don't you?"

"As I said, he's a pretty good kid," Tyler said. "And stabilization is going to be dead easy."

"Oh?" Nathan said. "Really?"

"Really," Tyler said. "Melt a couple of big patches. *Big* patches. Then get some tugs and pull out the metal as far as you can. Try to keep it straight."

"Horns?" Nathan said. "I thought this was the *Troy*, not the Viking raiders."

"Archimedes, Nathan," Tyler said, sighing.

"Levers," the small planetary objects physicist said, slapping his forehead. "Damnit."

"Why do I have to think of these things?"

"Do you know how hard it's going to be to do?" Nathan asked.

"No," Tyler said. "Easier than anything else that comes to mind, though?"

"Yes," Nathan said. "Easier than all our other thoughts. And the reason *you* have to think of things like this is that we worker bees are trying to figure out how to get your visions to actually work. But . . . damn. Levers. Heh."

"'Give me a lever big enough and I shall move the world,'" Tyler said. "Times like this I wish I had a time machine. 'Hey, Archy, come on into the future. We made a lever big enough.'"

"And . . . we have contact," Nathan said.

On the screen the six-hundred-meter asteroid impacted the side of the massive metal ball. Following the laws of physics, it then recoiled and bounced off. It was like moving a beach ball by hitting it with a fast-ball. The difference being that in this case the "beach ball" was a thousand times more massive than the baseball. The "fast-ball" bounced off with a spall of metal pinwheeling through space.

Troy didn't *seem* to move at all.

"How's our trajectory?" Nathan asked.

"Pretty good," the technician said. "About ninety-eight percent of nominal. We're going to have to adjust carefully on arrival."

"Do we know where the poor asteroid is going?" Tyler asked.

"Towards Jupiter orbit?" the tech said. "It's probably going to contact Ceres. We'd already planned to stabilize it."

"More nukes," Tyler said, sighing. "Those things are expensive, you know."

"And more at the other end," Nathan said. "The good news is that it also decreased the spin. Slightly. Hmmm . . . if we do the adjustments with a bit of English . . ."

"Space billiards."

"Apollo Mining and Tyler Vernon are up to it again, grabbing headlines across the world with a bank-shot in asteroid engineering! Here with us is Fox space analyst, Dr. James Eager. Okay, Dr. Eager. They hit Troy *with a nickel-iron cueball and now it's drifting into the space lanes! What's up with that?"*

"Well, Nick, it's clear that all of our initial estimates of Troy's *purpose were wrong. I'm not sure how big they were actually planning on* Troy *being, but it wasn't supposed to swell up to full size. And it wasn't*

ever supposed to stay in the asteroid belt. Given the course they set it on, there's only one target."

"Target? Is it a weapon?"

"I'm not sure if you'd call it a weapon, per se. But the name now makes sense. Troy is headed for a near collision with the gate. It's pretty unlikely they mean to hit it. They'll have to adjust its course at some point. But they're probably planning on parking it by the gate. And that has only one meaning."

"And the meaning is? Don't keep us in suspense, Doctor!"

"It's a battlestation, Nick. A massive fortress to protect the Solar System from hostile ships coming through the gate. And with kilometer-and-a-half thick walls and the SAPL... That's going to be one heck of a deterrent...."

"Levers," Tyler said. "Heh."

He'd gone ahead and gotten the ship even if Steren didn't want to get married in it. Smaller than if it was designed for parties, it was based on the Emergency Rescue Shuttles. He'd thought about getting a converted frigate but that just seemed too much overkill. The differences between a stock ERS and the *Starfire* being... many. ERS didn't have one wall replaced with optical sapphire. And they weren't nearly as comfortable.

He leaned back in the couch and watched with his naked eye as just about every tug in the system lined up on the two horns that had been extruded from the *Troy*. The melt area had left two large dimples at the base that were going to take some consideration. He didn't want two great big bull's eyes on the battlestation.

But getting the rotation out was the main problem at present. It wasn't like there wasn't lots of nickel iron in the system. They could melt the levers back into the mass easily enough. Take a while to cool, though.

Lining up on the levers was the tough part. The exterior of *Troy* was rotating at sixty-three meters per second. The levers, though, were five kilometers long, the longest Nathan thought they could make without seriously damaging the structure of the battlestation. That meant they were moving at *ninety-seven* meters per second. That was only two hundred and some odd miles per hour, a crawl at astronomical speeds. But it was *rotating*. It was like trying to catch the tire lugs on a snow tire. The tugs could barely keep up. The only reason they could was that there weren't any puny humans on board. They were pulling nearly forty Gs as they maneuvered into position.

"Tugs in place," Argus said. Tyler had taken one of the AIs he'd gotten from Gorku and installed it as the overall manager of the SAPL and other Apollo operations in the Solar System. The class II AI was necessary with the now thousands of clusters set up all over the inner system. He also managed civilian space traffic. At the moment, though, all such traffic was in holding pattern as the full resources of the AI were devoted to the job of stabilizing *Troy*.

"Here goes nothing," Nathan said over the circuit. "Initiate Delta One."

When they were at full power you could *see* the gravity field from the tugs. They distorted starlight. Ninety-six tugs, each with the same capacity as the original *Paws*, started to strain against the massive levers.

"Flexion," Argus reported. "Reducing power."

"Damnit," Tyler said. That was what they were mainly worried about. Nickel-iron was not as rigid as steel. The levers were tapered, a hundred meters at the end where the tugs were attached and six hundred at the base. But it still wasn't sturdy enough for the full power.

"This is going to take some time," Nathan said. "But it's working. We've already slowed rotation three percent."

"This will take about six hours," Argus said. "The tugs will exhaust their onboard fuel supplies before the evolution is finished. I will schedule rotations for refueling."

"I've got calls to make," Tyler muttered. At some point he *had* to find somebody to share things like this with. It was no fun by yourself. Maybe he should go on tour like Steve had done.

"Oh, the hell with it." He leaned back in the comfortable couch and watched the tugs work.

Before long he fell asleep.

NINE

"And we have burn-through," Nathan said.

There was no telling how much delta-V they were going to get from the gases in the interior. Since the *Troy* was running a bit high and fast to stop at the position planned, it had been decided to cut the door—which started with burning through to release the gases—on the "upper front." That wouldn't put the door in much threat from an enemy. *Troy* was planned to be "over" the gate. They planned to put the main opening "up" and "spinward" of the gate, well away from enemy fire. Not that Tyler planned on the door being open when an enemy was firing.

Tyler had had his fill of meetings in the last two months. The stockholders were up in arms, investors were rioting, and nobody knew quite what to make of the whole thing. And when Congress calls you to testify, you go. He thought he'd done pretty well. The Armed Services committee had been friendly, all things considered. And the ratings had been high. No death threats.

Troy was center of most news. People were still trying to grasp how large it was.

The Finnish corporation that was working on the crew quarters had managed to put it in perspective. They'd made a scale model. Then models, to scale, of various notable buildings, ships and landmarks.

The one that finally sank home was the model of the Twin Towers. They were still an icon, despite being gone for nearly three decades. And when STX pointed out that the *crew quarters* were nearly the same size, and those were the size of a *toy car* compared to the massive battlestation, the reality started to hit.

"That's a lot of gas," Tyler said. The *Troy* was spurting a gush of gases that looked for all the world like God's fire extinguisher.

"Not actually adjusting the delta that much," Nathan said over the hypercom. "We're going to have to do some adjustments."

"Are we going to be able to do that with the door cut?" Tyler asked.

"We've got it under control," Nathan said. "Our models say that we'll continue to have pressure for about two days. It's a small hole and a *lot* of volume. Then we'll get back to cutting. We're not going to be *done* before we have to do the final adjustments. The remaining material will hold it just fine."

They were using a VDA. It had taken two *hours* to cut the one-hundred-millimeter-wide, one-and-a-half-kilometer-*deep* hole. When they started on the door cut, they were going to use practically every VDA in the system. As they approached the gate, even the primary defense VDAs would be used. It was still going to take two months. If nothing went wrong. Something was *bound* to go wrong.

The amount of material they were planning on

extracting from *Troy* during construction was as bizarre as any of the other numbers related to it. Just the "bits" they'd gotten from the levers were tons and tons of material. They'd pulled sixteen tons just from cutting the exhaust hole. The main door was supposed to be a kilometer in diameter with "bits." It was going to be a lot of nickel iron burned out. *Before* they got started on the firing ports. Minimum diameter on the missile ports was three meters. If they went in a straight line, which they weren't, that was three hundred and thirty-five *thousand* tons of nickel iron. Most of which would be essentially discarded.

Tyler had people to do math like that for him. Bottom line, what they were planning on doing to *Troy* was going to make the Connie project look like a backwater. One estimate he saw was that they were going to have to remove five times more material from *Troy* in phase one than they'd mined off of Connie in *five years*.

And he planned on being done with phase one in six months from when the door was finally open.

Most of the nickel iron was just going to have to *wait* to be turned into useable materials. There weren't enough smelters and there wasn't enough market for all the material they were going to be pulling out of the battlestation. Some of it was going to go back in as "fiddly bits." Most of it was just going to have to sit in orbit until they had time to get around to it.

However, they were planning on doing some extracting. Because each port also yielded nearly a *ton* of platinum group metals. He had a *special* plan for those.

"Okay," Tyler said, as he gazed around the stupidly huge interior of the battlestation. "This is just silly."

There was some remaining atmosphere. It gave the interior a slightly yellowish cast. What you could *see* of the interior because...

"Big, huh?" Nathan said. He'd accepted Tyler's offer of the ride in the *Starfire,* since it was much more comfortable than a regular shuttle.

Cutting the door had gone easier than expected. With ninety-two VDAs working on the door it had been done on schedule. They'd even managed to park the *Troy* before they were done.

Then they had to get it *open*.

It was three kilometers across on the exterior, with three "bits" that might someday be hinges and a latch. It was a kilometer and a half *thick* and a kilometer wide on the interior. It was less a door than a cork. In keeping with the enormity of everything else about *Troy*, it weighed forty-one *billion* tons.

It took a lot of tugs. It stuck to the side of the *Troy* pretty well, though. They both had notable gravity.

"Not that," Tyler said. "I *expected* big. What I wasn't expecting was how hard it was going to be to navigate. You can't see a damned *thing*!"

Light did not "bend" in space. Shadows were absolute blackness, without any of the relief caused by diffusion of atmosphere on Earth.

The door wasn't pointed anywhere near the Sun. The *entire* interior was in shadow. Tyler could see a shuttle doing an interior inspection across the seven-kilometer sphere they were calling the main bay. It was a speck, and the only reason he could see it at all was that it had a nine-million-candle-power spotlight on it, which was reflecting off the interior walls.

"What's first on the agenda?" Tyler said.

"Start cutting the plug where we're going to insert the crew quarters," Nathan said. "Then there's the air and water tanks. That's going to be . . . interesting. We're going to have to bounce the VDAs in. We're also going to start on burning the firing ports."

"Right," Tyler said. "Two more things to put on the list. We're going to have to be able to rotate this thing. Maneuver is out of the question, but it has to be able to rotate at some point. We need some interior levers. Big ones. Use the wall material or what you're taking out, whatever makes more sense. I take it I don't have to suggest you be careful when you're doing this? Anyone stumbles through a VDA and—"

"You don't have to mention it," Nathan said. "We shudder about it every day. The power involved in this project is just crazy."

"Second thing. I'm going to go talk to Bryan about another special project."

"What's that?" Nathan said.

"Finding out how many laser engineers it takes to screw in a lightbulb."

"You want a *what*?" Bryan asked. "You're—"

"Insane," Tyler said. "I know. But you can't see your hand in front of your face in there. It's a safety issue. We need a light."

"You're not asking for *much*, are you?" Bryan said. "You want a light that will illuminate a seven-and-a-half-*kilometer*-diameter sphere. That's four and a half miles!"

"Very little diffraction," Tyler pointed out. "It really doesn't have to be that *bright*. There's nothing to attenuate it. There's what looks sort of like atmosphere in there but you'd die pretty quick if you tried to survive on it. Besides the fact that it's mostly ammonia. Point is—"

"You're right,' Bryan said. "It just has to scatter light well. But it's still going to take a lot of photons."

"We've got all these lasers," Tyler said, shrugging. "Can't we use them somehow?"

"Hmmm..." Bryan said. "I'm getting an idea crazy enough to be one of yours. I'll need to talk to Nathan about it."

"Which is?" Tyler asked.

"You're always being mysteeerrrious," Bryan said, waggling his fingers. "My turn."

"Bastard."

"Okay," Tyler said. "That's pretty damned crazy."

"We call it the Dragon's Orb," Nathan said proudly.

The Dragon's Orb was a one-hundred-meter-diameter sapphire that, yes, was held in place by what appeared to be an amazingly huge dragon's claw extruded from the bay wall. A simple BDA laser powered it. There were microscopic flecks of platinum mixed into the sapphire that scattered the sunlight. The result was a lightbulb big enough to illuminate the entire the main bay.

Shuttles and tugs floated everywhere. Well, almost everywhere. There were lines of red floating lights that marked laser paths. The ships kept *well* clear of those.

"Making it was good practice for extruding the control levers," Nathan continued. "We're going to start the first heat on those next week. We've determined we need at least three, preferably six. And they're going to be long enough to nearly meet in the middle. So things will get a bit more crowded."

"Firing lanes?" Tyler asked.

"Going slow," Nathan admitted. "Mostly because of all the material we have to extract. And then there's the jogs."

Creating lines that went straight into the interior was a recipe for disaster. Some knucklehead in an X-wing was bound to come along and drop an energy torpedo into your main power plant, and everyone knows how *that* ends.

So the firing lanes, missile and laser, had zigzags built into them. For the lasers, that was relatively easy. Just drill to a certain point, clear it out, put in a VDA mirror and bounce off that. Managing the drilled material was a pain in the butt, but it was doable. And it had a ton of heavy metals already partially processed.

The missiles that were planned for the *Troy* were only two and a half meters wide, but they were *fifteen* meters long. The zig-zag point, therefore, had to be large enough for the missiles to go sideways. And the tubes themselves had to be at least three meters. That was a *lot* of nickel iron to melt.

"Then there's the blast doors," Nathan continued. "Grav plates to move the missiles . . ."

"We're on schedule, though?" Tyler said. "*Troy* will be minimally operational in six months?"

"Barely," Nathan said. "If we can get the quarters installed. Just drilling out the plug . . ."

"I know, I know," Tyler said, sighing. "I *hate* fiddly bits."

"Crew quarters for four thousand and thirty shuttle crews is not *fiddly bits!*" Nathan protested. "And then there's the magazine for two hundred *thousand* missiles! Which are going to take longer to produce than we spent building this thing."

"Have you said two point two *trillion* tons to yourself lately?" Tyler said, grinning. "The *door* was fiddly bits."

"I knew it was big," Senator Lamarche said. "But this is . . ."

Tyler grinned and took a sip of champagne. He could afford it, he'd gotten the first installment on *Troy*.

The junket for the visit by the Joint Chiefs and the Select Armed Services Committee had been a nightmare to arrange. Which is why he'd left it up to his "Washington" people. The government had moved to St. Louis while the capital was being rebuilt. Which was going slow since they were still working on plans to fill in Lake Washington. But they were still "Washington" people.

One of the big sticking points was what to use as a conveyance. BAE had finally finished the *Constitution*, and the Joint Chiefs wanted to take that. Tyler pointed out that with the higher acceleration of the *Starfire* it was quicker. *And* more comfortable.

As usual with government, they'd compromised. The group had gone out to the *Troy* on the *Constitution*, which gave the captain and the admirals a chance to show it off, then transferred to the *Starfire*, which could fit in one of the *Constitution's* bays.

With almost the entire starboard wall of the *Starfire* being optical sapphire, the view was more than startling. The problem with the surface of *Troy*, though, was that it was just too hard to grasp. When they entered the main port, after the *Constitution* had time to go in and poke around its future home, it was different. *Columbia* shuttles and *Paws* provided some perspective. And the

Constitution had been moved down to a "safe" zone on the far side of the main bay. That really gave some perspective since the battle craft, as big as a skyscraper, looked just like the toy used for comparison in various videos.

"What are they doing over there?" Senator Gullick asked, pointing "down" in relation to the Dragon's Orb.

Changes were still reverberating through the body politic over the losses suffered in the Horvath attacks. Especially since the last census.

The plagues and the two Horvath bombardments had erased a vast swathe of the citizenry of the United States. The amount of damage the world sustained should have, by most lights, thrown it into a universal failed state.

However, it was pointed out that, relative to population size, the losses were barely *half* what Germany and Japan had suffered in WWII. There should, at least, have been a massive depression. But the world was so bent on rebuilding and rearming that money flowed. Factories had to be rebuilt. Places had to be found for the displaced population. And a nation that was experiencing a baby boom could be a surprisingly upbeat place.

Despite the fact that the attacks had been a calamity beyond imagination, entrenched political groups had resisted, for nearly two years, any major changes in industrial and environmental policy. Detroit was Detroit, even if it was a crater, and that was where the major auto companies had to be. That, at least, was the position of the powerful multiterm congressman from that district who was bound and determined to keep industry where it was *supposed* to be. No matter how much tax money it took.

Then the decade rolled around, the census was done, the nation was redistricted, the lawsuits flew and the arguments got down to fisticuffs in state houses across the nation.

And there was no district of Detroit and the Car Belt. It was gone. It was absorbed into the much more conservative districts that made up the bulk of Michigan's space.

It was like that everywhere. Nine districts in the L.A. basin became one. Five San Francisco Bay districts were merged. California, overall, had gone from fifty-three districts to thirty-five.

And things began to move. Environmental restrictions on "brownfield" construction were slagged. The entire Endangered Species Act was slagged because, in the words of the senior senator from Tennessee, "the most endangered species in this solar system is homo sapiens. When we've got that fixed, we can worry about the snail darter."

Gullick was Massachusett's junior senator, a firebrand hawk whose campaign slogan had been simply "Vengeance." He'd launched his campaign on the rim of the crater that used to be Boston. He won in a landslide.

Tyler had avoided getting entangled as much as he could. He was still registered in New Hampshire but he'd been in Wolf during the last election and voted absentee.

He'd been sure to provide as much graft—sorry, "campaign finance" money—as he legally could. And various gray areas.

He almost needn't have worried. The new crop of congressmen and senators wanted the money, no question. They had to have it to get reelected. But they were almost deferential to the man who had not only created Earth's one real defense, the SAPL, but had personally engaged the Horvath in battle and damned near died from decompression because of it.

"We're constructing one of the maneuvering levers," Tyler said, gesturing with his chin to the patch of cherry-red metal. "They're not technically in the specifications. We figured out it had to have them when we were making it."

"Like the horns," Congresswoman McEntyre said, nodding. The recent winner of Maryland's Third District, which included Lake Baltimore, was a veteran of the Iraq War. She had a heavily scarred right cheek and one arm that was prosthetic as souvenirs. She had run on a "Defense first" campaign.

"Actually getting them to work will require a lot of power and a lot of grav plates," Tyler said. "We won't be able to rotate it until we have about sixty tons of grav plates and the power for them. That's about sixty terawatts per minute. The entire Earth consumes four terawatts per year for comparison. And it will only rotate at about thirty feet per second."

"If nobody has mentioned it," Senator Gullick said, "we appreciate the power plants Apollo has been installing. Everything's still pretty messed up, but cheap power helps."

"I wish there was more I could do," Tyler said, shrugging. "But that was just a good long-term investment. I'll admit, my shareholders screamed about amortizing the plants over fifty years. But they should last at least that long. And when Wolf comes online I'll be able to drop the price of electricity even more."

"It's important," Senator Lamarche said. "More and more electric cars with these new nanny capacitors. They're using a lot of power. Of course, coal is a very important supplier as well..." he added, quickly. He was the senior senator from Pennsylvania, which still mined a lot of coal.

"Of course," Tyler said, trying not to grin.

"I was actually thinking about concrete plants," Senator Gullick said. "They use an *enormous* amount of power and we can't build them fast enough. And over there?" he asked, pointing to an area on the wall where dozens of tugs clustered.

"That was why I wanted to schedule this trip for today," Tyler said. "That is where we're going to be installing the turnkey operations center. It has quarters for crew, shuttle bays, the main command center, which is initially going to be using only ten percent of its allotted space, and resupply docks. We've cut the plug for it and are going to be pulling it out."

"Plug?" Congresswoman McEntyre asked.

"First we drilled a thirty-meter hole three hundred meters into the wall," Tyler said. "It was the first time I was happy we didn't get *Troy* to full size. There's still a good kilometer of nickel on the outside of the command center. Then we installed a reflector mirror and cut from within the hole to slice out the back. In the meantime, we cut out the edges."

"Where are the cuts?" Senator Gullick asked.

"Here," Tyler said, handing him a set of binoculars. "If you look down and to the left of the cluster of tugs you should be able to spot the initial thirty-meter hole."

"Oh, my God," the senator said, laughing. "It's a *dot*."

"Yeah," Tyler said. "And the cut lines are only eighty millimeters on a side so you're going to have a hard time spotting them. But..." He paused as he listened to his implant. "Right, they're going to engage the tugs. We're pretty sure we got all the edges cut out. But if not, we'll have to do some more drilling."

In the light from the Dragon's Orb, the rippling effect of the tugs' engines could be seen distorting the light. It was reflected in a waterfall of prismatic colors on the inner wall of the battlestation, the ripples of color reflecting and shining in a rainbow of light.

"That is... pretty," Congresswoman McEntyre said. "I hadn't expected it to be pretty."

"Neither had I," Tyler said. The effect was *damned* pretty. Beautiful even. And while there was immense satisfaction in the jobs he'd been doing, beauty, except for the unchanging starfield, was rare. "I just realized that if we ever *can* rotate this thing, it's going to have the same effect."

"Rotate, hell," Senator Gullick said. "What's it going to take to get this thing mobile?"

"Senator..." the Chairman of the Joint Chiefs said. "We'd prefer to keep our defenses up, thank you."

"Hell with that," Gullick said. "The best defense is a good offense. The Glatun negotiator on the Multilateral talks should be *shot*. It's worse than Chamberlain. When we lose E Eridani, the Horvath will have nothing to prevent them attacking at any time."

The combination of attacks against Earth had gotten the Glatun to at least provide assurances that no more Horvath warships would be allowed through the E Eridani system. When—at this point, not if—they ceded it to the Horvath, Earth might as well get ready for a pounding.

"Senator," Tyler said delicately. "Two point two trillion tons. The *Constitutions*, for way of comparison, mass three hundred *thousand* tons. Six orders of magnitude difference, and we have a hard time getting them to have more than five gravities of acceleration. The *door* is one billion metric tons and it took every tug in the system four hours to get it open."

"If we can't secure E Eridani, we're still open to attacks," the senator said. "I think that the *Troy* is amazing and vital. Don't get me wrong. I also think it's worth looking at making it mobile. You're usually the big idea guy, Mr. Vernon. Don't tell me you haven't thought of it."

"Well..." Tyler said, hanging his head and toeing at the rug in embarrassment.

"You're kidding?" Admiral DeGraff said, then belly laughed. "You *haven't*?"

"I've been setting aside ten percent of all extracted platinum group since we started," Tyler said. "It's getting to be a pretty big pile..."

"How big?" Senator Lamarche asked.

"Not big enough for the power plant we'd need," Tyler said, shrugging. "But it's getting bigger every day we work on *Troy*. We need two thousand tons."

"Two thousand *tons* of platinum?" DeGraff said, guffawing again. "Oh, Tyler, you're killing me! You're not *seriously* thinking of making this thing *mobile*?"

"We can't produce the grav plates," Tyler said, shrugging. "Or the secondary power converters. We need an *enormous* amount of both. About... two hundred years' worth of production based on current

Sol System output. And, of course, more *osmium* than has ever been mined in the history of the human race. Possibly in the history of the spiral arm. Most efficient power-plant material. Do you want to know how much *fuel* it will consume to go through the gate and into E Eridani?"

"No," Senator Lamarche said. "Yes. I guess I do. Just because the entire question is so absurd."

"Think of all the buildings we lost, sorry, in New York and Washington," Tyler said. "In one pile. And made of helium-three, which we don't even produce yet. That's three hours' fuel at one-sixtieth gravity of acceleration."

"That exceeds the requirements for the six-hundred-ship fleet we're envisioning," DeGraff said. "For about ninety years."

"So, yes," Tyler said. "I *have* thought of it. There are some alternatives. We could use an Orion drive. But I'd really rather not have to irradiate the surface, and such a drive is vulnerable to damage. I mean, more damage. Orion is damage in big numbers just as it exists. The big problem remains that we don't have any onboard weapons that match the defenses. Not by dozens of orders of magnitude. So...if I can get the grav plates for about six hundred Glatun super-dreadnoughts, a power plant the size of a small city and a laser emitter system that can match two hundred VDAs in power...we can get it to move at the pace of a very anemic snail and gut any fleet stupid enough to come in range," he finished with a grin.

"I withdraw the question," Senator Gullick said.

"We can't even figure out how to fill the *magazines* you've got planned," DeGraff said, shaking his head. "Not with any sort of reasonable budget."

"Are any of the defenses online yet?" Congresswoman McEntyre asked.

"Uh . . ." Tyler said. "Sort of. We have one laser firing port and collimator installed and testing. We're finding that there are all sorts of bugs. The channel has to be in vacuum and when we cut the firing lanes there was all sorts of microscopic material left behind, not to mention trace atmosphere. So we're going to have to grav sweep each of the ports. We're building bots for that in the Wolf system at the moment. Once the lanes are swept and we reinstall the focal systems, blast doors and collimator . . . it'll be able to fire. We're still waiting on Boeing for missiles."

"Looks like you're having trouble," Senator Lamarche said.

The tugs were reconfiguring towards the center of the plug, which *still* wasn't out.

"Argus?" Tyler said. "Status on the plug?"

"There are spot-welded points in numerous places," Argus replied. "I'm preparing to do a cut. We're moving the tugs to prevent confliction. I'm going to have them pull as we're cutting."

"This should be *much* more interesting," Tyler said.

"What is . . ." Congresswoman McEntyre started to say. "Oh. My. God."

Seven VDA mirrors were floating in a vaguely rectangular array within the main bay, SAPL power being fed to them by more VDAs aligned alongside the door.

The congresswoman's exclamation, and she wasn't the only one, was from the sight of all seven opening up at once.

There was just enough atmosphere in the bay for

the beams to be, for once, visible. They were incandescent lines of fire burning into the refractory nickel iron, portions of which went bright white at the very touch of the petawatt beams.

The enormous chunk of nickel iron finally started to move but the beams continued to cut, ensuring that no more spot welds formed as it was removed.

"Those tugs," Senator Gullick said. "They're about the size of the *Paws*, *right?* Two stories high, about five long?"

"Most of them," Tyler said. "Some larger."

The cluster of sixty tugs was centered in about one-third the area of the plug being removed. Which just kept coming and coming and coming.

"That's the size of a *stadium*," Senator Lamarche said. "A *big* stadium."

"Um . . ." Tyler said. "Bigger. *Much* bigger. Six hundred meters long, four hundred high, three hundred deep. Twice the length of a supercarrier, about the same length as a *Constitution*. The plug is going to have to be removed entirely and then cut. We're planning on almost totally sealing the center within the wall. So we'll put a fifty-meter thick section of nickel iron back on top of it. Maybe steel. We're working on some really big steel projects. But welding it is tough. Then we'll get to work processing the plug for materials."

"I thought there were supposed to be shuttle bays," Senator Gullick said. "How are you going to get the shuttles in and out?"

"Uh," Tyler said. "*Really* big doors? That's going to take longer to do than pulling the plug and cutting. I *hate* fiddly bits."

TEN

"This is really awesome," Tyler said.

"Even if it *is* a fiddly bit?" Nathan asked.

The tube was three meters in diameter with walls of iron that reflected the light from the space suits.

Tyler had just had to check out the first missile tube since it had been an unimaginable pain in the ass to build.

The basic concept was simple, a zigzagged tube that ran from the missile magazine, which was still being constructed, to the exterior of the battlestation. Put in grav plates to move the missiles. Since the missiles were pretty solid state and, with the exception of the capacitors, didn't tend to explode if they were hit, even if there was a major hit on a full tube, all the missiles were going to do was seal the tube. Shift to another and you were rocking again.

There were . . . issues. To make sure that an enemy couldn't get a hostile weapon in, the tubes needed blast doors. Just drilling the tubes was a pain. Putting in the blast doors had started to look like a deal killer. But by building some special mirrors and bots, they'd managed to basically cut out a chunk of the wall on either "side" of the tube. By cutting away some more, they ended up with two "sliding" doors that overlapped and, when closed, extended fifteen meters into the wall of the station. They were operated by grav plates, which had to be supplied with power and controls, and the base of the doors and the plate they rested on had to be perfectly smooth and...

Fiddly bits.

The missile magazine was going to take a while. Not only was it planned with more cubic capacity than the initial living quarters, which meant a bigger plug to pull, it had to have systems to move the missiles into the tubes. Fast.

More fiddly bits.

Troy was eventually planned to have *five* magazines, each capable of holding two hundred *thousand* missiles, and forty-eight launch tubes running off of each.

The missile complex was only a small portion of "Zone One." There were five planned zones. Each zone would be capable of independent operation. It would combine a purely military side, missile magazines, laser tracks, barracks, shuttle and eventually ship bays, repair areas, headquarters, supplies for thousands, support sections, air, water and, especially, a tremendously large fuel storage area.

There would also be a smaller "civilian" area that would house the dependents of the military personnel as well as civilian support staff and a "general support" area that was designed to grow organically just like a small town supporting a military base.

Five was going to take a while. Like, a couple of hundred years. Of fiddly bits.

For now they had one missile tube and one laser

tube. But the SAPL had started small, too. It now had twenty-eight *million* square yards of VLA mirrors capable of generating seventy-one *petawatts* of power. Doing so, including BDA, VSA and VDA production, had used up about half the "trash" portion of the Near Earth Asteroids. The SAPL division had been busy beavers and every year they just about doubled production while cutting costs. And to make matters better, the "good" part of the asteroids paid for the production.

"You're getting the new laser mirrors?" Tyler asked.

"Yeah," Nathan commed. "Capable of handling an exawatt? An *exawatt*, Tyler? The whole *VLA* doesn't put out an exawatt."

"I'm tired of never being able to concentrate enough power," Tyler said, running the waldo of the suit over the seal on a blast door. "And it will be capable of it eventually. Of course, we'll need several thousand VDAs by then."

"What does UNG stand for?" Nathan asked.

"What?" Tyler asked, continuing on.

"What does UNG stand for?" Nathan said. "Very Scary Array, Very Dangerous Array. What does UNG stand for?"

"Nothing," Tyler said. "The first time we activated it I got an actual button installed to fire it. And I went 'ung, ung, ung' just before I pushed the button. Everybody who had anything to do with it pretty much went 'ung' the first time they thought about it. I think the cover acronym is Unified Nuclear Grappler or something. But it really means just . . . ung."

"Ung is right," Nathan said. "Cooling them is going to be a bitch."

"'That is the other reason you're getting great big helium tanks," Tyler said. "Speaking of which: When are you digging the air and water tanks?"

"Next month we're *starting* on the water tank," Nathan said. "The main one, that is."

"I think it's time for us to have a little accident," Tyler said.

"I don't like accidents with stuff like that," Nathan pointed out. "People tend to, and I don't want to exaggerate this, vanish in a puff of volatiles."

"Not that kind of accident," Tyler said. "Just a little bobble with a VDA when you're digging out the plug."

"I understand you had a little bobble with digging out the water tank," Admiral DeGraff said. He had been in his position for three years and was just about to retire. But he wanted to stay around to see *Troy* activated.

"When you're throwing around that much power," Tyler said. "Sometimes these things happen."

"A very *suspicious* accident," Admiral DeGraff said. "A hollowed out point at the notional top of the water tank that looks, and I don't want to sound paranoid about this, suspiciously like a pool. A very *big* pool. With what looks like a bit of a water park with a little work. Melted out water runs on the *walls*?"

"I'm not sure how it happened," Tyler said. "Just a bit of a bobble with a VDA. The rest I ascribe to chaos theory. In an infinite universe... On the other hand, a pool will be a real MWR benefit to the crew. People may just be born, raised, live and *die* on *Troy*, Admiral. Surely they deserve something other than endless walls of iron and steel?"

"And do you expect us to *pay* for a pool, Mr. Vernon?"

"Of course," Tyler said. "Part of the contract specifications was a water testing area with Earth normal gravity, air and appropriate heating and cooling. You now have one."

Admiral DeGraff consulted the appropriate files and grunted.

"Hmph," the admiral said. "The 'water testing area' is listed as sixty thousand dollars, Mr. Vernon. You're going to sell us a sixty-acre water park for sixty thousand dollars? With 'Earth normal air, gravity, heating and cooling'?"

"There are various cost overruns so far, Admiral," Tyler said, smiling. "Most of which we've eaten. If for no other reason than we're getting nearly as much for the materials we're mining as we are for *Troy*. As long as we don't have to pay for all the fiddly bits, like the quarters and bays, I'm good. And I rather like the look of the pool, don't you? We call it Xanadu."

"Xanadu?" the Admiral said, then nodded. "So you think of yourself as Kublai Khan?"

"I understand he was below normal height as well," Tyler said, grinning and cutting the connection.

"Sir," Argus said over Tyler's com. "The Gorku manager Zih Temar has arrived aboard the *Galactic Miner*. He requests a meeting."

"Subject?" Tyler asked. Having an AI was better than any personal assistant. Among other things, you didn't have to turn down proposals of marriage. He'd switched to males after the first two female PAs and found that didn't help, either.

It also meant he could stay aboard ship. He'd more or less permanently installed himself in the *Monkey Business*. Since the *Business* was inside the *Troy* most of the time, it was also a damned secure place to work.

"It requests that the purpose remain proprietary."

"Interesting," Tyler said. "Do we know anything about Zih Temar?"

"It is listed as a special assistant to the assistant vice president of Entertainment and Design Management. Effectively, it is in charge of planning corporate parties and choosing which art to put on which walls."

"Could that be classed as sort of a corporate cultural affairs attaché?" Tyler asked.

"Yes, sir."

"Send a shuttle," Tyler said. "In fact, send the *Starfire*."

Zih Temar was so plain a Glatun it could have been chosen for an encyclopedia illustration: standard Glatun, one each. The harness was straight corporate drone. Skin tone was absolute middle. Ditto red on the eyes. Nose was a standard Glod short-nosed.

Tyler had never met a more obvious spy.

"The room is secure," Tyler said. "I have it swept weekly and there are, as I'm sure you noticed, large and bored 'miners' in the hallways that seem to have little to do."

"Sir," Temar said, setting a data crystal on the table. "A personal message from Niazgol Gorku."

Tyler set it in a player and a hologram of Gorku sprung up.

"Hello, friend," Gorku said. "With Horvath control of the E Eridani system and the support they are receiving from the Rangora, hypercom communication may no longer be secure. Thus...

"We're going to continue to buy materials, but production is slowing. The People's Council has firmly rejected further 'military boondoggles' and also have rejected every draft bill. So even if we build more ships, we can't crew them. They also refuse to yield on reductions of basic social spending, and taxes are already killing us. Thus, affording more ships is questionable. The production going to ships has impacted entertainment goods and services. The Benefactors are deadlocked and the peace movement is gaining strength. Federal Intelligence has solid evidence that it is heavily backed by the Rangora, but nobody wants to see it.

"The bottom line is that war is coming and we will not be prepared. With luck we will prevail. I have seen little luck for my people of late. I am not optimistic.

"I have prevailed upon certain people, I will not name them, to give certain releases. This good Glatun carries a shipment of not only updates for Granadica of the newest Gorku military and civilian technologies, but also releases. This effectively gives Earth the rights to produce any system of Glatun design, including military systems. There are also one hundred and seventeen blank AIs, the most I could sneak out. All of the rights and releases are authorized but it would be better for everyone involved if you could keep them somewhat secret. If...when war breaks out between ourselves and the Rangora, that will be less important. In the meantime, please try to keep it quiet.

"It will be some time before you can produce the

material, much less assimilate it. But you have it now. All legal but... it would be better if no one found out.

"The last item is the most troubling for your system. Certain of my ships have been somewhat upgraded in the sensor department. Also something I would prefer you keep quiet. But the *Galactic Miner* is one. When it last passed through the E Eridani system, they detected traces of large warships passing through the system. Since they did not go to Sol, they must have gone to Horvath. The traces indicated older class Rangora *Devastator* dreadnoughts. The Rangora produced forty-two. At least thirty have been mothballed or were. I'm trying to get information on whether they are still in retirement and what the status on the other twelve are.

"The *Devastators* have two-hundred-terawatt main lasers and thousand-gravity shields. They will shrug off your petawatt lasers. I hope you have upgraded. They also may or may not have the Rangora capital missiles. It depends on what technology the Rangora have shared with the Horvath. If so, they are fast and stealthy, and the *Devastators* each carry two hundred.

"If they reach your system I hope you have something that can stop them. *Troy*, alone, will not be enough.

"May peace be with us all. But I fear it will not. Good luck, my friend."

"Anything additional?" Tyler asked, pulling out the crystal. He walked over to his desk, took out a small hammer and crushed the atacirc.

"No, sir," Temar said. "By the time we returned through the system, the traces were gone. There is a Horvath battle cruiser on station but it didn't even hail us."

"How long do you think we can keep getting shipments through?" Tyler asked.

"The estimate is that the Horvath will not engage Glatun ships absent a declaration of war with the Rangora," Temar said. "But if we go to war with the Rangora, it can be assumed the Horvath will see us as an enemy."

"Glatun could trash the entire Horvath system in a day," Tyler said.

"But we would not do so," Temar said. "The Benefactors would never approve a simple annihilation raid."

"The Horvath are a poor, weak, oppressed polity that need comfort and care to bring them to a civilized condition?" Tyler asked.

"Yes, sir."

"And Earth?"

"Is a militaristic system bent on regional control," Temar said. "Its most notable personages are all atavistic barbarians. Probably it would be better under Horvath control."

"Is that a consensus?" Tyler asked.

"No," Temar said. "But the consensus of those who see the Horvath as poor and oppressed. Those factions would never have allowed this technology transfer. Fortunately . . . they do not control such things."

"We'd better get the transfer finished, then," Tyler said. "I'll personally carry the data to the Wolf system. Granadica can probably use it better than anyone in Sol. And it will be more secure there. We'll hold the AIs on *Troy*. We needed one, anyway."

"Yes, sir."

ELEVEN

✦

"Faster," Tyler muttered.

"Sir?" Byron asked, considering the progress of the mine with satisfaction.

Both washers were in place, the lower held up by what, from the distance the *Starfire* maintained, seemed the thinnest of strands. Single-strand carbon nanotube was incredibly strong stuff, but the strands weren't nearly as thin as they looked. Each was nearly a foot across, woven and rewoven about from individual strands thinner than a bacterium. Humans had finally cracked extruding continuous strands of carbon monomolecules. What defeated them, so far, was doing it as simply as the Glatun spinners, which moved at a rate of nearly forty feet per minute.

"I was just thinking," Tyler said. "This is going very well, Byron. How soon can we start installation of the separation equipment?"

"We're not even ready to start weaving the pipes, sir," Byron said. "The lines can only hold so much weight at this point. We'll need to spin more lines before we can start doing the actual mine portion."

"Think about ways to get around that," Tyler said. "We're running out of time."

"Sir?" Audler said, frowning and taking his pipe out. "We're *well* ahead of schedule."

"Byron," Tyler said quietly. "In no more than two years, maybe less, the Rangora and Glatun are going to get into a war that will dwarf anything that this region has seen in a thousand years. How that war is going to go is a big question. But one thing that's certain is that the Horvath are going to take the opportunity to cut Earth off from Glatun support. We've got the construction help we needed. We can build ships on our own. We can mine asteroids. We can build some pretty fair lasers and we have the SAPL. We can build anything we need and we can defend the Sol System pretty well and keep the enemy out of Wolf. *If* we have fuel."

"Oh," Byron said, putting his pipe back in and chewing on it. Tyler wasn't sure he ever actually smoked it.

"Get your team together and brainstorm," Tyler said. "We've got permission to make as many spinners as we want. We can make anything that Gorku has on its database. Get with Granadica and see about priorities because it's about to get *really* busy."

"Steren's not exactly happy being in the Wolf system," Tom Schneider said, looking out the crystal wall of the *Starfire*. "There's not much to do. And the medical facilities are . . ."

"State of the art but rough and ready?" Tyler said.

"I was about to say 'not designed around the pregnant daughter of the system owner screaming at the doctors.' But I'm far too polite."

Tom was not the head of Apollo mining in the Wolf system. His title was "Special Project Manager, Wolf 359 Division." The fact that he was the son-in-law of the boss had nothing to do with the fact that when he asked for anything he got it. But there was a reason that Tyler had put him in the position.

"She, and you, are safer in Wolf than in the Sol System," Tyler said. "And there's going to be more room to move around once some more habitats get made. The mine's going to have plenty of room to move around. I'll get you guys a little bungalow in the clouds."

"It will be pretty," Tom said. "But what's the point of us looking at this asteroid?"

"It's about the right size," Tyler said. "And the right composition. I want you to spin process it and get it down to iron and a bit of nickel. Then do a seal wrap like the washers. When you've got steel, make a shell about the size of Granadica."

"Which will be for ... ?" Tom said.

"That is the next conversation," Tyler said.

"Granadica?" Tyler said.

"You called?" the AI said, forming a hologram of a Glatun head in the *Starfire*.

"How are the repairs going?" Tyler asked.

"Just about done," Granadica said happily. "I don't exactly feel young, but I feel younger than I've felt in a while. I even got the rust smell out of the air processors. That took some time to run down."

Tyler was pretty sure it was just there to remind the users that the fabber was old. If it had really gotten the taste out of the air it was feeling young. Which might be good and might be bad.

"You got the updates from Gorku?" Tyler asked. "Are they really the releases we need?"

"They got the whole packet," Granadica said. "Terra, or rather the LFD Corporation, is now authorized to produce anything that Gorku had in its designs and patents database. Including military grade drives, weapons and inertics."

"Which is great," Tyler said. "Except we don't have the production capacity to use the data. Which brings me to my next question. You were using thirty percent of your capacity to do repairs. How much capacity would it take you to produce *another* ship fabber in, oh, about a year?"

"You want me to twin?" Granadica said dubiously. "Some of it I can't make. The shell, especially. Pretty much everything else I can make in a year or so using . . . oh, twenty percent of my capacity. If I have the materials. You need another fabber?"

"*Troy* does," Tyler said. "Yes. It needs a fabber to produce grav plates and drives, power plants, ships and especially missiles."

"The last one is the easiest," Granadica said. "There's a Glatun design of medium missile that fits pretty close to the Boeing Mjolnir specs. I can pump out a fabber that will be able to make missiles from raw materials in about a month. The output will be about . . . five missiles per hour."

"That . . . works," Tyler said. "Can they fly themselves to the bays?"

"Oh, yeah," Granadica said. "Easy."

"I still think *Troy* needs a fabber," Tyler said. "Does it bother you making a twin? I'd think of it more as a child."

"You're human," Granadica said. "No, it doesn't bother me that you want another fabber. I'm an AI. We don't have feelings."

"Granadica," Tyler said, nearly using the nickname that hovered in the back of his mind every time he talked to the AI. "Things are about to get very bad. I know you've been looking at the strategic situation."

"I'll admit that things don't look good, no," the AI said.

"Churchill, who was one of our great war-leaders, once said that the first year of a war you have nothing that you need, the second year you have half of what you need and the third you have all that you need, you just can't use it. In some cases, it's too *late* to use it. I don't want another fabber. Sol *needs* another fabber. And when that one is done, we're going to need a third. And a fourth. And a fifth."

"So you want me to churn out fabbers," Granadica said. "Just sit here in this system and churn out newer, competing, fabbers with all the latest gimmicks."

Tyler sat and thought about it for a moment.

"Granadica, I know AIs don't have feelings," he said. "But if you did, would you *like* humans?"

"Most of them," Granadica said. "Some of them are idiots."

"Agreed," Tyler said, grinning suddenly. "But, in general, would you say that you'd prefer that we not be wiped out of existence? Or, to put it another way, are you looking forward to a wipe to basic personality and then working for the Horvath?"

"I'll get to work on that fabber," Granadica said.

It was all about levers.

✳   ✳   ✳

Tyler checked the telltales on the air lock, *then* opened the door. One exposure to vacuum was all he ever wanted to experience. And while getting out in Granadica or the *Monkey Business* was one thing, Shuttle Bay One of the *Troy* had been built by the lowest bidder.

"Mr. Vernon, welcome to the *Troy*," Admiral Jack Kinyon said. The two-star commander of the *Troy* was of a size for it, standing nearly seven feet tall and probably pushing weight limit. He carried it well.

"Been around it a good bit," Tyler said, sniffing the air, then shaking the admiral's hand. "Sort of been hoboing in your bay, to tell you the truth. This is just the first time I've gotten out of a shuttle or ship."

"I had heard we had some homeless people hanging around," the admiral said, grinning. "But I understand there's a nice little compartment that somehow got slipped into the plans on the civilian side. Something about a three-thousand-square-foot apartment with a view of the bay?"

"Hey, I *built* the damned thing," Tyler said. "I figured I deserved a vacation get-away. The commander of the *Monkey Business* has also been making noises about how much room I'm taking up. I figure you've got the room."

"I suppose there's that," the admiral said. "And if I may introduce my senior officers?"

"Please," Tyler said, nodding to the group.

"Commodore Kurt Pounders," Kinyon said, trooping the line. "Chief of Staff."

"Sir," the commodore said. He was nearly as tall as his boss, but rail thin with a shock of black hair cut fairly long for the military.

"Commodore," Tyler said, shaking his hand. "I hope you have a good support team. Operations on this thing are going to be interesting."

"Which brings us to Colonel Raymond Helberg," Admiral Kinyon said. "Chief of Operations."

"Sir," the colonel said. He had a faint English accent. Tyler had heard that some of the crew and officers were from NATO units.

"Definitely got *your* work cut out for you," Tyler said, shaking his hand.

"We endeavor to provide, sir," the colonel said.

"Commodore Russell Marchant," the admiral continued. "Commander of Task Force One."

"Commodore," Tyler said, shaking his hand.

"Sir." The true "Navy" commander in charge of the *Constitution* cruisers and *Independence* frigates was medium height with pale blond hair and just as pale blue eyes. "This is one heck of a big platform. I'm not even sure what my group is going to do."

"Anything that requires moving, Commodore," Tyler said, chuckling. "The *Troy* isn't going anywhere any time soon."

"Captain James Sharp," the admiral continued. "Chief tactical officer."

"We throw rocks." The captain was black as an ace of spades and tall enough to have played college basketball. "And poke people with flashlights."

"I'll tell my people not to charge you for practice time with the SAPL," Tyler said, grinning. "You're going to have to pay for the missiles."

"I understand we're getting a missile fabber?" the tactical officer said.

"In about a month," Tyler said. "There may be more.

It's the usual problem of balancing infrastructure and actual equipment. For that matter, it will be a general fabber. So your bosses will have to decide how much of it goes to infrastructure versus weapons."

"We could use more missiles," Admiral Kinyon said. "That's for sure. Captain Chris DiNote, commander of the assault boat wing."

"We deliver the mail, sir," the captain said, shaking Tyler's hand. "When we have shuttles."

"They're on their way," Tyler said. "Until recently we were calling them emergency rescue shuttles because marine landing craft would have twigged the antimilitary design functions of Granadica. They're being redesignated as *Myrmidons*. Still the same capabilities for the time being. But we'll have about one a day coming in any time now."

"Looking forward to it," the captain said. "There's a training group down at Great Lakes doing work-ups. It's going to be interesting."

"I heard the Navy was insisting on enlisted personnel as pilots?" Tyler said.

"They're boats," the admiral said, shrugging. "Boats aren't run by officers. So, yes, the majority of the drivers will be coxwains."

"That will be interesting," Tyler said, raising an eyebrow.

"And the customer for Captain DiNote's boats," the admiral finished. "Colonel Daniel Bolger, USMC."

"Sir," the colonel said, nodding sharply.

"Have you tried out the micrograv ball court, Colonel?" Tyler asked.

"Yes, sir," the colonel replied gruffly. "It was a very interesting experience."

"I figured that if your personnel are going to be working in microgravity, it helped to have a place to get in practice that wasn't...practice if you know what I mean. Training doesn't always have to be serious. The more time they spend in microgravity..." Tyler trailed off since the colonel seemed to be suffusing a bit. He wasn't sure what he'd said...

"The colonel may be less than enthusiastic because the first platoon that tried it ended up with half a dozen serious injuries," the admiral said dryly.

"Oh," Tyler said. "Sorry."

"We're installing more padding, sir," the colonel said, his jaw working. "That's been a pretty interesting evolution as well. Superglue doesn't work the same way in microgravity as it does in gravity."

Tyler tried not to wince. Nothing liquid or semi-liquid worked the same in microgravity as it did on Earth.

"*Everything* about *Troy* has been a learning experience, Colonel," Tyler said.

"Second Platoon learned pretty quick that weight isn't the same as mass," the colonel said. "No pain, no gain, sir."

"And arguably the most important part of my command staff is still unable to be visually present in this bay," the admiral said, raising his voice. "Paris?"

"Here, sir," the AI replied from a PA box. "Welcome to *Troy*, Mr. Vernon. I will endeavor to do a better job than my predecessor."

"The big mistake of the Trojans was meeting the Achaeans outside the walls," Tyler said. "Let's not make the same mistake."

"Not a chance," Admiral Kinyon said, grinning. "I

don't plan to fight *fair*. With your permission, sir, I've arranged for a dining-out later. Yourself, the officers of the *Troy* and some of the senior civilian contractors."

"Sounds good," Tyler said, blinking. "I'm free this evening."

"In the meantime," the admiral said. "I'd like to let these gentlemen get back to their duties and I thought we could go inspect some of the more ... interesting aspects of the design."

"Okay," Tyler said, trying not to gulp.

"Gentlemen," the admiral said, nodding at the group. "Until later."

"And here we have the air mixing chamber," the admiral said, opening up the inner hatch.

All of *Troy* didn't yet have lifts or grav walks. The walk from the shuttle bays to the air recycling system had been nearly a mile. Tyler hadn't walked that far in *years*.

And then there were the *stairs*.

The air mixing chamber, because it was slightly over-pressured, had an air-lock system to enter. Sort of. There were two hatches to get through. But it wasn't a full air lock. More like a slightly more secure version of the sort of doors you found on big stadiums.

Beyond the door was a small patio with a waist-high railing. The whole thing was cut from solid nickel iron and Tyler could see some *actual* bobbles from the lasers. But, overall, it was pretty solid. Good enough for government work.

Beyond the railing was the main mixing chamber which was a five-hundred-meter-high, two-hundred-meter-diameter cylinder with more "patios" every six stories or so, stretching up from the base to the top. The admiral had trekked to a platform about midway and the view was more than spectacular. The gravity was also a bit low. While the platform had its own grav plates, the main chamber was under one-sixth gravity. You had to be careful not to hop over the railing. You'd definitely die from the fall.

It was also, unsurprisingly, windy. The air shot upwards and ruffled Tyler's beard.

"Very nice view?" Tyler said.

"Yes, it is," the admiral said. "Also, I might add, very interesting design. Some of the civilian contractors... Ah, a demonstration."

A man was flying *up* the chamber wearing a "squirrel suit" with textile "wings" spreading from ankle to wrist. As Tyler watched, he banked around in an arc and then up and back and around...

"Your point, Admiral?" Tyler asked. "I mean, if he works for me I can probably circulate a memo..."

"Don't tell me you didn't design it this way," the admiral said. "It's *made* for flying."

"Okay," Tyler said. "I won't. Or that the outlet system is designed so that nobody can get stuck on it."

"There have been accidents," the admiral said. "Several. One man died."

"And their contracts stipulate that any injury suffered during recreational periods are *not* covered by workman's comp," Tyler said. "We paid off the life insurance on the death and we're covering the major medical on the accidents. As we've paid off on the fifty-three people *killed* in the making of *Troy* and the literally *thousands* of major to minor injuries. Space is a very dangerous place, but people *are* going to find crazy stuff to do, Admiral. The make-up of the people who volunteer for space jobs leans heavily to the slightly insane. Or, at least, adrenaline junkies. Making a place for them to get their stupid out was a way to keep them from, oh, seeing how long they could breathe vacuum."

"That is . . . a point," the admiral said thoughtfully.

"What I'm worried about is the first complete *moron* to try to dive in the water recycler," Tyler said. "It's just as big and would be much worse than space since water absorbs light. We're not real sure about the physics, but there's not going to be much spatial orientation. Since it's a micrograv environment and water, the bubbles from SCUBA aren't going to go up. There's going to be zero, *absolutely zero*, spatial orientation as soon as you get far enough away from the walls, which you'll do quick, to see them. At which point anyone trying it is going to be lost in a void."

"I think we might have to put a ban on SCUBA gear," the admiral said.

"Their *suits* are SCUBA gear," Tyler said, gesturing outward. "This was intended to, at least for a while, keep these overzealous idiots from trying it. Eventually someone will. I just hope he brings a safety line. Or she."

"I've noticed the prevalence of shes," the admiral said, heading back to the door.

"If *Troy* and the SAPL can't hold Sol System, *Troy* won't survive," Tyler said. "Eventually they can starve you out or you'll run out of fuel. But if the Horvath or, God help us, the Rangora hit Earth so hard it's essentially destroyed . . . As long as *Troy* can keep fed, and we're getting ready to put in a big hydroponics section, humanity will survive, Admiral. *Civilization* will survive. So, yeah, we've used the 'equal opportunity' program to get as many females onboard as possible. The civilian side is going to have schools, including colleges and even a research university. We're going to try to get artists, sculptors, singers, entertainers, *comedians* when we get enough room."

"Battlestation and Ark?" the admiral said. "I had wondered."

"Don't sweat it," Tyler said. "You've got enough to worry about with getting the station up and running. But, yeah, it's an Ark. Let's hope we don't need it to fulfill its secondary function."

The admiral hadn't mentioned steak and lobster.

Tyler was polite enough to return the favor and not mention that as a resident of New Hampshire he knew the difference between good steak and lobster and the sort Yankee traders sold to the U.S. military.

"This is great," Tyler said, tucking in.

"And just a little weird," Commodore Pounder said. "I was a lieutenant commander when you sold your first load of maple syrup to the Glatun. Thirteen years later we're eating lobster on, face it, the Death Star."

"So that raises a question," Captain Sharp said. The tactical officer looked up and tilted his head to the side. "No press present and we've all got security clearances. How long *were* you planning *Troy*?"

"Heh," Tyler said, setting down his fork and wiping his mouth. "Since I was about nine. If you mean seriously planning it? Since the Horvath came through the gate. I never in a million years thought I'd be able to *do* it, mind you. And I didn't. A lot of *much* smarter people built this."

"Still a very long way to go," Colonel Helberg said, carefully cutting his lobster. Ripping it apart was clearly a barbarian American custom. "Combining getting the military side up and running with the ongoing construction has been an interesting chess game."

"Infrastructure versus direct production," Tyler said, resuming cutting the rather tough sirloin. "It's been a juggling act the whole time I've been doing this. I mean, face it, we've been at war with the Horvath since before I sold that first load of syrup. Figuring out how much direct war material to produce versus infrastructure has been the juggling act.

Fortunately, we've figured out how to make the VLA mirrors out of material for which we don't have much direct use. The rest is... tougher. Build fabbers or ships? If we build the fabbers now, we can build more ships later. We need ships *now*. We need mirrors *now*. Tugs or frigates? Tugs or launches? Granadica can produce one of the *Myrmidons* a day. It takes two days to produce a *Paw*-style tug. The tugs have an infinite variety of uses. *Myrmidons* have utility but they're more focused. Speaking of which. Captain DiNote?"

"Sir?" the boats commander said, looking up.

"The *Myrmidons* can operate rather well as tugs," Tyler said. "They only have about thirty percent of the operational power but they have magnetic grapnels which are, face it, the same tractor system as a tug. Just less powerful. You're probably going to get some requests for assistance in... well, construction, if you will."

"Doesn't bother me," the captain said, nodding. "It will give my people some operating experience."

"If it's work on the *Troy* ..." the admiral said, looking pensive. "I could see doing that. Direct commercial work...?"

"I understand the problem," Tyler said, smiling. "The flip side is that we'll be paying you guys for the time. So your people get boat-handling experience and the training time gets paid for by my company. And we then triple bill the U.S. government for it."

"That is..." the admiral said, looking thoughtful.

"Reality," Tyler said, chuckling. "And we get taxed on any profit we happen to make which then goes to pay for the triple billing on the shuttles we're borrowing from the government in the first place."

"My head hurts," Captain Sharp said.

"Hey," Tyler said. "I'm not charging you for laser time. Be happy."

"There is a charge for laser time?" Commodore Marchant said.

"Hmmm..." Tyler said, his mouth full. He cleared it with a sip of wine and wiped his mouth again. "About a penny a megajoule last time I checked. That's for purely internal charging, mind you.

"The SAPL is owned by a separate corporation from Apollo but they're both subsidiaries of LFD. So we have an internal charge rate. SAPL upgrades and maintenance, even R & D and overhead, and there's an *amazing* amount of overhead, get paid by charging for laser time.

"For external charging, cutting plates for the *Constitutions* and *Independence*, for example, the rate is about triple. That's standard, it covers overhead and secondary charges as well as a slight profit. I know about it, but I don't really get involved unless there's a dispute about charges between the different corporations. That's the sort of thing I, alas, spend too much time having to manage. It's like any other for-profit business. You have to find the price-point that will let you make the most money. Charge too much and BAE or Raytheon either tries to get into competition or figures out ways to not use our service. Charge too little and the SAPL corporation eventually goes out of business and you guys will have to buy it and run it.

"I'd rather prefer someone else was in competition at some levels. I'd like to see what other corporations would do with the same basic concept. And there are the usual mutterings in Congress about a monopoly. Fortunately, we're not incorporated in the U.S. so they can't technically force me to break up the SAPL or Apollo or any of the other places I'm in a monopoly position."

"You're not incorporated in the U.S.?" Captain Sharp said, blinking rapidly.

"Nope," Tyler said. "LFD is. Apollo, the SAPL, Wolf and all the rest are all incorporated in Tonga. We pay taxes as if we were an American corporation because most of the ground-side facilities are in the U.S. And corporate charges in Tonga that aren't chump change. But by being officially based in Tonga I avoid all sorts of hassles. No EPA telling me I can't melt asteroids because it changes the space environment."

"You're joking," Captain Sharp said. "Tell me you're joking."

"There is . . ." Tyler paused and shrugged. "*Was* a very active space environment movement. Humans have already raped the Earth, they shouldn't be allowed to rape space as well. I had to deal with them somewhat when I first started mining. Their tendency to concentrate in certain geographic localities means that the core of the movement is somewhat reduced."

"Yeah," the tactical officer said. "Like the joke about the Horvath targeting."

"Excuse me?" Tyler said.

"Um ..." the TACO said, looking uncomfortable. "Never mind."

"The joke about Horvath targeting methods is that they only ever read one thing written by a human," the admiral said, since the silence had gotten uncomfortable. "Shakespeare's admonition that the first thing we do is kill all the lawyers."

"Hooo ..." Tyler said, trying not to laugh. He'd noticed one time the statistic that the occupation most reduced percentagewise by the Horvath attacks wasn't police or firefighters or even secretaries, but members of the American Bar Association. "I guess that's one of those forwards I deleted. But, ooh, that's *cold*." He still couldn't help but chuckle.

"I guess you're not generally dialed in on such things," Admiral Kinyon said, shrugging. "But when the shock of the bombings and the plague finally wore off, it was laugh or cry until the rivers were tears. I guess the height was about two years ago. I remember because I was commanding the *Clinton* CVBG and my chief of staff was addicted to the things."

"I suspect that could have been taken badly by some of the other officers," Tyler said. "Especially those who lost people in Diego."

"His wife and three children were more or less dead center of the impact," the admiral said. "So nobody said anything about it. But every morning briefing he'd trot out the new list. And then just before we made port in Perth he ate his .45. Which is why I know a lot of bad jokes about the bombings and plagues and tend not to tell them."

"Yes, sir," Captain Sharp said. "Sorry, sir."

"Not a problem, Captain," the admiral said. "The term is *faux pas*. One of the purposes of social events like this is to find out each other's hot buttons. Also to talk shop because no matter how many meetings you have, all the information people need doesn't get passed around."

"Thank you for that explanation, Admiral," Colonel Bolger said. The Marine colonel was picking through the remnants of his lobster and didn't really look up. "I'd always wondered. Since I was a JO I'd just sort of assumed it was so you'd feel like a whore in church from time to time."

Tyler spit out a glass of wine, half of which went up his nose. But it wasn't really noticed as most of the group broke into relieved laughter.

"Are you quite well, Mr. Vernon?" Admiral Kinyon said, trying and failling to keep a straight face.

"Fine," Tyler gasped. "A little endive went down the wrong tube." He coughed and cleared the last of the wine, then shook his head. "Ahem. But on the subject of talking shop...Ah...Damn, I'm not sure if this is the right venue. It's about intel."

"As Captain Sharp pointed out, most of us have appropriate clearances," the admiral said, shrugging. "And *Troy* is, to say the least, a fairly secure environment."

"I passed on some intelligence to...um...higher?" Tyler said. "I'm just not sure if it got to you guys even though you're the main group that should have it."

"About?" Captain Sharp asked.

"Uh..." Tyler said. "Some ship traces in the Eridani system."

"I'd wondered where that tidbit came from," the admiral said, taking a sip of wine. "Yes, we got it. I'll just add that there is some..." He paused and his head came up as if he was listening to something.

The conversation slowly died away as, one by one, the officers all lifted their heads and looked off into the distance. Tyler recognized the attitude. It was someone unused to plants getting a—

"Mr. Vernon?" Argus said. "The Glatun free-trader *Partan Crossing* just came through the gate on an unscheduled run. There is a Horvath fleet in the E Epsilon system."

"How many?" Tyler commed, still picking at his lobster.

"Thirty *Devastator*-class Rangora battleships," Argus said. "Nine Iquka battle cruisers and seven Odiqa frigates."

"Mr. Vernon," the admiral said, setting down his fork and standing up. "A situation has arisen..."

"Which is difficult," Tyler said, taking a sip of wine. "We still can't close the door and use the SAPL internally. We haven't even started the bypass systems. So you have to decide whether to use it internally, and thus possibly protect the primary systems, or close the door and protect the soft materials in the bay."

"We're closing the door," the admiral said. "And with that, we need to get to work."

"So do I," Tyler said. "Since you can't close it without my tugs. And even then it takes some time. I need six, though."

"Very well," the admiral said. "Whatever you feel you need."

"And you'll want to assign Captain DiNote's people to assist," Tyler said. "I've already sent the order to scramble the tugs to the plug."

"My people are moving," DiNote said.

"And so must I," Tyler said.

"Nathan, you got the word about the Horvath fleet?"

"Got it," Nathan said. "And I just lost all my tugs to closing the door."

"Yeah," Tyler said. "Except six. They're going to pull the slag from a bypass. Now."

"We don't know when the Horvath are coming through," Nathan protested. "You're going to leave them out in the cold."

"They're just machines, Nathan," Tyler said. "We need a SAPL bypass put in, *now*. We've got the materials, right?"

"Yes," Nathan said. "I'm moving the tugs into position..."

"Use the Ung beam."

"Ung," Nathan said. "I don't really think of that as a *construction* system. But if you say so."

"Don't jog it," Tyler said. "We'll back-fill or something later. Just drive it straight into the bay."

"Yes, master!" Nathan said in a deep baritone. "It shall be done!"

"Not a time for levity, Nathan," Tyler said. "I've got other calls to make."

"Dad?" Christy said. "Do you know what time it is?"

"I'm on Greenwich, honey," Tyler said. "And I'd

call, anyway. There's a corporate helo headed to your condo. Get in it and go."

"What's happening?" Christy said, trying to wake up. It was 4 AM in Philadelphia and with the latest team report turned in, she'd been partying. Waking up quick wasn't happening.

"Horvath," Tyler said as the city alarms started going off. Her building had one of the new air-raid sirens and it started shrieking fit to wake the dead or even terminally hung over.

"Oh . . ." Christy said, grabbing her head. "Are you going to be—"

"I'm in a fortress," Tyler said. "You're not. Just get in the helo and *go!*"

"We're getting full power transferred to UNG 14 now," Nathan said.

"Let's be careful to avoid fratricide," Tyler said. "We're probably going to lose enough ships to the Horvath."

Six tugs were arrayed by a single spot, not far from the closing door, on the surface of *Troy*.

The requirement was, hopefully before the Horvath came through the gate, to blast a hole through the wall of *Troy*, clear away the melt during the burn, clean it of any debris left from the burn, install sapphire collimators in both ends and then get the hell out of Dodge.

In essence, all that was needed was a standard laser tube, just oriented to the rear to capture the power of the SAPL and feed it through *Troy*. The "mouth" needed to be wide enough that it could be fed from well away from the area of battle and systems needed to be in place to make sure the incoming beam or beams went into the laser tube and didn't damage the surroundings. And they were planning to go straight through because there didn't seem to be enough time to install all the crap for a jog.

Other than *that*, all they needed was a laser tube. Before the Horvath came through the gate.

The first tube, using a VDA, had taken nearly a week to burn.

Two light-seconds out was an UNG mirror waiting to go. About to receive the full power of the SAPL, as every other project in the system was shut down and every ship started to run for whatever it considered to be cover.

The six tugs were because if they were successful they were about to "mine" one-hundred-and-fifty-thousand tons of nickel iron with the usual admixtures. Nickel iron required about one point three megawatts of power per second per ton to melt.

The UNG beam was pushing about sixty petawatts of power. Neither Nathan nor Tyler believed the calculations they were looking at. What they said was they were about to burn all the way through *Troy* in a second and a half.

"Ung, ung, ung," Nathan muttered. "Argus . . . initiate burn."

"Oh . . . my," Tyler said as the UNG beam hit. A relatively small spot on the surface of *Troy* seemed to explode outwards.

"We're not cutting through in a second and a half," Nathan said. "Thank God. But we *are* cutting a one-meter tube at about ten meters per second. The first tug is already overloaded and we're getting significant spalling and dust."

"Arrange them in a circle," Tyler said. "Between all six they should be able to capture the full cut."

"Already done," Nathan said.

The take was coming from a BDA cluster, and there was enough refinement Tyler could zoom in. There was a *lot* of dust; the vaporized nickel iron was fountaining up out of the hole in a mushroom cloud.

"I'm going to let that subside for a bit," Nathan said. "I'm afraid the beam is bouncing around in the hole."

"Be careful when you get to burn-through," Tyler said.

"I've got sensors on the inside," Nathan said. "When we get close, I'm going to drop the power. I've also got a plate of steel on the far side. It won't last *long* but it will last long enough for Argus to cut power."

Even with breaks to let the gaseous iron clear, what had taken a day with the VDA took a bare thirty minutes.

"That is amazing," Nathan said. "And very very scary."

"Rout out the outer section for the collimator system," Tyler said. The tugs, which were staying well back, weren't full yet.

A quick blast of the UNG beam, carefully missing the hole at the center, had the area cut into a cylinder to accept the receptor collimator.

"Sending in the cleaner bots," Nathan said. "Tell the admiral we'll have a bypass set up in about another thirty minutes."

"It's taking longer to shut the door than to cut a hole," Tyler said, shaking his head. "I'll . . . Bloody hell."

The Rangora/Horvath battleship looked immense coming through the gate. It was bigger than the Glatun heavy ore freighters that had been plying their trade since Tyler started seriously mining asteroids.

It also was a mass of guns and missile launchers. All of which started belching fire as soon as it cleared the gate. Right at the *Troy*.

"Belay that order," Tyler said. "Get an UNG mirror in place to bypass."

"Moving the array into position," Nathan said. "It's going to take a minute or two..."

"Mr. Vernon?" Admiral Kinyon said mildly. "We don't seem to have access to the SAPL. And in case you hadn't noticed."

It took a lot to make a multitrillion ton piece of nickel iron ring like a tocsin. The hammer of arriving missiles from the Horvath ship was managing.

"We're bringing it online right now," Tyler said. "Permission to come to the command center."

"Granted," the admiral said with only a moment's hesitation.

"*Admiral,*" Captain DiNote commed. "*Issue.*"

"Go," the admiral said.

"*We have an inbound shuttle,*" MOGS said. "*Thirty-Three picked up the passengers from* Columbia Seventeen. *It's about two minutes out. Permission to slow door close.*"

The admiral looked at the icon of the shuttle and the notations on closing the door. And then at the notation on the inbound. He could do the math.

"I have six hundred civilians in various ships in the main bay, Captain," the admiral said. "And a swarm of Horvath missiles hitting the *Troy*. They're working their way to the door. Denied."

"*Roger, sir,*" DiNote said.

"Damn," Captain Sharp said softly.

"Captain?" the admiral said.

"That shuttle, sir," Sharp said. "The pilot just did a flip and is now inbound at max drive. He's trying to shoot the gap. Makes sense. Going to die *anyway*. Worst that happens is he misses."

"Going to make it?" the admiral said, looking at the icons. Without the SAPL up there wasn't much else to do but watch.

"Barely," Sharp said. "Even Paris is locking up. They can make it *into* the gap, but out? And that assumes the pilot can stay centered. Then there's braking in the main bay."

"How long?" the admiral said.

"This is going to be over fast, one way or the other."

"Visual."

"Out of visual," Sharp said. "It's in the gap already. Go baby, go . . ." he whispered.

"Staying nicely centered," the admiral said.

"And we have SAPL," Sharp said. "The laser is now online in the bay. But the damned tube is blocked."

"Missiles?" the Admiral said.

"No effect, sir," Sharp said.

"We're not being a very effective defense," Kinyon said. "And it *cleared*."

"Oh," Sharp said. "By a *whisker*! Damn this kid is *goo*—No!"

"Speaking of . . ." Kinyon said, then . . . "SAPL. Did he just *skew turn* that *Myrm* at four hundred gravities in *my* main bay?"

"*And* around the control lever!" Sharp said. "Yes! And slowing . . . slowing . . ."

"Ouch," Kinyon said. "*That* shuttle's a write-off. Going to be an interesting report on . . . Is it moving?"

"They can take some damage," Sharp said. "Outgassing, but they should make Bay One in time. So that kid just saved fifty-three passengers, sir. The *Columbia* has already been taken out."

"Well, back to the main battle," Kinyon said. "Paris, remind me to involve myself in the report on this incident."

"Yes, sir."

"Involve?" Captain Sharp said.

"I'm still trying to figure out if the kid should get a medal or a Mast."

Tyler had determined by the time he reached the command center that the next thing on the agenda for construction was grav walks.

"Door's closed," Colonel Helberg said. "No missiles entered the bay. Unless you count the *Myrmidon*."

"Ninety percent of missiles expended," Captain Sharp said. "We're not getting through their antimissile defenses. Eighth Horvath ship through the gate."

That was clear on the screens ringing the command center. As he said that, the ninth battleship entered the system, effectively unchallenged.

"Fortunately, they're expending all their fire on us." The battlestation rocked to another hammer of missiles. "Powerful stuff, too."

"The SAPL is moot," Admiral Kinyon said as Tyler bent over, holding his knees and panting. "Their fire had closed the firing port and they've destroyed every array within a light-second."

"Use it . . . anyway," Tyler panted. "Coming from two . . . light. It's . . . going to cut through."

"And we just lost the single missile port," Sharp

said, shaking his head. "This would *work* with enough guns and ports!"

"We could throw *Myrmidons* at them," Colonel Helberg said.

"Fire...the...SAPL," Tyler panted. "You...don't... FIRE THE SAPL."

"Do we have SAPL?" the admiral asked.

"Except for a slagged firing port," Captain Sharp said, "yes, sir."

"Fire the SAPL," the admiral said.

"Here goes nothing," Sharp said. "We don't have much in the way of aiming."

"Nothing," the admiral said. "As I said." There had been no effect.

"Wait," Tyler said.

The tenth ship exiting the gate suddenly seemed to ripple, its image distorting. Then the rear of the ship blossomed in fire and the ship listed off to the side. A moment later, it exploded in a flash of red and yellow.

"Yes!" Admiral Kinyon said.

"Burn through," Captain Sharp said. "The SAPL must have melted the damage." He stopped and shook his head. "That port was *closed*! The aiming collimator was totally slagged."

"You're pushing *sixty petawatts* of power," Tyler said. "What you just did was burn out the damage. Paris, can you adjust fire using the internal mirrors?"

"About three degrees," Paris said. "But it will be expended on the material of the tube... For about two seconds. I see your point."

The eleventh ship ran straight into the main fire of the SAPL. The shields held for a moment, going nearly black with power, and then failed. The heavy laser sliced through the refractory armor as if it were butter, and the ship cut in half from just abaft the bridge. It didn't explode, though, and the screen was suddenly marked with distress beacons as the Horvath crew abandoned ship.

"Athena is requesting power to engage the ships already in the system," Paris said. "I have argued that we should take out the additional ships exiting the gate. Especially since the emerged ships are concentrating their fire on us."

As the AI said that, the twelfth ship ran into the UNG beam. It had come in at an angle to take a VDA cluster under fire, and the beam cut it in half just forward of the bridge. The forequarters spun off in one direction as the rear spun in the opposite. Another shot from the UNG and the rear portion, which was still under power, exploded.

"Paris," Tyler said. "Pardon, Admiral. But if we aim carefully we can probably salvage more of these ships."

"Salvage is the least of my worries," the admiral said as the twelfth ship exploded. "I'm quite happy with scrap."

"We're taking out their shields in about three seconds," Tyler said, bringing up a schematic of the *Devastator* on the main holo tank. "If we then concentrate fire here and here," he said, pointing to two spots on the ship design, "we'll take out their primary forward and aft capacitor banks. That will leave them more or less powerless."

"Paris?"

"I may be able to do it," the AI said, shredding the next battleship.

"Ensure that they are not a threat," the admiral said. "To us, but especially to Earth. If you can do that and simply damage them..."

"We can easily convert them for our *own* use," Tyler said smugly.

"The beam..." Paris said as the *Troy* started to hum. "I have discontinued fire and transferred control to Athena. The enemy fire is sufficiently powerful to have shifted us off position, and the supplying UNG beam was impacting on the surface of the station."

"Looks like we're spectators for the rest of this," the admiral said, crossing his arms. Another flight of missiles rang the station and he grimaced. "I'd like to have more internal power. The SAPL is great, but I'd like to have my *own* firepower, thank you."

Tyler was looking at the drifting parts of ships and smiled.

"Admiral, there's four hundred terawatts of emitters drifting around," he said. "I think we might just be able to accommodate that request."

"That is all the ships that were reported on the far side of the gate," Paris said.

"Damn, we're going to be busy," Tyler said.

Parts and pieces of sixty ships drifted near the gate. Three of them were mostly intact. Athena, despite losing the two-second UNG cluster, had managed to not only destroy all the ships that cleared the gate but use Tyler's suggestion on three of them. They mostly related to meter-wide holes that went all the way through the ships' two main power transfer centers. Tyler was practically rubbing his hands in anticipation of getting his salvage crews on them.

"I'm seriously going to need some help from Captain DiNote."

"Noted," Admiral Kinyon said, his arms still crossed. "Status of the missiles sent Earthward?"

Towards the end of the battle the few remaining ships got the message that throwing missiles at the *Troy* was a losing proposition.

"Athena or Argus caught all of them, Admiral," Paris replied. "Earth is unscathed. Two personnel shuttles inbound to us were lost with all hands. Several manned construction sites were lost as well."

"Crap," Tyler said, his jaw flexing. "I *hate* losing people."

"Damage?" the admiral said.

"All the ports are closed," Colonel Helberg said. "And lasers from the ships that got around our backside have spot-welded the door shut. Other than that . . . scars."

"Chicks dig 'em," Tyler said. "Admiral?"

"*Yes*, Mr. Vernon?" Admiral Kinyon said.

"Do we have the SAPL returned to civilian control?"

"Under the circumstances, I'm almost loath to do so," Kinyon said. "This thing is too powerful for anyone to have control over. But . . . yes."

"Thank you," Tyler said. "Colonel Helberg, you're about to receive more damage."

"*What*?"

"Argus. Initiate program Ilius," Tyler said.

"What are you doing?" Admiral Kinyon asked tightly.

"It was supposed to wait for the commissioning ceremony," Tyler said. "But I think the *Troy* can be said to be officially commissioned."

"Incoming SAPL fire," Captain Sharp said. "Every direction."

"Mr. Vernon?" Admiral Kinyon asked.

"Watch," was all Tyler said.

From all over the system, VDA and UNG beams converged on the *Troy* in flashes of fire. It seemed, for a few seconds, as if the entire battlestation was being mauled apart.

When the fire cleared, on five hexants of the battlestation, there were meters deeply etched into the nickel iron, the clear silhouettes of a helmeted hoplite with a legend λιον. There was a smaller emblem on the door and under it the words "Born of Winter."

"Born of Winter?" the admiral asked.

"*For the warriors of Illium were those most powerful and fell,*" Tyler said. "*They were those born of winter.* Rough translation of a fragment they think is part of the original Iliad cycle."

"I'll take that," the admiral said.

"And you can have it," Tyler said. "The alternate translation is that they were cursed."

EPILOGUE

The *Starfire* drifted amongst the residue of the battle, so powered down as to appear as nothing more than more scrap, as "Per L'Eternita" played on the speakers and Tyler nursed a snifter of Centennial and a Cuban.

Paws and *Myrmidons* picked among the shredded ships, searching for survivors, moving the scrap into a more manageable configuration, salvage crews doing a survey to see what was still useable and what might as well be melted down for the fabbers.

Tyler had turned off the news after one glance. For the first time, Earth had emerged unscathed from a battle and the masses of people who would never set foot in space were dancing in the streets. There was, for a few minutes, nothing but praise for the *Troy* and the SAPL and even LFD. It pissed him off. Soon enough the mobs would be calling for blood again. Mobs were mobs, whether they were called hooligans or activists or pundits. They just followed the latest fad, the latest mood. They never looked at the future. They feared the sky.

The *Troy* had shrugged off the incoming fire and even if it had lost its own fighting ability, that was just a matter of completing phase one.

But if the enemy had fired all those thousands of missiles at Earth, some of them, many of them, would have gotten through the defenses. Senator Gullick had a point. Earth's defenses were on the wrong side of the gate.

Twenty thousand tons *of osmium.* Well, that was just a matter of infrastructure.

He stubbed out his cigar.

"Pilot. Set course for the gate. Destination Wolf 359."

"Aye, sir."

Time to visit the Night Wolves.

AUTHOR'S AFTERWORD

This is usually the part where the author inputs about things in the novel. From whence the idea originated (it wasn't illegal drugs, by the way) or something about the genesis of the novel.

In this case, it's going to be purely personal. My book, I can get away with it.

I don't exactly remember when Aunt Joan and Uncle Charles first came into my life. They just sort of appeared at one of Mom's parties in Iran and thereafter, for two years, were a fixture. After Iran I saw them little, once in England on one of the trips and the single time they were in the States when I was around at the right time.

But I can think of no two people other than my parents, and including my horde of brothers and sisters, who more affected my life.

Aunt Joan had been, prior to being married, one of those sorts of characters you only see these days in an Agatha Christie novel. She had settled into a life of being a professional barmaid and serving gal and seemed to have no issues. No more than she had issues with being of the "professional" class in a cosmopolitan city. She treated life as it came and never seemed to care if it was up or down. Of all the characters of fiction I have read, the one that most strikes me as similar to Aunt Joan is Nanny Ogg, the "Mother" character of the three witches in Pratchett's Discworld. She had that same permanently applied joie de vivre, "And top up my glass, there's a luv!" I cannot think of Aunt Joan and remember a single time when I saw her somber or anything other than on the cusp of a laugh.

What I learned from Aunt Joan:

- Serve from the left, take away from the right. Except drinks, which are both served and removed from the right.
- How to pile up food on an upside-down fork held in the left hand. "And mush up the peas!"
- How to properly serve salad with spoon and fork. (It's a bit like using chopsticks. Backwards.)
- How to properly pour beer. ("Nai! Tip the glass or you'll be all head!")
- Ice, scotch, soda. The order is important.
- How to bargain down a rug salesman.
- Proper language for addressing an Iranian taxi driver.
- How to bob curtsey.
- Corner folds on a bed. (Helped when I joined the Army.)
- "Ma'am" is pronounced "Mum."

And most of all, and the one that I forget all the time:

- Life is short, squeeze joy from every second.

I rarely drink but at my next event I intend to raise a pint of Guinness in her honor. I've missed you for years, Aunt Joan, I guess I shall have to go on missing you.

—John Ringo
Chattanooga, TN
August 2009

JOHN RINGO

Master of Military SF
The Posleen War Saga

A Hymn Before Battle   (pb) 0-6713-1841-1 • $7.99

Gust Front   (pb) 0-7434-3525-7 • $7.99

When the Devil Dances   (pb) 0-7434-3602-4 • $7.99

Hell's Faire   (pb) 0-7434-8842-3 • $7.99

Eye of the Storm   (pb) 978-1-4391-3362-0 • $7.99

Cally's War with Julie Cochrane   (pb) 1-4165-2052-X • $7.99

Sister Time with Julie Cochrane   (pb) 1-4165-5590-0 • $7.99

Honor of the Clan with Julie Cochrane
                                 (pb) 978-1439133354 • $7.99

Watch on the Rhine with Tom Kratman
                                 (pb) 1-4165-2120-8 • $7.99

Yellow Eyes with Tom Kratman   (pb) 1-4165-5571-4 • $7.99

The Tuloriad with Tom Kratman (pb)   978-1-4391-3409-2 • $7.99

The Hero with Michael Z. Williamson   (pb) 1-4165-0914-3 • $7.99

The Black Tide Rising Series

Under a Graveyard Sky   (hc) 978-1-4516-3919-3 $25.00
                                 (pb) 978-1-4767-3660-0 $7.99

To Sail a Darkling Sea   (hc) 978-1-4767-3621-1 $25.00
                                 (pb) 978-1-4767-8025-2 $7.99

Islands of Rage and Hope   (hc) 978-1-4767-3662-4 $25.00
                                 (pb) 978-1-4767-8043-6 $7.99

Strands of Sorrow   (hc) 978-1-4767-3695-2 $25.00
                                 (pb) 978-1-4767-8102-0 $7.99

Black Tide Rising anthology edited by John Ringo & Gary Poole
                                 (hc) 978-1-4767-8151-8 $26.00
                                 (pb) 978-1-4814-8264-4 $7.99

■ ■ ■

Citizens ed. by John Ringo & Brian M. Thomsen
(trade pb) 978-1-4391-3347-7 • $16.00

Master of Epic SF
The Council War Series

There Will Be Dragons (pb) 0-7434-8859-8 • $7.99

Emerald Sea (pb) 1-4165-0920-8 • $7.99

Against the Tide (pb) 1-4165-2057-0 • $7.99

East of the Sun, West of the Moon
(pb) 1-4165-5518-87 • $7.99

Master of Real SF
The Troy Rising Series

Live Free or Die (hc) 1-4391-3332-8 • $26.00
(pb) 978-1-4391-3397-2 • $7.99

Citadel (hc) 978-1-4391-3400-9 • $26.00
(pb) 978-1-4516-3757-1 • $7.99

The Hot Gate (pb) 978-1-4516-3818-9 • $7.99

■ ■ ■

Von Neumann's War with Travis S. Taylor
(pb) 1-4165-5530-8 • $7.99

■ ■ ■

The Looking Glass Series

Into the Looking Glass (pb) 1-4165-2105-4 • $7.99

Vorpal Blade with Travis S. Taylor
(hc) 1-4165-2129-1 • $25.00
(pb) 1-4165-5586-2 • $7.99

Manxome Foe with Travis S. Taylor
(pb) 1-4165-9165-6 • $7.99

Claws That Catch with Travis S. Taylor
(hc) 1-4165-5587-0 • $25.00
(pb) 978-1-4391-3313-2 • $7.99

Master of Hard-Core Thrillers
The Kildar Saga

Ghost   (pb) 1-4165-2087-2 • $7.99

Kildar   (pb) 1-4165-2133-X • $7.99

Choosers of the Slain   (hc) 1-4165-2070-8 • $25.00
(pb) 1-4165-7384-4 • $7.99

Unto the Breach   (hc) 1-4165-0940-2 • $26.00
(pb) 1-4165-5535-8 • $7.99

A Deeper Blue   (hc) 1-4165-2128-3 • $26.00
(pb) 1-4165-5550-1 • $7.99

Tiger by the Tail with Ryan Sear
(hc) 978-1-4516-3856-1 • $25.00
(pb) 978-1-4767-3615-0 • $7.99

■ ■ ■

The Last Centurion   (hc) 1-4165-5553-6 • $25.00
(pb) 978-1-4391-3291-3 • $7.99

Master of Dark Fantasy

Princess of Wands   (hc) 1-4165-0923-2 • $25.00

Queen of Wands   (hc) 978-1-4516-3789-2 • $25.00
(pb) 978-1-4516-3917-9 • $7.99

Master of Bolos

The Road to Damascus with Linda Evans
(pb) 0-7434-9916-6 • $7.99

■ ■ ■

The Monster Hunter Memoirs series
with Larry Correia

Monster Hunter Memoirs: Grunge
(hc) 978-1-4767-8149-5 • $26.00
(pb) 978-1-4814-8262-2 • $7.99

Monster Hunter Memoirs: Sinners
(hc) 978-1-4767-8183-9 • $26.00
(pb) 978-1-4814-8287-5 • $7.99

Monster Hunter Memoirs: Saints
(hc) 978-1-4814-8307-0 • $25.00

And don't miss Ringo's NY Times best-selling epic adventures written with David Weber:

March Upcountry   (pb) 0-7434-3538-9 • $7.99

March to the Sea   (pb) 0-7434-3580-X • $7.99

March to the Stars   (pb) 0-7434-8818-0 • $7.99

We Few   (pb) 1-4165-2084-8 • $7.99

Empire of Men   (omni tpb) 978-1-4767-3624-2 • $14.00
March Upcountry and *March to the Sea* in one massive volume.

Throne of Stars   (omni tpb) 978-1-4767-3666-2 • $14.00
March to the Stars and *We Few* in one massive volume.

Available in bookstores everywhere.
Or order ebooks online at www.baenebooks.com.

New York Times Best Seller

LARRY CORREIA
MASTER OF MONSTERS

MONSTER HUNTER SERIES
Monster Hunter International
9781439132850 * $7.99 US/$9.99 Can.

Monster Hunter Vendetta
9781439133910 * $7.99 US/$9.99 Can.

Monster Hunter Alpha
9781439134580 * $7.99 US/$9.99 Can.

Monster Hunter Legion
9781451637960 * $7.99 US/$9.99 Can.

Monster Hunter Nemesis
9781476780535 * $7.99 US/$9.99 Can.

Monster Hunter Siege
9781481483278 * $7.99 US/$10.99 Can.

The Monster Hunter Files
9781481483520 * $7.99 US/$10.99 Can.

MONSTER HUNTER MEMOIRS SERIES
with John Ringo
Monster Hunter Memoirs: Grunge
97814814826220 * $7.99 US/$10.99 Can.

Monster Hunter Memoirs: Sinners
9781481482875 * $7.99 US/$10.99 Can.

Monster Hunter Memoirs: Saints
9781481483070 * $7.99 US/$10.99 Can.

THE FORGOTTEN WARRIOR SAGA

Son of the Black Sword
9781476781570 * $8.99 US/$11.99 Can.

House of Assassins
9781481483766 * $25.00 US/$34.00 Can.

THE GRIMNOIR CHRONICLES

Hard Magic
9781451638240 * $7.99 US/$9.99 Can.

Spellbound
9781451638592 * $7.99 US/$9.99 Can.

Warbound
9781476736525 * $7.99 US/$9.99 Can.

MILITARY ADVENTURE
with Mike Kupari

Dead Six
9781451637588 * $7.99 US/$9.99 Can.

Swords of Exodus
9781476736112 * $7.99 US/$9.99 Can.

Alliance of Shadows
9781481482912 * $7.99 US/$10.99 Can.

Available in bookstores everywhere.
Or order ebooks online at www.baenebooks.com.

MICHAEL Z. WILLIAMSON

"This fast-paced, compulsive read, with its military action and alien cultures, will appeal to fans of John Ringo, David Drake, Lois McMaster Bujold, and David Weber."—*Kliatt*

For fans of David Drake and John Ringo, military SF adventures set in the Freehold Universe

Freehold (PB) 0743471792 · $7.99
The Freehold of Grainne is the last bastion of freedom in the galaxy. But things are about to go royally to hell . . .

The Weapon (PB) 1416521186 · $7.99
Kenneth Chinran infiltrated a fascistic, militaristic planet: Earth. He lived in deep cover for years, until Earth forces attacked his home system. Now Earth will pay the price.

Better to Beg Forgiveness
(PB) 1416591516 · $7.99
The deadliest mercenaries in the galaxy have suddenly become free agents, on a world that's ripe for the picking . . .

Contact with Chaos (HC) 1416591540 · $24.00
(PB) 978-1439133736 · $7.99
Caution: Contact with intelligent aliens can be hazardous to your health.

Do Unto Others (HC) 9781439133835 · $22.00
When your enormous wealth makes you a target, it's time to do unto others *before* they do unto you!

When Diplomacy Fails (PB) 9781451639117 · $7.99
High-tech mercenaries Ripple Creek Security must protect an obnoxious world government minister from the enemies who want her dead—and killed in the worst possible way.

Angeleyes (PB) 9781481482950 • $7.99
Angie Kaneshiro, once a veteran of the Freehold Forces of
Grainne, now tramp freighter crew woman. Angie was free
. . . then the war with Earth started.

Forged in Blood (PB) 9781481483537 • $7.99
Throughout history and into the future, those who wield
the sword show uncommon courage and a warrior's spirit.
These are their stories. Including stories by Tom Kratman,
Kacey Ezell, Larry Correia, and more.

Other novels by
Michael Z. Williamson

A Long Time Until Now (PB) 9781476781723 · $7.99
Ten U.S. soldiers find themselves in Paleolithic Asia. But
they are not the only time-travelers there. Groups from
throughout history have been gathered . . . but by whom
and to what purpose?

Tour of Duty (PB) 9781476781723 • $7.99
It's a tough universe out there. A hard hitting collection
of the best fiction of Michael Z. Williamson, along with a
generous helping of nonfiction truth-telling.

Tide of Battle (TPB) 9781481483360 • $16.00
The deadliest mercenaries in the galaxy have suddenly become
free agents, on a world that's ripe for the picking . . .

Available in bookstores everywhere.
Order e-books online at www.baen.com

IF YOU LIKE...
YOU SHOULD TRY...

DAVID DRAKE
David Weber
Tony Daniel
John Lambshead

DAVID WEBER
John Ringo
Timothy Zahn
Linda Evans
Jane Lindskold
Sarah A. Hoyt

JOHN RINGO
Michael Z. Williamson
Tom Kratman
Larry Correia
Mike Kupari

ANNE MCCAFFREY
Mercedes Lackey
Lois McMaster Bujold
Liaden Universe® by Sharon Lee & Steve Miller
Sarah A. Hoyt
Mike Kupari

MERCEDES LACKEY
Wen Spencer
Andre Norton
James H. Schmitz

LARRY NIVEN
Tony Daniel
James P. Hogan
Travis S. Taylor
Brad Torgersen

ROBERT A. HEINLEIN
Jerry Pournelle
Lois McMaster Bujold
Michael Z. Williamson

HEINLEIN'S "JUVENILES"
Rats, Bats & Vats series by Eric Flint & Dave Freer
Brendan DuBois' *Dark Victory*
David Weber & Jane Lindskold's Star Kingdom
Series
David Drake & Jim Kjelgaard's *The Hunter Returns*

HORATIO HORNBLOWER OR
PATRICK O'BRIAN
David Weber's Honor Harrington series
David Drake's RCN series
Alex Stewart's *Shooting the Rift*

HARRY POTTER
Mercedes Lackey's Urban Fantasy series

JIM BUTCHER
Larry Correia's The Grimnoir Chronicles
John Lambshead's *Wolf in Shadow*

TECHNOTHRILLERS
Larry Correia & Mike Kupari's Dead Six Series
Robert Conroy's *Stormfront*
Eric Stone's *Unforgettable*
Tom Kratman's Countdown Series

THE LORD OF THE RINGS
Elizabeth Moon's *The Deed of Paksenarrion*
P.C. Hodgell
Ryk E. Spoor's Phoenix Rising series

A GAME OF THRONES
Larry Correia's *Son of the Black Sword*
David Weber's fantasy novels
Sonia Orin Lyris' *The Seer*

H.P. LOVECRAFT
Larry Correia's Monster Hunter series
P.C. Hodgell's Kencyrath series
John Ringo's Special Circumstances Series

ZOMBIES
John Ringo's Black Tide Rising Series
Wm. Mark Simmons

GEORGETTE HEYER
Lois McMaster Bujold
Catherine Asaro
Liaden Universe® by Sharon Lee & Steve Miller
Dave Freer

DOCTOR WHO
Steve White's TRA Series
Michael Z. Williamson's *A Long Time Until Now*

HARD SCIENCE FICTION
Ben Bova
Les Johnson
Charles E. Gannon
Eric Flint & Ryk E. Spoor's Boundary Series
Mission: Tomorrow ed. by Bryan Thomas Schmidt

GREEK MYTHOLOGY
Pyramid Scheme by Eric Flint & Dave Freer
Forge of the Titans by Steve White
Blood of the Heroes by Steve White

NORSE MYTHOLOGY
Northworld Trilogy by David Drake
Pyramid Power by Eric Flint & Dave Freer

URBAN FANTASY
Mercedes Lackey's SERRAted Edge Series
Larry Correia's Monster Hunter International
Series
Sarah A. Hoyt's Shifter Series
Sharon Lee's Carousel Series
David B. Coe's Case Files of Justis Fearsson

DINOSAURS
David Drake's *Dinosaurs & a Dirigible*
David Drake & Tony Daniel's *The Heretic* and *The Savior*

HISTORY AND ALTERNATE HISTORY
Eric Flint's Ring of Fire Series
David Drake & Eric Flint's Belisarius Series
Robert Conroy
Harry Turtledove

HUMOR
Esther Friesner's *Chicks 'n Chainmail*
Rick Cook
Spider Robinson
Wm. Mark Simmons
Jody Lynn Nye

VAMPIRES & WEREWOLVES
Larry Correia
Wm. Mark Simmons
Ryk E. Spoor's *Paradigm's Lost*

WEBCOMICS
Sluggy Freelance... John Ringo's Posleen War Series
Schlock Mercenary...John Ringo's Troy Rising Series

NONFICTION
Hank Reinhardt
The Science Behind The Secret by Travis Taylor
Alien Invasion by Travis Taylor & Bob Boan
Going Interstellar ed. By Les Johnson

Available in bookstores everywhere.
Or order online at our secure, easy to use website:
www.baen.com